Betrayed by Europe's monarchs and a traitor's greed, they brazenly defied their captors with their passion and their blood

MARCEL HEBERT—As handsome as he was wild, he learned to fight at the side of savages, he learned to love by seducing an innocent young girl's heart... and he learned to hate by challenging the British who invaded his land.

NINA BABINEAU—Her young beauty blossomed like an Acadian spring; her passion swept her like a reckless sea into her lover's arms... but the tides of history would carry her to heartbreak and another man's bed.

GILLES HEBERT—A man too powerful to be broken, too proud to live as a slave, he would risk his life for freedom and his manhood for a woman's love.

HELENE HEBERT—Her golden loveliness was both a blessing and a curse as it led her into a rogue's ravishing embrace and into a notorious existence among the most powerful men of Cajun New Orleans.

JONAS AUDRY—His cruelty matched his craven desires as he ruled his Virginia plantation with a whip and a gun ... And his greatest passion was to take revenge on the Acadian brothers who tried to stop his mad schemes.

THE ACADIANS
by ROBERT E. WALL

Bantam-Seal Books by Robert E. Wall
Ask your bookseller for the books you have missed

BLACKROBE—The Canadians, Book I
BLOODBROTHERS—The Canadians, Book II
BIRTHRIGHT—The Canadians, Book III
PATRIOTS—The Canadians, Book IV
INHERITORS—The Canadians, Book V
DOMINION—The Canadians, Book VI

THE ACADIANS

a novel

by

Robert E. Wall

SEAL BOOKS
McClelland and Stewart-Bantam Limited
Toronto

THE ACADIANS
A Seal Book / December 1984

ISBN 0-7704-2010-9

PRINTED IN CANADA

COVER PRINTED IN U.S.A.

U   0 9 8 7 6 5 4 3 2 1

*This book is dedicated to Anna Porter
for her willingness to take a chance*

Part

Part One

ACADIA

CHAPTER ONE

Saint John River, March 1755

The young man crept quietly through the fanlike bushes that
grew in abundance along the banks of the brook. Sunlight
penetrated the cover of the giant trees and struck the waters,
breaking into hundreds of ephemeral jewels. He stopped and
listened. Only the chirps of the birds fluttering from tree to
tree and the bass gurgle of the water sweeping over rocks
broke the silence.

He was dressed in deerskin, his shirt decorated with
porcupine quills. The skins were old and well worn, and
many of the quills had broken and fallen off. The young man's
wavy black hair fell in a gentle sweep over his light blue eyes.
He pushed it away from his forehead with his hand. He
touched his lip. He was trying to grow a moustache. It was
slow work when you were only eighteen.

He took another step forward. He heard the snap of metal
and the whimper of an animal in pain. His instincts were
right again. He had been following his traplines with his
partner, Benoit, the half-breed Penobscot. Most of the trapped
animals were close to death, if not already dead. But this
time the complete ease of the birds and the rustling in the

1

bushes near the brook had warned him. He rushed to the trap.

"*Merde*," he exclaimed, "it's only another raccoon." The skin wasn't worth much money and its meat wasn't worth chewing. The animal growled at him, bared its teeth, and pulled at the trap chain that pinned its leg. The limb was not broken. The young man looked around furtively to see if Benoit was in view. Then he reached down and released the trap spring. The raccoon scurried away with just a slight limp. The young man watched it run and was then startled when two smaller raccoons broke from the cover of the ferns and went chasing after their mother.

Marcel Hebert smiled. He told himself he released raccoons because they didn't bring as much as silver or red fox and certainly not as much as beaver or muskrat could bring from the merchant. But deep inside he knew it was the almost human expressions and behavior of the 'coons that touched him.

He heard Benoit's whistle. He covered the raccoon tracks and reset the trap before he returned the whistle. Benoit was wading in the brook. His green pants were drenched up to his knees and his beige-colored linen shirt was soaked at the armpits. The most striking feature of his attire, however, was a fine three-cornered hat trimmed with ostrich feathers. Sticking from the middle of the hat was a giant eagle feather. The hat itself, minus its final adornment, would have been appropriate at Versailles or the Court of St. James's. To see it in the midst of the Acadian wilderness was only slightly less shocking than finding it atop Benoit's braided black hair.

The Penobscot tribe roamed to the south of the Saint John Valley, in the eastern province of Massachusetts which some called Maine. Benoit, however, was no longer welcome among them. He never went home and rarely spoke of his origins. The young Frenchman knew only that his partner was the son of a French storekeeper and the grandson of the Penobscot chief known as the Rat. The chief's daughter had run away with the Frenchman to the mission of St. François, where many Christian Indians had settled in a quasi-European life-style. Somehow the Rat found them and they were killed. Benoit had been only a toddler at the time, but he never forgot their fate. As a young man he kidnapped the Rat and executed him. One night while sharing a jug of brandy with Marcel, he treated him to a vivid account of how he had skinned his grandfather alive. He cackled while describing the Rat's disgraceful screaming. His parents were avenged but Benoit was now a man without a tribe. The whites rejected him for his Indian blood and he rejected the Christian mission where his parents had lived. He had an equal contempt for both priests—whom he called men without pricks—and ministers—whom he called men with pricks who don't want anyone to use them except to piss. This last was rendered in one tongue-twisting Penobscot word that Marcel suspected Benoit had made up.

The half-breed greeted his boy partner with an ugly smile. His face was long and narrow, making his bulbous nose and large ears seem all the larger. He was not sure why he trapped with this young French novice except that the boy worked hard and learned quickly and it was lonely on the trapline. He had met the boy at Fort Beauséjour and had gotten drunk with him. He liked a boy who could get drunk—man drunk, not boy drunk, puking and hiccuping, but drunk deep within so that it lasted the day. Later they had gone out to find women. While drunk the boy had admitted to Benoit something that he could never have said sober: he was a virgin. Well, that was a problem that once cured would never return, and Benoit set out to cure him. He found the ugliest, dirtiest squaw among all the hangers-on at the French fort and he brought the intoxicated boy to her mat for his first good lay.

It was Benoit's theory that the first one should be the worst in your life. That way your sex life could only improve and there wouldn't be any nostalgia later. It was unfortunate that the squaw also gave the boy his first case of clap, but that hardly hurt Benoit's theory about the first time. Even today, a year later, he smiled when he thought of the youngster, far from home, sleeping on the ground not in his own bed, no *maman* to feed him, only Benoit's crude efforts with fresh meat and an open fire. But worst of all, there was the pain and the burning pee. The boy had groaned every time the urge came to him, and it seemed to come every five minutes. It was all right so long as he could pee. If the flow stopped, they would have had to go to the fort, where there was a doctor who could open you up. Benoit worried about that. He had had that operation and never wanted it repeated. That might, in Marcel's case, push his theory about the first time just a bit too far.

But the pain ceased finally and the boy showed no ill effects. And how he thrived in the woods! Within a year his muscles had developed and his shoulders had broadened. He had turned the corner of boyhood to become a man—a good trapper who could still drink. When he thought about it, Benoit was grateful to have found such a companion.

He raised his hand in greeting. He was sure the trap was empty. He had set it hoping to take raccoons. This was a good spot for them, near the stream where they would take their food for washing. Yet he almost never took anything here. He would have to rethink the placement. But it was of no matter. He had a sackful of muskrats, and they had cached a whole winter's trapping in a cave several miles down the Saint John. They had also agreed that this would be their last trapline inspection. They had to take the furs to Fort Beauséjour.

Marcel took the sack of dead animals from his partner. They would be busy skinning them and drying the skins over the next few days. The half-breed led the way back to the clearing farther downstream where they had constructed a lean-to and drying racks for the skins. The pelts were an annoyance because with the coming of spring they attracted flies. The flies annoyed Marcel but left Benoit alone. In fact, Marcel had noted that everything left Benoit alone. Mosquitoes did not like him, nor did the black flies that would be coming as soon as spring was at hand. Body lice drove Marcel to distraction during the winter. He scratched until his skin was raw. The first warm day of spring he had torn off his buckskins and jumped into the icy stream. He scrubbed himself all over with sand from the stream bottom. Then he soaked his buckskins and let them dry on his body so they would not shrink.

Marcel was sure that Benoit was immune to everything, even to the clap. He was sure that the older man had bedded the same squaw as he had, yet nothing had happened to him. A grimace crossed his face when he remembered that encounter. He had sworn he never would be with a woman again. He had survived up to seventeen without a woman and he could

4

survive forever without one. His resolve had melted the first time Benoit had taken him to the Micmac camp at the mouth of the Gaspereau. There he had met a girl who was young and pretty and just as willing as the old hag. This time he had been sober—well, at least partly sober. They had stayed together for his two-week visit to the Micmac camp. Last month a chance encounter with a small hunting party from that same village brought the news of the birth of a boy with blue eyes to the Micmac girl. At first he thought there would be anger from the members of the village, but the girl's new husband viewed the son as his own and as a blessing to their marriage.

Marcel had breathed a sigh of relief and then started strutting about. Benoit had laughed and teased him for weeks and had insisted that the first girl he had gotten pregnant had given birth to redheaded triplets. Marcel ignored him. When Marcel suggested that they return to the Gaspereau in the summer to see the baby, Benoit warned him to mind his own business. But Benoit had been wrong before; it could do no harm just to look at his own son.

Marcel flopped down into the pine-bough mats in the lean-to while Benoit began to skin the muskrats. He looked up at his friend. "I hope you're not planning to serve those things for dinner," he said.

"There's nothing else," the half-breed responded.

"They stink," Marcel said with disgust.

"Well, get something better and I will dispose of these little fellows' carcasses." Benoit brought one of the muskrats right in front of Marcel's nose.

Marcel needed no further encouragement. He jumped to his feet, picked up his musket, and ambled off toward the brook. It was getting late in the day. He knew the deer would be coming down to the water to drink and eat. Yet if he shot a deer he would waste the meat. In only a few days they would be ready to leave for Fort Beauséjour to sell their furs. Benoit had tried to talk him into taking the furs to Albany, where the New York English paid almost four times as much. But Marcel wanted to go home for the spring fête. He had never missed one in his life.

He rested against a giant spruce tree. All its lower branches were dead or broken off. Very little light penetrated the forest cover to nourish new growth. He would wait here for the game to come down to the brook to drink. It was better for the hunted to come to the hunter.

He watched the few patches of open sky that could be seen from the forest turn from a gray white to a gold. There would be only an hour or two of daylight left. Maybe it was wrong to take the lazy approach; he might end up eating muskrat.

Thoughts of Port Hebert, his home down the coast from Beauséjour, kept coming into his mind. Maman Adele, small, dark, and tough, had no sympathy for a scraped knee or a cut finger. You only went to Maman with serious things, for she was a *traiteur*, a healer, adept at curing the croup and mending a broken leg or, even more mysteriously, driving the evil one from the possessed. Marcel crossed himself, frightened by the thought of the power his mother on occasion had demonstrated.

When he or Helene, his little sister, had bangs and bruises, they went instead to Lucien, their father, even though it was hard to steal a moment of his time. Everyone in Port Hebert sought Lucien's counsel. He was a large, gentle man, yet in his quiet way he was every bit as powerful as Adele, his tiny wife. He gave of himself freely—too freely, Marcel thought when someone else monopolized the time that Marcel felt should be his.

Gilles, Marcel's giant of a brother, dwarfed even Lucien. He never seemed to need his father's advice. Marcel liked to joke that Gilles was so dumb that he sought his mother's wisdom and his father's healing. Marcel and Gilles had never gotten along. Marcel thought once it was because he saw Gilles sneaking looks at Nina, Babin's daughter, but he knew the rivalry was older than that. As a boy Marcel had teased his older brother until Gilles could stand it no longer and began to beat him up. With Helene screaming that Gilles was trying to kill Marcel, Lucien would come running and beat Gilles for "picking on his little brother." Afterwards, while Gilles stormed out of the house to sulk, Marcel would have to pay off Helene by stealing some sugar from his mother's cherished supply. No one in the family ever got free assistance from Helene.

He and Helene had been great friends despite her greed for sweets. She looked so unlike him. She had golden hair and fair skin while he was dark and swarthy like his mother. But in spirit they were one. Both would die rather than give up. Both were able to live off their wits. They fooled Gilles continuously, and Lucien, too, on occasion. Only Maman Adele seemed to be onto their tricks. But then she had the power and could rarely be fooled. Yes, he missed his sister most of all—except maybe for Nina, the Babineau girl.

He felt a tension in the pit of his stomach and his groin when he thought of the pretty brown-haired girl. He imagined her lying on her back, her soft-skinned thighs parted. He shook his head to clear it. He could not think of Babin's daughter as if she were the squaw at the mouth of the Gaspereau, especially not if he was contemplating a return to the village. Nina Babineau would be someone's wife. Maybe she would be *his* wife—not now, but later.

He saw something move in the bushes. He raised his musket. Whatever it was, it was not particularly wary. He saw a sharp nose and two beady eyes peer out from some blackberry bushes. Then the animal pushed forward and Marcel realized why the animal moved so boldly. It had few enemies since few would dare to risk the quills that covered its body. The porcupine, like the skunk, walked the forest with little fear. But Marcel thought this one just about the right size for dinner, especially if he could get Benoit, the expert, to skin it and there was little in the porcupine to remind him of people.

He fired and the animal leapt into the air and landed on its side. Marcel would have sworn that a look of surprise crossed its face, but soon any life, much less expression, was drained from it. He gave his whistle to Benoit to indicate that he was all right. Benoit would know it anyway. He could recognize the sound of Marcel's musket and distinguish it from any others.

Marcel picked up his dinner with great care and retraced his steps back to camp. Benoit greeted him with disgust when he saw the porcupine. Then with resignation he began the difficult task of preparing the beast for the fire while Marcel pulled off his buckskins and walked naked across the clearing for a quick dip in the brook.

"Marcel," Benoit teased, "you know why insects are always biting your ass?"

Marcel ignored him and continued to walk to the stream.

"Well, for one," Benoit continued, "it's uncovered a lot more than it should be. And then there is the smell. You smell bad."

Marcel turned to look at his friend. He sniffed himself. "No worse than usual and a lot less than you."

"That's the point. You smell like a man. Sure, you wash everything else but you can't wash away man's smell except temporarily. Now me, I don't wash away anything. I smell like smoke and dung and dead animals left out in the sun to bloat. All those things cover my man smell so that insects' little noses pass right over me and land right on you and bite your ass because they recognize you. You stink like a man and man is tasty food for them little bugs."

"You're telling me I shouldn't wash?"

"Now I know your *maman* said different."

Just then Marcel slapped a giant mosquito that had landed on his forearm. Maybe there was something to what Benoit said. He was sometimes right about things that didn't have to do with women. The young man went back to the campfire and redressed.

Benoit smiled. He would make a real trapper out of this boy yet.

"What about going off to Isle Royale after our visit to Beauséjour?" Benoit suggested. "I'd like to show you the fortress of Louisbourg."

"No," Marcel said. "I'm going to Port Hebert. You're welcome to come with me."

"And sleep in a house and eat woman-cooked food? It would be the death of me and you, boy. It takes six months off your life for every day you live in a house."

Marcel struggled with the arithmetic to figure out how much sooner he was doomed to die. But he gave it up as a stupid effort. The only figures he had learned involved sous and livres.

"Where shall we meet?" Marcel asked Benoit, despairing of getting him anywhere near Port Hebert.

"How about on the Gaspereau?" Benoit said, smiling at him.

"Do you mean it?" he said, giving Benoit a quick glance.

As soon as he saw the smirk he knew that he was being teased.

"I'll meet you at Beauséjour. Besides, your chances of seeing her are better there anyway. Many of the mainland Micmacs come to the fort to trade for the summer."

Benoit had butchered the animal as easily as most men sliced bread. He prepared strips of meat on sticks and placed them over the fire to roast, then pulled his brandy bottle from out of his bedding.

"The last of the lot," he said, holding the dark bottle up to the light. It was half full. He poured a tiny bit on each piece of the meat. The flame leapt slightly as the alcohol dropped off the meat into the fire. It gave off a delicious aroma. Benoit took a slug and passed the bottle to Marcel. Marcel opened his throat and allowed an enormous swallow to warm his throat and belly.

"Hey," Benoit complained, "for that I get to take two gulps." He proceeded to imitate the boy. "Here," he said, handing one of the sticks with the roasted meat to Marcel. The young man wolfed the meat down.

Benoit ate more slowly. "So you're determined to go back to that town of yours?"

"Yup," Marcel said through a mouthful of meat.

"I despair of making an Acadian into a real woodsman. Too much farmer in him or too much fisherman in him but no real love for the woods."

"What do you mean? We French go everywhere. We live with the Indians, we explore the rivers, all in search of furs. Why you're half-French yourself."

"French, yes. All you say about the French is correct, but not Acadians. Their minds are down in the dirt. They are up to their ankles in sea muck."

Marcel smiled. "We love the land and we love the sea."

"You love it so much you'll never get beyond the sound of waves without becoming homesick."

"It's always been that way. My father's ancestors came to this land with LaTour well over a century ago. We have been at Port Hebert for four generations. The town is named after us."

Benoit made a noise of disgust. "Four generations, bah. My Indian ancestors can no longer count back how many

9

generations have hunted and trapped this land. Yet we roam where we please and the only thing that stops our movement is a stronger tribe."

"You don't understand how it is with my people," Marcel said. "We came to a wilderness. We cleared our fields. We drove back the sea and we reclaimed acres of salt marsh to feed our cattle and sheep. We have left a mark on this land of Acadia. It did not matter who our masters were. We plowed the land under Louis XIV and when he gave us up, we plowed the same acres under King George of England. Nothing changed. We still have the land and the sea."

"I thought you wanted to be a fur trapper and an adventurer just like me."

Marcel shrugged. "I'm different, I don't know why. I just couldn't stay cooped up in Port Hebert."

Benoit belched loudly. "Not so different. You're going back, aren't you?"

"Just to visit for the fête."

Benoit grinned. His smile went unnoticed in the gloom. Then he grew serious. "But *mon ami*," he warned, "don't believe that things will be the same under the Bastonois as under the Canadiens."

"What do you mean?"

"The Bastonois are greedy for land. They gobbled it up to the south of us. They drive the tribes from their hunting grounds. First it was the Pequots, but soon after the Naragansetts and the Wamponoags and the Nipmucks and even the Mohegan. Now only the powerful Abenacki tribe survives, but they will go eventually. The Bastonois look at your dike marshes and your plowed fields with the eyes of greed. Somehow they will make all of it theirs."

"We were granted our land by treaty between England and France. We are subjects of the English king just as are the Bastonois. Yet because King Louis did not wish to abandon us after he lost the last war with the English, he signed treaties giving us the right to receive his missionary priests. He protected us from having to bear arms against our fellow countrymen across the straits in Isle Royale or Isle St. Jean."

"And what did those priests do in 1745?" Benoit asked. "Did they not come across the border and urge you not to remain neutral in this new war, and did they not urge you to take up arms against your new king? And did not the men of the Minas Basin and Grand Pre do just that?"

"No one from Port Hebert did. My father persuaded everyone to stay home and send no one to attack Port Royal."

"I'm sure the English king made a note of your loyalty."

"His governor, Mr. Mascarene, did. He commended my father in an official proclamation."

Benoit laughed. "He's not governor anymore."

There were long moments of silence broken only by the snap of sparks rising from the cooking fire. Finally Marcel spoke.

"Do you really think there will be trouble for my people?"

Benoit chuckled again. "I thought you were different. It should not concern you."

"Answer my question."

Benoit grew serious. "I know *les anglais, mon ami*. The only thing more greedy than the English are wolverines and New Englanders. And when the English join with their Puritan colonists from New England they eat innocents alive."

"And the Acadians are innocents?"

"*Oui.*"

"But by culture and language we are French. Did not our countrymen in New France come to our assistance?"

This time Benoit guffawed. "Only a few moments ago, *mon ami*, you were saying that you were subject to King George. Your own words sum up the very troubles your people will face. You are caught in a no-man's land. No one will claim you, no one will defend you, and both sides, English and French, will attack you." Benoit yawned. "But not tonight, Marcel." He rose and crossed the shelter until he came to his own bedding. He flopped down on the ground and pulled the gray-blue Indian woven blanket over his body and up around his shoulders.

Marcel was left alone by the fire. He suddenly felt cold and lonely. Now he felt even more compelled to return to Port Hebert. If anything were to happen to his family they would need him.

Marcel left the fire to relieve himself. He walked several paces into the darkened woods. He heard a small animal scurrying away into the underbrush. Off to his left he heard the hoot of the night owl. He said aloud, "Run, little fellow, whoever you are, back into your burrow before the horned one sees you and makes you his supper." As he spoke it occurred to him that there were a great many hoot owls in the woods tonight.

The sun broke through the early morning mist and bathed the shelter in warmth. Marcel groaned when the sunlight struck his face. He pulled his blanket up over his head. His mother would be coming to get him up to help in the marshes any minute now. He sat bolt upright in his bedding. He had been dreaming that he was in Port Hebert and a boy again.

Benoit sat across the shelter grinning at him. He was fully clothed. But then he never removed his breeches, even when he slept.

"Overslept? You are reverting to town ways even before you get back into town." There was a disapproving tone in his voice. Then suddenly Benoit stiffened. Marcel reached for his musket. He knew enough to trust Benoit's remarkable senses and even more remarkable instincts. He cursed himself under his breath. After he shot their dinner, he had failed to reload his musket, a beginner's mistake that Benoit had warned him about before.

Benoit rose to his feet and walked out into the clearing. Marcel knew that attention would be drawn from him by this gesture and that Benoit was giving him time to reload. He reached quickly for his powder horn and his pouch with the lead balls.

Benoit called a greeting in Micmac but there was no response. Finally the bushes parted and two Indians and a white man entered the clearing.

"Well, well, you old half-breed," the white man said in French, "I thought you were up on the Gaspereau still. How was your winter?"

"What are you doing around these parts, MacMichaels?" Benoit said, rushing over and throwing an arm around the newcomer.

"Jean," he called out to Marcel, "this is my old friend Timothy MacMichaels, out of Saco to the south. Do we have any meat left for him?"

It was a signal between them. Whenever Benoit called him

by the wrong name it meant immediate danger. Marcel had completed loading his musket. He picked up his friend's skinning knife and stuck it into his waistband. He knew the trouble. Benoit had warned him about roving bands of Indians, sometimes led by white men, who murdered trappers carrying a winter's work to market. From his strange-sounding name, Marcel guessed that MacMichaels was from the English settlements. The Indians were probably Abenacki. Marcel searched the bushes across the stream for signs of any more members of this raiding party. When he looked back at Benoit, he noticed that the older man was keeping MacMichaels between himself and a clump of bushes along the bank on the opposite side of the brook. He had seen something there. Marcel studied the bushes more carefully as he picked up the last sticks with roasted strips of meat. He was sure of it. There was just the slightest rustling in the bushes. He studied the rest of the far embankment as he walked toward Benoit and MacMichaels. He handed the sticks of last night's meat to Benoit. The Penobscot pretended it was hot and dropped it. Out of instinct MacMichaels bent down to grab the food and Benoit's knee came crashing into his face.

Marcel picked his target. It was not the Indian who stood next to the fallen MacMichaels. Instead he aimed his musket at the Abenacki who rose from the bushes across the stream. He fired. The Indian leapt into the air. The ball caught him in the throat. Then Marcel swung his musket toward MacMichaels's companion, but the Abenacki had sprung into action. He dodged out of the way and raised his own weapon to his shoulder. Benoit charged into him and the musket fired harmlessly into the air. The two men went crashing to the ground. More Abenacki stood across the stream but MacMichaels, back on his feet, yelled out to them. He staggered away from Marcel toward the brook. He entered the water.

"Get the bastard," Benoit called to Marcel.

Marcel pulled a knife from his waist and moved toward MacMichaels, but then he hesitated. The man was staggering. He could do no more harm to them. There was no need to kill again. MacMichaels reached the far bank. Two of the Abenacki picked him up under the arms and dragged him away. Marcel turned to aid Benoit. The Abenacki was already dead and about to be scalped. Benoit took his knife from Marcel's hand.

"You should have killed him. There will be more ambushed trappers in the woods because you let the son of a bitch live. He would have had no mercy for you."

"Who is he?"

"He operates out of Maine. He kills trappers and takes their furs and sells them. Nice work. He sits on his ass at home before the fire and lets some other poor clod trap and skin for him. All he has to do in the spring is trap and skin the trappers and he gets rich."

"But he seemed to know you," Marcel objected. "If he planned to kill us why would he walk into our camp with greetings? He must have known you recognized him."

"Know him! I used to work for him."

Marcel waited for a further explanation. Surely Benoit had not ambushed trappers. But the grin on his face was ample testimony that he had.

"He's your friend and you wanted me to kill him?"

"Hell, yes. Now I'm a trapper."

Marcel could not deny the logic. He tried to ask Benoit what had converted him to the honest trade of trapping, but the older man would not tell him. Instead he complained that he would have to bury the dead Indians or they would drive them from the clearing.

"Nor have we seen the last of MacMichaels," Benoit said softly. "You should have killed him while you had the chance. And damn it, I don't feel like burying any Abenacki. Let's break camp. They'll follow us looking for our cache. And if they have any concern for kin they will bury their own dead and we'll escape."

CHAPTER TWO

Port Hebert, March 1755

The icy Fundy wind bent the green marsh grass low before it. The cows that made up the Port Hebert herd turned their backs on the sea and munched, bending their necks lower, to reach the tender blades of salty grass. Nina Babineau walked warily through the grass. She wanted to take off her shoes so they would remain dry for the festival tonight. The whole village would be there and she would be miserable if she had to dance in wet shoes. But the thought of her feet sinking into the cold mud dissuaded her.

"TiJoe," she called out toward the herd. Her ten-year-old brother was supposed to be watching over the herd. She called again. Still no response. TiJoe was never where he was supposed to be. She pulled her woolen shawl about her shoulders more snugly. The pail she carried contained slices of smoked ham and a small jug of beer—the boy's lunch. She had taken some of Papa's tobacco and hidden it in the pail. TiJoe would have his pipe with him. Her parents were old, too old to understand how important it was to TiJoe to be able to smoke his pipe with his friends like a man. At sixteen she still felt closer to TiJoe than she did to her strict parents. Again she called his name. She had almost reached the herd by now. Several of the cows turned their huge brown eyes on her as she called out, but most continued to ignore her.

"Well," Nina exclaimed out loud. "He is not here." She tried to ignore the sinking feeling TiJoe's actions so often produced in her. If the neighbors' cows wandered off and TiJoe was on watch, Papa would strap him. She could not bear those times. She searched the horizon out toward Chignecto Bay—an arm of the Bay of Fundy. She could see men working far out on the mud flats. In this part of the bay the tides were so great that in a few hours from now the flats on which men stood would be covered by twenty-five feet of sea. But the tide did not impress Nina. She remembered not so long ago when their village of Port Hebert had been closer to the sea, and she could recall when the marshlands she now stood upon had not even existed. They had been reclaimed from Chignecto by hard work. The men out on the mud flats continued that work, wresting more and more acres of valuable and fertile marshland from the sea for their cattle. With grain growing on dry fields and cattle in abundance in the marshlands and additional bounty provided by the sea all about them, the people of Port Hebert, while not as rich as those of Grand Pre across the Minas Basin, could still think of themselves as blessed.

Nina walked toward the sea. Perhaps TiJoe had been drawn toward the workmen. She left the thick grass. Now only tufts of marsh grass struggled up through the fresh mud. She knew her shoes would be ruined. She pulled them off and shivered as her toes touched the cold mud. Although it was spring the water was cold. In midsummer it would not be much warmer.

Nina recognized the huge form of Lucien Hebert and the even larger frame of Gilles, his son. Lucien was a direct descendant of the founding settlers of Port Hebert in the last century and was the village's wealthiest farmer.

"Papa Hebert," she called out to him. "Have you seen my brother, TiJoe?"

Lucien waved back at her. It was clear that he had not heard her. But Gilles replied.

"That little rascal. We sent him to the village to Maman Adele to bring us our lunch. He has not returned."

Nina felt embarrassed. She always felt embarrassed in the

16

presence of the Heberts, especially the male Heberts and most especially the absent one, Marcel, the younger son.

"What is that you are carrying in the pail?" Gilles inquired as Nina approached.

"TiJoe's lunch," Nina responded.

"Good, let's have it," said Gilles, reaching for Nina's hand.

Lucien slapped his son's wrist. "You oversized oaf. Did not Maman Adele teach you anything? You don't reach for what belongs to someone else."

Gilles' face clouded. Had any man other than his father spoken to him in that tone, much less slapped him, Gilles would have broken him in two. But his father was not just any man.

"Please." Nina offered the lunch pail to Lucien. "Please take it. But I am sure it will not be enough for the both of you."

The older man bowed gracefully to the girl. "You are most generous, Mademoiselle Babineau, and certainly far more reliable than your little brother. My friend Babin has his hands full with that son of his."

"The brat deserves a warm bottom," said Gilles gruffly as he slammed a pointed stake into the oozing mud and drove it deeper into the slime. The muscles on his arms bulged with the exertion and the veins in his neck swelled and appeared all the more blue in contrast to his flushed face.

Lucien started to laugh at his son's display of brute strength. He ate some of the ham and took a swig of the beer, leaving the rest for Gilles.

"Step aside, *mon enfant*," he chuckled. He raised his huge wooden mallet high above his head and brought it smashing down atop Gilles' stake. Five stakes had already been embedded deep in the mud flat. Long after they left this spot for the day, the surging waters of the bay would return and wash over the freshly implanted logs. They would be covered throughout the high tide and then, as the water ebbed, drawing debris, sand, and mud back toward the sea, the logs would catch some of it, much as a weir trapped fish as the sea retrenched. Gradually the trapped mud would rise high enough to emerge out of the sea and more salt marsh would be reclaimed to feed more cattle. Acadia was a land of the sea. Few other farm communities in the world were so closely bound to the rise and fall of the tides.

Lucien swung the mallet again and Gilles continued to hold the stake firmly in place. Gradually its pointed end sank deeper and deeper until it was firmly embedded. Nothing, not even the force of the Chignecto—Fundy tides could dislodge it. Gilles relaxed as the thud of his father's last swing of the mallet echoed out onto the mud flats. The wind had changed and the tide was beginning to turn. Soon it would be time to leave the mud flats for the relatively dry footing of the salt marsh behind them.

Nina searched the swaying grass again for some sign of TiJoe. Her rich brown hair blew across her face. She brushed it away with her hand. Her face and her neck were tanned golden by exposure to the sun and wind, and her high cheekbones glowed. At sixteen the effect of the elements on her complexion was strikingly beautiful, yet those same elements, if they continued to beat against her, would turn her skin as tough as shoe leather by the time she was thirty.

Gilles took the mallet from his father and swung it over his shoulder. The older man watched his son stare at the girl. He smiled and remembered what it was like to be twenty.

"You two go on ahead of me," he said to them. "I'll round up the cows and perhaps TiJoe as well."

Gilles took Nina by the elbow and started to lead her back toward the marshes. Nina hesitated. She should not let Monsieur Hebert, the leading farmer of their village, do the task assigned to a ten-year-old boy. Babin, as the other men called her father, would be furious and TiJoe's tiny bottom would smart for a week if he ever found out.

Lucien tossed his head back and laughed. "I don't go about snitching on mischievous boys," he said, reading her thoughts. "Old Babin need not know what a scoundrel his son is. After all, I raised one just like him."

A look of anger appeared on Gilles' face and he opened his mouth to protest. Again Lucien laughed.

"My God, Gilles, you are dense."

Gilles' expression grew even darker. He brushed his black hair from his face.

"It is your little brother I refer to, my son," Lucien said at last as he dropped his own massive forearm across Gilles'

18

broad shoulders. "You are slow. Slow to anger, slow to cool off. It is your brother, Marcel, who is the scoundrel."

Gilles did not know how to react. He knew somehow he had been insulted and exonerated at the same time.

"Run, children, the tide comes," the older man joked. "If we stay planted here like stakes our feet will soon get soaked."

The wind swirled again directly from the sea. High above them white clouds raced across the gray sky toward the hills beyond Port Hebert.

Gilles and Nina turned their backs to the gale and trudged up into the marsh grasses.

"Are you going to the fête, Nina?"

Nina nodded excitedly. She had been able to think of nothing else all day until her mother had sent her out with TiJoe's lunch pail.

"May I call on you and escort you?" Gilles blurted out. He had been preparing himself for a week to make this request.

Nina stared at him in some confusion. She had hoped to be asked by a Hebert but she had hoped against hope that it would be Marcel, if only he would return. She had never considered that this bull of a man, so dark and brooding, would be interested in her. The brothers were such contrasts. Marcel was handsome and witty. He continually shocked the whole village with his indifference to family and his rejection of their way of life. He had fled Port Hebert and taken up with the Indians in the wilderness across the bay. Poor Gilles was so loyal to family and tradition, strong and quiet. He would be a good husband some day to some village girl, but surely not to her.

"I don't think my father would hear of it," Nina said finally.

"Oh, no," Gilles said, shaking the dark curls that covered his head. "My papa has already spoken to Babin, your father."

Nina started to laugh. She did not need to be told that Babin was her father. Papa Hebert was right. Gilles was slow. But then her laugh faded as the implication of his words sank in. A father did not talk to another father just to allow a daughter to go to the fête in the company of his son. That her father was talking to Lucien Hebert about Gilles frightened her deeply.

"May I?" Gilles repeated.

Nina was still lost in thought and did not respond.

"Nina?"

"What?"

"May I escort you?"

"I guess so," she said wistfully.

Gilles flashed one of his infrequent smiles. He had a blackened front tooth. Four years ago, when he had been Nina's age, he'd gotten a toothache. He could still remember the throbbing, blinding pain that had surged through his face. He had told no one, and the pain had finally ceased. He could remember the relief almost as well as the pain. But then the tooth had turned gray and finally black. It embarrassed him and he grew even more solemn than normal. He noticed that Nina was staring at his face. He pretended to cough and covered his mouth.

"I'll be by your house right after sunset," Gilles said from behind his hand.

They continued to walk through the marsh grass. The village of Port Hebert now came into view. It consisted of about fifty small wooden houses spread out along the banks of the creek. Each had a small garden plot and a barn for the cattle. The creek, which in earlier days had emptied directly into the sea at the edge of the village, now meandered across the reclaimed marshlands and finally spilled onto the new mud flats into Chignecto Bay. Its banks were lined with boats, some no more than canoes, others much larger and able to forge out into the waves of the Bay of Fundy. They were a reminder to any observer that these farmer-fishermen were never far removed from the sea.

They entered the village. Nina hoped that Gilles would stop at his own house, but he did not. He continued instead to hold her by the arm and lead her toward her own house.

Nina opened her front door and stepped through. Gilles had to bend low to enter the foyer. The Babineau house was very much like his own. The foyer was an unheated, tunnellike extension of the house. Its interior wall was the back side of the fireplace and chimney. The front door leading to it was always unlocked. Tradition allowed any traveler to seek shelter in an Acadian home without disturbing the owners. A traveler, caught in foul weather, could always find a dry anteroom with some warmth from the chimney stones. In the morning, when his unwitting hosts arose, he could be sure that Acadian hospitatity would provide him with a hot breakfast.

Nina opened the door to the interior of the house. Gilles held back until Odette Babineau, Nina's mother, called from the hearth where she was baking bread and small rolls for tonight's festival. Her coarse linen apron was covered with cornmeal, as were her hands. Babin himself sat in a straight-back wooden chair watching his wife knead the flour. A column of white twisting smoke rose from the clay pipe he held in his hand.

Nina went to her mother and kissed her.

"Stay clear of me, girl," said the older woman. "I'm a mess."

Babin greeted Gilles with a nod of his gray head. "Hebert."

"Monsieur Babineau," Gilles responded, not quite daring to greet the older man by the nickname that everyone used in his absence but that only his own age group used to his face. Gilles did not know what Babin's first name really was, and sometimes he wondered if Madame Babineau would not have to stop and think about it if asked. It never dawned on him to think that if TiJoe, or Little Joe, was his son, that perhaps Babin's name might be Joseph.

"Join me in a pipe?" Babin asked him.

"No, sir." Gilles declined politely. "I have to go home and wash up for the fête."

"Are you going with anybody special?" the older man teased.

Gilles' blush was almost instantaneous. He tried to stammer an answer. Before he could respond, however, Babin interrupted him.

"You take good care of my daughter. You understand, young man? She's a good girl and I want her to stay one. Young bucks start coming around and trouble begins. I know. I was one myself once. Maman and I strayed not one bit, though. She was every inch a virgin when we went before the curé, weren't you, Dette?"

Now it was Babin's wife who flushed. She ignored him and went back to her dough.

"I must go now," Gilles said nervously.

Babin stood. He was a short, thin, wiry man whose head reached only to the top of Gilles' shoulders.

"Why run, boy? Do I frighten you?"

"No, sir," Gilles said defensively. In truth, very little frightened him, but this stern little man did make him nervous.

"Didn't my son return with you?"

Nina tried to send Gilles a warning with her eyes but Gilles' attention was riveted on the face of the man who stood in front of him.

"No, my father went looking for him."

"Your father went looking for the cowherd? That means the whole village may have to go looking for its cows. The little brat. I'll tear his hide off."

Nina looked at her mother in dismay. She got no comfort there. Her mother's face showed only fear.

Gilles, looking terribly uncomfortable, started to back out of the house. He turned to Nina.

"I'll be here at sunset," he said, moving away from her.

She was about to cry out a warning to him as he reached the doorway, but almost instinctively he ducked his head at the last moment and made it safely out to the entryway, closing the interior door behind him. He raced down the dirt road to his own house.

The Hebert house was a larger version of the Babineau home. It too had an outer foyer built about the exterior of the fireplace and chimney. But Lucien Hebert was the richest farmer in Port Hebert and he had added a sleeping loft, a food storage attic, and a lean-to kitchen to the right side of the hearth.

Gilles had warned his mother of his intention to bathe this evening, and sure enough, a blanket had been strung across the room to hide the tub from the kitchen so that he might enjoy some privacy.

"Maman," he called out. "Is the water ready?"

"You're damned right it is," answered a male voice from behind the blanket.

Gilles pulled the blanket away angrily to reveal his younger brother, Marcel, luxuriating in the tub of hot water meant for him.

"When did you get back? Why did you get back? And what the hell are you doing in my bath?"

"Why, brother, I returned for the spring fête. I wouldn't

miss it. Maman took one whiff of me, and she ordered me into the tub, dropped a cake of her soap in, and left." He scratched his armpit and began to soap up his chest and his neck. "Hey, big brother, would you mind scrubbing my back. I can't reach it."

"Up your ass," Jacques said angrily.

"So you're doing that? I knew it would come to that, all of this farming and the curé coming to town to worry you about girls and girls about you."

"Get the hell out of my water while it's still hot," Gilles demanded.

"Whatever you say, *mon frère*." Marcel grimaced and seemed to raise his rear off the tub bottom. An odd groan was heard, and large bubbles appeared on the water. Relief crossed his face.

"You farted in my bathtub!" Gilles shouted. He reached for Marcel's shoulders but his hands slipped off the other's skin.

Marcel rose to his feet. He was smaller than Gilles, but not much. He was heavily muscled in his chest and thighs. The inner door of the house opened and Maman Adele entered. She was a dark woman with a brown golden complexion, black hair, and a faint trace of a moustache on her upper lip. It seemed incongruous that she could have given birth to the two young giants who faced off against each other just behind the blanket. But they were not beyond the range of her voice.

"Marcel," she yelled out with her peculiar nasal twang. "Get out of the tub. Gilles, get your clothes off and get into the water. I can smell you from here."

Marcel started to chuckle.

Gilles protested. "He's already dirtied the water."

"What do you expect from me?" the little woman yelled again. "Am I supposed to haul heated water for each of you? What do you take me for? You used the same water when you were boys. You can use the same water now."

She grabbed a large cotton cloth and pulled aside the blanket. She handed it to her naked son.

"Maman," said Marcel, looking uncomfortable for the first time, "you should not be back here with me like this."

She slapped his bare bottom loudly and laughed. "I saw

23

you all the time when you were not much to look at," she joked, "and by the way, you're still not much to look at."

Marcel wrapped himself in the cloth and started to laugh.

Gilles' anger gave way to embarrassment. He did not like the familiarity that existed between Marcel and their mother. He started to remove his clothes. He stopped when Maman Adele pushed the blanket and hauled a cauldron of heated water to the tub. She poured it in and steam rose from the water up to the rough-hewn wooden rafters. Gilles waited until his mother had disappeared behind the blanket once again. Marcel had dried himself off and was putting his buckskin leggings back on.

"Why put those smelly old things on?" Adele called to him from the open hearth.

"You're peeking," Marcel responded.

"No, I just know you."

"I haven't any other clothes."

Adele walked to the high chest next to her large double bed. She rummaged through it for a few minutes and pulled out a pair of homespun breeches and a linen shirt. "Here," she said tossing them at the blanket.

"Maman, these were mine two years ago. I've grown."

"Not from what I saw," she laughed.

Marcel tried the breeches first. He had to suck in his belly but he was able to button them.

Gilles ignored his brother. He thrust one leg into the reheated tub water. He hated the first touch of hot water on his body almost as much as he loved the glowing sensation that surged through his limbs and torso once he became used to the warmth. He hesitated a moment and then placed his other leg into the tub. Just as he started to lower his rump into the water, Marcel made a disgusting sound with his mouth. Gilles glared at him, but the younger man merely laughed and went to join his mother on the other side of the blanket.

Gilles sank into the water. The water rose up to his neck. He sighed and allowed the back of his neck to rest against the rim of the tub. The tension in his muscles began to slip away. He was ashamed of himself for wanting to lash out at his brother. He was supposed to love his brother but, by God, Marcel made it difficult. He shook his head. Tonight he would think only of Nina. He would confess his feelings about Marcel to the curé next time he arrived at Port Hebert from Beauséjour.

Lucien had cut himself a switch from a sapling that had sprouted among the marsh grasses. The cows moved reluctantly before him. They would need milking soon. The little Babineau boy was courting a lot of trouble by shirking his responsibilities. He saw the tiny cloud of smoke arise from the gully to his left. At first he thought there might be a brush fire. He left the cows and moved toward the smoke. He heard the sound of boys laughing and decided to get on his hands and knees and sneak up on them. They were all village boys and he recognized all of them, TiJoe Babineau, one of the Mouton boys (they all looked alike and Lucien could never remember names), Felix Arseneault, whose father had been lost out on the bay two winters ago. There was a Dugas, a Bernard, and Gilbert Broussard. He recognized all of them, and he knew also what they were doing in addition to smoking. He rose to his feet.

"You'll all grow hair on your palms," he boomed out loudly like an avenging angel.

Never were six boys more frightened and never were six pairs of breeches buttoned more quickly. Poor Louis Bernard dropped his pipe and some of the lit tobacco fell into his open breeches as he fumbled with the buttons. He started to howl and jump up and down. Several of the boys began to run away from Lucien and back toward the village. Lucien, however, grabbed TiJoe by the cowlick. The boy squealed in fright and tried to pull away. But it was useless. Lucien's grip was viselike.

"Ah, Monsieur Babineau, the exquisite herder of cows for the village, how can it be that your responsibilities were spread all over the marshland while you were sent for lunch for the marsh workers? How can it be that I discover you and your friends pulling on your puny peckers instead of watching over your father's and my prized milk cows? How can it be?" Lucien repeated as his fingers gripped TiJoe's hair even more tightly.

The boy's eyes were wide with terror. Lucien looked into the child's face, tanned by .days in the sun, wide eyes so brown as to appear black. He was a smaller version of his pretty sister.

"Have you no explanations for me, TiJoe?"

"I didn't think..." the boy stammered.

"That is quite clear," Lucien exclaimed.

The boy was so frightened that he could barely speak.

Lucien took pity on him. "'TiJoe, sit down with me here." He pulled his pipe from his pocket and stuffed it carefully with tobacco, then patted it neatly with his thumb. He sparked his flint and his taper caught. The smoke soon rose lazily until it reached above his head.

Lucien took a puff. He glanced over at TiJoe, who sat tensely waiting for the blow to fall. Lucien offered the boy his pipe for a puff. TiJoe reached up to receive it hesitantly.

"Go ahead, take a puff," Lucien said calmly. He watched TiJoe puff away expertly.

"Now, young man, we must discuss the notion of responsibility."

The boy nodded solemnly.

"This village," Lucien continued, "can never survive as a collection of individuals who never think about each other. We are the people of Port Hebert. We help each other. We come to each other's aid when needed whether asked or not. Men farm, fish, and reclaim marshland from the bay. Women cook and make clothes and keep house and if necessary farm and fish and reclaim the new lands from the bay. Even boys like you and your friends Mouton, Arseneault, and the others, you are given tasks for the benefit of the whole. TiJoe, when you run off and leave all our cows unattended, you hurt all of us, including yourself. Do you understand me?"

"Yes, Monsieur Hebert. Are you going to tell my father?" the boy asked timidly.

"Should I?"

TiJoe shook his head.

"Why not?"

"Because he'll beat the shit out of me," the boy said. He looked sheepishly at Lucien, suddenly embarrassed by the vulgarity he had used.

"Well, then, I think I could be persuaded to keep my mouth shut."

The boy sighed with relief.

"If, and only if," Lucien continued, "you promise me there will be no more 'I did not think' excuses."

This time TiJoe nodded solemnly.

"Be off with you, then, and get those cows back in their barns. I graduated from cowherding when I was only slightly older than you, and that was a very long time ago."

Lucien tossed his sapling switch to TiJoe. The boy caught it and scrambled up out of the gully.

The older man smiled and watched TiJoe disappear into the high grass. Lucien continued to puff on his pipe. Finally he rose and climbed up out of the gully himself. Off in the distance he could hear the jingling of cow bells and he could see the last of the herd making its way into the village.

Despite the disappearance of the snow from the hills around the harbor Lt. Audry Hastings thought the new town of Halifax was still cold beyond human endurance. The wind coming off the ocean pierced his greatcoat and cut through the wool of his jacket. He shivered as he crossed the muddy street to the Lord Halifax Inn.

"Good God," he mumbled, "wouldn't his lordship piss in his boots if he knew what a flea-bitten tavern and a flea-ridden hole of a village these special projects of his have created—and all bearing his vaunted name."

The wooden steps to the tavern entrance were blocked by a mud puddle at least six inches deep. Hastings looked up and down the muddy lane that passed for a street in this village. There seemed no easier way. The horse-drawn military carts rode through these streets like a never-ending parade. It had devastating effects on the efforts of the road builders—especially when the rains came in off the sea.

"There is nothing else to do," Hastings said aloud. He leapt forward. His right boot sank into the cold mud. His foot felt the chill as the leather became soaked. Hastings leapt again and the effect was repeated, but this time on the left foot. One more step and he would be beyond the puddle and up onto the wooden porch of the tavern. He could feel some of the water seep through the stitching of his boot. He cursed. He hated to have cold, wet feet. In all his months in Halifax he never seemed able to avoid it.

Once on the porch of the tavern he stomped his feet to

remove some of the mud. But he would get very little off in this fashion. Poor Johnston, his orderly, would have his hands full of caked mud when he polished the lieutenant's boots this evening.

He hesitated, unwilling to enter the tavern with muddy boots. Then he remembered he was in Halifax—in godforsaken America, not back home. He opened the door and stepped inside.

His nostrils were greeted almost immediately by the familiar odor of roasting mutton and English beer. It was a hint of home and warmed him almost as much as the blazing fire in the tavern hearth.

The calendar might say it was spring and the snow might be gone in the hills, but when the surf crashed against the stony shore beyond the harbor and the chilly North Atlantic winds poured down the hills onto the village, then Audry Hastings would demand a fire in the hearth even if the calendar claimed it was July. Apparently the rest of the patrons of the Lord Halifax agreed.

There were two other men in the taproom waiting for him. They sat at a table not far from the fire. One had a black patch over his eye. He rested his hand on his cheek, but it did not cover the scar that ran along his cheek to disappear under the patch. The scar twisted his lip into a sneer. The other man wore a powdered wig, but it was his only claim to elegance. His clothes were shabby and he had the appearance of a clerk.

"Cousin," Hastings greeted the scarred man. He was Jonas Audry, the son of his mother's brother, a branch of the family that had contributed his first name—a gift of dubious merit as far as he was concerned. He barely knew Jonas and he had heard some petty scandals about the scar, but it had all been hushed up. The Audrys were Virginia planters and rarely got this far north.

"The governor appreciates your coming to this meeting, Lieutenant Hastings." The clerk, whose name Hastings could never remember, bowed slightly as he spoke.

"Governor Lawrence is my patron, sir, my commander. I am always at his service."

The clerk seemed to fidget a bit, pulling at his neck cloth in discomfort.

"But there remains a problem," the clerk said finally, his eyes darting toward Jonas Audry.

Hastings smiled. "Governor Lawrence is not my cousin Audry's patron, is that your problem, Evans?" he guessed.

"It's Ernst, John Ernst." He said this last without even a hint of annoyance. He was accustomed to people like Hastings forgetting his name.

"Ernst," Hastings repeated. "You wonder what role cousin Audry is to play?"

"I do."

"It's simple. Governor Lawrence is not the fool that Mascarene and the other administrators of His Majesty's poor colony of Nova Scotia have been. Even though he supported Lord Halifax's colonization move, the real British subjects are still the minority in this colony."

"That is all known to me, sir, and to Governor Lawrence," said Ernst.

"The French Acadians still constitute a majority of the population and without doubt have the best lands along both the Fundy shores."

"I have heard Governor Lawrence speak highly of the potential of the Annapolis Valley as farming land," Ernest said piously.

"Potential versus reality," Audry said, speaking for the first time. He dabbed his chin with a scented handkerchief.

"As usual, my cousin gets to the heart of the matter. Governor Lawrence is prepared to drop the policy of placating our French subjects and acknowledge them for what they really are—traitors. Every time France and England have gone to war the Acadians have shown their true colors. They have sided with France, despite their feigned oaths of allegiance to Great Britain. It shall be Governor Lawrence's policy to remove the Acadians from Nova Scotia."

Ernst looked over his shoulder as if afraid Hastings might be overheard. He finally looked again at Hastings. "That is the secret policy that the governor has revealed to the council after permission from London was received," he said, almost in a whisper.

Audry smirked. He had been informed by Hastings that London had advised caution—a warning that Lawrence had no intention of following.

"The plan is simple," Hastings continued. "First we move against the French at Beauséjour, a retaliation for their intervention in the Ohio Valley. No war need be declared, although eventually our masters in London and Paris will surely get around to it. Next we disarm the Acadians. Then, once any possibility of assistance for them from France is crushed, we round them up and ship them out. Their lands, livestock, treasure, all are forfeit, and that's where my dear cousin fits in."

Ernst turned his attention to the man with the eye patch.

"There are two things I want," Audry said in his slow slurred speech, which betrayed his origin far south of Nova Scotia.

"In Virginia we raise tobacco," he said, "a crop that uses a great deal of labor. We seem to have an insatiable need for black slaves, but when they become impossible or far too expensive to get, we take white convict labor. I'd like to see a couple of shiploads of these frogs head toward the auction block in Williamsburg."

Ernst nodded to Audry. "I'm sure Governor Lawrence would have no objection to such a destination."

Audry stared at Ernst. It upset the clerk being stared at by a one-eyed man.

"We can count on it, then?" Hastings said.

"Well." Ernst fidgeted in his wooden chair. "There are no guarantees, of course. His Excellency might intervene."

"Not likely," interrupted Hastings. "You just said yourself that the governor could have little objection to the destination. Besides, Governor Lawrence doesn't give a farthing for the details. They are all in your hands."

The clerk sat still in his chair. His face broke into a grin. "Yes, they are, aren't they?" he said finally, after savoring the moment.

"And you expect something for considering our request, don't you?" Audry chimed in.

Ernst said nothing, but he continued to grin.

"There will be a package delivered to your rooms which I am sure you will appreciate," Hastings continued.

"I hope I appreciate it," Ernst interrupted. "I wouldn't want to feel unappreciated."

"You'll be satisfied," said Audry.

"And the second request?" Ernst said directly to the southerner.

"My cousin Hastings is not a rich man. Good family, of course, but no lands. I was thinking that some of these Acadian lands might come to him. Of course, with my knowledge and my wealth I could back him." He glanced at Hastings. "For a share of his profits, of course."

Hastings knew the man would want the lion's share but he was in no position to argue. He needed cousin Jonas Audry if he was ever to be anything more than a garrison officer in some godforsaken outpost of the empire.

Ernst sat quietly. "I am a secretary, gentlemen. What you ask is beyond my ability to give. The governor will oversee what is distributed. It will be done carefully and to his own advantage."

"Agreed," Audry exclaimed. "But it will do us no harm if you are there to remind him of Lieutenant Hastings's good offices. You, of course, can expect an even more significant package delivered to your rooms should this work out."

Ernst smiled and rose from his chair. "I'll do my best, and my best includes not leaving Governor Lawrence too much on his own. I'd best be off."

Neither Audry nor Hastings rose with him.

"Good day to you, sirs," Ernst offered.

Hastings responded but Audry merely gave a slight wave of his hand.

Ernst turned toward the door and then stopped to face the cousins.

"Yes?" Audry inquired.

"My rooms, sir," Ernst said smiling, "they are on Hollis Street." He turned abruptly and left the tavern.

Audry reached over and touched his cousin's arm. "Now you do your part, Lieutenant, and we'll all prosper. All but the frogs, that is."

Antoine Dugas was a fiddler without peer in the whole of Acadia. His fingers moved unerringly along the strings with such speed that some had suggested that he had a pact with the evil one. The curé from Beauséjour admonished the villagers not to partake in superstitious gossip, but most of the time the curé was not in Port Hebert and it was hard to

31

remember his admonitions when one listened to Antoine and his fiddle.

Dugas was in rare form for the fête. He was sitting on a wooden platform. His music resounded throughout the village center and his foot pounded on the plank platform and provided the percussion for the jig that danced from his bow.

The village was lighted by torches. As each wife arrived for the festivities she deposited her offering to feed the hungry mob on a huge trestle table. The men walked off together toward the marshland on the edge of the bay but soon returned carrying iron pots filled with sea water. These were hung over fire pits. The evening air was chilly and the new arrivals thronged about the fire, all except the young unmarrieds who made their way toward Dugas' music. Soon several couples were dancing in time to the Breton Celtic rhythm that filled the night air. Children raced from the dancers back to the fire pits playing tag, their dark forms darting from torchlight to darkness and then into the light of the cooking fires. It gave them an appearance more ephemeral than real. Yet no one could deny the reality of the squeals, the laughter, and the utter glee that came from these moving shadows.

The water in the cooking pots hissed. Giant cloth sacks were slit open with knives and out of them slithered huge lobsters and crabs and some shellfish—clams and mussels primarily. The children darted at the lobsters, teasing them and jumping back with shouts of fright mixed with anticipation as the crustaceans raised their wicked-looking pincers in self-defense. But soon stronger hands grabbed the creatures and dropped them unceremoniously into the boiling water. For a few seconds the sounds of hard shells scraping against iron were heard, and then nothing but the bubbling of the water.

Lucien stood off to the right of the steaming cooking pots. He was famished from his day's work. The light lunch he shared with Gilles had not really satisfied him. He smiled to himself and then puffed on his pipe. The boy TiJoe had diligently rounded up the cows and led them home. If he had not, Lucien was not sure he could have maintained his dignity driving cattle through the village. Any more than he was sure he could keep himself from grabbing the iron tongs away from Madame Arseneault, who guarded them, and dipping into the pot for a lobster.

Old Broussard came up to Lucien and asked for some tobacco. He had left his at home. He had sent his son, young Broussard, home to fetch it for him. Without tobacco the night of the fête was not to be borne.

Lucien gave generously from his leather pouch. Many Acadians mixed other weeds in with the tobacco, but Lucien preferred his tobacco undiluted.

Broussard and Hebert stood silently smoking and watching the whole village assemble.

"Where's Babin?" Broussard asked finally. "I have seen none of his family yet."

Lucien smiled. He knew Broussard was more of a gossip than any woman in the village. He was looking for a tidbit tying Gilles Hebert to Nina Babineau. "I've not seen any of the Babineaus either," Lucien said honestly.

Broussard fell silent for some more moments. André Mouton, Maman Adele's cousin, joined them as they waited patiently for the Widow Arseneault to give the word. She lifted the lid of the great iron pot. Steam rose up into the night sky and the air was filled with the aroma of cooking shellfish. She grinned at the three men.

"Aha!" exclaimed Lucien. "We feast."

The woman pulled a large bright red lobster from the pot and deposited it on a pewter plate. It was followed by a second and a third. Each man had his own. Lucien grabbed his gingerly with his hand and pulled off the claws. He cracked the shell with his viselike fingers and pulled out the meat and plopped it instantly into his mouth. He burned his tongue but hardly noticed it as the delicious taste of the lobster flooded his mouth.

"Ach," complained the cook, "don't your wives feed you at home? You act like hungry pigs. Here, wait for the butter sauce."

"Ah, Dominique, my love," Mouton said, taking a pinch of the woman's behind, "my wife feeds me all the food that I want but she does so little for my other appetites."

The woman squealed in shock and delight.

"Mouton, stop it," Broussard complained. "Dominique is my sister. Have you forgotten?"

Mouton started to laugh. "She's a grown woman, a widow, a mother. You cannot protect her like Babin protects his virgin daughter."

"Yes, Georges," Dominique Arseneault interrupted angrily, "watch out for your own children. I don't need your protection."

"My friends." Lucien tried to calm tempers. "Let's enjoy the food and the music and let the good times roll."

The others grew silent. Dominique followed the example of the men. She would have liked to continue to attack her brother. She was fed up with his interference. It had been lonely for her these past two years. She would have liked a man in her bed. But there was no one. No one, that is, who did not already belong to someone else. Well, the other women should be willing to do a little sharing, but no man would come to her with Broussard hanging around like a watchdog. But so be it. Lucien was right, as usual. They were here tonight to enjoy themselves and not to fight. She returned to her cooking.

"They say that LeLoutre, the priest, has visited Grand Pre," Broussard said, repeating a rumor that all already had heard.

Lucien nodded. "He'll be coming to Port Hebert before too long. That can do us no good," he continued as he pulled a handful of lobster meat from its shell and dropped it into the pot of melted butter that Dominique Arseneault had set out for them.

More and more hungry people were lined up in front of the pot waiting to be fed. But all acknowledged the primacy of the three village elders.

"I too prefer it when the curé from Beauséjour visits. Those missionaries from Isle Royale are too intense, especially this one. We will be on our knees doing penances for the rest of the spring," Mouton complained.

Broussard looked worried. "If that's all he does. His Indians leveled Beaubassin when the villagers would not leave their land and retreat across the border onto French soil."

Lucien shook his head. "We're like Grand Pre, too far across the line for him to demand that of us. He prefers us to stay here, a constant threat to English security."

"But this new English governor, how will he like that?"

"Not at all," Lucien said, laughing. "But what can he do about it? We're here and we're staying here."

"But if there's a war?" Mouton said.

"There's always a war," Broussard interrupted wearily.

"We stay neutral, just like last time," said Lucien.

The other two men looked admiringly at Lucien as he spoke. Both had objected to the policy of neutrality the last time the priests had come with their Indians, demanding the Acadians fight with them against the English. That was almost a decade earlier. Hebert had been right then. The French had been defeated, even Louisburg had been captured. Only Port Hebert had been commended by the English governor. They had been left in peace ever since. But now the appearance of the dreaded LeLoutre had the villagers worried.

Lucien was confident, however. He had been right ten years ago and he was right now. Let the priests come. He wiped his butter-covered fingers on his pants, then looked around for Adele, hoping she wouldn't scold him for his poor manners. Tonight was a night to enjoy. His whole family was together. Gilles would be coming later with Nina. She was a pretty girl, quiet and shy, not like his Helene. He would have no trouble finding Helene tonight. All he would have to do would be to look for a crowd of young men and the beautiful fair-haired Helene Hebert would be in the middle of them. He had to watch her. Gilles would marry the Babineau girl, of that he was certain. The old fool guarded her like choice wares, yet it was he, Lucien, who should be guarding his own daughter. She worried him. She was too much like her brother Marcel. Willfulness was acceptable in a son but never in a daughter.

And Marcel, his prodigal son, was home at last. This time he would stay.

The sound of the fiddle wafted out to where the elders sat.

"My friends," Lucien said, "we neglect our colleague Dugas. He wears his fingers to the bone providing music for us." Lucien snatched a lobster from the outstretched hand of a hungry young reveler. The young man backed away respectfully. "Don't fret, lad," Lucien said, laughing. "There are plenty more, and I must go feed old Dugas before he faints from exhaustion."

Nina walked beside Gilles Hebert. He held her hand in his own as they strolled down the dirt street toward the music and lights. In front of them Babin and Dette, his wife, walked, but not together. Babin had whipped TiJoe unmercifully before they left their home. Nina could still hear the screams and then the awful sobbing that had followed even after the strap had been put away. Odette Babineau, for the first time in her life, had begged her husband to stop. Babin was deeply displeased with Odette and showed it by walking ahead of her, forcing her to run to keep up.

Nina was still furious with Gilles. TiJoe had returned on time. The cows were safely in their barns. No harm had been done. But Gilles had given the secret away. Nina thought him a fool. There would be no fête for TiJoe tonight, only salty tears.

Babin entered the festival area first. He was greeted by several pipe-smoking cronies and a mug of ale was shoved into his fist. Dette went to the trestle table and deposited her loaves of fresh corn bread. They were still warm and would soon be smothered with melted butter and maple syrup and devoured by the hungry celebrants.

Gilles led Nina to where the young couples danced to Dugas' fiddle. He was not much of a dancer but he had little choice. He could hardly force a young girl over to the crowds of married folk. There she would be swallowed up by the ladies preparing food while he would soon be guzzling beer or ale with his father's friends. He wanted none of that. He wanted to be with Nina.

He could see Nina's face come alive in the glow of the torches as she watched the couples face each other and shuffle their feet expertly in time to the music. She led him by the hand toward the dance platform. All memory of her anger toward him was shunted aside by the magic of Antoine Dugas' fingers.

Gilles followed her reluctantly. Several of the girls called out a welcome to Nina. Helene, Gilles' sister, started to tease her brother about his girlfriend. The young man glared at her angrily, but Nina ignored Helene. Her face was now alive with excitement. She threw her head back and soon her toes and heels began to tap. She was grateful that she had had the good sense to go barefoot in the mud that afternoon. She didn't care if she caught a chill. At least she would dance the night in comfort.

Gilles tried to follow her example but he couldn't get his body to feel the rhythm of the music. It was almost as if his stiff muscles acted as a barrier between the notes and his soul. He saw several of the girls snicker as they watched him. He grew even clumsier. He would have known what to do if it had been the young men who had laughed at him. They knew better and would not dare.

Gilles stopped dancing. Nina did not even notice it. She was not even looking at him.

"Let's rest a bit," he said to her. She turned toward him, disappointment filling her face.

"Gilles, we've just begun."

"I'm tired," he complained. "I've worked hard all day."

"So did everyone else!"

But he had already begun to leave the wooden dance platform. She could not remain there by herself. She followed him out of the torchlight.

"I'll get us something to eat," he offered. "What would you like?"

"Nothing," she said, still pouting.

"Something to drink?"

She had already turned her back on him and was looking back at the dancers. Her feet began to tap out the rhythm on the bare dirt.

"I'll get us some cider," Gilles offered finally, walking away.

She barely noticed his departure. She was shocked when the mug was shoved into her hand. How could he have returned so quickly. She turned and was startled to see the handsome face of Marcel Hebert.

"How come you're not dancing?"

She smiled coyly. "How come you're not?"

"I'd like to." He took the mug back from her and set it on the ground. Taking her hand he led her back into the torchlight and onto the dance platform. He caught her about the waist and whirled her about. It was a tricky and unusual maneuver. Normally the couples did not touch each other.

Marcel's daring encouraged several other youths to place their hands on the waists of their partners. The older folk were too busy to notice. Nina started to laugh as Marcel showed off his fancy footwork. His breeches were incredibly tight, she noticed, and she worried briefly that they might split.

Dugas, inspired by the spirited dancing, picked up tempo and the dancers twirled, their lower bodies a frenzy of motion while their upper torsos and arms remained in the usually static posture of the Celtic dancers of Brittany from whom these Acadians descended.

Suddenly Marcel's raised arm was grabbed as he held it aloft and his whole body was swung around.

"What the hell?" Marcel exclaimed.

"Keep your bloody hands off my girl," Gilles snarled through gritted teeth.

From long experience Marcel knew what would come next. Gilles would never back away now. Marcel relaxed his own tense muscles and started to turn away from Gilles as if to speak to Nina. Then suddenly he spun around, and with all his might he slammed his fist into Gilles' belly.

Gilles' breath came whooshing out of his mouth and his face turned a bright red. He sank to one knee, his face a grotesque mask of pain. But he did not fall. Helene screamed for their father.

"Damn," Marcel said aloud. He had hoped to end it all with one surprise blow, but Gilles had already began to struggle to his feet. Marcel slammed his booted foot into Gilles' shin. The giant merely bellowed in anger and dived at his brother.

Several girls started to scream. Dugas' fiddle finally struck its first errant note and faded off in a dissonant wail. Marcel tried to step aside, but Gilles' enormous fist struck him a glancing blow on the cheek that sent him spinning backward. He tripped over his own feet and landed with a crack on the wooden platform. Through the pain he heard a loud ripping sound as he fell. He had split the seat of his breeches wide open.

He looked up and saw his brother looming above him ready to pounce. It had happened many times when they were boys. Gilles would pummel Marcel, screaming for him to give up, but Marcel never would. He tensed now, awaiting the assault.

"Marcel, Gilles."

Both men were startled by the voice whose authority they had both recognized since childhood.

Lucien entered the torchlit area followed by Helene.

"You disgrace me, both of you," he shouted.

"The bloody bastard took my girl, Papa," Gilles pleaded. "He put his filthy hands all over her. I saw him. And when I tried to stop him he attacked me." He turned toward Marcel.

Lucien grabbed his older son's shoulders and spun him around. With his hand he struck his son's cheek. Tears of humiliation sprang to Gilles' eyes.

"My sons will not brawl in public like common riffraff. You disgrace me before all of our neighbors. Gilles, go join the men."

The older brother's rage returned but he did not challenge his father. As he stalked away from the dance area, Lucien turned to his younger son.

"Marcel, is what he said true?"

Marcel rose to his feet. He heard several of the girls start to giggle. He reached behind himself to try to draw together the ripped seams. Suddenly Marcel's embarrassment turned to amusement. He could not help himself; he grinned from ear to ear. Even Lucien could not remain solemnly patriarchal while his son tried to cover his exposed posterior. The older man started to laugh. His laughter was contagious. Soon the dancers joined in and made him laugh all the harder. He slapped his thigh with glee and his eyes filled with tears.

From the shadows Gilles heard the laughter and it filled him with anger. They laughed at him. He was clumsy. He was slow-witted. He knew what they said about him. It didn't matter that he did the work of three men without complaint while Marcel scampered off to lead the lazy life of a savage. Whatever Marcel wanted he got. Well, not this time. He would not let Marcel steal Nina from him. She was so beautiful, so warm and soft, unlike any creature he had ever known. He loved her and he would not lose her.

*   *   *

Marcel retraced his steps from the village center back to his family's cottage. He had seen enough of the festival.

He did not hear Nina's footsteps until she was almost beside him. He smiled when he saw her.

"Come to get another peek?" he teased.

She blushed.

He saw he had embarrassed her and he regretted it immediately.

"I'm sorry. I think I've ruined the festival for you. Why don't you go back and make up with Gilles. Forget about everything else that happened. I'm going home to bed."

"Don't!" Nina surprised herself by her boldness.

Marcel looked at her and an amused grin crossed his face. "Do you want me to walk around with my rear exposed?"

"Change," she suggested.

"I have no other clothes. This pair of breeches were about the first I ever owned after my mother stopped putting me in dresses," he exaggerated.

"Come to my house. I'll get a needle and thread and stitch you up," she offered.

He smiled and wondered if the offer involved anything more. Then he discounted it. She was barely sixteen and not the type to lead a man on.

"All right," he offered. "Stitch away."

They walked down the dark road together until they came to the Babineau house. Nina opened the outer door. She told Marcel to wait in the foyer while she went in to the house to find her mother's sewing kit. After a second she reappeared at the doorway and leaned her head out.

"Take off your breeches and pass them to me. I won't look," she said.

Marcel laughed. "Tonight seems to be my night to be bare-assed," he said as he started to unbutton his pants.

"Sssh! TiJoe is asleep inside. I don't want to wake him."

Marcel lowered his voice. "Here, don't run back inside. Take them." He handed her the torn breeches. He felt very foolish standing in the foyer of the Babineau house naked from the waist down. He began to grow nervous. What if Babin himself should return home? How would he explain his presence to that stern old man? Then he thought he heard voices outside on the road.

"Damn it!" he exclaimed. He pushed open the door to the inner house and ducked inside. Nina sat before the glowing embers of the hearth trying to thread the needle by their light. She looked up at him in surprise. He stared sheepishly at her and started to cover himself with his hands. He felt like a complete fool.

"I heard somebody out there on the road," he offered lamely. "Maybe I should go back outside."

"Not if someone comes," Nina said, the worry in her voice clear. "Especially if that someone should be my father."

"There's always the storage room," he said, looking over at the door behind the girl.

Nina rose and went to the small window that looked out on the road. "I don't see anyone," she said, almost to herself.

Marcel sat down on the stone step by the fireplace. The surface was rough but it had been warmed by the fire. He picked up the breeches that Nina had discarded while she readied the needle and covered his lap with them.

Nina returned and sat down beside him. She smelled of fresh-baked bread. The smell of her combined with the aroma of burned birch in the fireplace. It was a good mixture.

She finished threading the needle and turned and looked him in the face expectantly. Her eyes were black in the darkness of the room but the glow from the hearth reflected golden highlights in her brown hair.

"Well?" she said.

"Well what?" Marcel repeated.

"Your breeches—give them to me."

Marcel passed them to her without taking his eyes from her face.

The room was silent except for the steady breathing of TiJoe, who slept in the corner on a floor mat. Nina sewed swiftly and expertly while Marcel watched her profile. He could feel the tightness developing in his groin and he knew he had better cover himself. When she finished, Nina passed the breeches back to him. Her hand touched his. He caught it and raised it to his lips.

"What was that for?" she asked shyly.

"A gentleman must thank his lady for her favor."

"No gentleman would sit with his lady like you're sitting."

He moved his hands to her breasts, half expecting her to

41

pull away. He rubbed his hand gently across her firm flesh. He felt her nipple beneath her blouse and he squeezed it gently between his fingers. She gasped with pleasure.

He was fully aroused now. He brought his mouth to the nape of her neck and kissed her. She tossed back her head with pleasure.

Marcel stood, drawing her to her feet with him. He picked her up in his arms and carried her toward her parents' bed and placed her on the down and feather quilt.

A look of panic crossed her face.

"Not here," she whispered. "It wouldn't be right."

"It won't be right anywhere, my love," Marcel whispered. His hands were busy tugging at her blouse. Once he had pulled it out of her skirt, he pushed the front of it upward and uncovered her small breasts. His mouth closed over one and then the other, sending bolts of pleasure through Nina's body.

He reached down and tugged at her skirt. She reached behind herself and undid the button. Her skirt was soon down around her knees and then finally on the floor. Marcel rose on his hands and knees and loomed over her. He could not stop this even if he wanted to, but he knew he should stop. He placed himself into position and moved forward slowly but firmly. Nina cried out with pain. He stopped and listened. He could hear her gasping breath and his own but that was all. He lowered himself again and pushed forward, this time covering Nina's mouth with his own.

Nina lay still for some minutes after he had finished. She could feel him still inside her, although as the moments passed she felt him slipping out. She had wanted this moment. She had wanted Marcel to make love to her more than anything else in the world, and it had happened. The evening that had begun so badly with Gilles had ended in ecstasy with Marcel. The lovemaking had been nothing to her, more pain than anything else, but the feel of his body on top of her, the strength of his arms when he placed them about her and pulled her close to him, the musky smell of him in the midst of their lovemaking, all of it had filled her with a joy. Now she planned to have all her nights filled with him. Now that he had taken her, taken the greatest gift she had to offer, she would be his and he would be hers forever. But they could not remain like this. Her parents would return at any moment. Marcel groaned when she moved.

"Get up, my love," she teased him. "If Babin returns and finds us like this we will both be very unhappy."

The mention of her father's name brought Marcel crashing back to reality. He rose from the bed and reached for his breeches. Nina's stitching had been expert but she had had to tuck in the seam of the pants and they felt even tighter. He dared not bend over. Nina finished straightening out the bed. When her parents returned, they would never guess what had occurred here.

Marcel reached for her and pulled her against his chest. He kissed her.

"I'm going home now. By the time my family returns, I shall be sound asleep. I suggest you do the same." He kissed her on the nose.

She nodded. Walking very carefully, he stepped out of the door into the foyer and then out onto the road. She went to the window to watch him. He knew she would, and even though he could not see her, he waved good-bye as he strolled down the road toward his own home.

She went back to the hearth. She picked up her skirt and blouse and she hung them on her clothes hook. She had bled a bit. She took a cloth and dipped it in the pot of water next to the hearth and washed herself with it. She took her long white cotton nightgown and drew it over her head. She went to her sleeping mat on the opposite side of the room from TiJoe's. She slipped under the covers. As she drifted off to sleep, her mind wandered back to those moments on the bed just across the room.

TiJoe had watched everything they had done. He knew a lot about it from the other boys. It was related to what the older boys had been demonstrating when Monsieur Hebert caught them. He knew that Mama and Papa did it sometimes in the middle of the night when they thought he and Nina were sleeping. Some nights he deliberately stayed awake and hoped that they would do something. But most often he would hear Babin's snore and a disappointed TiJoe knew he might as well fall asleep. He was glad that Nina had done it with Marcel and not with Gilles. He didn't like Gilles very much, but his feeling for Gilles was nothing compared to the animosity he held against his father. Every time he moved in his bed, the pain that shot up from his back reminded him that he hated Babin all the more.

Marcel closed the inner door of his house softly. He did not know who might have-returned. He was nevertheless surprised to see his sister asleep in the wooden rocker that was Maman Adele's pride and joy. The moonlight poured through the windows and struck her face and blond hair. Not until this moment did he understand just how truly beautiful Helene was. He knew that almost every young man in Port Hebert had a crush on either Nina Babineau or Helene Hebert. And now he understood why. The girl awoke with a start and looked up.

"I'm glad you're home," she said.

He could see she was alarmed.

"What's wrong?" he asked.

"It's Gilles. He's getting very drunk. He looked all over for Nina and couldn't find her. Then he went looking for you and couldn't find you. He decided you were together. He is saying terrible things about you, Marcel. I am afraid of what will happen when he finds you."

Marcel took his sister in his arms. "I can take care of myself, Helene."

"No, you can't. Not with Gilles. He is stronger than you. He is stronger than anyone. If Papa hadn't saved you, Gilles would have beat you to a pulp."

"Maybe I can hide behind Papa again tonight." He chuckled.

"It's not funny, Marcel. Papa is drunk too. The curé LeLoutre has arrived for the festival with his Indians. Papa attacked him for his burning out the settlers at Beaubassin four years ago. The curé was furious. Mama had to step between them."

"You mean the old man was going to strike the priest? I don't believe it." He laughed. "I would have loved to see that."

"Where were you? You must have been the only person in the village to miss it."

Marcel coughed nervously. "I was getting my breeches stitched. What a night this has been!"

"Please, Marcel," Helene pleaded with him, "don't take

Gilles lightly. He's crazy with drink and Papa may not be able to handle him."

Marcel's smile was almost a grimace. "I think perhaps I've stayed too long. Maybe I should get my skins back on and return to the Micmac villages. Things are certainly less complicated there."

Marcel walked across the room to where he had left his buckskins. He quickly changed into them. He helped himself to a cooked and half-eaten leg of mutton and half a chicken, which he stuffed into his pack. He reached into the corner by his bed and pulled out his musket and powder horn. He rolled up his blanket from the bed and crammed it into his pack as well. Then he strapped it onto his back. Helene watched him sadly. There were tears in her eyes. She hated to see Marcel leave and she knew her mother would be crushed.

He kissed her. "I'll come back later this summer," he said. He thought of Nina. He would miss her. But they had time, and it was best for the Heberts that he depart.

"Helene," he whispered, "tell Nina that I will return later in the summer." Then he stepped out of the house and into the moon-drenched night.

Abbé LeLoutre read the gospel quickly in Latin. These simpleton farmers would not understand a bit of it anyway. It had been years since he had been in Port Hebert. Certainly, he had not been here since he had punished the Beaubassin Acadians for failing to rally to the cause of their king. Curé Leger from Beauséjour came on occasion to Port Hebert. It had been his report of the town's indifference to France that had decided LeLoutre to come himself. His task was not an easy one. Those fools in Paris had surrendered much of Acadia, certainly everything south and east of Fort Beauséjour, to the British. It was his task to keep the population of this British cession loyal to His Most Christian Majesty of France. The people were French. Their hearts were with the mother country. He would appeal to their loyalty, but if that failed then he would cater to their fears.

That was why the first row of pews in this dingy meeting hall chapel was filled with his Micmac warriors, his devoted disciples. No one at Port Hebert could forget what happened to their neighbors at Beaubassin when they insisted on remaining in their homes instead of retreating across the line into purely French territory. But Port Hebert was like Grand Pre—too far into this British-held province of Nova Scotia to force its residents across the border. But even here, within the fringes of British territory, they could serve their Lord of Versailles.

LeLoutre turned to face the congregation to read the Gospel to them in French. Before he began he surveyed the congregation. The Micmacs, all ten of them, were dressed in their finery. Their buckskins were decorated with porcupine quills and beads. From their braids they had dangled pieces of ribbon. They stank of the bear grease that they rubbed all over their bodies to drive away insects. The smell filled the whole chapel. Many of the Acadian women had covered their faces with their handkerchiefs. That arrogant bumpkin, Hebert, the one who had too much to drink last night, had actually left the pew in order to open all the windows.

Behind the Indians, and clearly resenting their presence, were the leading families of the village. Behind them were the rest of the "gentry" of this pestilential piss-hole. They complained about the Indians while in fact they all smelled of cowshit and fish.

He finished reading the Gospel and waited for the congregation to seat themselves before he began his sermon. He stared wide-eyed when the males in the congregation began to move toward the exit, many stopping to light up their pipes while still in the chapel. One of them actually lit his from the taper beside the vigil light.

"Where are you going?" the priest called out, his voice echoing through the hall.

Several of the men stopped to look back at him, while others kept on walking toward the door.

"I've come to preach the word of God and you run out to have a smoke? Is this how the people greet the word of their Maker?"

Hebert came back down the aisle. "It is our custom to smoke during the sermon. We always do it with Curé Leger," he said. "And besides, have you come to preach the word of God or is it the Gospel according to Louis?"

"Don't speak of your monarch with disrespect, Hebert. I know your treasonous heart."

"I'm not sure that King Louis is my monarch. I recall when I was a boy another Louis decided to give us, lock, stock and barrel, to a Queen Anne. And just last month messengers from the new English town of Halifax on the ocean side came to tell me to swear anew my allegiance to Anne's successor, a King George. I didn't pay attention to them and I won't pay attention to you. If you don't mind, I'll go out for my smoke. When you start up the mass again, I'll come back. I like the mass. It's not that bad if you don't have to go too often, and I've not been to mass more than three times in the last four years. It's not bad."

"We cannot get priests for you," LeLoutre reported. "The English block them."

"Stop, priest. If you continue I'll be forced to swear allegiance to King George out of gratitude."

Several of the women in the congregation blessed themselves when they saw the rage in the priest's face. Some of the men began to look about nervously, and old Broussard quietly sat down in the pew. Most thought Hebert went too far. It was best to placate priests, especially priests with Indian acolytes.

Hebert looked about him. Several of the older men and boys had returned to their places.

"Is this when you tell us that it was the English who crucified our Lord?"

"Quiet, blasphemer," LeLoutre shouted.

Even Helene looked at her father nervously and Adele stared at him wickedly. It was a warning he rarely ignored. He sighed and sat down to hear the priest preach.

"Hebert mocks my attack on the English. But even his mocking is not so far off the path. We know it was the Pharisees and Scribes aided by heathen Romans who murdered our Lord. But Christ our Savior, through a mystery fully understood only by the Trinity itself, is united for all eternity with the Godhead. It is our sins which crucify our Savior, and those who commit the foul sins of heresy are far more responsible for his death than those who sin from weakness but whose faith is firm. Yes, Christ was murdered by us all,

47

but the burden rests heavier on those, like the English, who deny the true faith."

Lucien yawned, and again received a warning from Adele. He yearned for his pipe. Soon LeLoutre began to preach to them about the coming war. The English had attacked "their king's" possessions somewhere in the western place called the Ohio Valley, and now "their king" was going to call upon them to rally to his cause.

"I knew it," Hebert mumbled. The last war had ended only five or six years before. The Acadians had been dragged into it against their will. The priests had promised much but in the end they had left, leaving the Acadians to face the anger of the English government. That anger still simmered and now this priest was preaching war again. Lucien rose from his pew. He announced loudly that he was going to have his smoke after all.

The Heberts spent Sunday afternoons together. Maman was always busy. The women of the village came to consult her. She was the niece of Frufru Mouton—the greatest *traiteur* in all Acadia. Once her own mother realized that Adele was left-handed, she knew that the gift had been passed on. As a young woman, and now as a middle-aged woman, Adele had laid hands on the sick. She prescribed herbs and helped those in labor. She said nothing to the priest, but she saw no conflict between her deep religious piety and her belief in her skills. She attributed all her healing powers to Our Lady of the Assumption.

Today few came. Most had been scared off by the priest's visit. But by next Sunday they would return in their usual numbers. The priest would be departing today.

Marie Broussard came seeking advice on how to make the young Gregoire Mouton, Adele's cousin, pay attention to her. Adele was patient with Marie. She did not dally in witchcraft. There would be no spells. She advised patience and prayers to the Virgin and perhaps some cloths tucked into her bodice.

Next Dette Babineau arrived, leading TiJoe. Dette's problems were far more serious. She insisted that TiJoe exasperated his father and now had come between her husband and herself. He had a *couchemal* or evil sprite, his mother insisted. Adele must cast out the wicked one from her son. Her last baby had been stillborn and not baptized. She was sure TiJoe's problems had begun just at that time.

Adele thought Dette's theory a bit farfetched. She had heard of cases of the spirits of the unbaptized causing mischief in a household, but she doubted they had powers to possess. Nevertheless, she had to do something for her friend. Anyone forced to live with that tyrant Babineau needed all the help and sympathy she could get.

She went to her special cabinet beside the hearth. She kept her herbs in the front of it. Behind the special glass jars she kept her tools, holy water and the even more potent Easter water blessed at the ceremony of the New Fire on Holy Saturday morning. They had not had a priest for Easter in Port Hebert in almost ten years, and her supply was running low. TiJoe's *couchemal* would require only regular holy water she decided. Next to the holy water was the most precious commodity of all, ashes from burnt palm, come all the way from the West Indies for a Palm Sunday celebration well beyond her memory. Her aunt Frufru had given her the ashes, her most sacred legacy.

"Take all the boy's clothes off," Adele ordered.

Dette hesitated.

Lucien glanced over at the women and the boy. He did not put much stock in these incantations but he dared not say anything to Adele. She had a good marriage, three strong and beautiful children, a husband who loved her and never strayed, well at least not that often, and she attributed all her prosperity to the Virgin, her patron, who blessed her powers. Far be it for him to suggest otherwise.

"Helene," Lucien called to his daughter, who was peeling the last of the winter's potatoes for their dinner.

"Papa?" she responded.

"We are going to have naked boys running about the house. Why don't you go and search out the places where your brothers normally sleep it off after a festival drunk. They should be sober by now. Lucky louts, they didn't have to listen to LeLoutre spout his dung all over the chapel. I should have stayed out all night myself."

Helene had not told her parents of Marcel's departure. She did not wish to ruin their one free day in the week, but she knew she would have to tell them now.

"Papa, Marcel left to go back to his trapping last night."

Lucien looked at her. His face sagged with disappointment. Adele, who was chatting with Dette Babineau as she stripped her squirming son, halted in mid-sentence.

"Why did he leave?" she asked Helene.

"He didn't say, Maman."

"This is not a season for working traplines. Marcel had already traded his catch at Beauséjour," she protested. "It was the fight with Gilles, wasn't it?"

Helene looked away from her parents. "He didn't want to cause any more trouble. I'm going now to find Gilles," she said throwing a shawl over her shoulders and leaving the house.

Dette was relieved that Adele's attention was distracted. Perhaps she would not require her to remove all of TiJoe's clothes. In her opinion, which of course Adele had not solicited, the Heberts were better off without that lazy Marcel. They should be grateful for Gilles, who was hardworking and dutiful. She was delighted when Babin told her of his plan to unite Nina and Gilles. Her daughter would be provided for, and they could look forward to a more secure old age.

Adele turned back to TiJoe.

"Dette, I told you to strip the boy," she said, her annoyance clearly visible.

Dette's heart sank. They would know. Her pride demanded that she leave this house but desperation required her to remain. TiJoe tried to pull away from her but she grabbed the back of his breeches and pulled them down.

Adele gasped. The boy's back and buttocks were festering and oozing. He had been beaten with a whip of some kind.

Dette started to cry.

"He's not a bad man, my Babin, but he is so hard, so unforgiving of the errors of others."

Lucien rose from his chair.

"God's blood," he exclaimed, as he stared at the boy's wounds. "Adele, you treat the wrong Babineau for an evil spirit."

Adele went back to her cabinet. She would have to clean the boy up and give Odette a poultice to draw the poisons out of the sores. She signaled Lucien to hold TiJoe and lay him down on the bed.

The man placed his powerful arms about TiJoe's chest. The boy looked up at him.

"Monsier Hebert, you promised me and Gilles you would not tell my father. You lied to me. He beat me. You said..." His voice caught and he could not finish his complaint through his hiccups.

"I did not tell, TiJoe. I am sorry. Gilles complained to your father. He didn't know about our talk."

While Adele and Dette administered to the boy, Lucien left the house. He covered the distance between his home and the Babineau cottage quickly. He entered their foyer and knocked on the inner door. Nina answered it. She looked radiantly beautiful in the late afternoon sun.

"My child," Lucien greeted her, "I want to speak with your father alone."

"He's not here, Monsieur Hebert. He is working on his boat down at the river."

"*Merci*," said Lucien. He turned to leave but Nina halted him.

"Monsieur Hebert, I must speak with you. Your son..."

"Gilles has not yet returned home." He said with some annoyance, "I suspect he is sleeping it off somewhere. It is just as well. His behavior was awful last night. This way I don't have to see him for a while and I can cool off."

Nina allowed him to finish. "And Marcel?"

"Ah, that one! The fool. I'll have a long time to cool off about him. He left last night to go back to his damned savages."

Nina was shocked by this news and it showed in her face. Lucien was puzzled, then suspicious, but he had other problems more pressing to deal with.

Nina closed the door behind Marcel's father. She could barely breathe. The news had struck her with the same shock she had once felt as a child when she had been pushed into Chignecto Bay. She went over to her parents' bed and sat down. He had simply gone away without even a word to her. Is that all it had meant? One night, just like with a whore. She looked down at the bed, and the memories flooded back. She remembered the passion. She stood up quickly as if separation from the bed might still the memories. But an enormous wave of loneliness engulfed her and she collapsed onto the bed and wept.

Lucien found Babin caulking his boat. He walked up behind the other man and laid his hand on his shoulder. Babin jumped in fright.

"Holy Jesus," he exclaimed, "I thought you were LeLoutre or one of his savages catching me working on the sabbath." He looked into Lucien's furious face and his voice trailed off. "What's wrong?"

"Your wife is at my house now with TiJoe."

"So what!" Babin said defensively.

"She showed us how you beat the boy."

Babin stood up straight and stared Lucien in the eye.

"He's a bad boy. It was for his own good. If he is ever to grow to manhood and assume responsibilities he must be taught his lesson. Besides, neighbor, it is none of your business."

"Your wife made it our business by bringing the boy to us. Discipline the boy if you must, but do not injure him. You go too far, Babin."

"As I said," the other man responded coldly, "it is none of your business."

"We are one community," said Lucien. "We are neighbors, relatives. One day we may be in-laws," he added pointedly. "We are all our brother's keepers. Do you understand my meaning, Babin?"

"You need not fear," the other man responded. "I understand you precisely."

Lucien turned and left the other man beside his boat. When Lucien was out of sight Babin kicked at the boat with his foot.

"Son of a bitch," he mumbled, "threaten me and my plans for Nina, will he? Well, we'll see who wins this struggle." But his words were mostly bravado. He had not the courage to stand up to Lucien Hebert.

CHAPTER THREE

Port Hebert, July 1755

Warm weather came to Port Hebert at last. The perpetually gray skies of March and April gave way to a deep blue. The acres of marsh grass turned golden and the plowed fields of the mainland sprouted corn shoots and dark green potato plants.

But with the summer came the English. About two thousand red-coated troops arrived by transport from Boston and Grand Pre, and later from Halifax. Once again the British had determined to seize the French fort of Beauséjour and rid Acadia south of Cape Breton of French influence.

Port Hebert received a contingent of twenty-five redcoats under Lt. Audry Hastings. They marched in ranks to the village center, a bagpipe and a drum accompanying them.

The women and children of the village were drawn instantly to the sound of the pipes. Men working in the fields and the marshes and even those out on the mudflats heard the faint wail and walked toward the sound.

Within half an hour of their arrival the British force stood surrounded by the entire population of Port Hebert, men, women and children.

Hastings stepped forward.

"Does anyone here speak English?"

He was greeted with blank stares.

"It was too much to hope for," he said. Then he broke into his own atrocious French. "I have come to alert you that it is His Majesty King George's intention to drive the interloping forces of the French from the soil rightfully ceded to Her Majesty Queen Anne of happy memory in 1713. In short, we are attacking the French fort on the Missaquash. We require the assistance of the males of this community."

Lucien listened to the lieutenant as long as he could. He had heard this all before in the last war.

"Lieutenant," he interrupted, "the men of this village have all sworn allegiance to King George on the proviso that they would not be forced to bear arms against their former countrymen."

"I see nothing to that effect in the oath."

He reached into his breast pocket and pulled out a large piece of paper. Lucien walked over to the lieutenant and the officer handed him the document. Lucien glanced at it.

"The document we signed was in French," he said. "This one is in English, I presume."

"The official oath must, of course, be in English," responded Hastings. "And this document says nothing about exemptions."

"The French one did," Lucien responded defiantly.

"I see," said Hastings after some seconds. "Well, Governor Lawrence expected as much from you. You will not be required to bear arms."

There were audible sighs of relief from the men in the crowd and some of the women began to clap.

"But." Hastings had to raise his voice above the applause. "Since you will not bear arms we must protect the flanks of our army. You will all be required to surrender your arms. I want every musket, pistol, pike, and sword delivered to this square within the next half hour."

"I must protest, *monsieur*," Lucien said angrily. "That leaves us absolutely defenseless. What if Abbé LeLoutre's savages turn on us? What if a pack of wolves should attack our cattle? Our losses would be severe."

"You're not likely to see that savage LeLoutre or his henchmen. Not while the British army advances on their den of thievery. As far as wolves are concerned, a few dead

Acadian cows is a price I am willing to pay to secure the flanks and rear of my compatriots against any potential treason by you fellows. Weapons, gentlemen, all of them, in this spot in thirty minutes. And if I don't see a sufficient quantity we'll begin a house-to-house search."

Broussard, Mouton, and Babin crowded around Lucien as soon as Hastings had finished his speech. The younger men stood apart waiting for the decision. Gilles urged several of his friends not to surrender their guns. But Lucien, his face creased with worry, soon emerged from the spontaneous council.

"We will comply and surrender all weapons."

There were some sounds of disgust from the younger men.

"All weapons, did you hear me? All of them," Lucien repeated loudly.

That afternoon the British gathered the weapons in the village center, packed them into crates, and loaded them into their boats, then disappeared again in the direction of Beaubassin and Fort Beauséjour.

It took the village several days to quiet down after the British left with their weapons. The younger men were still angry about the decision reached by their fathers. They mumbled but they did not have the nerve to confront the older men. But gradually the men, young and old, went back to their work in the fields and the marshes. Several even took to the bay to gather fresh fish.

Nina walked past the Hebert cottage several times trying to determine if Adele were alone. Finally she saw Helene leave, carrying lunch for her father and brother. As soon as Helene disappeared around the bend in the dirt road toward the chapel, Nina entered the Hebert's foyer and knocked on the inner door. Adele opened the door. Her warm brown face broke into a smile when she saw the girl.

"What a pleasant surprise, Nina," she said, "but if it is Gilles you are looking for, you know you will not find him hanging about his old mother."

Nina smiled warily. She knew the other woman enjoyed teasing but she was in no mood to be teased.

"What is it child? Are you ill?" Adele asked, sensing Nina's anxiety.

"I think so," Nina responded and instantly broke into tears.

"What is it? Now there, come sit in my chair. I'll brew some herb tea. You'll feel better in no time."

"I've tried to talk to my mother but I'm so frightened."

Adele poured hot water over the herb leaves. Then she strained the leaves from the tea.

"Here, drink this. It will calm you." She gave the girl a mug of her brew. "Now, tell the *traiteur* the symptoms."

"I am sick to my stomach," Nina said through tears, "constantly."

"The tea will help that. But it is only a symptom. We must find the cause. Have you been eating shellfish? I won't eat them on the second day. They must be fresh. Hold out your hands—no, palms down. Let me look at your fingernails." She reached over and pulled down the skin below Nina's right eye, revealing the reddened veined underside.

"How are your flows?" Adele asked.

"They've stopped," Nina responded.

Adele looked at her with concern. "When was your last flow?"

"At the end of the winter."

Adele went to the teakettle and poured herself a mug. She returned to Nina's side and took a loud slurp.

"I'll have to ask you this question, child. Please don't be angry with me if I am wrong. Have you been with a man?"

Nina's face went white. "Do you think I'm pregnant?"

"It is a possibility, but only if you've been with a man. Have you?"

Tears began to flow down Nina's cheeks. She nodded. "I've been with your son," she cried.

Adele smiled comfortingly at Nina.

"I thought as much. I think you've explained everything, the stomach sickness and the flows stopping. Did you not think of that possibility?"

"My mother never told me that the monthlies stop when you are with child. Besides, it only happened once, I mean being with a man. Oh, Maman Adele, what do I do now?"

"You do nothing. You will recover from the stomach sickness, probably without any assistance from me. But take some of my herbs just in case."

"But what about the baby?"

"You do nothing about the baby either. You let it grow and in the fall I predict you will have a son or a daughter. I predict it and everyone knows I have the gift," she joked.

"But the shame! I have no husband. The child will have no father!"

Adele became suddenly angry. "What kind of a man do you think my son is? Do you think he will shirk his responsibilities and abandon you? Think again, missy."

"But how can he marry me?"

"Girl, you don't need a priest. You've seen many a couple exchange vows before the village in the chapel on a Sunday morning, and often enough the bride is a little too thick in the middle by the time she reaches the altar. A majority of the first babies in this village arrive early."

"But he's not here, Maman!"

Adele's face clouded. Then her confusion was replaced by surprise. "You mean Marcel, don't you? Oh, my God, I always assumed it was you and Gilles."

She held Nina's face against her chest. She pulled one of the straight-back chairs away from the table and sat down on it. The problem had suddenly taken on an entirely different dimension.

For a moment Adele began to think of the herbs her aunt had mentioned in the greatest secrecy—those that could induce the little one to come before its time. But she rejected that course quickly. The Virgin would certainly punish her and Nina if she resorted to those medicines. Besides, the little one she referred to was her own grandchild.

"Nina, we must not panic. Marcel told us he would return in the summer. That will be before that little one is born. You may marry then. I am sure he will stand by you. He is the son of Lucien Hebert and therefore a man of honor."

"But what do I explain to my parents when I begin to grow large?"

"Oh, child, I don't know. If only your father was like my husband. He would listen to a child's trouble and give his support. But not Babin. I've seen what he has done to TiJoe. I swear, child, if he puts a hand on you . . ." She paused. "If he touches you, you come to me. Lucien and I will protect you. In the meanwhile I will try to reach Marcel. Some trappers used to spend the summer in Beaubassin but with the English there I doubt they will this year. But I will send one of my cousins across Chignecto just in case he shows up there. Maybe we can reach him."

In the days that followed Nina waited for word from Adele. But the only word that came from across the bay was the news that Fort Beauséjour had fallen to the English and that Abbé LeLoutre had disappeared. Most of Port Hebert greeted the news with indifference. The young men speculated that now that France had been driven off, maybe the English troops would give them back their weapons.

Nina cared not a whit whether the guns were returned. Every morning when she awoke she tiptoed out of her house to the privy behind the barn. She did not want anyone to know about the morning sickness. She would lift her nightgown and stare down at her white belly. She swore it enlarged before her very eyes and terror would grip her.

One morning late in July, TiJoe caught her looking at herself. He snickered. She dropped her nightgown into place and turned around.

"You little brat," she yelled at him, "what is so funny?" But before she could reach out to grab him he was gone.

She went back to the house and crawled back onto her sleeping mat. Usually the nausea went away after her trips out back. She lay quietly, waiting for the spasms to pass. She glanced over at her brother's bed and noticed that he had not returned. She guessed that he had waited until she left and then returned to the outhouse to finish his business.

She had just fallen back to sleep when she was awakened by a shout. Someone was yelling out on the road. The house seemed smoky. Nina jumped from her mat. Babin sat bleary-eyed in his bed and shoved his wife.

"Dette, get up. I think the house is on fire."

Nina ran to the door. Smoke billowed over the roof from the backyard.

"Oh, my God! The barn, my cattle," Babin shouted as he joined Nina. He raced back into the house, grabbed the iron cauldron by the fireplace, and dashed to the back of the house. Nina and her mother followed.

Babin stopped dead in his tracks. It was not the barn after all. It was the privy. Smoke bellowed from the open door and flames shot upward from the little window. Babin had made such a racket screaming with fear for his cattle that half of the village was awakened. Babin's neighbors, Lucien and Gilles Hebert and Gaston Bernard, were the first to arrive on the scene. Gilles bent in half with laughter when he saw what was on fire. His guffaws struck Babin as offensive.

"You got the whole village up at dawn," laughed Gilles, "just to save your shithouse."

Lucien smiled indulgently at Gilles. "Let's put it out anyway," he said quietly. "It could spread."

Soon a long line of villagers spread from the village well to the Babineau fire and pots of water were poured over the burning boards—too late. The privy collapsed in a heap of burning, wood sending sparks up into the morning air.

"How did it happen?" Adele asked, standing next to Babin and Nina.

"I don't know," Babin said angrily. "But I've not seen TiJoe."

"Oh, my baby," Dette screamed and started running toward the burning wood.

Nina panicked. "I saw him at the privy this morning when I was there. I chased him away."

Lucien made his way toward the fire, covering his face with his arm to protect himself from the heat.

"TiJoe is not in the fire," Gilbert Broussard called out to Lucien. "I saw him behind the barn about ten minutes ago. I yelled at him for not helping with the buckets."

Odette Babineau fainted from relief. Lucien caught her and lowered her gently to the ground.

"I've got him," Gilles yelled as he dragged TiJoe from behind the Babineau barn. The boy was kicking and fighting but he was no match for Gilles, who set him on his feet before the villagers. TiJoe's eyebrows were singed slightly and he had an ugly burn on his right hand. Babin looked at his son.

"Do you have an explanation, Joseph?" Half the village did not realize whom he addressed.

The boy started to stammer.

"I'll bet you were smoking and the straw caught fire," Gilbert shouted out.

TiJoe gave the other boy a wicked glare.

"You were in the privy, weren't you?" Babin said sternly to him.

TiJoe shook his head.

"Don't lie to me," Babin shouted. "Your sister saw you there."

"I didn't do anything wrong," TiJoe screamed as his father grabbed him. "Nina is a liar. She gets away with everything. I saw her and Hebert doing it together on your own bed but she never gets whipped, not like me."

A murmur ran through the crowd. Babin smacked the boy viciously across the face, knocking him senseless.

"Enough," Lucien yelled at Babin. "It was a dumb mistake, and you've lost very little as a result. Don't hurt the boy."

Babin ignored Lucien. He was close to hysteria. He stared wide-eyed now at Nina. "Is what the boy said true?" he shouted at her.

"Papa!" Nina cried out. "How can you shame me before the whole community?" She began to cry.

Gilles came to her side.

"The little pig is a liar. We all know that. No one would believe his lies. He put his own arm around Nina's shoulders.

For once she was happy to have him touch her and she did not pull away. She needed someone. Oh, God, she thought, where is Marcel?

Gradually the crowd dispersed. Dette took TiJoe to Adele for treatment of his burns. Gilles walked Nina back to her house. Babin followed them. He was silent until Gilles left Nina at the door after kissing her on top of the head. As soon as Nina closed the door, however, her father began to yell.

"What the boy said was true, wasn't it? Trust the little bastard to speak the truth only when it is bad news and then in front of the whole village."

"Papa, I'm pregnant," Nina blurted out.

Babin looked as if he had been slapped in the face. "Have you told him?" he asked.

"I will when I can."

"What do you mean when you can? Do you plan to exchange vows in between your labor pains? What are you waiting for? Hebert is a good match. I intended you to marry him. Tell him now or I'll tell him myself."

"It's not Gilles, Papa, it is Marcel."

Again Babin was taken by surprise. His face changed from the red of anger to the pasty whiteness of shock.

"Why in God's name would you choose that ruffian—a man who has never done an honest day's work in his life? Why? Answer me why." His anger was returning now. He lunged for Nina, but she stepped quickly from his path. "You slut," he screamed.

She knew he would beat her as he had beaten TiJoe in the past if she stayed. She ran to the door and threw it open. He yelled at her to stop.

"Nina, if you leave this house you are no daughter of mine. Never enter my home again if you leave now."

Nina bolted through the doorway then out into the road. She heard Babin trip as he started to follow her. She ran as fast as she could toward Heberts'. They would help her. She heard her father shouting behind her. She could see the Hebert cottage looming ahead of her, only a few more feet. She heard her father's feet behind her. She dared not turn back to look. He was gaining on her. He was breathing heavily. She could hear him. She opened the Heberts' outer door and raced to the entryway of the house. It was bolted from the inside. She pounded on it. Her father was at the outer door now. Suddenly the bolted door swung open and Helene Hebert emerged carrying an ancient blunderbuss. She pointed it at Babin.

"Get out of my father's house," she shouted.

"Don't you point a weapon at me, you sniveling brat."

"I'll say it a second time but no more, child-beater, woman-beater. Get out of my father's house. The foyer is for welcome guests and you are not welcome."

"My wife and son are here."

Helene shook her head. "They went with Maman Adele to the chapel to give thanks to the Virgin that TiJoe was not badly hurt. I am alone here, but if you want to try to harm me I'll blow your head right off your neck. And what do you think Gilles would do to a man who harmed his sister or the woman he loved?"

"She's already been loved," Babin sneered. "And I would like to see what Gilles Hebert will do to the man who beat him to it. It will serve this family right." He turned and slammed the outer door behind him.

Nina collapsed into Helene's arms. Helene patted the back

of the girl's head and soothed her as a mother soothes a hurt child even though she was barely a year older than Nina.

"Come into the house. I am glad your father wasn't willing to risk anything. I don't know if this old thing is even loaded. Papa brought it down from the storage loft after the British confiscated all our muskets. He says it belonged to his grandfather, the first Hebert here in Acadia. What a morning!" Helene said, trying to keep a conversation going. She wished her mother would return. She would know what to do next.

Nina wept quietly. Helene led her to her mother's rocking chair.

"I always seem to end up here when troubles overwhelm me," Nina said.

"What is wrong with Babin?" Helene asked.

"He's discovered that I am carrying your brother's child, your brother Marcel's child."

Helene's face broke into a huge smile. "Good for you!"

Nina could hardly believe her ears.

"You love him, don't you?" Helene asked. "And I'm sure he loves you. So it's all set."

"How do you know?"

"What?"

"That Marcel loves me."

Helene was sure of her brother's feelings—any fool could look at him and tell. But she knew Nina would need more. "He told me he loved you," she lied.

"Oh, thank God," Nina sighed. "Most people, including my father and your mother, thought it would be Gilles."

"Mother knows? Well, that's good. You know, you picked the right brother. I know if I were not their sister and had a choice I would pick as you did. Marcel is handsome and charming and exciting. Life with Gilles would be dull and boring."

The outer door of the foyer was opened. Helene picked up the blunderbuss once again. Adele entered the house. She looked at the two girls.

"Babin knows!" was all Adele stated.

"What do we do now?" Helene asked.

"We wait until your father and brother return for lunch and we seek counsel."

* * *

The next morning when Nina awoke she could not remember where she was at first. She looked about and realized that she shared Helene's bed in the Heberts' storage loft. Her mind flashed back to the events of the previous evening. Gilles had screamed at his parents and at Helene when he learned the news. Finally he had stormed from the house. She had not heard him return and assumed that he had stayed away. His hatred for his brother alarmed her, but she knew that everything he said about Marcel he meant for her as well. She was sorry that she had hurt him so deeply.

Later that evening Nina's mother had come weeping to the Heberts' carrying some of Nina's clothing. Nina had hugged Odette and the two of them had cried together. They talked for some time before Dette became frightened that Babin would take offense at her staying at the home of his enemy. In all the excitement, she mused finally, everyone had forgotten about TiJoe and the fire, and he had not been punished. At least one blessing had come from all of this pain.

Soon, Nina expected to hear Maman Adele stir below. Instead she heard sounds she remembered from the not-so-distant past, the far-off wailing and the sound of the drum. She sat up in the bed and pulled the covers tightly around her neck and chin. Helene stirred next to her.

When he heard the sound Lucien leapt to his feet and hastily drew his breeches up over his ample rear. "Damn it," he called out to no one in particular, "the British are back." He pulled on his shirt. "Gilles," he called out, but then he remembered last evening. He took hold of the blunderbuss that rested next to the hearth. He raised it over his head toward the loft. "Helene, take this and put it out of sight." He did not notice that it was Nina who took the gun from him.

He opened the door to the foyer and was startled to see the massive form of his son Gilles in the doorway. He had taken advantage of the old tradition of spending the night in the foyer like a traveler come upon the house too late to wake up the occupants.

The older man looked at his son and extended his hand in greeting. Gilles had to fight back the tears as he took his father's large hand into his own enormous paw.

"It's the British again, Gilles. I wonder what they want this time."

Robert E. Wall

"Perhaps they bring us back our weapons."
"I don't think there's much chance of that, my son," said
Lucien. He reached over and grabbed Gilles by the shoulder.
"It is good to have you back in the fold, Gilles."

CHAPTER FOUR

Beauséjour, July and August 1755

Marcel sat in the tavern at the fort sipping his brandy. Benoit had not yet appeared but it was still early in the summer. The date on which they had agreed to meet was still weeks away. Marcel ran his hands through his hair and pushed it from his eyes. The wench who served him the brandy was eying him now. If her bodice had been pulled any tighter her breasts would have exploded from their confines. But her face was pockmarked and her teeth showed black when she smiled. She was almost as ugly as the squaw Benoit had procured and her black teeth reminded him of his brother, Gilles, but her breasts intrigued him.

He thought back ruefully to his visit to Port Hebert. He had shamed his father by brawling publicly with Gilles. He suspected that if he had also been caught with Nina, his father would have skinned him as neatly as Benoit skinned a rat.

His mind wandered off to the night with the girl. He smiled when he thought of his split pants and the girl's offering to stitch them. A more open invitation to what followed he could not have received. Gilles would have kissed his own ass for such an invitation, but it was he, Marcel, the little one, who received it. His smile broadened into a grin as he realized he was not so little any longer. The wench with the black teeth approached the table next to Marcel's and bent to wipe it. Her rump was directly in front of his face. He slapped her hard. She yelped and straightened up.

"Get your ass out of my face. It's not your best feature."

She turned, a look of mock hurt on her face. She leaned forward as if to reach across the table and presented a full view of her best feature to him.

"Now what do you think?"

Suddenly it dawned on him that he did not think too much. She disgusted him. He looked away and sipped his drink. The barmaid withdrew, her face a picture of disappointment. She had hoped she'd attract him enough to get him to pay, but he was a handsome one and she would have been willing to give him anything he wanted without charge.

But Marcel had already dismissed her from his mind. He was thinking of Nina, her soft brown hair with the reddish highlights, her breasts not nearly so large as those he had just seen, yet so soft. He remembered the sweetness of their coming together. It was the first time for her. He laughed aloud when he thought about it. He hoped her first time had better memories for her than his did for him.

He could not shake the feeling of loss that had descended upon him after leaving Port Hebert. Sometimes he dismissed it by attributing it to his boredom here in Beauséjour. Other times he confessed to himself that he missed his family. He had looked forward to the visit and the brevity of his stay had left him dissatisfied. Yet, late at night, when he lay by himself in the low light of the spent cooking fire, his mind drifted back again and again to the girl with the brown hair and the soft breasts. He tried to be callous about their lovemaking, just as Benoit would expect of him. But that moment with her, her stitching his pants, and then his lying atop her on the soft down guilt in the dark of her parents' home, that could not be reduced to simple jest. Nor could it be forgotten. He certainly knew that at Beauséjour he had tried to put it all behind him, but to no avail. He did not know it yet, or if he did he could not articulate it to himself, but Marcel Hebert was in love.

There was a commotion out on the parade ground. Marcel

rose to his feet and looked out the window. Large numbers of Micmacs were pouring through the gates. A bugle began to sound. Marcel went to the door of the tavern. Soldiers were running across the yard and officers had started shouting.

He caught one soldier and spun him around. "What the hell is happening?" he asked.

"It's the damned English. They are approaching overland from Fort Lawrence and there are sailing ships in the basin."

"I didn't know we were at war!" Marcel said.

"We are not, *monsieur,*" an officer responded. "We are merely settling boundary disputes by resorting to violence. We chase the English from the Ohio so they must chase us from Beauséjour. It and our position at Baie Verte are the last two French posts on the mainland of Acadia—drive us off and it all becomes Nova Scotia for good.

Marcel ran back into the tavern. There was one fact he was very sure of. He did not wish to be confined inside a fort during a siege. He would get his pack of personal possessions and leave before the English blockade began. He saw the barmaid sneak around the corner. His eyes darted to where he had left his possessions. They were gone. He raced around the corner of the taproom after her. She had gone through the kitchen and out the door into the back alley.

"Damn that slut," he yelled out. "Stop her. She's taken my belongings."

In the confusion on the parade ground, however, there was no way to discover which way she fled. His money was in the belt around his stomach but his razor, a bar of his mother's brown soap, an extra shirt, and knitted woolen stockings, some of the things he had missed last year, had disappeared with the barmaid and he would have to spend another year without them. He cursed when he thought of the lice and the burning itch they produced. There was not a louse hatched that could stand up to Maman Adele's brown soap.

He turned abruptly when he heard his name called out. At first he saw only a group of Micmacs behind him. Then he noticed the tricorn hat. Benoit had returned.

Marcel went over to his friend and clapped him on the back.

"What are you doing dressed as one of the Indians?"

"It's a disguise. A certain fellow we met back on the Saint John has been following me."

"How could he miss that hat? Not much of a disguise."

"Well, I couldn't get rid of it."

Marcel looked around at the commotion about him. "Let's get out of here. I don't think your disguise will help you very much if the French army gets the bright idea of forcing all of us to enlist for the siege."

"But I wanted you to see him," Benoit interrupted.

"Who?"

"Your son, Tetagouche. The girl named him after a river she liked."

He pulled a fat squaw over to him. She had a baby strapped to her back. Benoit pulled the blanket away from a squalling little boy. His skin was light brown and his eyes were steely blue.

"That's not his mother," Marcel said.

"Bad news. She died," Benoit said nonchalantly. "And her husband ran off with LeLoutre and was killed."

"Then who is she?" Marcel said pointing to the squaw. "And what are they doing here?"

"They were on their way to Beauséjour for summer trading. They had just got here when the English arrived. She's the man's mother. I don't think she regards the little fellow as her favorite grandson. But she lost a baby herself not so long ago and she has milk. I told her you'd take him off her hands."

"You told her what?" Marcel shouted, still trying to absorb the news about the baby's mother.

Benoit lifted the carrying cradle off the squaw's back. She broke into an instant toothless smile as Benoit handed the squalling child to his father.

"What am I supposed to do with him?"

"I don't know. You said you wanted to see him. You strutted around like a bantam rooster. So now you're seeing him."

"He's nice," Marcel said, a note of panic creeping into his voice. "Now what do I do?"

"I suspect Old Gums here would take pretty good care of him if you was to see to it that she ate regular. It's part of your education, boy. Fathering a child is serious business."

"What about your redheads? Did you do your duty by them?"

"Funny you should ask that," Benoit said. "We never had any red hair in my family so I was not prone to accept that responsibility."

Marcel heard more noise and looked up to see the large gates of the fort closing. There was no chance to escape now—not with a fat squaw and a little baby. They were in Beauséjour for the siege.

The Micmacs and Benoit were placed under the leadership of Father LeLoutre. Marcel was enlisted in the militia. Benoit sat on the parade ground drinking a special issue of brandy that LeLoutre had ordered for all of his warriors. The trapper cackled and howled with delight as Marcel was paraded up and down the parade ground until his buckskins were soaked with sweat. Old Gums took the baby to the woman's quarters, where she was issued rations as a nurse-maid for a militiaman's child.

The enemy were mostly Bastonois, undisciplined and row-dy volunteers off the docks and out of the jails of Boston, Salem, and Portsmouth in New Hampshire. They came off the transports as soon as the ships were sitting high and dry on the mud flats at low tide. Then they proceeded to get drunk and fire muskets indiscriminately at the fort. Later, redcoats from Fort Lawrence (just across the border, on the English side) arrived with their officers and order was restored.

Marcel was posted to the fort walls that first night. Everyone knew there would be no attack. Still it was exciting to watch the fires of the enemy encampment. It was less exciting the second night and still less on the third. On the fourth night the entire garrison was on edge. The English seemed to do nothing but parade all day outside the walls while the French paraded with equal noise and confusion inside.

The British regulars and the New England militia spent their days building gun emplacements. Marcel would not have known what it was exactly that they were building except that one of the French officers let it slip. Soon word spread to all the militiamen. Gun emplacements meant big guns, heavy cannon. A sense of dread descended upon the entire garrison. It was merely a matter of time before those death-dealing iron tubes were brought to bear on all of them.

Every day Old Gums brought the blue-eyed boy to see

Marcel. He knew he should thank the woman. He should be grateful to her for the care she gave to his child, but he had difficulty thinking of anything but the cannons.

Every evening Benoit arrived with a portion of the ration of brandy that LeLoutre gave to his Indians to bolster their courage. It bolstered Marcel's as well, but it could not dispel his depression. He had wanted to avoid being trapped like this to begin with. He resented being a pawn in the struggle between France and England, between Catholic and Protestant. He wanted to be no one's pawn; in truth, he wished to be back in Port Hebert with Nina Babineau. But how, he wondered, would he explain Tetagouche to Nina? The thought depressed him even more.

On the tenth night LeLoutre decided to preach to the garrison. Marcel still stood his evening watch. Benoit escaped from the Micmac section of the congregation and joined him.

First the priest said mass for all of the defenders—Indians, whites, regular soldiers, officers, militia, and hangers-on. Word was sent to the British commander that the French were at mass and that it would be considered the act of a gentlemen if a truce could be arranged. No word was received back and so the guard was kept in place and had to watch from a distance. LeLoutre's voice penetrated every nook and cranny of the fort anyway. His voice seemed to carry beyond that of a normal man. His words dripped venom about the heretic English who had chased their rightful Catholic king out of England into France and replaced him with a German heretic.

Benoit listened briefly, then he spoke to Marcel as he offered him a swig of brandy.

"You know, those English are smart. Kicking a king off his throne is not a bad idea if he isn't doing his job."

Marcel had inherited much of Lucien's ambiguity about kings and was not inclined to disagree with his friend.

LeLoutre continued on with his pet theme of the everliving God, Jesus Christ, nailed to a cross by heretics like the English.

"Do you think the English killed Jesus, Marcel?"

"No," the young man responded.

"Why not?"

"I know. My mother read me the story. It was Romans."

"No English?"

"No."

"Then Romans must not like Frenchmen."

"Why?"

"Because they kill them. LeLoutre says Jesus was French and you say the Romans killed him."

"Jesus was Jewish and they killed him for claiming to be a king and claiming that he was God."

"Not French?" Benoit looked at Marcel in astonishment. "Of course Jesus was French. Everyone knows Jesus was French. Everyone loves Jesus and everyone hates Jews, although I am not sure why. I've never met one but I know I hate them. LeLoutre hates them but then he loves Jesus."

Marcel started to laugh.

"So you tell me that Jesus was Jewish and not French and that the Romans killed him not the English."

"That's what the book says."

Suddenly the air was shattered by the sound of cannon. Benoit looked at his friend.

"I think the time has come to put an end to soldiering. All the fun is out of it now the English have started with these cannons. A person could get killed here."

"You can't desert," Marcel protested.

"Boy, you are smart enough about most things, but you do lack a certain vital ass-saving instinct."

"I can take care of myself," Marcel said defensively.

"Oh, in a fight you can. I'm glad to have you on my side. But you won't go that one step beyond to guarantee your advantage in the next fight. Right now the English are about to kick the shit out of us. They have brought heavy cannon to bear on this wooden fort. You know the outcome already. So do I. So does Captain de Vergor, our commandant. So does Father LeLoutre. Now just you watch. De Vergor will surrender, if honor is served. He'll surrender his arms and promise not to fight the English for a year or something like that. But LeLoutre, he isn't going to give up his weapons and he isn't going to make any promises not to fight. And next time the English come up against him he'll be ready for them and give every bit as good as he gets."

"You admire LeLoutre?"

"No, I think he's a snake."

"Then what is this lecture all about?"

Again cannon crashed. There was a small panic among the militia on the parade ground as cannonballs found the range of the walls and splinters went flying in all directions.

Benoit grabbed Marcel's arm and shoulder. "The point is that a man who changes the Bible to suit his own ends isn't going to sit here and be shot to pieces. I'm keeping my eyes on the man with no prick. When he makes his move to get out of here, you, Old Gums, the boy, and me are going with him."

They escaped that same night. The priest would have objected to the woman and the baby had he seen them. But he was first through the escape hatch and out among the ditches and pointed stakes that made up the outer defense of Beauséjour. The dark forms of the Micmacs followed the priest.

Benoit led his little party. Old Gums had to be pushed through the hatch. Marcel held his son. He then passed the child to her and followed.

They slipped past the sharpened stakes, over the covered way beyond the outer ditch, and scrambled down the side of the enbankment to the open fields that surrounded the fort. Ahead of them the fields were clear. The priest and the Indians had already made it to the cover of the forest.

Benoit crouched low. The night was dark. The fires of the British encampment seemed to darken the rest of the night about them. There were sentries, but most seemed to be drunk. The American militia was notoriously undisciplined. If they could keep away from the British regulars they would escape unseen.

Marcel pushed Old Gums ahead of him. They were half-way across the field now. Up ahead he saw Benoit halt and stiffen. He grabbed the squaw and shoved her to the ground. The baby let out a whimper. Marcel whispered to his son to be quiet.

Benoit straightened up again. He began to walk forward with a nonchalant gait. It was enough of a signal to Marcel to remain flattened out on the ground. He crept forward past Old Gums and crouched cautiously behind Benoit.

"I thought you'd be sneaking out with that lunatic priest,"

said an English-accented voice. "I knew you were hiding out with the goddamned Micmacs. And I sure as hell knew they didn't have balls to face English cannon. All I had to do was sit here and wait for the Indian in the leathered hat and I'd have old Benoit."

"I've sold my furs, MacMichaels, so why waste your time with me?"

"You'll have the money on you, and if you don't, one of my fellows here"—he pointed to two burly white men behind him—"will get it out of you. They used to be fishermen back in Saco. They can do things with fish hooks—not little ones, but big ones—that would absolutely amaze you to see."

"Given up running with the Abenacki, I see," Benoit goaded him. "I guess losing two of them the way you did didn't sit too well with the Abenacki chiefs, eh?"

"Give us your belt, Benoit, and I'll tell the boys to make it quick."

"Go bugger yourself," Benoit retorted.

MacMichaels rushed toward Benoit. Marcel knew he had to strike now or his friend would be dead. He rose to his feet. The movement in the darkness caught MacMichaels's eye and he turned in fear to face a second assailant. Marcel pulled the trigger and the ball slammed into MacMichaels's head, tearing half his skull off and sending a shower of blood, bone, and brain in all directions. The fishermen started to move toward Benoit when from out of the darkness, from the direction of the campfire, someone yelled out in English, "A sortie from the French."

Someone else yelled as well and suddenly a drum started to beat. The two men took another look at their dead leader and turned and ran. They had been saved by the massive confusion and lack of discipline of the New Englanders.

"Let's run for it," Benoit called out. "There'll be dozens of redcoats rushing this way any second. No need to try to stay hidden. Just run."

Marcel turned behind him to look for Old Gums, but she was not there. Benoit had already started to run. He caught sight of the woman bending over MacMichaels's body. He came up behind her and shoved.

"Let's go!"

She was scalping the dead man and nothing would deter

her from her task. Panic started to grip Marcel. Normally he would have left her to her own fate, but she carried his son on her back.

Finally she was successful in ripping the scalp free from the skull. She looked up at Marcel. He could swear she was smiling at him although her lack of teeth made it difficult to tell in the dark. He gave her another shove. This time she started to run. They were not far from the woods now. Behind them there was some more shouting and a volley of musket fire. Musket balls tore over their heads into the leaves and tree trunks.

"Over here," Benoit called out.

Marcel gave Old Gums her last shove in Benoit's direction and then dived into the underbrush. He was breathing heavily and it took a few seconds for the fear that had built up in him to subside. He got to his knees and crawled to where Benoit sat.

Old Gums was brandishing her trophy, which she still held clutched in her bloody hand. Marcel moved around to the back of her. The baby's blue eyes stared into his face. The child played with its own hands.

"Damn your feather hat, Benoit. You almost got us all killed." He shoved the squaw's hand away from him as she persisted in showing him MacMichaels's hair.

"My hat would have made no difference if you had finished MacMichaels off like I told you to on the St. John. But there's hope for you yet, boy." Benoit laughed. "You sure didn't give that bastard a chance to say his last prayers this time."

"Killing MacMichaels was no thrill, Benoit. He stumbled on us twice. The first time he got his face bashed, the second time his head blown off. He was a mighty dumb fellow."

"You're right. That's why I never worried about him. If somebody smarter had been chasing me, I'd have worn a different covering for my head. But what impresses me, Marcel, is that you might just have the killer in you after all. No questions asked. Just *pow,* and his head comes off." Benoit started to laugh. "And for God's sake, would you take the scalp from Old Gums. She took it for you. You killed him. You're father to the baby. She must be taking to that little fellow. She wants to make sure his papa has all the trophies he has earned."

"Tell her to stuff that thing," Marcel said in disgust.

Benoit spoke rapidly to the Micmac woman. She smiled and nodded.

"You didn't tell her what I said?"

Again Benoit cackled. "No, I told her to prepare it for hanging by your lodge."

"Shit," Marcel said in disgust.

Benoit laughed. "The blue-eyed son of the chief with blue eyes will have to have some scalps hanging before him when he grows up so that he knows how to be a man."

"Let's get away from here," Marcel said, ignoring Benoit. "The English will search the woods after they discover MacMichaels's body."

They kept to the woods and out of sight from then on. They were not alone. LeLoutre and his warriors had disappeared, but they encountered many trappers and some militia farmers who had also escaped Beauséjour.

The cannons roared for two days and then were silent. The English offered Captain de Vergor terms that allowed his regulars to march out with the honors of war and return to Isle Royale. The militia would surrender their arms and return to their own homes.

Several days later Fort Gaspereau on the Baie Verte facing Isle St. Jean surrendered on the same terms as Beauséjour. Its militiamen were also disarmed and sent home. Once again the neutrality of the Acadians had been violated by their French masters and once again they had been left to the mercies of the English. Only this time, English mercy had given way before English frustration and greed.

Marcel took no part in these events. He and his new little family continued to live in the woods on the Chignecto Isthmus. They allowed the days to pass. They hunted occasionally, just enough to keep away hunger. Little Blue Eyes—Marcel could not think of him by his Indian name—seemed to thrive on the care he received from Old Gums. Marcel was amazed by the way Benoit took to the little boy. In return, the baby cooed and laughed any time the Penobscot half-breed picked him up. He even allowed the baby to grab his prized hat off his head.

Many trappers now started returning to the fort for the summer as they had every year. Only now it was an English fort. It mattered very little to them. The Acadians had changed sides frequently in the endless wars between England and France. But in late summer strange reports began to circulate from Beaubassin and Beauséjour. Militiamen were being rounded up and arrested. English transports had been sighted coming up from Fundy.

At first Marcel and Benoit ignored the trappers who visited their camp with these stories. Finally, though, Benoit went out to find out for himself. As a half-breed they would never take him for an Acadian.

After Benoit left, Marcel watched Old Gums nurse his son. He had racked his brain for a new name for the boy. He could not even remember what it was that his Indian mother called him. He liked the name Lucien, his father's name, but he was not sure the old man would appreciate having his name given to a grandson born out of wedlock. Marcel shrugged his shoulders. He had time to work it out. The squaw yelped, indicating that Benoit's pet name for the boy, Little Gums, would soon be inappropriate.

They needed some firewood. He picked up his ax and went into the woods. He found a fallen balsam of good size. The wood was soft and would burn quickly but that hardly mattered out here in the woods. He began by slicing off the branches. With most, one good swipe with the sharp ax was all that was needed. Near the base of the trunk he had to apply more strength. Finally he rested the ax on the ground and wiped his forehead with his arm. He sensed someone watching and he swung around, grabbing the ax. He relaxed instantly when he saw it was Benoit. But the man had a stricken look on his face. Marcel tensed again.

"What is it?" he asked his friend.

"It's very hard to believe."

"What, Benoit?"

"It's true. They've rounded up all the men in the church of Beaubassin. They are to be transported."

"Where?" asked Marcel, disbelieving.

"Anywhere, everywhere. The English have decided to drive every Frenchman out of Acadia."

Fear gripped at Marcel. "That means Port Hebert as well." The thought raced through his mind. "Are the people resisting?"

"They have been disarmed this summer."

76

"They have hands." He picked up his shirt and put it on. "I've got to get to Port Hebert."

"It's already over," Benoit said softly.

"What do you mean 'over'?" Marcel said in near panic.

"The transports have been to Port Hebert and they are heading here to pick up more people."

"We have to stop this." Marcel began to walk swiftly back to their camp. "Grab your musket, Benoit. Fire the signal. I want to speak to the trappers in these woods."

Benoit smiled. It looked like he was going to have himself a fight.

The corporal of the guard marched his men in their heavy red coats despite the heat. He would not have done it that way, but corporals did not argue with lieutenants, and Lieutenant Hastings had been insistent that the men dress in full uniform to contrast their discipline with the rowdiness of the American troops. With this last point Corporal O'Hagan was in complete agreement. The Yanks had no order about them, no pride in belonging to a fine-tuned military unit. They were worse than the Irish, his own people, and he never thought he would discover a more undisciplined people than the Irish. But his troops were soldiers, good for more than wenching and drinking. He did not care that it was only a wood detail that he commanded. The lieutenant had assigned the task to his troop and he intended to have it done properly.

"Private Henry," O'Hagan called out, "you're out of cadence."

"Have a heart, Corporal," the private responded. "We're only going to get some bloody wood."

"Bloody wood, is it?" Corporal O'Hagan shouted back. "It's a bloody back I'll be giving you for your bloody mouth."

There was now silence in the ranks. O'Hagan had been about to give the order for his men to load muskets on the march. It was a drill they had practiced often as there had been some reports of Frogs hiding out in the woods, but they had time.

"We're to enter those woods and get some kindling and logs so that Lieutenant Hastings can sleep nice and warm tonight," O'Hagan called out.

"It was as hot as hell last night," someone else complained.

"Silence," he commanded. Damn them, O'Hagan thought,

they were behaving just like the Americans, calling in the ranks like that. He was sure that Hastings followed them with the glass from the Fort *Bowsayjaw,* as the French called it. Well, be damned with them and their heathen language. He would never learn to pronounce it. All he had to do was to get some wood and get back to the fort smartly. Then he might be on his way to becoming a sergeant, especially with all the talk that Lieutenant Hastings would soon be Captain Hastings.

They were a hundred feet from the edge of the woods. He searched for a path in the foliage. He was becoming nervous. He thought he saw the bushes moving.

"Damn," he cursed. He had forgotten to give the order to load. He could not think of so many things at the same time. His eye was caught by the glint of something in the sunlight. It came from the woods.

"Spread out and load up," O'Hagan yelled. Just as the men started to fan out there was a devastating blast of musket fire. It cut them to pieces.

O'Hagan kept his head. The lieutenant would be watching. Everything depended now on how he behaved. "Fix bayonets," he called out above the random explosions of single muskets from the woods.

"Close ranks," he ordered. The redcoats stepped over the bodies of dying comrades and formed one solid rank of steel. "Forward march," O'Hagan screamed. Once again the woods erupted with a musket volley. O'Hagan staggered as a ball entered his stomach. He fell to his knees. He should order his men to retreat and save themselves except that none of them were left standing. They were beyond receiving orders. His eyes were clouding. He could not think straight any longer. He wished he had not been given this command. His defeat would surely mean that he would fail to make sergeant.

Marcel stepped out of the cover of the timber. He checked each body. They were all dead. He heard the skirl of pipes coming from the fort. The ambush of the wood party had aroused the English. A relief party would be coming forward soon. They would get the same treatment.

"Marcel," Benoit called to him. "Come back under cover. The English will be here soon."

Marcel returned to his friend. There were twenty of them—refugees of the woods. Marcel could not stay still. He paced back and forth behind the line of marksmen that he and Benoit had set up.

"We should be charging the church at Beaubassin and releasing all the men," Marcel said.

Benoit merely chuckled. "They'd mow us down. But this last was a turkey shoot."

"Don't expect it to be easy this time," a trapper from the Miramichi called out. "Look what's coming."

The gate of Beauséjour had opened and a pipe band followed by one hundred redcoats came marching out. They were led by an officer on horseback.

They came forward in a wide file, their muskets at belt level with fixed bayonets.

"I think it's time to get out of here," the Miramichi man said. He picked up his powder horn and began to move deeper into the woods.

"You're going to run away from them?" Marcel called.

"You bet your ass I am," said a second trapper.

Benoit took Marcel by the arm. "You'll die if you stay here. We did a little damage to them. There is no sense in getting ourselves killed. We have to flee so that we can fight again some other day—in some other place."

Marcel pulled away from Benoit. He stepped in the opposite direction, from out of the cover of the woods. He stood in the bright sunlight amid the dead bodies of Corporal O'Hagan's wood detail. He stared at the British officer who rode a gray horse so elegantly. Then he raised his fist in defiance. But he knew Benoit was right. Gestures of defiance were satisfying but purposeless. What he was really waiting for were the transports from Port Hebert. Maybe, if he could get aboard one with some of his company, he could not only strike a blow against the English but he might also do something for his father, for Maman Adele and Helene, and even Gilles. And for Nina—for all of them.

CHAPTER FIVE

Port Hebert, August 1755

Lieutenant Hastings knew he would soon be a captain, his reward for disarming the settlers of Port Hebert. Colonel Lawrence, the governor of Nova Scotia, was extremely generous with battlefield promotions, even if they would never hold up once the peace came.

"Damn it," Hastings said aloud as his troop of fifty heavily armed men entered the village center once again. "He had better make me a major right on the spot if I pull this one off."

Once again, just like last time, the village had turned out and all were assembled before the pipers, who brought up the rear as the troops came to a halt. Again the white-haired older man came forward to speak for the town.

Hastings walked over toward Lucien. "It's Monsieur Hebert, isn't it?"

The old man nodded. "Have you brought back our possessions?" he asked.

The captain was annoyed with his impertinence. "As you know, sir, France and our country are not yet at war, despite the fighting. I am sure we will receive word from London at any moment that a state of war exists. It would hardly be

81

sensible for me to rearm a whole population of potential enemies."

"Need I remind you that we have all taken the oath to King George?"

"I know you have, and I also know that it will last just as long as we keep the priests away."

"We have a treaty right to have our missionaries," Babin shouted out from the crowd.

"Treaty rights will be worthless just as soon as we have received word of the war," Hastings responded angrily.

"Why did you come back?" Lucien asked.

"I am authorized by Governor Lawrence to make an offer to the men of this community concerning the oath."

"Let's hear it," Lucien suggested.

"Not now," Hastings responded. "I will address the men and boys over fifteen this afternoon in the meeting house or chapel, whatever it is that you call it."

Lucien entered the chapel in the company of his son Gilles. He was nervous about this meeting. Why had Hastings insisted on delaying the discussion until this afternoon? And he was nervous, very nervous, about the fifty armed British troops in the village. Were they to become permanent guests, draining the resources of the village? The British had a long tradition of quartering troops.

Lucien went to the front of the chapel and sat in the family pew. Lieutenant Hastings and two noncommissioned officers strolled down the aisle. They were followed by ten armed soldiers. There was a murmur of protest among the Port Hebert men. It was improper to bring weapons into the Lord's house.

Hastings pulled a folded piece of paper from his breast pocket. He looked up at the men in the church.

"I have the following instructions from Governor Lawrence. You will have to bear with me as I translate.

"By the King's orders you are called here to listen to His Majesty's final solution concerning the French settlers of the Province of Nova Scotia who for more than half a century have had more indulgences than any of his subjects in any part of his dominions."

"I'll believe that when I get my musket back," old Dugas the fiddler called out.

Hastings waited until the laughter subsided.

"His Majesty's instructions are that your lands and your cattle and livestock are forfeited to the Crown with all your effects except money and household goods and that you are to be removed from this province."

There was a deadly silence in the chapel. Suddenly at each window a soldier appeared with musket aimed directly into the congregation, and more soldiers spread out in the back of the chapel.

"I must inform you," Hastings continued, "that it is His Majesty's pleasure that you remain in security under the inspection of my troops until the transport ships arrive to take you away."

Lucien stood. "You are mad!" he called out. "This is our home. We have lived here for generations. We have tilled the soil, watered it with our sweat and blood. We have even carved it out of the sea. Do you know what it is like, Lieutenant, to wrest an acre of land from the Bay of Fundy?"

"I am sure I do not," Hastings replied coldly. "You will be transported before the week is out."

"To where? And why us?"

"I have no idea. That's not in my orders," Hastings replied. "And it's not just you, it's Beaubassin, Grand Pre, all of you Acadians."

"We must be allowed to appeal to the king. We are British subjects. We cannot be treated in this way." Lucien was now shouting in desperation.

"I am afraid, Monsieur Hebert, that it is a bit late to discover that you are British subjects. But I do hope you will remember it in the future. I suspect you'll be sent to other British colonies. And now you must forgive me. I have much to ready for your departure."

Lucien collapsed into his seat. As Hastings started to withdraw down the aisle, however, Gilles lunged for him. The butt of one of the soldier's muskets came crashing down on his head, knocking him to the floor. Hastings continued on down the aisle, seemingly unaffected by the scuffle behind him. The British soldier who had hit Gilles followed behind

Hastings, but he looked back in consternation when he saw Gilles rise to his feet, rubbing his bleeding scalp. Any other man would be lying dead with a crushed skull from such a blow.

The men crowded around Lucien and Gilles. There was panic in most of their faces.

"They wouldn't do such a thing to us," Babin said, but there was no conviction in his voice.

"What about my wife and daughter? How will they prepare for the departure? They'll need me," shouted another man.

Lucien silenced them all. He was concerned about Gilles, who still had a glazed look in his eyes. But his responsibilities to the village had to be met.

"I will ask for a meeting with Lieutenant Hastings. There are several paths open to us." Lucien spoke with patience and assurance. "We must send an appeal to Governor Lawrence and ask for time. I'm afraid the price we must pay will be an unconditional oath of allegiance to the English king, which means bearing arms against our own people, maybe joining an attack on Isle St. Jean or Louisbourg."

"I think they're bluffing," Babin said.

"You may be right," Lucien responded, "but I'm not sure we can afford to test them."

"We could always fight them," Gilles added.

Lucien attributed his son's remark to the blow he had received. "We have no weapons, Gilles, unless you want to count our old blunderbuss. Also, they hold our families. It is not just we in the church who are held hostage. The whole village is under the gun."

Lucien managed to convey to the sergeant in charge of the guard detail that he needed to speak with the captain once again. The day grew hotter and the old wooden chapel grew more sultry with over eighty sweating men crowding into its narrow confines. Hastings entered the back of the chapel and was immediately struck by the stench of nervous perspiring men. He raised a perfumed handkerchief to his nose.

"You desire to speak to me?" he said in French.

"We have agreed to sign the oath," said Lucien, capitulating.

"I am afraid you've agreed to yesterday's policy. Today's policy is transportation."

Lucien could tell from the tone of Hastings's voice that he

meant precisely what he said. For the first time Hebert became frightened.

"You will let us send a written appeal and a signed oath to Governor Lawrence?"

"You sign it and I'll send it," said Hastings, "but I think it only fair to tell you that our naval forces at Beaubassin have sighted the transport vessels from Boston. They are within the Bay of Fundy already. When they arrive here you will be loaded onto them and transported, petition pending or not."

He turned, and without waiting for Lucien's response, he left the chapel.

Word about the fate of the community spread quickly through Port Hebert. The women began to collect in the village center about the large community well. Helene and Nina remained behind in the Hebert household. It was too hot to light a fire, so they sat by themselves with pieces of yesterday's corn bread. Helene held her father's old weapon across her knees. Nina busied herself with a mug of milk, which was warm and not terribly appetizing.

"Where is Maman Adele?" Nina asked.

"She's staying with your mother. Dette is near hysteria. *Maman* thought to calm her down," Helene said absent-mindedly.

"I offered to come home," said Nina with some bitterness, "but she said she was afraid Papa would find me there once he was released and she could not defy his wishes by bringing me back into the household."

Helene paid almost no attention to Nina. How could she go on about her own troubles when the fate of the whole village, of all Acadia, was being decided around her? She shrugged her shoulders. Perhaps she was too hard on her friend. She was pregnant by a man who showed no signs of returning to her and she had been tossed out of her own home by her father. She had a right to indulge in a bit of self-pity.

"I would not concern myself with your father coming here, Nina. The British are not going to release the men. They are going to transport us. All we can do is sit here and wait for them to do it."

"But why?" Nina asked.

Nina's question started a chain of thought in Helene's

mind. She hated inaction and she hated to be dependent on the men. And that was the key to the British action—immobilize the men and paralyze the entire village. It angered and frightened her at the same time. Why did she have to remain immobilized? She had a gun. There were probably some other hidden weapons in the village. They had to organize.

"*But why* is right," she said finally.

Nina stared at her uncomprehendingly.

"We can't just sit here and wait for it to happen."

"But all the men are prisoners."

"So what? We could rush the chapel and free them. There are a couple of hundred of us and only fifty of them."

"They have the guns."

"We have some weapons. Besides, they won't shoot women and children."

"I don't know," Nina said with some uncertainty.

"Well, I do." Helene rose and started to the door, the blunderbuss under her arm. "Are you coming?" she tossed back at Nina. But she did not wait for the other girl's response.

Nina looked about the empty room in dismay. Finally she grabbed a stick and a pile of kindling and began to run ufter Helene.

The women frequently congregated at the village center. Many of the families had dug wells near their own homes years before but the old well in the village center was still a gathering spot for gossiping or showing off a newly stitched dress or just to see one's friends. On this day there was a larger crowd than usual. The women of Port Hebert sought each other out for comfort.

Helene moved among the women in the crowd. The fact that she openly carried a weapon startled some. Others seemed to be given strength by her boldness.

"We must free the men," she repeated again and again. "Go home, get any weapon you can find. I know your men. I know they withheld something in each and every household. Get your children, bring them here. We'll line them up in front of us and we'll march on the chapel. The British won't dare fire on us."

Women slipped away from the old well in small groups to return moments later with children in tow. Many had strange bulges under their skirts or behind their aprons. Finally, when Helene thought the crowd large enough, she stood up on the stone rim of the old well itself and called out for silence. A hush fell over the crowd, except for the lonely wail of a frightened child awakened from the warmth of a nap by a determined mother.

"My friends," Helene called out, "our husbands, brothers, and fathers are locked up by a cruel enemy who would remove us from Port Hebert and take us God knows where."

"We're not going anywhere," the widow Arseneault called out. She pulled a fireplace poker from behind her apron and began to swing it about, cracking at imaginary British heads and forcing several of her neighbors to back away from her to avoid the cracking of some very real Acadian heads.

"To the chapel, free the men," Dominique called out, pointing her poker in the wrong direction.

"Christ," Helene swore under her breath, "the old bawd has been nipping again."

She called out to the crowd. "We must organize. Some must march on the Mouton house where the English commander is. Some of us must march on the chapel, and some of us must block the path to the English soldiers' camp."

But no one was paying much attention to Helene at this moment. The crowd of women and children surged ahead toward the main objective, the chapel where the men were being kept.

Helene jumped down from the well. Nina rushed to her side, a stick resting on her shoulder.

"We should get away from here," Nina said in fright.

"You're probably right," Helene shouted. "But I've started it and I'll have to see it through to the finish."

She grabbed her skirt to prevent herself from tripping and ran as fast as she could through the throng of women and children. She pushed some aside and elbowed her way through others until finally she reached the head of the crowd and brought her blunderbuss down with a thud on Dominique Arseneault's foot.

"You bitch," the widow shouted at her. "What's the matter, I thought you were in favor of this?"

"We'll get nowhere with a mob," Helene called out.

Several women gasped. Helene turned in the direction they looked.

About fifteen British redcoats, their muskets topped by steel bayonets, were approaching them. Behind them walked Lieutenant Hastings, his sword drawn.

Helene could feel the tension in the pit of her stomach. It seemed to be working its way up to her throat. This all had seemed so simple back at the well.

The troops continued to advance.

"Lock your arms together. Place the children up front." Helene felt Nina's arm grab hers. Several of the younger boys came to the head of the group. Their mothers cried out in fear. The boys were determined to carry on their roles as the only "men" in the village to protect them from the treachery of the British. Nina stifled a cry when she saw her own brother at her side. TiJoe looked frightened, but he would not allow little Bernard and Felix Arseneault and the Mouton boys to be there without him. He would be with his friends even if they were slightly older. He was proud to be up in the front—that is, until he got his first glimpse of the British coming toward him.

Helene also grew frightened. She had wanted smaller children up front, toddlers, no one the British could rationalize killing as armed and dangerous boys. She wanted babies and very young girls. Damn their male egos, she cursed. She didn't want anyone hurt, but as things now stood the boys were in grave danger. Their mothers sensed it too. They began to waver and fall back, calling to their sons. Helene could feel the tension in Nina's hand.

Hastings stepped in front of his own troops and advanced on the crowd of Acadians.

"Disperse this group," he yelled in his bad French.

The women were frightened. Hastings sensed it.

"Who's in charge here? Who's responsible for this challenge to His Majesty's authority?" He watched the eyes of the women. Without realizing it they betrayed their leader. Even the young boys in the front rank turned to look at the young woman with the strikingly beautiful face and blond hair. Hastings smiled. They have not the resolve to pull this off, he thought to himself. One show of force and they would be finished.

He turned to his troops. "Fire over their heads," he called. "On my command, ready, fire!"

Fifteen muskets roared at once. The women screamed and the crowd broke ranks. The women stepped backwards—slowly at first, then faster as the panic grew.

"Seize the blond-haired woman," Hastings ordered.

Helene knew it was hopeless. She started to run. She tripped and fell on the ground. Nina screamed again and again with fright when a soldier lifted her friend to her feet. Quickly Helene's arms were bound behind her back and soldiers led her to the Mouton house, which the lieutenant had confiscated as his headquarters.

Night fell. There were few hot meals served in Port Hebert that evening. The moaning of unmilked cows started at sunset. Some women went home to take care of them but others seemed transfixed and waited at the village center for word of their fate and that of their men.

The British troops lit campfires about the chapel. The night was warm and the fires were extinguished as soon as the meals were prepared and served to the soldiers; then the night became black again. There was no moon. A fine mist began to fall. It was difficult to tell if it rained or if they had become enveloped in a night fog bank drifting in from the bay.

There were no lamps in the chapel either. Someone lit the tiny votive candles, but they gave off almost no light individually and there were not enough of them to make any difference.

Most of the men began to curl up on the wooden pews to sleep. Gilles removed his shirt and folded it and tried to make it into a pillow for his aching head. Lucien followed his example. Soon the chapel was filled with the sounds of men sleeping—a dozen different and varied snores and snorts. Occasionally someone would cry out in the night as some dark fear penetrated into the world of his dreams.

Babin could not sleep. He could not believe this was happening to him. His disbelief had given way to an ardent desire to get out of this trap—to return to his own home, to his own fields, to his own cows. No one was going to take these things from him. He had to go home to Dette and TiJoe and even to his daughter, his dear daughter who carried the wrong man's child. He had dishonored her by driving her out of his home almost as much as Marcel Hebert had dishonored her. He must make his peace with Nina.

But first he had to get out of the chapel. He crawled from the dark corner behind the altar where he had placed himself for the night. He reached the window, which the British in a foolish act of kindness had left open as some small relief from the summer's heat. Now fog had rolled in and the chapel had cooled down. Drops of water dripped rhythmically from the eves of the chapel to the muddy and puddled ground of the yard.

Babin peered cautiously out of the window. It was black outside. The window was narrow. It would be impossible for one of the huge pompous Heberts to get out, but he could squeeze through. He hoisted himself with his arms up to the level of the bottom of the window. His shoes kicked against the wall but there was no hold. He fell to the floor of the chapel with a thud. He waited a few seconds to see if anyone was awakened by his efforts, but the snoring and mumbling continued. He reached again for the window ledge and pulled his small frame up a second time. His arms ached and began to quiver. He made one last effort. His knee caught on the ledge and rested on it. Within a few seconds he had slipped through the window and dropped to the ground outside. His feet landed in a puddle of water. There was a loud splashing noise. In front of him a black form loomed.

"A little runaway frog," said a voice in English.

Babin leapt forward. His head struck hard into the soldier's thighs, knocking him off his feet. As he fell, he dropped his musket, which discharged, sounding like thunder on a summer night. Babin reached for the gun. Holding it with both hands, he raised it high over his head and brought it smashing down on the skull of the soldier before he could struggle to his feet. The soldier fell silently backwards to the ground.

The musket's discharge awakened the men in the chapel and the sleepy guard detail as well. Babin dropped the weapon and began to race toward the village center and his own home. He was terrified now. He was sure he had killed the Englishman. If they caught him they would kill him. He must get to his house. If he could reach his wife and children they would make it to the boats and flee across the Bay of Fundy to the western shore. As he ran wildly down the street he heard shouts in English. Muskets were fired and lead balls went whining over his head. His heart sank. He had been spotted. He thought of going directly to the river and saving himself, but pride overcame his fear. Even in a moment of terror he was an Acadian and he would not abandon his family.

He ran past the Hebert cottage. No lights were showing. There was more musket fire behind him. He swerved off the road as his house came into view. He cut through his yard and crashed against the outer door. He opened it and entered the foyer. The inner door was unbolted. He opened it and slammed it behind him.

Dette and Adele shared the large bed. Both sat upright, staring in fright at him as he leaned against the bolted door gasping for breath.

"Get the children, Dette," he gasped at her. "We must make a run for it to the river."

Helene was kept bound and under guard. After she was seized, she was dropped unceremoniously in the foyer of the Mouton cottage. She had pulled herself up against the stone wall of the hearth and prepared to spend the night. Just as she drifted off to sleep, she was awakened by the sharp prick of a bayonet against her leg. She pulled her legs up under her. As soon as her eyes began to focus clearly she identified a pimply-faced boy of a soldier motioning for her to rise.

She did as he signaled. He pointed to the house proper. She entered, and the soldier closed the door behind her. She stood alone facing Lieutenant Hastings.

He sat at a small camp table, a candle illuminating his face and the paper on which he worked. He looked up at her as she entered. "Mademoiselle Hebert, isn't it? The little lady who tried to start a riot? You know it is a capital offense, but then of course what isn't?"

Helene refused to speak to him.

He rose from the desk and approached her. "I could make it easier for you." He raised her chin with his fingers. "You are very beautiful."

She pulled away from him.

"I suppose," he said, smiling, almost leering, at her, "that a real cad, someone who would truly take advantage of a situation like this, would say something like 'I like spirit in a woman.' Well, I don't. Nor do I regard myself as a real cad. I will make a straightforward proposition to you. Come to bed with me and I will make sure that your parents and relatives are transported as suits their rank."

Helene was angered by his suggestion at first. But then she began to think.

"Lieutenant, you offer me very little for something I have been taught to treasure greatly."

"Oh, my God! Don't tell me you're a virgin. They are so hard to deal with and so bloody," Hastings complained.

Now Helene was frightened that she would lose the opportunity he had given her. Her own reaction shocked her.

"Of course I'm no virgin," she lied.

"Good. Now what is it you demand for the price of your already lost virtue?"

"A piece of paper signed by you as an agent of the governor granting Lucien Hebert and his heirs the right to live on this land forever."

"You're a cocky little bitch," Hastings said in English. Then he continued in French. "What makes you think you're worth that much to me?"

Helene was really frightened now. She knew from the tone of Hastings's voice that she had hooked him. He wanted her. If she was clever enough and strong enough she might just be able to save her own family. To hell with the others, she thought, those stupid people who had gone off on their own and had not followed her lead. As might be expected, they had panicked at the first show of force. Well, she would save her father and her mother and Gilles, and even Nina. Why not Nina? She carried Marcel's child. Marcel, damn you, she thought, if only you had been here.

Hastings came toward her. His breath was bad. She stepped backwards.

"First the paper," she said.

"Ah, yes," Hastings said, turning to his writing desk. He scribbled something with his quill and poured sand from a shaker onto the wet ink. He approached Helene again and handed it to her.

"It's not in French," she guessed, not letting him know that she could barely read in her own language.

"Bloody right it's not in French," Hastings responded. "It's got to be in English if it's to be official."

"Put it in French on the back and sign both," she demanded.

"I can't write well in French," Hastings complained.

"It's not hard to say," she insisted.

"Oh, all right." Hastings went back to his desk and wrote some more. Again he poured some sand, waiting a minute for the ink to dry. Then he held up the letter. He waved it at Helene. "Now you come and take it from me."

Helene remained riveted where she stood. She really did not know what to do next. She wanted that paper but she did not want to pay the price that Hastings would demand of her. He stood there holding it up in the air, the one chance the Heberts had to remain on their land. Why should she have to pay? It was their land. What right had the English to chase them from it? What right had this pig of an English officer to demand she sell herself to retain what was rightfully hers?

Hastings picked up the candle from the desk and brought it closer and closer to the paper. Just as the paper began to smolder Helene yelled out, "No," and raced to him, snatching the precious passport in her own hands and shoving it into her bodice.

"I hope you don't think it will be safe from me there of all places." Hastings laughed. He grabbed her about the waist with one hand and thrust the other between her legs.

"Jesus Christ," he screamed as her knee slammed into his groin.

It was a foolish reaction, a stupid reaction, she realized just as soon as she had done it. Now she would lose everything.

"You bitch!"

Suddenly there was musket fire coming from the direction of the chapel. Hastings grabbed his sword. The sentry opened the Moutons' door just as soon as he heard the captain yell. Hastings called to him.

"Soldier, keep your eye on this woman. Make sure she does not escape, and for Christ's sake, keep away from her knees."

He hobbled out into the night. "Sergeant," he called to the soldier who ran to meet him, "what has happened?"

"One of the prisoners escaped through an open window,

sir. We've cornered him in one of their huts. He has killed Private Rourke."

"Show no mercy, Sergeant," Hastings responded instantly. "If he surrenders, take him to the nearest tree and hang him immediately. If he refuses to surrender, burn him out and then hang him."

"Yes, sir."

Adele looked out the front window and turned to Babin. "There is no escape," she said. "You'll never get to the river. The yard is filled with redcoats."

Terror gripped Babin. He turned to his wife. "They'll hang me for sure. I killed one of them."

Just then TiJoe awoke and sat up on his mat, rubbing his eyes. He heard the noise of soldiers outside the house and jumped up to go to the window.

"TiJoe, no," Adele called out to him. She stepped forward to block his path to the window. A volley of musket balls rang out, tearing through the windowpane and splattering glass in all directions. A huge sliver of glass smashed into TiJoe's throat, severing an artery. Blood gushed from him. A look of hurt surprise crossed his face, and he sank to his knees, his life's blood pouring out of him. Adele stared in disbelief at the growing circle of red that stained her skirt just above her navel. She too sank to her knees. Odette did nothing but scream and run from one victim to another. Babin stood motionless. He knew without looking that TiJoe would die within seconds and that Adele's belly wound was fatal. He knew instinctively that his beloved Dette's mind had snapped. She could never recover from the sight of her baby's blood gushing from him.

Just at that moment Hastings called out for him to surrender. He was numb. There was no use resisting. There was nothing to resist for. He opened the door and walked out into the yard. He was seized roughly and his arms were tied behind his back. He heard Nina scream out his name. He could not even look at her. He was pulled almost off his feet by a rope that had been tied around his neck. Twenty-five years before he had planted the maple tree in the front yard. It had grown sturdily. Its roots had sunk deeply into the soil of Acadia. The loose end of the rope was tossed over a high limb of the maple. Five soldiers hauled on the rope, walking away from the tree. Babin felt the hemp tighten around his neck. Then he was jerked off his feet. His legs kicked a gruesome dance in the air. His face turned red and his eyes bulged. He could not breathe. Finally there was nothing but blackness.

Lieutenant Hastings ordered the corpse to be left hanging from the maple tree until sundown the next day. He turned to his sergeant and smiled.

"About that girl back at the headquarters, see to it that she sails on the first transport that arrives and that she sails separately from the rest of her family."

The sergeant didn't like hangings. He had no stomach for them, and he didn't like what the officer suggested about the girl.

"The first ship is likely to be Captain Rofheart's sloop, sir."

"So?"

"He's a bad one. There are few sailors in Boston who will sign on with him, and there isn't a whore in any seaport on the Atlantic Coast who will sleep with him."

"Luck of the draw, Sergeant."

"I don't like it," the sergeant responded.

"It's not for you to like or dislike, Sergeant. And while you're at it, add the screaming widow to Rofheart's list as well. Maybe he can shut her up."

He turned away from the other man and smiled to himself. "I guess I am a bit of a cad after all," he said aloud.

They buried the victims of Babin's escape in the chapel yard the next evening. Gilles dug a grave for his mother. Lucien stood watching. His shoulders sagged and his eyes seemed to have clouded over. He saw nothing. Adele's small body was placed gently into the four-foot-deep grave by her giant son. Then he stood next to his father with his head bowed. The sun's setting rays struck the hills across the bay and then reflected directly into their eyes. They could see no farther than the gravesite. Gilles squinted and held his hand to shield his eyes. Then he saw them. Three schooners and a sloop lay anchored in Chignecto Bay. He placed his arm about Lucien's shoulders, for he was afraid his father was going to collapse. He seemed drained of all strength by the death of his wife. Gilles decided not to mention the transports to him.

Nina stood behind Lucien. The British dug a single grave for her father and little brother. Both were placed in it—the boy on top of the man—united in death as they never had been in life. Nina seemed as paralyzed as Lucien. No one had seen her mother or Helene and all questions about them were carefully ignored by the British.

Lucien stepped to the open grave of his wife. There had been no time to build coffins and Gilles had wrapped his mother in the blanket from the bed she had shared with his father for so many years. Lucien stared down into the hole as if staring into an abyss. He picked up a handful of dirt and sprinkled it on top of the still form. Then he turned away and allowed himself to be led back to the chapel.

Gilles was crushed by the loss of his mother but he was terrified by what had happened to his father. Lucien seemed drained of all emotion. Where was the man that all looked to as leader of the village? Certainly it was not the broken old man he followed. If Lucien could not lead, whom could they look to? Who would lead them out of this tragedy? Before his eyes all he could see were those transports out in the bay. Suddenly it dawned on a terrified Gilles that they might not be able to avoid the fate that the British seemed determined to mete out to them. Gilles could feel a cold sweat break out all over his body.

That night the men slept fretfully. They were told that some families were to leave on the next day. The sergeant called out the names of those to leave for Virginia. When the name of Joseph Babineau was called, Lucien called out, "*Mort.*" The sergeant knew the word and asked, "Any family?"

"*Mort,*" old Dugas said.

Gilles walked over to the sergeant. "Babin has a daughter and she's with child."

"I don't speak French," the sergeant said, shaking his head with annoyance.

Gilles pointed to his belly and made a sign as if holding a protruding abdomen.

Now the sergeant nodded with understanding.

"Wives go with their husbands."

Gilles began to grow panicky. No one had yet called out the Hebert name. He again questioned the sergeant.

"Hebert?" he asked.

The sergeant ran down the list of names.

"No."

Gilles stepped quickly to his father's side.

"Papa, Nina will be split from us. She is scheduled for a different ship, one scheduled for Virginia."

Lucien stared blankly. "She has her mother," he said finally.

"No one has seen Dette since..." He could not bring himself to mention the incident that had cost Adele's life.

"What do you want of me, Gilles?"

"I don't want Nina to go alone. She's pregnant. And I don't care if my brother is the father. The baby will be my nephew or my niece and it will be Nina's son or daughter."

"Go with her, then," the old man said with no emotion whatsoever in his voice.

"I can't leave you, Papa," Gilles said, tears filling his eyes.

"I'll have your sister."

Gilles could not bring himself to say it, but no one had seen Helene either. He had a lot of thinking to do. He sat behind his father's pew and stretched out his limbs.

Dugas' fiddle began to play. The tune was dirgelike and incredibly sad. Gilles fell asleep to the music and did not later recall hearing the last notes.

In the morning they found old Dugas dead, his hands still gripping the fiddle. They could not pry it from him. Gilles could not get even a flicker of response from his father when he told him the news. Lucien's heart still beat but he was closer to old Dugas than he was to his son. Gilles went to his mother's family, the Moutons, and asked their advice. He could see that they thought he should stay with his father rather than run off with a girl who was not related to him, but they did promise to watch out for Lucien should Gilles decide to try to go with Nina.

When the sergeant appeared to release a handful of men at a time to go to their homes to collect their personal goods and families and then reassemble at the riverfront, Gilles confronted him and pointed to himself and said "Babineau."

The sergeant looked at him and smiled. He was not fooled. He knew what the giant of a man was doing. He let him go.

Gilles stared for a moment at his oblivious father, who sat looking blankly at the church wall.

He took a deep breath and then left the chapel. The dirt road was crowded with people. British soldiers with their muskets at the ready, and men, women, and children carrying packs on their back and heading toward the river where the transports now stood. The tide was high. As soon as it began to turn the transport captains would be leaving. The British would see to it that all the passengers were aboard. The tide would determine how much time they would have to ready themselves for the trip.

Gilles raced down the dirt road toward his house. He opened the door to the foyer. The inner door stood open.

"Nina," he called out.

She sat in his mother's chair. She had been sleeping.

"Have you seen your mother or Helene?" he asked.

She shook her head. A moan escaped her lips. "Oh, my God," was all she could say in her grief.

"We are going together," Gilles said. "I love you, Nina. Despite what you and Marcel did I will not abandon you."

She looked up at him. She was too weak to protest that she and Marcel had done nothing wrong as far as she was concerned. He ran about the house, packing some clothes for her and some for himself. He remembered that his mother had kept her children's baby clothes—a foolish gesture until now. They might need them. He found the old trunk in the sleeping loft. He grabbed a few baby dresses and underneath he saw something glitter. There were seven gold pieces. He picked them up in his hand. He could use them all. His father was too far gone, even to think of them. But he and Helene might need them. He put four of them back into the trunk and closed it.

He stuffed their clothing and food in a knapsack and returned to the main floor. Nina still sat where he had left her. He raised her to her feet and took her hand in his own. "I'm not going," she said feebly. "Just leave me alone. Let me sit here. Let me die like Papa, like TiJoe." The mention of their names released a flood in her. It began with a low moaning sound, then swelled into a pitiful wail of despair. Finally she began to cry great sobs of grief and defeat.

Gilles stood holding her. How he wished he could transfer

98

his strength to her. He loved her so much. He did not care if she drained him in her need.

Slowly he led her out of the house and into the road, where they joined the shuffling crowd of refugees trudging toward the village center and then on toward the river.

As he walked, Gilles wondered how it had come to this. All over Acadia a race was being torn from the soil of its birth, yet there had been no resistance. They were a peaceful people who wished only to be left in peace.

He helped Nina into the small boat. The crew began to row and the boat leader kicked Gilles in the rump.

"Sit down, you giant. You want to tip the boat?"

In the past Gilles would have broken the Englishman into two equal pieces and then into quarters with ease. But now he meekly took his place and aided in the rowing.

The climb up the side of the ship was difficult for Nina, but Gilles followed close behind her and supported her whenever she faltered. Once they arrived on deck, she looked back toward the shore, toward the village, toward her home. She shuddered. Gilles held her by the shoulder.

"You two, get the hell forward into the hold. No gawking. You there, seaman, get those Frogs on the move."

Gilles could not understand the words but he recognized the tone. He pushed Nina gently with his hand. They climbed down a ladder into the cargo hold. Three levels had been constructed, each one no more than four feet high. Nina and Gilles were directed to the lowest level. It was dark in the hold and moisture dripped from the rafters. Beneath their feet they could hear the lapping of the river against the hull. The whole compartment stank of bilge water. Nina bent low to enter, then turned in panic. Gilles caught her in his arms and held her as his ears filled with her screams.

Half the village of Port Hebert departed with the change of the tide. The rest remained behind. The men were still confined in the chapel while the women and children worked together to pack as many of their belongings as possible. On the high tide the next day more transport vessels arrived. These were already crowded with deportees from the Grand Pre region. They had room for only a few families or single individuals. Lucien was selected and marched out to the riverfront. He had not bothered to go to his home to collect any of his belongings. He walked into exile with only the clothes he wore.

He was rowed out to a small schooner, the *Pembroke* from Boston. He nearly fell into the sea boarding her and would not have tried to swim had he fallen. The ship departed with the tide for Beauséjour where more refugees were loaded aboard. They had room for no more and headed out to the greyness of the Bay. Lucien was shoved up against the bulkhead and was kept standing by the crush of people. There was no room to lie down unless everyone did it together, and it wasn't time for that.

Some women wailed hysterically when the hatches, the only source of light and air, were closed finally and the hold fell into darkness.

Lucien barely heard the din that echoed deeply within the bowels of the ship as hundreds of Acadians voiced their complaint. Few cried out in anger at their fate; instead, one could hear the sobs of the hungry, the moaning of those who grew seasick once the *Pembroke* hauled in its anchor and sailed out onto the waves of the Bay of Fundy. Some retched from deep within their guts in sympathy with the seasick. A mother cried out in terror because she had been separated from her child.

Food was dropped to them in buckets. After it was devoured, those same buckets were to be used to take care of their bodily necessities. At first the women complained and several would come together to shield each other and provide privacy, but after a while no one seemed to care, nor did anyone look at anyone else with anything other than desperation in their faces.

Lucien had not eaten. Let the food go to the young, who had a chance of surviving.

After the food buckets had been sent up through the hatches, many people began to slump to the floor. Suddenly Lucien was startled to hear a voice ring out through the darkness.

"My friends," the voice said, "we need some organization. Everyone must lie down. Now, all together. Then everyone must stand when the signal is given. We must appoint captains in charge of food distribution. We must assure that the old and the weak, nursing mothers, and little ones get food. That means even distribution. I appoint Georges and Louis, because they are named after the two monkeys that got us here."

There was some faint laughter at his words.

"Marcel," Lucien called out into the mass of people and darkness.

The voice halted. Someone else started to give instructions about allowing the food captains to get near the hatch openings to receive the food when it was passed down. There was a pushing among the people who tried to lie down next to Lucien. A dark form crossed over some and stepped on others, to loud complaints.

"Papa." Marcel reached out and clasped his father to himself. "I can't believe my luck to find you on the same ship."

"Gone," the old man said, and he started to weep bitterly.

"What do you mean, Papa?"

The old man could not answer.

"Maman Adele?"

Lucien merely nodded.

"Helene?"

"I don't know," he said. "I buried your mother." He put his face in his hands. "But your sister vanished. I have not seen her."

Marcel sat dazed for some minutes. He wept openly for his mother. Deep within him an anger seethed, an anger that could be satisfied only by revenge. Finally he choked back his tears. "And Gilles?" Marcel asked.

"He is a good boy," Lucien responded. "He accompanied Nina. She was to go to Virginia. She was alone. The British killed my Adele and little TiJoe and then they hanged Babin."

"My God, it sounds like a massacre at Port Hebert. It was bad enough at Beaubassin. The cruelty was unbelievable, but there were no murders. On the contrary, a fellow named Hebert led an attack on the British and killed quite a few of them." He lowered his voice to a whisper. "We have a few of the troop here in the hold. We entered this ship deliberately at Beauséjour and we intend to take it and sail back home. We will kill the bastards, so help me God. I will avenge my mother; I promise that. And I will avenge my sister if need be, although I pray to God it need not be. There are no British troops aboard to guard us. They have left us to the tender mercies of the merchant sailors."

Lucien did not hear his son, although he had grabbed Marcel's arm and held it in his grip.

"The girl is pregnant, Marcel. Gilles did the right thing to go with her."

Marcel looked at his father in surprise. He felt suddenly very ill. She had gone on to Gilles' arms after he left her. The news hurt. It surprised him that anything at all could still hurt. He had planned to come back to Port Hebert to be with Nina Babeneau. He had lost almost everything now—his mother, his sister, even Nina. All he had was his father and his son.

Lucien grabbed hold of Marcel's shoulder. The grip was feeble—so unlike the touch Marcel remembered. "You must bring them all back to Port Hebert, my son. Promise me." Marcel nodded. He heard his name called out by one of his compatriots. He reached down into his boot and felt the razor he had hidden there. He was happy only in the thought of the damage he would do with it in the morning.

At first light the hatches were opened and the stale mixture of body odor and rancid air seemed to rush through the opening. As the sea breeze blew over the top of the hatch, some stray winds were caught and sucked down into the hold, where they were greeted with sighs of relief.

The ship's cook leaned down into the cargo hold with a bucket of gruel. Just as he was about to lower the bucket on the rope, a man in buckskins leapt on the shoulders of Marcel Hebert and reached up for the bucket.

"If that's the way you Frogs want to do it, that's the way it will be." The cook leaned forward to pass the bucket to the top man.

Suddenly his arms were grabbed and he was yanked into the hold. The man on Marcel's shoulders leapt for the edge of the hatch. Catching it with both hands, he pulled himself up onto the deck. Then he reached down. Marcel made a step with his hands. Another buckskin-clad man stepped into Marcel's hands and was lifted up until his arm was grabbed by the first man on deck. He too was hauled upward. And then a third made it to the deck.

Marcel looked around the hold in desperation. He signaled to his father to help him, but the old man merely stared at him. Finally a farmer made a step with his hands for Marcel. The young man bounded upward and was caught and hauled out of sight.

The people in the hold heard nothing but silence on deck for some moments. Finally there was the sound of bare feet running along the deck above their heads. A musket fired and someone screamed. The people in the hold waited patiently, almost breathlessly. Suddenly a rope ladder was dropped down and the somber face of Marcel Hebert reappeared.

"They are all dead," he yelled.

A great roar rose from the hold and several people tripped over each other trying to be the first up the ladder.

"One at a time," Marcel cautioned, "but first send up fishermen or sailors, anyone who knows how to handle a schooner."

They beached the schooner at St. John at the mouth of the harbor. The English had not struck here yet, but they would come. Of that Marcel was certain.

He felt he must go back and look for Helene or at least find some record of where she had been taken. If he could liberate his brother and Nina he must attempt that as well.

When he mentioned returning to Port Hebert to Lucien, the man became obsessed with the idea. But, unlike Marcel, he had no concern for the living. He wished to go back so that he might sit by Adele's grave.

"It will need a cross, or maybe even a stone. Some flowers should be planted," he said. For the first time Marcel saw some interest flicker in the old man's face.

The night they arrived in St. John, Marcel stole some food and a leaky canoe. He placed his father in the front of the craft and turned its nose north toward the top reaches of the Bay of Fundy. He traveled only at night. The transport vessels dotted the bay, carrying more and more Acadians from their homes. At times Marcel felt he was paddling not only against the bay tides but also against the tide of history and human affairs. Those tides drew the people of his race away from their home. Still he continued northward.

At dawn Marcel pulled into an inlet not far from Beaubassin. They were only a few hours from Port Hebert, but he could not chance being spotted. He gave his father some cold ham and washed it down with water from the creek that flowed to the inlet. It was slightly brackish. Lucien had said nothing the whole night of traveling. His face was ashen, and Marcel worried about him. He picked at the ham and refused the water.

"Papa, you must eat something," Marcel complained.

Lucien sighed wearily and like an obedient child began to chew his meat more vigorously. Then suddenly he grabbed at his chest. His face folded into an agonized grimace. He vomited up the recently eaten ham.

Marcel rushed to his side.

"I hurt," the old man complained.

Marcel laid his father on his back. "Don't move. Rest here. Can you breathe?"

The old man nodded. "But the pain is awful."

It was not until midafternoon that the pain in Lucien's chest began to grow weaker, but by then the old man too had begun to weaken.

Marcel knew they would have to remain where they were until his father's strength returned, but as soon as Lucien realized his son's intention he began to berate him.

"I wish to return home. I am dying, my son. Don't deny your father his last wish."

Marcel too believed that the old man was dying, and there were still several hours of daylight left. He could make it to Port Hebert before sunset if he really paddled. He didn't really care now if the English spotted him. He had escaped them once and he would escape them a second time if need be. The only thing that mattered now was to return home.

He lifted his father and laid him down gently in the canoe. He propped his head up with the bundles of food he had taken at St. John. He turned the bow of the canoe toward Chignecto Bay, the northern arm of Fundy.

The afternoon was warm and hazy. The eastern shore was visible from the very beginning of their journey. As the minutes wore on, Marcel could make out familiar sights. He called them out to his father.

"I can see the mud flats you worked on in the spring."

Lucien smiled.

"The marsh grass is spreading that way already." The

mouth of the Hebert River came into view. "It's the river, Papa. We're coming to it."

"Lift me up a bit, Marcel," the old man cried out, his face alive with excitement.

They were at the river's mouth now. They rounded a curve.

"I see the village," Lucien called out. "Look how the smoke rises from the chimneys. The women are preparing a meal. Soon we shall return home from the fields. Maman Adele..." he called out.

His body stiffened and slowly slumped down. He slipped off the bundle, his face landing in the water in the bottom of the canoe. Then he lay still.

Tears streamed down Marcel's face. He stopped paddling and allowed the canoe to glide. What Lucien had seen as smoke rising from happy homes, a sign that all was right, was in fact a black smoldering ruin. Every building in Port Hebert had been put to the torch.

Marcel found the chapel yard. He buried his father among the Heberts beside a freshly dug grave that he assumed to be his mother's. He knelt before both of them and recited the almost forgotten prayers Maman Adele had taught him so many years before. He was truly alone now. He had been alone many times in his life and at times he had sought out solitude, but never before had he felt lonely. He knew he should be making vows of revenge, as he had aboard the *Pembroke* when he first learned of his family's suffering. But he felt little now but numbness. He wanted to find Helene. He wanted to find his brother and Nina. Yes, Nina, even if she was Gilles' woman. He needed them all.

He rose. At least his parents would rest together in the soil of Acadia. They would know no exile. He turned his back on the ruins and walked through the village center. He stopped at the old well. A dead cow had been dropped into it to spoil the water. He followed the road until he came to the site of his old home. The rafters of the roof had collapsed. The ashes were still hot and some sections of the building still smoked. He kicked aside some rubble and saw the charred armrest of his mother's rocker.

The storage loft had collapsed and spilled its contents onto what had been the main floor. But this must have happened late in the fire, after the flames had died down, because very few of the loft's contents had burned.

Marcel noticed the old trunk. He touched the metal latch and quickly pulled his fingers away. It was very hot. He used the charred armrest to lift the latch. There were some old mementoes in the chest and in the corner there were four very hot gold coins. He couldn't pick them up. But he was in no hurry. He would come back for them in the morning.

He walked out into what had been the foyer. The hearth wall still stood. He sat down on the ground with his back to it. He needed to sleep. He would not awaken the household. Maybe if he slept, maybe in the morning residents of this Acadian house would rise and find a guest in their foyer and provide the weary traveler with a hot country breakfast.

CHAPTER SIX

Off New England, September 1755

Dette had finally cried herself to sleep, but the stench of the cargo hold kept Helene from drifting off. She lay on the compartment's damp wooden floor, her body cuddled against Dette for warmth. Stretching away from her in all directions were the dark forms of sleeping bodies. Men snored, some older women like Dette joined them. Every once in a while someone would break wind, adding to the denseness of the atmosphere below decks.

The schooner seemed to be tossed aimlessly by the giant waves of the Atlantic. So rough were the seas that no one had come to lift the hatch covers all day, and now with night no one would. Helene shivered in the dampness. Yet she could feel the beads of sweat on her skin beneath her clothing. She felt the paper—the Hebert passport—a useless paper, still stuffed into her bodice. She was tempted to tear it up and toss it into the sea. Except there was no sea visible to her. Instead she removed Hastings' scribbling and folded it and placed it back next to her skin.

They had been trapped like this for three days now as the sloop headed along the coast of New England. On that first day she and Dette had been rowed out to the schooner along with a handful of other deportees. They were forced to climb rope ladders up to the main deck. A huge redhaired, red-bearded man stood on the quarterdeck watching the new arrivals. As they stepped up to the first officer and gave their names, Helene looked up to see the giant staring at her. His face broke into a grin as he watched her. She pulled the shawl Dette had given her even more closely about her, but still she could sense the man's hands on her flesh just from his glance.

She felt relieved when they were shoved down into the compartment already crowded with Grand Pre folk. But the relief did not last long. The hold was filled with seasick people, and the smell of vomit and unwashed bodies almost made her sick as well. Dette barely noticed it as she shuffled along looking for space. She had not left that space since the first day. They had all cried at first, but now most were beyond tears. Despair had settled their emotions and only lethargy remained. The old lady next to Dette died the second night at sea. She had not been ill, just old. Helene hoped no one would die tonight. Last night, despite the rough seas, they signaled the crew and passed the woman's body out of the hold. There would be no contact with the crew tonight.

Dette had told Helene about the deaths of Babin and TiJoe. Almost as an afterthought she added the news that Helene's mother had died as well. Helene did not blame the distraught woman for that. She could not have known how much the news added to the turmoil Helene already felt. She had loved her mother deeply, and her death was a terrible loss. But there were so many others: Maman Adele, already cold in the earth; Gilles and Papa transported like herself, God knows where. Only Marcel was free, she hoped, but separated from Nina, who bore his child—a fact he did not even know. Port Hebert, her home, was now hundreds of miles away, and except for Dette and a few other Port Hebert deportees she was among strangers. But they were Acadians like her and joined in her misery. Together they all bore the burden of exile.

She felt a hand touch her own. She started in fright at the cold and clammy touch. She turned to look into the wide eyes of an older man. His breath was foul and his face was covered with black whiskers mingled with a sprinkling of gray.

"Mademoiselle," he whispered, "we have some people with fever on the other side of the hold. Can you help us?"

Helene stared at him uncomprehendingly. Why did he approach her?

"Are you not the daughter of Adele Mouton, the *traiteur*? That is what some Port Hebert people have told us."

"I am," Helene responded, "but I have never claimed the gift."

"I am sorry," the whiskered face said, "but they also told us of Madame Adele's death, God rest her," he said, blessing himself. "Sometimes the gift passes at that moment. Besides, we have no one else." This last was said with a note of pleading in his voice.

"I'll do what I can," she said and sat up.

Dette awakened as soon as she felt Helene stir. She cried out in fear when she felt Helene get up.

"Ssh," Helene soothed her. "There is fever in the hold. I have been asked to look at the sick."

She saw the look of wonder cross Dette's darkened face.

"Because of *Maman*," Helene added.

"I knew it," Dette said loudly. "I could feel the power from you course through my body. Why else would I have awakened in fright from my dreams just because you moved? I knew your *maman* would not abandon us even in death. She passed it all on to you."

"So you're the one who spread the story, Dette. I'm not even left-handed."

"That worried me at first," the older woman responded, "but then I heard the story of a woman on Isle St. Jean, a right-handed *traiteur*, the most powerful of them all. The priest was sent to rout out all the healers from the island. He rounded up the left-handed in each parish and read the prayers for exorcising the devil over them. But he missed one, and it was as if all the powers taken from all the others were stored in the one. She was the grandmother of all *traiteurs*. It is said she was the teacher of Fru Fru Mouton, who taught your mother. It all fits, Helene."

Helene saw the man waiting patiently. She was annoyed with Dette for putting her in this position. She cursed under her breath and followed the man who disappeared rapidly into the gloom of the hold. As she crawled over the sleeping people, some complained while others merely groaned and turned to go back to sleep.

She did not realize she had reached the far end of the compartment until her head struck the low beam. She thought she would faint with the pain. She grabbed her skull and gritted her teeth. Finally the pain began to subside and she started to chuckle to herself. She had begun her career as a *traiteur* by healing herself.

"Over here," said the man she followed.

She moved to the left.

"This is my sister," he said. "She is very weak."

Helene squeezed between the man and his sister. The woman was about thirty-five. She was covered with a woolen blanket and there was a sour smell about her. But then, everyone smelled poorly now.

Helene felt awkward. She had assisted Adele too often not to know what was expected of her. She had no herbs or medicines. No one would expect much more than a touching. She felt that would be the least effective remedy, but she knew there were at least a dozen pairs of eyes watching her. They would expect much from this first touch.

She placed her hands on the woman's fevered brow. What her mother had thought at those moments Helene would never know. She remembered only to say an "ave" and hope the Virgin, her mother's patron, would have pity on all of them.

There were two more fever victims. Helene followed the same treatment with each of them—hands on the forehead and a prayer to the Holy Mother. Other hands reached up to touch her. She grasped as many as she could. It was as if touching her somehow was a link to them all, the last tie to home. She could almost feel the pleading in their grasp, the desperate longing that all the horror around them was a dream and that by touching the *traiteur* the pain of that illusion would disappear.

She made her way back across the compartment, but the whispers preceded her and again and again people reached out and touched her. She regained her place by Dette and collapsed onto the floor. She was exhausted. She did not know how or why, but they had drained her strength.

She leaned back against the bulkhead. Once again the face of the bearded man loomed out at her in the dark.

"I was not able to thank you, mademoiselle."

"Helene," she sighed.

"Maurice, Maurice Bertrand from Grand Pre," he responded.

She squeezed closer to the sleeping Dette to make room for Bertrand, who clearly wanted to talk.

"Do you know where they take us?" Helene asked him.

"No, I've heard only that Captain Rofheart, the master of the sloop, is the devil himself. I fear he will try to take us to the West Indies and sell us as slaves."

As he spoke his voice broke and his body trembled. Helene was not sure if he was sick like his sister or if it was fear rather than fever that had touched him. He leaned his back against the bulkhead. The two of them sat side by side in silence.

Helene felt herself slipping off. Her head jerked and she awoke.

"I'm sorry," Bertrand apologized. "I am keeping you awake and you are exhausted."

"No." Helene denied the truth. She knew the man was desperate to speak to someone. "Tell me about Grand Pre," she said. "I have never been there. In fact, I have never been anywhere—until now," she added wistfully.

"It's gone" was all that Maurice could say. "They torched it—eight hundred homes and other buildings all gone." His voice broke again as he spoke. "Oh, God, what have we done to deserve this?" he cried out. "My wife and daughter, I don't know where they are. I was lucky to be transported with my sister at least. Now I don't know what will happen to her."

"I did the best I could," Helene said sleepily.

"I did not mean to imply anything else."

But Helene did not hear Maurice's apology. She had drifted off to sleep. Her head and shoulders gradually slouched toward Maurice until finally her face rested against his upper arm. He was startled at first by her touch, but then the closeness of her filled him with a warm comfort. It was the same as when his Marie Paul rested her head on him at night when they were alone together under the feather quilt. Now he was surrounded by a stinking mass of snoring humanity and it was not Marie Paul. But he closed his eyes. Somehow, even in the dark and fetid hole, that seemed to help. With the softness of a woman's hair against his skin, the loose strands reaching up and touching the underside of his jaw, he could pretend he was somewhere else and she was someone else. For just a moment he could forget all that happened. But then he heard someone cry out. It reminded him of his responsibility to his sister. Maurice moved gently away from Helene. Her head sagged a bit and Maurice very gently turned her body toward the other side, where Odette Babineau slept between her fits of tears.

Helene stirred but she did not awaken under his soft touch. He allowed his hand to linger on her shoulder and then her hip as he moved her. Finally he took one long last look at her and, turning, began the long crawl back to his side of the hold.

In the morning the hatches were removed and fresh air was sucked into the hold. Helene was awakened by the light that streamed into the compartment and struck her face. Sailors dropped several rope ladders down into the old and began to yell at the Acadians. By their gestures it was clear they wanted the prisoners to climb up to the deck. Helene desperately wanted to feel the sea wind in her face. She struggled to her feet and grabbed the bulkhead to steady herself against the pitch of the ship. She moved toward the ladder and found an easy path through the crowded compartment as people moved aside to make way for her.

The deck was cluttered with the remnants of the rough seas of the night before. Some sailors were cleaning up the mess; others kept muskets and one swivel cannon trained on the prisoners.

Helene stared off toward the stormy horizon. A faint band, the New England coast, extended north and south as far as she could see. They followed the coast and had not ventured very far from it. Perhaps these New England sailors feared French privateers sailing out from Louisbourg.

Helene walked with Dette and others at first, but then she

leaned against the railing of the ship. The seas were still a bit rough and the bow of the sloop repeatedly struck the waves with a smashing thud, sending spray in all directions.

Helene deliberately allowed the wind-blown spray to strike her, hoping it would wash away the stench from below deck. She paid no attention to those around her and was surprised when Bertrand stood next to her. In the light of the day she could see that he too had the flush of fever about him.

"Your sister, Monsieur Bertrand?"

"She seems better this morning, although I have not allowed her to come up into the air. I am afraid of chills. We are very grateful to you."

She smiled at him. "I am happy I could be of any service, although I am afraid my talents were exaggerated."

"No," Bertrand interrupted quickly. "All the sick are feeling better this morning. Everyone is talking of your powers."

"You," the man at the swivel gun called out.

Both Bertrand and Helene looked up. Behind him on the quarterdeck stood the man with red hair and beard.

"Go back down," the guard called out in English. Neither Helene nor Bertrand understood his words, but his gesture toward the hold was clear enough.

They both started to move forward but the redhaired man called out in French, "Not you, my love, only the man. You may stay on deck longer."

Helene resented his familiarity and his leering smile. She felt suddenly frightened and moved forward to join the others who were starting down the rope ladder. From the corner of her eye she saw a blur of motion. The man had leapt from the quarterdeck and landed heavily on his feet. He reached out and grabbed her by the shawl, snagging a loose strand of hair with it. Helene yelped in pain.

"Sorry, my lovely, but I said you were to stay on deck. And since I am the captain of this bloody ship I expect to be obeyed, even by a French slut like you."

Bertrand reached out his hand to steady Helene then screamed as the captain's foot rammed into his crotch. As he bent forward, a musket ball exploded from the gun of the quarterdeck sentry and struck his face. With complete indifference the captain lifted the now limp, bleeding body of the

Frenchman and tossed it over the railing into the sea. He looked up and grinned at the sentry who had fired the shot.

"Mark him down as attempted mutiny and get a mop and swab up the blood. Can't have my ship looking like a filthy slaver."

Helene watched horrified. She shrank back when the captain reached out to touch her. He grabbed her wrists and led her tripping and tumbling up the steps to the quarterdeck.

"No need to go back down into the stench, my pretty."

Helene shivered.

"McIntyre," he called out to his mate in English. "Get the little lady a chair so she can enjoy the morning. And, Mac, get her a sea coat. She seems to have the chills."

Helene watched Rofheart command his ship from the quarterdeck for the rest of the morning. He paid almost no attention to her, and she even imagined that he had forgotten about her. Then at noon he took her by the hand and led her down to his cabin.

There were two places set at a small table. Steaming hot cups of freshly brewed coffee mixed their aroma with the pungent odor of grease that came from the pan-fried potatoes heaped high onto the two plates.

Rofheart bowed toward Helene and pulled out the captain's chair for her. Then, still standing behind her, he wet his palms with his tongue and plastered them against his unruly windblown hair. Next, he ran his fingers through his beard and smoothed his moustache. As he came around to face her and take his seat, Helene watched Rofheart warily. She was famished and the hot food, poor fare though it was, seemed like a royal banquet.

Rofheart began to eat his fried potatoes. Helene did not require any further signal. She wolfed down the contents of the plate and then began to gulp the hot coffee.

"Don't care much for the gruel we feed you, do you?"

Helene shook her head.

"Can't say I blame you. But there's no need for you to eat anything but the best, the same as I eat, right here in this cabin. Fact is, you can spend the rest of this trip right here in the cabin or up on deck in comfort for the right price."

Helene knew precisely what he wanted. It was Hastings all over again. What she didn't know was whether his words constituted an offer that could be rejected or were merely a polite statement of her fate.

"Do I have a choice?" she asked.

"No," he said smiling at her.

"I'll fight you," she said.

"I don't think you will. You like to eat and you sure as hell don't like the stench down there in the hole. And besides, if you fight me you'll never win, and I don't give no quarter. That is something you should learn from me: never give any quarter. When you got somebody, finish them off."

He stood up from the table and came round to Hélène. He extended his rough and calloused paw toward her. She did not reach out for it. Suddenly she found herself pulled to her feet. Rofheart grabbed her by the shoulders. Helene tried to pull away from him, but his massive arms resisted her pull. He swept her off her feet and carried her to the cot on the opposite side of the small cabin. She tried to kick out at him unsuccessfully. He dropped her unceremoniously onto the cot and began to remove his breeches.

"You're going to have to pay for your meal now, my fair one," he said in English.

Helene stared up at him. Her mind was in a turmoil. She knew she would help herself by allowing him what he wanted, but she had never been with a man and this was not the way she had pictured it.

He reached down and pulled off the coat she still wore. As he touched her breast with his large hand, she made up her mind. She began to undo the buttons of her blouse.

The red face above her broke into a smile. "So you want it after all?" he said. He knelt on the cot, which seemed to sag under his weight. His red-bearded face came closer to Helene's. His beard was coarse and scratched her face. The smell of the potatoes and coffee still lingered in it. His mouth clamped onto hers and his tongue began to shove against the barricade of her lips and clenched teeth. She could feel her skirt shoved up roughly about her hips and his hands touching her. His mouth now covered her nose. She couldn't breathe. She gasped for air, but as soon as her mouth opened his tongue penetrated her. She felt sick to her stomach. She tried to pull her mouth away, but his full weight pinned her to the cot.

The smell and the coarseness of him revolted her. He

tasted of grease and decaying teeth. She wanted to escape, to flee his invasion of her. Still his tongue bored into her. She bit down hard on it. She heard his muffled scream and her mouth was flooded with his blood. He pulled away. Her body was free of his weight. Then his fist crashed into her jaw and she remembered no more.

Helene awoke in the hold. It was dark and the hatch-cover was shut. She moved her legs and cried out in pain. Bolts of pain stabbed from her groin up to her stomach and her breasts, which she realized were raw and bruised. She saw faces in the dark hovering over her. Dette was weeping. Damn her, Helene thought, she is always weeping. So she lost her dwarf of a husband. He was a man of violence and he died in violence. Even TiJoe had been a strange child. Helene had more to weep about than the forever teary Dette.

She recognized the face of Maurice's sister and several of the others she had treated for fever. Someone had uncovered her. She was grateful for the dark. Cool female hands touched her where, before Rofheart, no one else had touched her. A cool cloth was placed between her legs, replacing the warm fetid one. She realized what had happened to her in Rofheart's cabin. She started to weep.

"Ssh," Dette whispered to her.

"You'll be just fine," said another voice Helene could not recognize.

But they did not understand. They had not tasted the potatoes and the coffee.

The waves seemed to heave up from the ocean's depths. The sloop was pounded by them. Everyone in the hold was sick and there were no buckets left. At first in her feverishness Helene noticed nothing but the throbbing pain in her groin and the agony that screamed from every muscle when she tried to move her beaten body. But then the fever and the pain subsided and her senses began to function. The nausea was ever present in her gut and several times she could taste bile in her throat.

Every time the vessel listed, moans escaped from the lips of the Acadians lying on the floor of the hold. Helene tried to shut out the cries of the suffering by covering her ears with her hands. Dette was calling out, urging the Virgin to help her. Helene saw Denise Bertrand kneeling by her side, hovering over her, healing the healer, yet clinging to her patient as if to some last vestige of her brother. A particularly violent lurch of the ship sent Denise sprawling against Dette and brought a curse from the older woman. The horror of it all filled Helene. She turned away from her friend and finally gave up the bitter-tasting contents of her stomach.

As the days passed, the stormy seas calmed. Still the sloop flew southward away from the gray-and-black waters of the Bay of Fundy, away from the chill waters of New England. Helene's bleeding stopped and the bruises on her breasts and buttocks turned purple and then yellow and finally faded. There had been no further visits to the deck, and she began to believe that the deck outing had been an excuse staged by Rofheart so that he might get his hands on her without entering the hold. Perhaps he was afraid to come down among the poor wretches he transported while he amused himself with rape and murder.

But Rofheart was afraid of nothing and no one. As the sloop tacked against the southwestern wind some hundred miles off the coast of Montauk Point, the eastern tip of Long Island, a rope ladder was again dropped into the hold and the captain descended. He had a dueling pistol in one hand and a large knife shoved into his belt. The Acadians near him scattered.

"I want the blond girl," Rofheart called out.

Dette screamed in fear at his words, but Helene smiled. It was clear from his speech that teeth wounds in the tongue took longer to heal than bruises on the skin.

Denise Bertrand tugged at Helene's arm. "Quick, come with me over to the Grand Pre people. It's darker there. He won't find you."

Helene smiled at the girl. "Where will you hide me?" she said. "From him there is no hiding."

She rose to her feet, steadying herself against the roll of the sloop. Rofheart caught sight of her as she moved into the sunlight that streamed through the open hatch. She walked toward him. He glared at her, but at the same time the throbbing in his mouth warned him to be wary with this girl. He gestured toward the rope ladder. Helene grasped the rungs above her head and pulled herself up. Her muscles still ached from the beating she had received at the captain's hands, but the rest of her had healed. She wondered for how long.

She could feel his presence beneath her on the ladder. She dreaded him, yet this time she would not resist. It was not the rape and the beating she feared, rather she could not face going back into the hold.

Helene lay on the cot in Rofheart's cabin. She pretended to sleep, hoping he would leave her be. He sat at his table plotting the sloop's southward course on his charts. She had been in the cabin for three days and nights. She preferred to remember the days. He allowed her to stay in his bed and to sleep, but most of all he had allowed her to bathe.

There was a knock at the door and a crewman entered. Instantly the cabin was filled with the aroma of bacon and eggs and coffee. Rofheart rose from his desk. Helene could hear the scraping of the chair against the floorboards of the cabin. Then she felt his presence looming over her. She opened her eyes and looked directly into his face. How she hated him.

"How about some grub," he said, touching her breast. Helene looked over at the crewman, who was removing the charts and setting the table for their breakfast.

Rofheart laughed aloud. "Henry," he called out, "the little miss doesn't want me feeling her up with the hired help around. Look you, little whore, count yourself lucky I don't strip you bare-ass and march you around the deck for my whole crew to admire because, after all, when I am through with you that's who will be getting their hands on you."

Henry stood smiling at the captain and Helene. He was gap-toothed and unshaven. She shuddered at the thought of Henry's hands on her.

Rofheart continued to touch her. She began a slow motion with her hips. The captain's eyes widened slightly in surprise. "You are a hot little bitch, aren't you? And I do pleasure you, don't I?

Helene smiled.

"But first we eat and then we fornicate."

He pulled the covers from Helene's body. She was naked,

118

and Henry's eyes nearly popped from their sockets as he took in the beauty of her body.

"You've had your fill for today, mate, probably for a year, you bilge rat. Now get the hell out of here," Rofheart yelled at the crewman. Henry withdrew from the cabin, still glancing backward as he left.

As Rofheart pulled Helene to her feet she reached for her dress, which had fallen to the floor. Rofheart kicked it aside. "No," he said, "eat with me just like you are. It will make it easier, later."

Helene forced a smile. "If you'll do the same."

Rofheart laughed. "I'll be damned. Why not?" he said and began to peel off his breeches and shirt. "It's a helluva hot morning."

When he was as naked as she, he pulled her roughly to him, forcing her face into the rough red hair of his chest. "You like this, don't you?" he growled into her ear.

"Yes," she lied.

"Maybe we could postpone breakfast for a short while," Rofheart suggested.

"Cold eggs and bacon are hardly warm comfort," she offered.

"True enough, but then you can take care to warm me while I eat, can't you? And if you do it right, I'll see to it that you get a bit here and there."

Helene steeled herself for what would happen next. But she knew now that she would do whatever was required of her to survive this ordeal.

The wind had disappeared two days before. The sails of the sloop lay limp against the mast, while overhead the sun beat down upon them with such force that Helene wondered how the occasional swell of the ocean could defy its pressure. But even the sun was preferable to the oven that Rofheart's cabin had become. Helene sat on the quarterdeck. Over her was an awning of sailcloth that Rofheart had ordered constructed for her comfort. She could only imagine what it was like down in the hold. She had asked Rofheart to leave the hatch open during the night, and to her surprise he had agreed. Emboldened by her success, she asked to have Dette and Denise Bertrand join her in the cabin. Rofheart had laughed

and said that she was enough woman for him at this moment.
But he had allowed both of them to walk up on the deck for
an hour.

But that had been yesterday. Helene could not think about
yesterday. Only today and tomorrow counted. She would live
today in such a way as to guarantee tomorrow. Maybe Rofheart
would leave her alone tonight as he had done the night
before. The heat made touching almost unbearable. But
then, if he did not approach her for two nights in a row
perhaps that was a sign that he wearied of her and would
dump her back down below with the others. She panicked
momentarily.

"No," she said aloud.

"What?" Rofheart turned from the railing. "What did you
say?"

"Nothing," Helene lied. She rose from her canvas chair
and walked to the captain's side. "You seem to be nervous,"
she observed. "Is there anything I can do to calm you?"

"Calm me," he laughed. "Almost nothing you do calms me.
Quite to the contrary."

He reached down for her hand and thrust it into his crotch.
"You see," he sneered, "you keep me constantly hard."

Helene wanted to pull away from him but she did not.
Instead she massaged him.

"Not now," Rofheart said, pushing her hand away roughly.

Helene's panic, calmed by his first interest, began to grow
within her again. She had to gain control of herself. She could
not allow the man's whims to drive her to despair. He had
control of her, even over her life and death, but she could
control his passions.

Again he stared out at the sea.

"What is it?" she asked after some moments of silence.

"It's too calm," he responded. "I don't like it. Not in this
season. Late summer is a time of trouble in these waters."

"Where are we?" Helene asked.

"A few hundred miles off Hatteras, the Carolinas."

"Where are we going?"

"Charleston, South Carolina."

"And what is to become of us?"

"I dump you all and return to Boston to pick up my
reward."

"But how do we live? We have nothing."

"Ah, hah." Rofheart laughed. "There is no shortage of masters in Charleston looking for field hands for the rice and indigo plantations. They are also known for recognizing a choice piece when they see one. You'll have no trouble moving from my bed to an even more comfortable one, my lass."

"But we are not blacks to be enslaved," Helene said with some fire in her voice.

Rofheart looked at her in surprise. Had he misjudged her passivity? Perhaps he had not broken her yet. "No, you're not black to be enslaved. You're Frogs to be indentured."

Helene turned away from him. She did not want him to see her anger. They were silent for some minutes more. Then Rofheart slammed his hand down on the railing and turned abruptly toward his cabin. He reemerged moments later.

"Mr. McIntyre," he yelled for the first mate.

"Aye, sir," the mate called from behind a pile of rope on the deck where he had fallen asleep.

"The glass is falling rapidly. I want everything in readiness for a storm, and a big one."

McIntyre rose to his feet and started issuing orders. Men began to appear from various hiding places. The sun was now forgotten, to be replaced by a far more deadly enemy. They secured every loose piece of tackle; they closed the hatches despite the roar of protest that rose from the hold. Other sailors climbed into the rigging to furl all but the most necessary sails. Within twenty minutes the ship was prepared for the worst.

Rofheart remained on deck. A breeze began to stir the few sails in place and the sea grew choppier.

Helene was frightened. Since Rofheart was ignoring her, she decided to go down below to his cabin. She found the room bare. The cot and table had been folded and stowed. The stern window seat was the only place to sit. Helene climbed up onto it, folding her legs beneath her. Outside the window the sea rose in swells, lifting first the bow and then the stern and sending the ship plunging down until the waves seemed to rise on all sides. Helene turned her head away. She could not watch. Then suddenly the rains came, smashing, driving rains that sounded like thunder as they beat upon the decks above her head. Soon the ship's list became even more pronounced, and Helene had to hold onto the sides to prevent herself from being tossed onto the floor of the cabin.

The cabin door flew open, and Rofheart, his face and beard dripping with water, entered. His eyes searched the darkened room until he saw Helene at the stern window. She was startled to see the look of relief on his face.

"You stupid bitch," he shouted at her, "why didn't you tell me you were going below? One minute you were next to me and the next you had disappeared. My mind should be on my ship, not on a piece of trash like you."

He walked to her and placed a piece of line about her waist and looped it through the hooks on each side of the stern seat, effectively tying her into the seat. Then he turned and left the cabin, slamming the door behind him.

Helene was astounded. He had actually worried about her. Maybe she would not end up on the auction block in Charleston after all. But the alternative struck her at exactly the same moment. Suppose he should decide to keep her. Could she face a future of his pawing, of his demands that she do things she never knew of before she was forced to do them? And what would the end be? To be turned over to crewmen like Henry when he grew tired of her? But what if he did not grow tired of her? She did not have time to think it through. The storm cut short her contemplation of her future.

Lightning streaked through the black sky, drawing Helene's attention to the rain-battered glass. What she saw terrified her. All around were moving cliffs of water that crashed down upon them. The sloop climbed up the side of a cliff, then teetered on the precipice, and then finally tumbled down the other side with a dizzy speed, only to began the process all over again.

Helene held onto the restraining cord to keep herself steady. She closed her eyes, but the dizzy rise and fall frightened her even more. She heard shouting above her and a terrifying call of "Man overboard."

Her first thought was for Rofheart. What if it should be he? What would happen to her then?

"My God," she said aloud. "Now I'm worrying about him, a man whose very appearance sets my skin to crawling."

She tried to sleep, but the noise and the wind kept her

awake. She thought of Dette and the others in the hold. They must be terrified. She tried to blot out the picture of them from her mind.

Once again the cabin door opened and Rofheart entered, followed by McIntyre, the mate. The captain carried a hurricane lamp, which he fit snugly into a holder in the cabin bulkhead.

"Damn it, Mac," Rofheart cursed, "the winds are driving us westward toward the cape. That's a graveyard for ships if there ever was one."

He threw off his raingear and tossed it onto the floor. The clothing beneath was soaked. He pulled off his shirt and then his breeches. He stared at Helene. She rose out of the window seat and untied the securing lines. She picked up his discarded clothes and went to his sea chest. She picked out another shirt and another pair of breeches. He was sitting on the floor pulling at his stockings. She reached in to get him another pair. The cabin door flew open and Henry lunged through it into the cabin.

"You asked for a brandy, sir," he said, handing the still naked ship's master a jug. Rofheart took an enormous swig of the liquor and then belched. He stood and began to put on the dry breeches. As he slipped his arms through the sleeves of his shirt there was a loud cracking from above. Rofheart threw on his raingear.

"Mac, get up above," he shouted. "I think that was the mast. If it was and we can't jury-rig something, we're done for."

McIntyre's face went pale and he did not move.

"Damn you, sir," Rofheart screamed at his mate as he ran past him toward the doorway, "I never took you for a coward.

"Woman," he called to Helene, "we may flounder. If it looks like we're going under I'll send word for you to come on deck. I'd rather be swept over than trapped like a bilge rat below."

Helene thought immediately of the prisoners in the hold. If the ship went down, would anyone think to release them? But before she could protest to him he was out of the door. Henry followed him. The terrified mate turned slowly and went up on deck like a man walking to his own execution.

Rofheart's comment about trapped bilge rats finally sank

in. Helene looked about her. The cabin seemed to dance as the ship listed from port to starboard and then back again. The hurricane lamp flickered and its feeble light barely illuminated the small cabin. The bulkhead seemed to be pushing toward her as the seas crashed into them. She could not stay here any longer. She allowed herself to slide with the tilt of the ship toward the cabin entrance. She pulled open the door and was immediately drenched by sea spray. But the waters of the Carolinas were warm compared to the seas she was used to. She climbed the steps to the main deck, grabbing the rope railings on either side of the steps. The rain and the sea crashed all over the deck, and she stood ankle-deep in sea water.

But wet feet were not Helene's concern. She had donned no raingear and she was already soaked through to the skin. She needed to get up onto the quarterdeck, yet she was terrified to let go of the ropes and climb upward to the main deck. She reached out of the stairwell and grabbed for a handhold in the stairs that led up to where Rofheart and his helmsman steered the sloop. She screamed as her hand was grabbed and she was dragged up the stairs to the quarterdeck.

"Where the bloody hell do you think you're going, bitch?" Rofheart screamed into her face over the howl of the winds. "There's no place to escape, you stupid slut, except into the sea."

"I wasn't escaping. Where would I go? I just didn't want to be trapped."

He pulled her to her feet and lashed her to the railing of the deck. Now that she was above deck, she began to regret her decision. The mast of the ship had split in two and lay across the deck. Several sailors attempted to chop through and dump the top of the fallen mast, but the work had to be accomplished with small hand axes and the sailors' lives hung in the balance with each wave.

The dripping form of the first mate, McIntyre, appeared at the top of the stairwell to the quarterdeck.

"Mac," Rofheart yelled, "I told you to stay with the poor bastards working on the mast. What are you doing back here?"

"It's useless, Captain. They can't cut away the cordage, much less get at the mast itself. It's like trying to saw through an iron bar with a file. Those hand axes just can't do the job. Why can't we just throw the damn thing overboard?"

Again a wave crashed over the deck, swishing water about Rofheart's boots and forcing Helene to hold the railing even more tightly.

"If we do that, you idiot, we won't be able to get a sail on after the storm."

"There ain't going to be an after the storm," McIntyre screamed. The panic in his face was now obvious. "Henry reports seeing some reefs off the starboard. We're already in among the cape's sandbars."

"Shut up," Rofheart roared at his mate. "Just do your job. Get the mast up out of the water so that the goddamned butt doesn't pound a hole into the deck. Go back to your job."

McIntyre did not budge.

Rofheart went to the head of the stairs. He kicked out viciously. His foot caught McIntyre in the chest and shoved him back. McIntyre lost his footing and fell onto the lower deck. He reached for something to hold onto as the water crashed over the deck and threw his body against the railing on the port side. Again he grabbed for a handhold and again the waves crashed over the deck. As the ship's bow cleared the waves and the deck came into view again, there was no sign of McIntyre, only little eddies of water splashing against the wooden railing.

"Shit," Rofheart yelled up at the black sky. "Now I've got to go up forward myself."

He leapt down from the deck and grabbed the rope lines that were strung along the lower deck. A wave crashed over him but his grip was firm. Pulling himself hand over hand and holding on for his very life when the waves struck, the captain reached the crewmen struggling with the mast.

Helene could catch glimpses of him only as the bow rose. She saw him teeter precariously on the mast, then sit astride it. His arm raised a small ax again and again. Helene watched it. She searched for the sight of his arm each time the bow rose. If she saw him, she was sure they were safe for one more onslaught by the angry sea. If he was lost, then they were all lost.

For a while it seemed that some angry sea god had condemned Rofheart to chop away at the mast for all eternity, but finally Helene heard a tearing sound. The wood of the mast splintered, the underside fell away and disappeared unceremoniously into the waves, leaving Rofheart hanging precariously on the jagged edge. He grabbed the mast splinter and began to inch his way back toward the bow. Helene lost sight of him again as the ship listed and rolled. When it was righted he was gone. Helene felt as if all hope had gone with him.

Then the helmsman shouted. He too had been watching Rofheart and had been caught unaware by a wave that struck him broadside. The wheel spun out of his grasp, snapping the spokes that held his lashing. The helmsman flew across the deck and went crashing into Helene. She was too dazed to reach out when the man desperately grabbed for her hand. The next wave smashed even more violently into them, and the wheel spun aimlessly and no longer maintained the bow into the course that Rofheart had set. Helene reached for the helmsman too late. He had been swept away. She knew she should get to her feet and try to make it to the wheel to steady it.

She struggled to her knees and then to her feet. She loosened the line that held her to the railing. The next wave knocked her off her feet but the loosened knot still held. She struggled again to raise herself, this time bracing herself for the wave. As soon as it had passed she staggered to the wheel and started to lash herself to it. The next wave struck, knocking her to her knees. She felt herself tumbling toward the stairway of the lower deck. She could grab nothing. Maybe the railing would hold her. She crashed into something hard. She looked up into the red-bearded face of Captain Rofheart. He had not gone overboard but had been struggling back to the deck fully aware that the helmsman had lost control. He grabbed Helene by the blouse and hauled her with one hand back to the wheel. He put her between the wheel and himself, pushing his body against hers with his full strength. When the next wave crashed against them they did not move. Rofheart relaxed a bit and maneuvered the bow into the wind. Again he pressed against Helene, holding her and the wheel securely.

They remained pressed together for the next half hour. The waves continued to smash at them, but the captain kept the helm steady.

Suddenly he stepped back from her and shoved her aside. She fell to the deck. He swung the wheel wildly to port. Too late. There was a grating sound as the sloop touched sand. The ship lurched ahead slightly, the remnant of the mast fell forward with a clatter, and the ship's timbers seemed to moan in pain. Helene went sliding along the deck toward the quarterdeck stairs once again. Then the ship came to a halt.

Helene rose and reached out for Rofheart. He took her hand and roughly pulled her to him.

"Well, you might say we've come to harbor," he said sarcastically. "Except that the harbor ain't a harbor, it's a sandbar off Hatteras. If this storm lets up we just might float off with a change of wind. But if it don't, the waves will kick the shit right out of this tub."

He watched the skies for the next hour. Even Helene could tell that the storm was abating. Finally Rofheart started for the stairway. Helene followed.

"The wheel," she called out. "Aren't you going to stay at the helm?"

"Why?" Rofheart asked. "We ain't going nowhere and the storm is lessening. We're not going under, my girl. I'm going to bed. Come morning we'll rig a new mast and get off this reef. In the meanwhile, come," he ordered her.

Helene was huddled on the edge of the stern window seat. Rofheart lay sleeping on his back, his knees bent. She looked over at his naked body. He had kicked off the coverlet. She looked away again, back across the cabin. Their wet clothes were strewn from the cabin door to the seat in the order in which they had been removed. She would have to sew the blouse. Rofheart had been none too gentle removing it from her. She looked back at him again. His body was so coarse. It was covered with freckles, and his chest, arms, stomach, back, and shoulders were covered with a matting of red hair.

She tried to close her eyes again and get a bit more sleep. She did not want to think of last night, neither the storm nor what had happened afterwards.

She heard the patter of bare feet on the deck overhead.

The crew was about the business of the ship despite the obvious lack of motion. The surf crashed into them, but with much less intensity than the night before.

Helene wanted to go up on deck. She began to crawl over Rofheart's sleeping form. Just as she placed her hand across his body he reached up and pulled her down roughly on top of him. He crushed his stale-tasting mouth into hers. She tried to pull away from him, but there was no resisting his strength. She felt him begin to grow large between her legs. She groaned at the thought of what would happen again. He grew ever more passionate, mistaking her dread for desire.

But suddenly there was a commotion on the deck above them. More feet were heard running and there was a shout.

"What the hell?" Rofheart said, pushing Helene off of him. He stepped awkwardly from the seat and stepped into his breeches.

The door of the cabin was shoved open and Henry stuck his head through. "A sail off to port, Captain!"

Rofheart did not bother with the shirt but followed Henry up on deck.

Helene dressed more slowly, then went up onto the quarterdeck herself.

Rofheart had his glass to his eye and was searching the lines of the fast-approaching schooner. He slammed the glass shut with some anger.

"I don't like it," he said to no one in particular. "Too many men and too many guns for a merchantman. She may be flying the British ensign but I'm damned if she's not French."

"She's got French lines," said the dour seaman who had replaced last night's helmsman at the wheel.

Helene's hopes soared. If the schooner was a French privateer, she and her friends below deck might be released from their captivity. They might even be returned to Acadia.

The schooner came about and now approached them directly. It would pass broadside along their stern. Rofheart opened his glass again. The British ensign dipped first in salute, then was swiftly lowered and replaced by the maritime ensign of the Bourbon monarchs.

"Damn your soul to hell," Rofheart cursed.

The schooner belched black smoke and a ball went flying

across the sloop's stationary bow. The helmsman looked toward Rofheart.

"Do we strike?" he asked.

"No, by God. He can't board us in these seas and he'll not want to risk our fate. He'll stand off."

"He'll stand off and blow us right off this bloody reef," the helmsman objected.

"You have a point there, mate." Rofheart thought for a moment. "Henry, get all the prisoners up on deck." He turned to the helmsman. "If he's a pirate he'll still blow us out of the water. If he's a kingsman, he'll be wondering about the prisoners. He may have second thoughts about firing on us."

The hatches to the hold below decks were opened. The stench made Helene want to vomit. Suddenly the people of Grand Pre began to appear on deck, crowding out of the hold like specters from another world, bent in half with seasickness and covered with filth. Helene searched for a familiar face but saw none she recognized.

The schooner raced past the sloop's stern. When she did not fire her broadside, Rofheart breathed out with relief. The captain would not fire until he understood the meaning of decks crowded with men, women, and children.

"Now if the seas stay up until he gets tired of tacking, we may just get out of this mess." Rofheart laughed.

"If the seas stay up we'll probably break up," the helmsman reminded him.

The schooner came about and began another run past the sloop's stern. Again Rofheart held his breath and watched his foe in the glass.

Once again the schooner rushed through the waves and passed them, this time cutting much closer to the sloop.

"He's a good seaman, that French," Rofheart exclaimed. He turned toward the lower deck. He heard the woman's voice scream out.

"Murderer!"

Helene recognized Denise Bertrand instantly.

"Kill the bastard," she screamed again up at Rofheart. She moved from the crowd toward him. Several people moved along with her.

Henry had the swivel gun aimed at the prisoners. He did

not wait for Rofheart's command. He pulled the lanyard. The swivel spat grapeshot into the crowd. Denise staggered as if punched in the stomach and then sank to her knees. Three other women and a man also fell, and screams of terror filled the deck. But rather than cowering in fear, the crowd surged forward as an angry mass. By the time Henry had pulled the pistol from his belt and waved it at them, the front of the surge was already at the stairway to the quarterdeck. Henry pointed his pistol at the first face. He fired. The farmer he struck fell backward into the crowd, but another man came forward. The crowd's angry roar filled the air now. Henry panicked and tossed his empty pistol at them.

Rofheart had drawn his sword and was soon backed against the railing, swinging wildly at anyone who dared approach him. Most of the crowd ignored him at first. Instead they reached for Henry, who fell to his knees and then disappeared among the flailing arms of the angry Acadians.

Next, the helmsman was picked up bodily and tossed into the sea. Several of the crowd recognized Helene. She was pulled away from Rofheart and handed off the quarterdeck into the crowd below. One by one the rest of the crew were tossed into the sea, but Rofheart held his ground. None of the farmers dared approach his sword.

Finally an old man, bent in half with rheumatism, called off the men who surrounded Rofheart.

"You are beaten, Captain," the old man said. "If you surrender to us we will not murder you."

Rofheart was no fool. He saw in this offer his only chance to avoid the fate of his crew. He bowed clumsily to the old man. And he handed him his sword hilt first. Then rough hands grabbed the captain and shoved him forward. A fist came crashing through the crowd and struck Rofheart in the face. He staggered.

The old farmer shouted out, "He has surrendered. Let us not behave like the English pigs. We have given our word that we will not kill the captain, but, by God, we will bring him to justice."

The crowd roared its approval. Rofheart was shoved forward and thrown into the filth of the now empty hold.

Helene breathed a sigh of relief. She was now in the hands of her people. She was free. She sank to the deck and placed her face in her hands and started to cry. She was startled by a voice from the crowd crying out to the others.

"What about his whore?"

Helene looked up at the angry face of an old hag. "What do you mean?" she half whispered in surprise. The other woman's face was distorted with rage.

"While we sat in puke and shit in the hold this one was living in the comfort of the beast's bed. All she had to do to survive was to keep her legs spread."

"That's not fair!" Dette shoved her way up to the quarterdeck. "She is a *traiteur*, a healer, and she helped us when we needed help."

The old man who had subdued Rofheart stepped between the two women. "We must not fight with each other," he said.

"I accuse this woman of being the Englishman's whore. She must also answer for the deaths of Denise Bertrand and her brother Maurice. Rofheart killed them for just looking at his woman," she continued to yell. "I bet she was a whore back in Acadia also."

Helene could not believe what she was hearing. How could these things be said about her? The mind of this woman must be truly warped.

Someone yelled, "Throw the bitch overboard." There was some angry agreement from the crowd, but that was followed by a few protests.

"No, she's a *traiteur*, she touched us," someone else cried out.

The old man merely shook his head. It was a problem beyond his ability to solve. "Put her in the captain's cabin," he ordered. Then he turned toward the schooner, which was on another tack toward them. He waved his arm and cheered. He was soon joined by the entire crowd of freed prisoners.

When the cabin door was slammed on Helene she nearly screamed. She walked to the stern seat and collapsed on it. The covers still smelled of Rofheart's dank and musty odor. She thought she was going mad. She had been terrified and exhilarated at the same time by the prisoners' daring revolt. But now to be turned on by her own people because Rofheart had used her was too much for her to bear. What had they expected of her? She had done what he wanted in order to

131

stay alive. Had they expected her to give up her life along with her innocence?

She looked out the window toward the sea. Again the schooner swept past. She heard more cheering on deck. This time the schooner responded by dipping her colors. It was clear that the Frenchman was not going to abandon them. He would remain in the vicinity until the seas calmed and the stranded sloop could be boarded.

Locked in the cabin, Helene drifted off to sleep. She was awakened by the blast of a cannon off to port. She looked out the window. The sun just peeked over the eastern horizon, chasing away the gold and pink of the sky with its brilliance. The seas were much calmer now. The cannon must have been the schooner's warning that a boarding party was heading out for the sloop.

She saw the longboat pass behind the stern. It was rowed by six heavily armed seamen. And in the stern of the boat sat a man with black curly hair and a rakish black moustache. He was richly dressed in a pair of black breeches, with a white silk shirt covered by a black vest. About his waist he wore a red sash with two pistols and a sword stuck in it.

"My God," Helene said aloud, "he looks even more like a pirate than Rofheart."

The boat disappeared from her view, but within minutes she heard cheering from the deck above. Then she heard the noise of booted feet on the deck above her head. She did not know what was going on, and after a while she began to fear that everyone would leave and abandon her in the cabin. Fear began to clutch at her.

Finally the cabin door swung open. The man in black with the red sash entered.

"Mademoiselle Hebert?"

Helene nodded.

"Let me present myself. I am Captain Lionel Robichaud of His Most Christian Majesty's privateer *Giselle*." He bowed graciously in her direction.

"Captain." Helene acknowledged with her best curtsy.

He spoke with an accent she could not recognize. She was sure he was not Acadian, but he didn't speak like the priests who came fresh from France either. His demeanor, despite the flourish of the bow, was serious, almost angry.

"Your presence, Mademoiselle Hebert, is required on deck. We are about to begin a trial."

Helene felt the fear grip her. "Whose trial?" she asked.

"The misbegotten son of a bitch who captained this slave ship, Rofheart, will be tried for murder. I must warn you there is some sentiment for placing you on trial as well. You will be questioned and your answers may determine your fate, mademoiselle."

Helene's fears quickly turned to anger. "I have done nothing wrong!" she said with some heat.

"Then you have nothing to fear, Mademoiselle Hebert. I will see to it that the guilty are punished, but I assure you that no one will lay a finger on the innocent. If Rofheart forced you, mademoiselle, I suggest you swallow your pride and admit it. It will be one more crime for him to answer for."

"I should not be forced to admit my shame publicly. It is not the way of our people to punish the innocent by having them admit that they have been raped, monsieur. I will never be able to live among my own people or to marry if I must acknowledge that someone else took me, even if it was against my will."

"If you don't admit to being forced, mademoiselle, they will condemn you as the slaver's whore."

"Could I not claim that nothing happened?"

Robichaud looked at her. She could see the pity in his expression.

"It's not likely that anyone will believe me, is it?"

"It is not unlikely that everyone will believe that you were raped," Robichaud responded. "He threw you bleeding and bruised back in the hold after the first time. Many people have said that."

"That is true."

"Make the claim," Robichaud advised her. "Worry about the consequences later."

"What happens to Rofheart?"

"He will die, and before the sun sets if we can get up on deck to the business at hand."

"Will he die as a result of what I say?"

"He will die if he is guilty of capital crimes, and I assure you, mademoiselle, he is guilty of capital crimes."

Robichaud opened the cabin door and stepped aside to

allow Helene to precede him. Helene climbed the stairs up to the deck. The former prisoners lined the railing of the sloop three deep. In the center a large trunk had been set up as a desk, and a chair had been placed behind it. Robichaud went to the chair and sat down.

There were several sneers from the crowd when Helene appeared on the deck, but there were some whispers of encouragement as well. Almost immediately she was flanked by two seamen from Robichaud's schooner.

Rofheart was dragged out of the hold. Several men tried to reach him with fists, but the schooner's sailors pushed them back with the flat of their swords. Rofheart's clothes were covered with filth and his face and beard were dirty. He sneered at Robichaud, then glanced over at Helene and winked at her.

Several people in the crowd yelled at Helene as a result of Rofheart's familiarity.

"Rofheart," Robichaud said in French, "since I understand that you speak our language, this trial will be conducted in French."

"Trial?" Rofheart spat out contemptuously.

Robichaud ignored his insolence. "You are the master of this schooner?"

Rofheart did not respond.

Robichaud looked up. "You must respond!"

"I *must* not do anything, shit-eater," Rofheart reported.

"You are the master of this schooner. Your papers indicate that you were authorized to deliver these prisoners to ports along the Atlantic Coast. Yet I find you off the Carolinas with a full complement. Where were you heading?"

Rofheart looked slyly at Helene. "As far as I remember, even though I don't have the charts with me, the Carolinas are on the Atlantic Coast."

"Where were you heading, Rofheart?" Robichaud repeated. "And what were you planning for loyal subjects of King Louis? Was it the auction block?"

Rofheart did not respond.

"Ask his whore," a Grand Pre woman shouted out. "Maybe she can remember."

All eyes turned toward Helene. Even Rofheart glared at her.

"Mademoiselle Hebert," Robichaud shouted over the din of the crowd, "do you know where Captain Rofheart was taking this ship?"

"She won't tell the truth," a voice interrupted. "She was to share in the profit." There were more angry shouts between Helene's friends and enemies.

"We will establish Mademoiselle Hebert's relationship with Captain Rofheart," Robichaud spoke out. "Mademoiselle, are you Captain Rofheart's mistress?"

"No," Helene responded quickly.

Rofheart's face broke into an amused smile.

"Did you ever sleep with him?"

"Don't lie, bitch!" Rofheart anticipated her response.

"I'll not lie," she said heatedly. "Yes, I slept with him. The first time he kissed me I nearly bit his goddamned tongue off, and in turn he beat me and he raped me."

Dette gasped at Helene's admission of rape. She and the others in the compartment in the hold knew it was true, but to admit rape publicly was to condemn oneself.

Rofheart laughed. "Aye, a goodly tumble that first one was. I still have the sore tongue, but it's been my cock that has been sore ever since she first felt it. She squirms her arse every time I come near her. There's not been rape since that first one, not with that hot bitch."

"He was taking my people to Charleston to sell them as slaves," Helene shouted angrily.

There were more gasps of surprise in the crowd.

Again Rofheart laughed. "Niggers are sold as slaves," he said. "Frogs are sold as indentured servants. They could pay off their time with their labor."

"It's a fine point," Robichaud uttered in disgust. "The fact is you were about to sell the subjects of His Majesty King Louis into slavery, Christians enslaved against their will. You are no better than a Barbary pirate."

"Fine words coming from the scum of the Spanish main. Christ, condemned by a pirate and a whore. But have it your way. I'm sure you will do so anyway."

"No," Helene said softly, "it is your way, Rofheart. When you win, never give quarter. It is the one thing about you I hope to remember."

Rofheart stared at Helene for what seemed to her like an

eternity. Then he threw his head back and howled with laughter.

"Did Captain Rofheart kill Maurice Bertrand, as has been claimed by others?"

"Maurice Bertrand? Who the hell is Maurice Bertrand?" Rofheart called out.

"He was the man with me that first day," Helene said.

"Oh, you mean your first lover?" Rofheart sneered.

"You lie, you were the first and you know it."

"First? At least a dozen stallions and a score of rams had been there before me, you country slut. Bertrand, now I remember. Attempted mutiny. We shot him."

"It was simple and pure murder," Helene corrected him. "You kicked him into submission and then you shot him and threw him overboard."

Rofheart shrugged his shoulders.

"I've heard enough," Robichaud exclaimed. "Hang him!"

The crowd cheered.

Rofheart did not even blink an eye when two of Robichaud's sailors grabbed his arms and tied them behind his back. The noose had been prepared in advance. It was thrown about his neck and the other end of the line was passed through a yardarm. His huge body was lifted up and set down on Robichaud's former desk—the trunk.

Helene looked away.

"Winners never shrink from the results of their victory," Rofheart yelled at her.

She turned back and stared at him defiantly.

Robichaud offered the captain a mug of rum. Rofheart kicked it out of his hand with his foot.

Robichaud nodded to his crewmen. The trunk was roughly pulled from under his feet. He fell and there was a sickening snap and then a gasp from the crowd. The rope, not Rofheart's neck, had given way. The dazed captain rose to his feet and stared about at the crowd. Then he roared again.

"You Frogs can't even hang a man right," he croaked harshly, the tight noose cutting off his air.

Robichaud yelled at his crewmen. "Get a decent piece of rope and do it right this time."

Rofheart's face was bright red. He was choking. Spittle

mixed with blood appeared at his mouth, and his eyes were bulging.

Helene turned in panic and started to run from the sight, but it was Robichaud who put an end to it. He did not wait for a new noose to be tied. He took his pistol from his belt and placed it against the squirming Rofheart's temple and pulled the trigger. Rofheart's head jerked backwards, his eyes glazed over, and he sank to his knees.

Helene turned back in time to see Rofheart's final fall. This time the crowd cheered. Several of the Acadians rushed forward, some kicked at him, then others grabbed at his body and raised it over their heads and tossed it over the railing into the sea.

For Helene it was a release. Rofheart was gone. She started to weep. Several of the Grand Pre women sneered at her, but Dette and the women of her own compartment in the hold surrounded her. Dette took her into her arms and hugged her.

Robichaud came over to her. "I am glad you testified against that animal, mademoiselle. It took courage."

Helene merely shrugged.

Robichaud bowed to her. Then he swiftly jumped the stairs to the top of the quarterdeck.

"Ladies and gentlemen," he called out.

The crowd moved toward him. They were still covered with the grime and filth of their suffering. But now that they were free once again, they no longer seemed so stooped and so dirty.

"I'm taking you off of this wreck."

Several in the crowd clapped their hands.

But the old man who had led the revolt called out. "Where are you taking us, Captain Robichaud? We want to go back to Acadia."

"That's impossible," Robichaud responded.

"We're not going anywhere else," the old man exclaimed.

Now several persons cheered.

"Look," Robichaud softened his haughty tone. "You've suffered much—too much. If you go back to Acadia, the English will round you up and ship you off somewhere else. Then you might not be so lucky. You might not run into a Captain Lionel Robichaud the second time."

Some Acadians started to laugh.

"No," Robichaud continued, "I sail for New Orleans and the king's Louisiana Colony. My tour of the American coast is over. I've taken prizes enough. My crew is down to a minimum. I have room for all of you to come with me. I want you to come with me to New Orleans. It is King Louis' land. The English cannot reach you there."

It was Dette who yelled out at first.

"I'll go to New Orleans. Acadia is a land of pain now, and I'll not be shoved down into that filth again. I'll do anything, I'll go anywhere, so long as it is French, to avoid repeating what has just happened to me."

"Me too," Helene shouted.

Soon most of the women were shouting support of Robichaud's New Orleans. Some men grumbled, but they too realized that a return to their home was impossible.

Captain Robichaud smiled, showing his brilliant white teeth behind his full moustache. "Good," he called out. "We'll be crowded on the *Giselle* but we'll share and share alike as brothers, subjects of our good king."

Before the sun set, longboat after longboat made the journey between the grounded sloop and Robichaud's schooner. Helene went in the second boatload. The crewmen of *Giselle* had rigged pumps on the deck of the schooner to allow the Acadians to bathe. They screened off an area for the women and children. Helene stood naked beneath the spray of sea water. She was clean compared to the others. As she allowed the water to course over her body and run down her legs, she felt as if the last remnant of Rofheart was drained from her. She dressed and dried her hair. Some women set up empty barrels and began to wash clothes in sea water. Then they hung them from the rigging to allow them to dry in the weakening sun and the slight sea breeze. Helene watched as the last boatload of prisoners came alongside *Giselle* and the Acadians clambered up into the lines and onto the ship's deck.

Robichaud stood beside his helmsman, watching the last passengers come aboard. When all were on deck he gave a call to his crew. Suddenly men appeared along the railing. The schooner's guns were run out by their crews while men climbed into the rigging to get more sail and allow *Giselle* to gain some speed.

Robichaud manuveured *Giselle's* broadside across the sloop's stern. He shouted, "Fire," and instantly the five guns on the starboard battery broke the stillness of the golden evening with their roar.

Helene watched as wisps of smoke curled out of the shattered stern windows of the sloop. Robichaud's men had set fires aboard the sloop before leaving with the last boatload of refugees.

The wind had shifted at last, and Rofheart's sloop finally floated free. But the new breeze also fanned the flames, which caught quickly on the cordage and dried timbers of the vessel. Within minutes it was a drifting inferno.

Helene stared at the ship and did not realize that Robichaud was beside her until he spoke.

"No death is pretty to watch, not even the death of a slaver."

She did not look at him. She knew he was referring to more than the death of the sloop.

"I have no regrets," she said finally, just as the sloop rolled onto its side. The flames made a hissing sound as they touched the darkening sea. They both stared at the sloop until it seemed to groan and slowly sink into the waves.

"Will you share supper with me in my cabin?" Robichaud asked.

Helene turned to look at his face. My God, she thought, did it begin all over again? But she did not care.

"What are you serving?" she asked.

"A fine cut of salt meat, pickled really—I took it from a prize—and some good red wine. I even have some ripened bananas and oranges. I took them aboard while they were green. They matured right in my own cabin."

Helene searched his face for his meaning. His smile was obvious and she nodded to him. He took her by the hand and led her toward his cabin.

Lionel lay quietly at last. His back and buttocks were wet with his sweat. His breathing relaxed at last. His lips no longer parted with ecstasy and no moans escaped between them. Never in his life had he experienced anything like what she had done to him. She lay still now beneath him. He had grown limp again and had slipped from her. She played with the curly black hairs on his chest and nipped at the hairs of his moustache with her white teeth.

"More?" she whispered huskily into his ear.

"Oh, yes!" he said softly back to her. "More indeed, but give me a rest."

Helene smiled. He could not see her smile. It was not meant for him to see. She had won again. And she would give no quarter.

Part Two

LE GRAND DÉRANGEMENT

CHAPTER SEVEN

Virginia, September 1755

The cart bounced along the rutted road. The driver, a gray-haired black man, ignored the holes that were filled with water from the last evening's rainfall. He clucked and talked to the bow-backed plow mule in a language only he and the mule understood.

Nina did not care if she bounced a foot into the air with each jolt. To be on dry land again offset any of the discomforts of the journey. It was Gilles who complained out of concern for Nina. She did not show much, but she was six months along. The two of them and ten other Port Hebert folk sat as if linked in the back of the wagon.

"Do you deliberately look for the potholes and steer for them?" Gilles called out in French.

"Now don't that beat all," the black man laughed. "White folks that don't speak nothing but gibberish. No wonder they be in this cart going to market in Williamsburg."

The mule stumbled in a rut and the cart twisted to the left. The wheel on that side splintered with a loud crack.

The driver sighed. He smacked the rump of the mule, then climbed down from his seat and studied the splintered wheel, scratching his gray head.

Captain Rodney Elliot, who commanded the ship *Bridget*, which had brought Nina and Gilles and most of the Port Hebert prisoners to Yorktown on Chesapeake Bay, came up behind the wagon. The horse he rode stamped its foot and snorted at the black wagon driver. Elliot leaned forward in the saddle.

"I've got five more wagons coming up the road, Jubal, and they can't go around you into the mud."

"I don't know how to fix a wheel nohow, Massa Elliot," the black driver said with his saddest expression on his face.

"Damn," Elliot cursed. "Then you can all walk. But, Jubal, I hold you responsible for the wagon and the horse. You see to it that no one runs off with them."

"Yes, Massa Elliot." Jubal nodded slowly. "I knows the region. I be growing up on plantations in James City County before they sell me up the river to King George County and Massa Audry. I got me a heap of cousins about in this county."

Elliot looked at Jubal suspiciously, then he turned to the Acadians who still sat in the cart. "Out," he called in English and then in French.

Gilles was the first to react. He climbed down, then reached up and helped Nina out of the back of the wagon. The second wagon, heavily loaded with Acadians, was in sight down the road.

Jubal took the wagon mule by the reins and led him off the road, pulling the crippled wagon into the gully. The displaced Acadians began to complain as the wet mud soaked their shoes. Several removed them in order to protect the leather. Gilles approached Elliot, who was looking back down the road toward the oncoming wagons. Gilles called to him but Elliot ignored him. Gilles reached up and grabbed the horse's bridle. Elliot turned with a start and raised his riding crop and brought it down with a snapping sound on Gilles' shoulder. Gilles staggered backward and looked up at the captain in mixed surprise and anger. Seeing the Frenchman's angry face, Elliot drew a dueling pistol from his belt.

Nina cried out and stepped forward, pulling at Gilles' arm. He stared defiantly at the horseman, but his anger was abated by Nina's pleading and the black muzzle of the pistol that was pointing directly between his eyes.

144

"Don't ever do that again, not if you expect to live," Elliot said through clenched teeth at the uncomprehending Acadian.

The second wagon was now directly behind them. Elliot's mate rode up to the captain and looked quizzically at the drawn pistol. But Gilles ignored both of them. He took Nina by the hand and walked directly to the second wagon.

"You there, where are you going?" the mate called out.

Elliot's pistol followed Gilles, but Gilles ignored him. He lifted Nina onto the back of the second wagon. Several of the Port Hebert people shoved backwards to make room for her. Then one of the men jumped down into the mud to join Gilles. He motioned to another of the women displaced by the broken cart, and one by one the women were given places to ride while the men they displaced walked beside the cart in the mud.

Captain Elliot, who had been prepared for an insurrection, breathed a sigh of relief. Once again the wagons moved on toward the capitol. As they passed old Jubal off to the side of the road, each of the black wagon drivers greeted him with a knowing smile. Jubal was the best wheelwright in King George County and he was about to be off to see his kin. He would be coming home, but it might just take a few days to fix the wheel right.

The little caravan entered the city of Williamsburg from the southeast along the York road. It turned right into Waller Street and entered the open area called the Exchange. The Acadians stared wide-eyed at the numbers of people transacting business and selling wares. Wigged gentlemen and ladies rode by in carriages drawn by well-groomed and well-fed horses. Planters haggled in the streets with merchants, and soldiers in blue militia uniforms mixed with the red coats of regulars. There were more people in the square in the late afternoon than there had been in the whole village of Port Hebert.

The carts stopped before a large wooden tobacco warehouse, and the prisoners were ordered out and herded into the darkness of the wooden shed. Some of the women cried out in anguish at being placed once again in confinement. Any reminders of the *Bridget*'s hold overwhelmed them with horrifying memories of the journey south. The fragrant aroma of cured tobacco filled their nostrils. At first its smell was a pleasant change from the stench of the ship's holds, but soon its vapors seemed to seep into their clothes and their pores. There was no escaping it.

Gilles helped Nina find a place on the warehouse floor. He and several other men rolled huge thousand-pound hogsheads loaded with tobacco away from the walls to make space for the women and children to sit and to rest. Nina's cousin, Renee Babineau, started to cry out, half in prayer to the Virgin and half in a curse. Nina took her cousin's hands in her own and tried to soothe her.

Several of the men came to sit beside Gilles. They needed to speak to Lucien Hebert's son. They needed him to lead them, to tell them what to do. Roland Gilbert and Antoine Broussard had come to him aboard the *Bridget*. They had a plan for taking over the ship. Gilles had agreed to try if they were allowed on deck, but the ever-suspicious Captain Elliot had never allowed them any exercise. Now these same men again turned to Gilles for leadership. Gilles studied their questioning faces. It frightened him when they did this. He would fight the English, he could tear the limbs from any man who might try to lay a hand on Nina. But he was frightened when these men, his friends, some of them older than he, looked at him in that trusting way. He had no idea what to do. Suddenly he realized that old Broussard had been speaking to him.

"What?" Gilles said. "I wasn't listening."

"Tabernac," the old man cursed, "what do I have to do to get your attention? Hit you between the eyes?"

Gilles bristled.

"I was saying that we can't escape," the old man said impatiently. "We don't even know where we are. For all we know, France and England are at war again. Did you see all those people out there? There were soldiers. Did you see all of the soldiers?"

"But there were very few redcoats," said Gilbert. "I tell you we should break out of here." His young face was almost gleaming with excitement. "One of the black men who drove our wagon was from the West Indies. He spoke some French, although I could barely understand him. He told me we were to be sold just like black slaves."

146

"They would not do that," Gilles exclaimed.

"Nor would they have torn us from our beloved land and shipped us to this hot, stinking warehouse," old Broussard responded.

"No," Gilles repeated, "they will not do that. We are prisoners of war. They will return us to a French land."

"Then why bring us here?"

"We are here until the war is over," Gilles argued.

"The war hasn't even started yet," Gilbert said in exasperation.

Once again there was silence as the group of men stared at Gilles.

"I have to go to Nina," he said finally. "She needs me."

He crawled over to the girl's side and took off his jacket for her to sit on. The others waited for a few moments, then without looking at each other they dispersed to their own corners. Young Gilbert took Renee Babineau by the arm and led her to the other side of the warehouse. It was clear they had become close on the journey to Virginia.

The next morning the doors of the tobacco shed were flung open, letting in the brilliant fall sunshine. A small man dressed in black with a white wig and a three-cornered hat perched on his head entered, followed by three militiamen with muskets at the ready.

The man in black began to read from a paper. It was Nina who first realized that he was attempting to communicate with them. His French was so atrocious that none of them had recognized a word he read. It was only when he began to read what sounded like a list that she nudged Gilles.

"These goddamned heathen names are unpronounceable," the Virginian said finally to the three militiamen. "Bring all of them outside."

The blue-clad soldiers moved into the crowd and by pushing and shoving conveyed to the Acadians that they were to walk out into the sunlight. There was a large crowd of people already milling about the open yard of the Exchange. Most were businessmen and some planters with smaller holdings. On the fringe of the crowd there were elegant horse-drawn carriages where the very well-to-do sat out of the sun and heat. The Acadians were made to stand in a long line at the foot of a raised platform. The black-clothed man walked down the line and offered his ink quill to each adult male and showed him where to make his mark on the paper. Old Broussard was the first to refuse to sign. Gilles also stared at the clerk when he approached him.

"What's the matter with these people? Don't they know they must sign the contract?" the clerk said to no one in particular.

"What's wrong, Lawyer Pike? Let's get on with the auction," one of the planters called out.

"What's your rush?" said a well-dressed older man. His pale blue coat and white breeches were tailored perfectly of the finest cloth.

"Mr. Ludlow, sir, we have been looking for choice field hands. Most of us can't afford to bid on a black man. They cost too much. But convict labor, that's within my range. I've got fields to prepare for spring and my acreage along the river is just about worn out after only four seasons of planting."

"We all share that problem, my friend. The wicked weed has enslaved all of us, not just poor unfortunates like these French convicts. We are all doomed to a life of clearing ever more acreage for that thief of the soil—tobacco."

"Very well said, Mr. Ludlow. We all got to work clearing them fields. Perhaps you can get Lawyer Pike to start the auction."

"I cannot, sir," said Pike, who had listened to the argument. "They refused to sign the indenture papers."

"Have you explained it to them?" Ludlow asked.

"Of course," responded the lawyer, "and in their own gibberish."

Ludlow smiled. "Let me try," he said and walked over to the crowd of Acadians.

"Listen to me, please," he said in impeccable French. "All of the heads of families must sign or make their mark on these papers before you can be released."

"What do you mean, released?" Old Broussard said sarcastically.

"Released to the care of your masters—the gentlemen who buy your contracts."

"And what then?"

"You work for them for fourteen years and then you are released with a new suit of clothes and a set of tools so that

148

you can begin your own farm and become planters like these gentlemen." He pointed toward the crowd that surrounded the platform.

Gilles slammed his fist down on the wooden platform with a smash.

"We are not criminals to be bought and sold."

Ludlow looked embarrassed. "I am afraid, sir, that His Majesty's government has judged you potential traitors and has transported you a long way away from the familiar setting of your homeland so that you might cause no mischief. Now you will be forced to pay for the cost of that transportation by the sweat of your brow."

"We're not to be sold as servants," said Gilles.

"You will be sold as servants or you'll be sold as slaves," Pike said after Ludlow translated Gilles' words.

"Perhaps a display of the difference would help here," Ludlow suggested. "We do have some blacks to display and sell, don't we?"

Pike smiled and soon disappeared in the direction of a smaller building with barred windows.

Soon moaning sounds came from that direction, followed by the cracking of a whip. Five blacks, four men and one woman, came out the front door of the little jail, followed by Pike and another burly man dressed only in breeches and a white linen shirt. Twisted about his arm was a stout brown leather whip.

"You niggers, hurry up," the auctioneer yelled from the platform. "We haven't got much more time for nonsense."

The blacks were forced up onto the platform. The men were told to strip to the waist to show off their muscles. The crowd surged toward the platform when the bidding began, even though most could not afford to participate. When a planter purchased a black slave, he purchased not only a man's or a woman's labor for life but also the lives of any offspring they might produce. The prices were high and most of the bidding came from enclosed carriages via messengers.

The first to be sold was the woman. She was young, about sixteen, and very beautiful. Her brown skin glistened in the Virginia sun and she perspired through the calico blouse she wore, revealing the hint of firm and full breasts. She stood defiantly facing the crowd as her health, strength, and child-bearing potential were extolled. She glared across the platform at one of the black men who was also up for bidding, but he did not meet her glance. He was darker than she, well muscled, with a broad chest and shoulders. He was a prime field hand, but there was something in his muscle tone and demeanor that most had already noted. Few wealthy planters could resist a strong yet docile worker. But this man projected an aura of defeat; someone had gone too far with him.

The other three men flexed muscles on command and flashed broad grins to reveal healthy teeth, but not the darker man. He merely stood staring blankly ahead.

The bidding on the woman moved ahead rapidly. When it ceased, the auctioneer pointed to a poorly dressed white man in a black felt hat and brown homespun. He let out a whoop of victory and raced back toward one of the carriages on the fringe of the Exchange to collect his fee. The woman was led from the platform, her gaze still falling on the silent, almost motionless man. Finally, desperately, she called out to him.

"Nathan!"

The man's body stiffened, but he did not look at her.

"It don't matter," she called out. "It was them that did it. It was not fault of ours."

Still he stared ahead.

The woman began to cry out now. Her cries rose over the din of the Exchange.

"Nathan, you still be my husband," the black woman cried out. The man in the black felt hat returned from the carriage to claim his prize. He looked nervously at the motionless black man on the platform, then quickly hoisted up the skirts of his new slave and snapped leg manacles on her. The hem of her dress lingered in his hand.

By now the woman's screams and cries of anguish were beginning to be drowned out by the auctioneer's calls for bids on the prime field hands still on the platform. But none of the Acadians could take their eyes off the unfortunate black woman who was pulled and dragged from view.

Nina instinctively moved closer to Gilles. His looming presence was now her only protection from the irons and the leers of the slavedrivers. She was not alone. All the women in the French group clung a bit closer to their men.

Ludlow saw that the sale of the black woman had affected

the prisoners. He stood next to Gilles and commented direct-ly to him.

"By signing our contracts you will protect your family. Indentured Christians have protection under our laws that these poor blacks don't. Those who make their marks will, of course, be protecting their families."

Gilles ignored him, but he could feel Nina's terror in her trembling body.

The auction continued. Several white men climbed up onto the platform, some of them in homespun like the bidder for the woman but others in finer clothes, planters bidding for prime field hands and wishing to examine the goods personally. The men's mouths were opened and teeth examined.

"I am given to understand that one of these men has been, ahh, has been neutered," one of the planters addressed the auctioneer.

The man with the whip nudged the dark silent man forward. "Clean as a whistle," the auctioneer joked, making a cutting motion with his hand.

"Why?" the planter asked.

"Troublemaker. Him and the woman that was just sold was from the Audry place up in King George County. They ran away and talked about insurrection and fleeing to the Indians now that war has broken out on the frontier. Mr. Audry punished them as examples to the rest of his people. The man has completely recovered, however, no infection at all. You can take a look if you choose." The man with the whip moved toward the silent black man.

"It won't be necessary," said the planter. "I have no need for eunuchs on my farm. I need little ones to replace the older ones. Audry is a beast anyway."

"Don't deny us our fun," a man in homespun called out. "We want to look at the gelding."

The planter turned away in disgust. But the overseer dropped his whip and started to remove the trousers of the slave.

Nathan pulled away from the overseer. He grabbed at the string that held up his threadbare pants. His eyes flashed in anger.

"No man's going to see what they did to me," he spoke finally.

Several of the people crowded about the platform began to back away. The three other blacks looked at their companion with astonishment mixed with fear.

Nathan screamed out his woman's name, then picked up the startled overseer's whip and lashed out with it. A gash appeared on the overseer's bewildered face. Blood gushed out of the wound and splashed onto the man's shirt. Again Nathan struck with the whip; this time the lash tore into the auctioneer's shirt. The man screamed in fright. Other screams and shouts were heard all over the Exchange as people ran from the scene.

Nathan stood like a cat, his feet spread, ready to spring. The howling, swirling mob of panicked planters moved rapidly away from him. All, that is, but Ludlow. Calmly the elegantly dressed planter walked toward Nathan and his whip.

"My dear fellow," Ludlow called out to him, "please put down that whip. You can only do more damage to yourself and that poor woman who was just taken from you. Don't make it worse."

The other three black men had fallen to the ground to avoid Nathan's whip. They also began to call out to him in pleading voices.

"Nat, take it easy. Nat, you're going to get yourself a skinning if you don't drop that thing. Nat, you sure is going to be in a heap of trouble now."

"Nat," Ludlow called, picking up the pleading tone of the blacks, "hand the whip to me. Don't make it any worse."

Nathan looked about and realized there was no avenue of escape. Just as quickly as the flash of defiance had appeared in his eyes it was extinguished. His shoulders slumped and his head bowed. He dropped the overseer's whip with a clunk on the wooden platform.

"That's a good boy," Ludlow said as from behind his back he drew a loaded pistol. He pointed it directly at Nathan's head and pulled the trigger. The impact of the lead ball spun Nathan around and he fell into a heap. Several of the women among the Acadians began to scream. Their husbands and brothers, themselves trembling with terror, attempted to calm them. Mr. Ludlow handed the pistol to the blood-soaked auctioneer, then walked over to examine Nathan's body.

"Pity," he said shaking his head. "Audry had no business doing that to a man. Drove him to desperation. But he'd attacked a white man. There was no way he could be allowed to live."

The crowd now surged back toward the platform. Several of the whites began to crowd about Ludlow as he descended from the steps of the platform. Some tried to clap him on the back but he shook off their congratulations. He walked toward the crowd of Acadians.

"Are you prepared, Lawyer Pike, to have the contracts again offered to the prisoners?" he called out.

The man in black quickly emerged, carrying the papers for Gilles and the other men to sign. One by one the men of Port Hebert signed away their freedom in order to avoid the auction block and to keep their families together.

Pike came finally to Gilles. The Frenchman wanted to refuse. He wanted from the depth of his soul to punch this man in black who thought he could speak their language. But Nina, gentle Nina, was by his side and large with child. Even if it was his brother's child, it had to be protected. He marked the papers where the lawyer pointed.

"Nicely done," Ludlow said to the Acadians. "The time of your debt will go by fast. Soon you'll all be free." He turned to the lawyer. "Pike," he said finally, "do go and ask the constables to pick up the body of that poor man. I'll be at my town house if they need to question me."

"I don't think there will be a need to question you, sir. Everyone in the Exchange saw what you did. Very courageous, sir, in defense of all that our society holds dear. These darkies must be kept in place or they'll murder us all in our beds."

"I think we had better keep a watch on these Frogs as well, my friend," Ludlow offered. "Especially the large ones. They have the same defiance in their eyes that I saw briefly in poor Nathan. They'll all bear watching. Nevertheless, I'm sure they'll bring a good price, especially accompanied by those young wenches."

"Do you intend to bid, sir?" Pike asked.

"Me?" Ludlow laughed "Not I. Not for any of these. I don't think it would be at all wise to have any of these fellows as your enemy. And surely they would become your enemy if you purchase their bodies, much less contemplated touching their wives. There is more trouble here than I need. It will have to be a different kind of man who tames one of these wild dogs."

Nina reentered the warehouse with all the Port Hebert people after the men had signed the papers. She had been listed as Gilles Hebert's pregnant wife. The two had been sold to the same bidder. It was clear to all their former neighbors that they now would be splitting up; some perhaps would never see each other again. They clung to each other, allowing eyes and hands to linger long on faces that they hoped never to forget.

Nina went through the good-byes almost mechanically. Almost everyone she loved occupied a shallow grave in the soil of Acadia. Perhaps her mother still lived; she hoped so. And there was Marcel. But now there was also Gilles. She was confused. She loved Marcel so, yet it was Gilles, not the father of the baby squirming in her belly, who protected her from the horrors all about her.

She shook herself to clear her head. She was not thinking straight. Marcel had been off in the woods when the English had come. If he had known what horrors the English planned, he would have returned. He did love her. He had confessed his love to Helene, her best friend. He would come looking for her someday. She was sure of it. Helene would never have lied to her.

She felt Gilles' hands on her shoulders. The confusion returned. Gilles loved her too. He protected her and she and her baby needed him.

"Our contract has been purchased by Jonas Audry. They say he has a large plantation to the north and west of here," Gilles whispered to her.

She looked at him, the fright showing in her face.

"Don't fret, girl," he said to her. "I'm not going to let anything happen to you or to the baby." He had almost said "our baby" but had caught himself at the last moment. His face flushed red.

"Gilles, you don't owe me anything. You have done more than enough already."

"Quiet, hush. I owe you everything. I love you."

"It's not fair," she said with some ambiguity. "I can't pretend to be your wife. I can't go with you."

"Did you see what happened on that platform today? These people are heartless. The man in the blue coat who spoke French seemed to be the best of them, yet he struck down the black man, Nathan, even after he had given up the fight. It was as though he was some insect, a louse you discover in your clothes and crush between your fingers. These people have no feelings. They would do to us what they did to those blacks. They would do it without a second thought. Would you like to face them alone? Would you like the child you bear to deal with them without the protection of a man, a husband, a father?"

"But you're not . . ."

"I'm not Marcel," he interrupted. "Oh, God, I know I'm not Marcel. I've been aware of that these many years. I'm also not your husband and I won't demand anything of you, Nina. Just let me take care of you."

He placed his arms about her. There was nothing sensual in his touch, yet Nina could not ignore the sense of strength it contained. She did not pull away from him.

CHAPTER EIGHT

The Meadows, September 1755

The road through Williamsburg ran past the houses of the
legislature and the governor's residence. Once outside the
main town it cut in front of the buildings belonging to the
College of William and Mary, after Harvard the oldest school
in the English colonies. Nina and Gilles sat in the back of the
mule-drawn cart. Jubal, the black man who had first driven
them from Yorktown and who had then disappeared, was
again driving the cart. He chatted away without seeming to
mind or even notice that they didn't respond. Nina clung to
Gilles. Except for him she was now totally alone.

"You folks is some of them foreign folks we took from
Yorktown, ain't you?" Jubal questioned. He got no response
from the uncomprehending Acadians. "Well now, we don't
see too many white folks taken for slaves, so I guess you are
time-servers. I don't suspect I would like to be 'dentured like
you folks. Can't say I think much about being a slave either. If
I had my ways I'd be sitting up in Da Home ruling the devil's
own like me grandpap before me." He scratched the worn
seat of his pants and laughed a high cackling laugh. "Now I
don't rightly know, seeing as you're 'dentured, if I should give
you the 'struction I give good nigger folk. Because you sure is

going to need 'struction working for Massa Audry. Now there is one mean son of a bitch. How come you folks don't talk much to me?"

There was a moment of silence as Jubal looked first at Nina and then at Gilles, awaiting their reply.

"Je ne comprends pas," Nina said finally.

"What's that you say?" Jubal said, leaning his gray head toward the girl.

"Je ne comprends pas."

"You say something about your pa? Don't look to me that man be anything like your pa. Seems to me you folks got a lot to worry about. For one thing, you better start thinking about what's in your belly, girl. You're gonna have yourself a'dition and that's sure gonna piss off old Massa Audry good." Again Jubal squealed, absolutely delighted at the thought of Massa Audry's annoyance.

"Now don't you worry none. My woman, Luck, she's had her hand in delivering a mess of babies and she'll take care of you when the time comes. You'll be back in the fields in two days. Course, if I know Massa Audry, you'll be working there when the pains start. If he loses only two days' work from you, sister, he might not cut your man's balls off for getting you with child to begin with. Massa Audry, he sure has a thing about balls. Seems to be working on a scheme that leaves him as the only one who's got any." The jovial expression fled from his face. He could not forget the fate of the slave Nathan.

Jubal fell silent for the first time since the trip began. Nina leaned back against the side of the cart. She rested her head against Gilles' massive shoulder. The morning air was chilly. All about her the trees overhanging the dirt wagon road seemed to sag. Some of the leaves had turned a pale yellow and a handful drifted to the ground each time the breeze stirred the branches.

Nina disliked the blandness. At home the countryside would be ablaze with red, yellow, orange, and violet colors. But there were compensations here. There were birds in Virginia like none she had seen in the northern climate of Acadia. Tiny blue birds with red breasts, yellow-and-black birds, and birds that looked almost like insects, their bodies tiny and their wings moving rapidly. They were a delight to the girl and their presence brought a smile to her face.

"You're laughing," Gilles commented to her.

Nina looked up at him and shook her head. The birds were only a momentary diversion for her; they would offer no solace to a man of Gilles' gruffness.

"Where is he taking us?" Nina asked, nodding her head toward Jubal.

Gilles shrugged his shoulders and held his palms up in exasperation. "Who knows?" he muttered. "I heard the black man speak of Port Royale, but they can't be taking us home to Acadia."

"Maybe they have a place here of the same name."

Before Gilles could respond a carriage drawn by a sleek chestnut horse came thundering up behind Jubal's wagon.

The black man rose in his seat and turned. He pulled the mule and wagon to the side of the road and into a ditch. Once again the wagon lurched to the left and the wheel cracked under the impact.

"How do, Massa Audry?" Jubal shouted out, removing his cloth hat from his gray head.

The open carriage passed the wagon. The driver was clad elegantly in a beige coat and brown riding breeches. He wore a patch over his left eye, and his mouth was twisted into a perpetual sneer by a scar that ran through it and up to his eye, disappearing behind the patch. He hauled in on the reins and brought his chestnut horse to a halt.

"Jubal."

"Yes, Massa?"

"I expect you at The Meadows in four days."

"But, Massa, I done broke a wheel, and old Black Edgar ain't a purebred like you got. He ain't nothing but a tired old mule. It will take time."

"A lash for every hour you're late, you lying old scoundrel. You won't pull off a visit to friends and relatives on me as you did on Captain Elliot. You fix that wheel damned quick and you get to The Meadows just as fast as your old black ass will take you."

Audry laughed at his own joke, then glanced for the first time at Nina and Gilles. His eyes lingered long on Nina. She tried to ignore his stare, but she could not continue to look away. Finally she stole a glance at him. She shivered. He was ugly. Yet the eye patch and the curl of his lip seemed almost fascinating. He noted her stolen glance and grinned at her as if in triumph. He said nothing. He raised his whip and brought it down viciously on the back of the chestnut. The horse reared slightly in fright and then bolted down the road.

"Shee . . . it," Jubal exclaimed in disgust. "That mean son of a bitch means every word he says. I damned well better get to Port Royal and the Rappahannock in four days. It makes no difference to that devil that my Luck gave him the nipple just after he stuck his ugly face out of his mama. What am I talking to you two for?" Jubal said finally in annoyance. "You two don't understand good English. Too busy speaking that mush you talk."

He sighed and then slipped down from the driver's seat into the mud. As he did the black mule struck out with his hind foot, nearly kicking Jubal in the leg. The black man danced out of range just in time, his footing gave way and he fell to his knees. He rose to his feet and stared at the animal. The mule seemed to shiver in anticipation. The old man moved slowly; his whole body seemed to be at rest as he walked; his stride was graceful and totally lacking in tension. Nina and Gilles were completely deceived but not old Black Edgar, the mule. The animal bellowed in panic as Jubal came into its field of vision. Jubal swung his fist and struck the mule a staggering blow in the nose. Again the animal screamed, but this time in pain.

"You dumb bugger," Jubal yelled. "You broke the truce on this trip. Thought I wouldn't be 'specting you, didn't you?"

The animal glared at him with hatred.

Now Jubal turned his attention to Nina and Gilles. "You two planning to stay in the cart while I fix the wheel?"

As he spoke he waved them out of the cart. Gilles jumped down into the mud. He swung Nina down after him but held her feet off the ground and carried her to the damp grass that grew beside the road.

Jubal stripped off his shirt and reached into the driver's seat for his tools. He bent down and examined the wheel.

"Cracked the frame and busted a spoke," he said. "Could be worse." He reached down and attempted to pull the wheel out of its rut. It would not budge. He tugged harder on the wheel, and as he did, muscles rippled all over his arms and chest. The wheel began to move off the ground. The muscles strained even more. Now the wheel was inches off the ground. Jubal whistled to Black Edgar and the mule walked a few steps forward. Jubal moved forward with the mule while holding onto the wheel.

Jubal didn't see the second rut in the road. His foot caught in it and he stumbled forward. The wheel slipped from his hand and came crashing down on his leg. It glanced off his calf but pinned the cloth of his pants to the muddy ground. Jubal cursed in pain, but his real problem was not with the wheel. Once again Edgar saw his chance to even the score. The mule's hind foot again shot out, catching Jubal in the chest with a sickening thud. Edgar struck a second time, narrowly missing the black man's head. Jubal called out, half cursing, half screaming. Gilles leapt to the side of the wagon, and with one heave of his enormous arms he lifted the wagon's wheels off the ground. Jubal scrambled to his feet just as the mule kicked a third time. This blow struck harmlessly into the air where, but a few seconds before, Jubal's face had been. Gilles set the wagon back down. The black man looked at him with awe.

"Now that be something," he whispered. "You be some strong nig . . . fellow," he finished.

"What's they call you?" When he received no reply, he pointed to his own chest. "Jubal," he said.

Gilles stared dumbly. It was Nina who understood his gesture. "Zhubel, Zhubel," she repeated.

"That's close enough," said the old man. "What's your name?" he asked, pointing toward Nina.

"Nina."

"Nina, that be a pretty name," he said.

Gilles finally caught on and spoke his name.

Jubal scratched his head. "A good name. I 'spects your mother wanted a filly. I'll call you Jack instead. Well, I'm Jubal and this is old Black Edgar," he said as he swung around and kicked the mule as hard as he could with his bare foot. The animal stared ahead stoically, but not Jubal. He hopped around holding his toes until Nina could stand it no longer and burst into laughter. Her mirth was contagious and

Gilles joined her. Before long Jubal's tears were a mixture of pain and laughter.

"I can't affore no more of this foolishness," Jubal said, his chest still rising and falling with laughter. "I got me a wheel to fix and I got me a run to Port Royal. When Massa Audry says he'll give me a beating, he'll treat me a lot worse than I treat old Edgar here. Come on, Jack, you be a strong man. You lifts and I pull the wheel off."

They crossed the Rappahannock River into King George County at Port Royal. The Audry plantation, The Meadows, was on the north bank opposite the ferry.

Jubal drove Black Edgar up the poplar-lined gravel road toward the great house. It was three storey high and constructed of red brick with chimneys at each corner. Its lead-paned windows were framed in white. The double oak doors at the main entry looked down upon a manicured green lawn that ran to the river's edge on one side and toward some marshes on the back side. The view of the river was obscured intermittently by the graceful drooping branches of the willow trees.

Jubal continued past the main entry of the house and down the yellow gravel road. A short distance from the house the road branched off to the north, away from the river, and the gravel road disappeared and gave way to red mud. Now they could see the north face of the house. It was identical to the river side except it faced the surrounding acres which were filled with topped and stunted tobacco plants, the remains of last summer's harvest.

The air was heavy with the smell of curing tobacco. Nina was reminded of her father's pipe. She shuddered as the memory of Babin came floating back into her mind, including the grisly sight of his feet dancing grotesquely in the air.

Edgar kept moving ahead, now with no urging at all from Jubal. The curing shed from which the odors emerged came into view at the edge of the harvested fields. Then came an even more pungent odor, the odor of marsh gas that wafted up from the meadows along the curve of the river.

Jubal saw Nina wrinkle her nose and he laughed and slapped his thigh.

"Never fails! Massa Audry can call this place The Meadows

all he pleases, but we gots the right name. The Stink Hole is what every right-thinking nigger calls this place."

Edgar moved into a trot, the fastest the animal had moved during the whole journey from Williamsburg. Beyond the curing shacks and beyond sight of the river, the dirt road entered the slave quarters. It was a tiny town of fifteen wooden one-room shanties, each with a board- and mud-lined chimney. Smoke rose lazily from about half of them.

Jubal hauled on Edgar's reins and the mule came to a halt. "There goes my house," he said pointing to one of the gray-and-brown shacks.

The door of the house squeaked in protest as it was opened, and a thin, bony black woman with gray hair partially concealed by a red bandanna came out into the yard. She ignored Jubal but went immediately to the mule.

"There's my fine fellow," the black woman said and slipped half an apple into the mule's mouth. The animal shivered with pleasure and nuzzled the woman with its snout. The woman laughed, then turned to Jubal.

"You been beating up on the mule again?" she asked.

"He damned near killed me. If it wasn't for the fact that I had me a Samson right out of the Bible that mule would like to kick my brains all over the Port Royal road."

"Then the road would be empty, 'cause your head be." She scowled, then walked over to Nina, her interest heightened by the girl's swollen belly.

"I be Luck. Massa Audry's own mammy and this no-account's woman."

"No use talking God's talk to them. They be like Africans brought over fresh. They talk only gibberish. Her name is Nina and his be Jack."

Luck pointed to herself and spoke her name while looking directly at Nina.

Nina repeated the sound. "Luck."

"Nonsense," Luck said to Jubal. "This girl speaks English."

Jubal shook his head.

"Didn't you just hear her? She spoke my name. Least that's a beginning. All you got to do is keep speaking to her. Before long she'll speak just like you and me. Now, what they doin' here?"

"Massa Audry, the devil take his soul, bought their contracts. They be 'dentured folks. Field hands, I 'spect."

"You stop picking on the Massa. I raised that boy. He is mean sometimes, but deep down inside him is the little one I nursed at my own breast."

"Yup, and he shared that teat with our own child. But just as soon as he got control of this stinking hole he sold his playmate up Alexandria way and then he put his mammy to work in the tobacco fields. He sure is somethin'. You call that mean, I call it a devil."

A look of pain crossed Luck's face. Jubal had touched an unbearable wound.

"I don't want to talk 'bout that," she said, shaking her head as if the gesture would drive away the pain. "Where are we going to put these two? We ain't got no empty houses. What was Massa Audry thinking about?"

"If I knows the Massa, he was thinking about screwin' with the lady just as soon as she is able."

Luck did not respond. Her silence, Jubal knew, was an admission that his evaluation was correct.

"We'll take them in for the time being," she said finally.

Jubal was about to complain, but before he could say a word she settled the bandanna more firmly on her head. It was a gesture of finality that he knew well. There was no arguing with her now. There would be four of them, all in the same cabin.

Luck returned to Nina's side. She placed her arms about the girl's shoulders.

"By the looks of you, child, I 'spect this little one is to be a girl. Some folks have their own theories, but I don't put no stock in any of them but mine. When you be carryin' a man-child, you stick out in the front. There's no doubt about it. You be carryin' that girl all even in the belly."

Jubal had heard Luck expound on an unborn child's sex before. For some reason he could not understand such speculation was important to womenfolk, and there were those who put much faith in Luck's predictions. He paid little or no attention to his wife's success rate. All he knew was that she had not predicted accurately the sex of their own child. Luck had predicted a daughter. That was the boy that Massa Audry had sold upriver and the boy she had not seen in fifteen years.

Jubal had managed one or two visits. He reported to Luck but told her only what he thought she wanted to hear. Right now his big task was to find straw for a makeshift mattress for his guests.

Nina undressed behind the blanket that Luck had strung across the cabin. She sat in her flimsy shift on the straw bed. Gilles had stayed outside smoking his pipe in silence with Jubal. She was determined not to cry again tonight. The woman Luck had been kind to her. God knew these poor black folks had little enough of their own, but Luck had presented her with a sacklike shift that she had covered herself with during her own pregnancy so many years ago. Luck had said nothing, but the threadbare condition of the shift indicated that it had been lent out before—many times.

They were good people. She was relieved to have arrived in their midst. She was more upset now about Gilles. The fiction that they were husband and wife had served the purpose of keeping them together. But now that they were to share the same bed, would he want more?

The blanket was lifted at the corner and Gilles stepped under it. She blushed and he quickly looked away. He took off his badly stained and torn shirt. He looked about for some place to hang it, but seeing no hook of any kind, he folded it neatly. Nina smiled at him. He caught her expression, and shrugging his shoulders, he broke into a grin as he set his shirt gently on the rough board floor of the cabin.

"We're lucky," he said to her softly in French. "These two blacks are leaders. She's a former wet nurse and he is the field boss, from what I can discover from his gestures. He showed me some of the other cabins. They all have dirt floors." He spoke to distract her attention from the fact that he was removing his woolen breeches. He dropped them on the floor next to the shirt. Then he flopped down on the straw beside Nina. He noted that she shifted her body weight and moved slightly away from him.

"Our marriage is a fiction, Gilles," she said nervously.

"I know that," he responded. "But we will have to maintain that fiction unless you want to be sold off to another farm or have me sent away. And I don't like the way 'Massa' looks at you."

Again Nina shifted uncomfortably. She did not know which made her more uncomfortable, the prospect of maintaining her pseudomarriage to Gilles or not having his protection.

Gilles lay back on the straw and began to pat his belly with his hands. The noise annoyed Nina. She was tired and wanted to get some sleep.

"Nina, lie down," he urged her. "I am not going to touch you. We'll say you have had trouble and we're worried that you might not be able to continue to carry, so we've stopped having sex until the baby is born."

Nina finally lay back in the straw.

"You know, time is on my side," he said, smiling at her. He turned toward her and rested on his elbow. She started.

"Relax," he said, "I don't bite." He picked up a piece of the straw and placed it between his teeth and fell back again.

"Eventually," he continued, "you'll think less and less of my brother. You'll see me sweating in the fields to earn the food you put in your belly. You'll see me a father to the child and I'll be lying by your side at night and eventually you will accept me—in every way."

Nina said nothing. She made a secret promise to herself that it would never happen. Marcel was her lover and the father of her child. Someday he would find her and reclaim her love.

Gilles started to beat out the same rhythm on his stomach again. She reached over to stop him. Her hand rested on his stomach. His hand fell quiet and he looked into her eyes. She pulled her hand away quickly. She had frightened herself. The touch of his body had sent shivers through her. It was not going to be easy to keep her resolve to be true to the child's father.

Before the first rays of the sun lightened the sky, Luck pulled back the blanket that divided the two couples. There was a fall chill in the early morning air and the black woman had lost no time lighting her fireplace and warming up the cornmeal gruel she had prepared the night before.

"You folks must be up," she said to the sleeping forms of Nina and Gilles. But only Nina sat up, startled by the black woman's call. Gilles merely moaned and turned over.

Luck laughed. "Ain't that just like all mens. Womanfolks is

supposed to get up first and get the world started, that is unless it crosses his mind to give the old war horse a morning workout. Then we is supposed to lie back and spread 'em. *Then* we is supposed to get up and get the world started."

Nina smiled at the woman. Her chatter seemed friendly to the French girl and the smile seemed appropriate.

"Child, you and I sure do understand one another. That old Jubal telling me that you don't understand. That smile tells me plenty. I bet that's just how that hunk of a man you sleep with got you with the girl-child in the first place. That early morning time when he's not quite sure whether he wants to make love or make piss. Just your luck on the wrong morning he chose love. Don't get me wrong now, child, I ain't got anything against babies. I wish in fact I had me more than the one, but being with child in a harvest season is no small thing. That's something I had to go through. You's lucky the tobacco is all in and all we'll be doing now is grading and stacking it in the curing shed. Heavy lifting, but not so hard on the back, not like weeding or bugging the tobacco plant."

Nina rose and went over to the fireplace to enjoy the warmth of the fire. She saw the water bubbling in the pot and four mugs set out on a small wooden board table that rested against the far wall of the cabin. Its legs were uneven and a small wooden plug had been set under the leg closest to the hearth to keep it from wobbling. Nina gestured to Luck as if to pour water into the cups; perhaps Luck had tea to add to the water.

Luck nodded to Nina. The girl poured, but the water was greenish in color and smelled rancid. Nina thought for sure Luck must have confused last night's dishwater with her cooking water. She wrinkled her nose.

Jubal came up behind Nina and reached around her to take one of the steaming mugs into his large hands. He sipped the contents and smacked his lips together.

"Some folks like their pot likker later in the day, but I like it with my corn bread, 'specially if I got me a long day of stacking to do. Makes the meal stick to your gut and puts some zip in these old tired muscles."

Luck offered a mug to Nina. She sniffed it and only pretended to drink it. Gilles, who had arisen and put on his breeches, came over to where Nina and Jubal stood. He took the mug from Nina's hands and took a gulp. He made a grotesque face at Nina beyond the older couple's vision.

"That's horrible," he said to Nina.

"I knew you'd like pot likker," Luck said to both Nina and Gilles. "We had some fresh greens yesterday. I knew my man would be home and so I give him what he likes."

"What is that stuff?" Gilles asked.

She sniffed it again. "I think it is the water they cook their vegetables in."

"No wonder their skin has turned black. I used to think it was because they had been too long in the sun, but now I am sure it's the food they eat."

"These are good people, Gilles," Nina protested, "and they have been kind to us."

"I have no doubt about their goodness," Gilles laughed, "only about their taste."

By now the sun was shining in the eastern sky and warming the air, making the heat from the fireplace unnecessary. Gilles and Nina ate the corn bread but refused to take any of the liquid that Luck offered them.

When Luck went out to feed the mule, Jubal threw his arms about Gilles' shoulders.

"Friend, I believe you are about to work your first day in bondage."

A shadow fell across the doorway and both Gilles and Jubal turned to face a thin black-haired white man dressed in homespun. He had a leather whip circled over his left shoulder and under his armpit.

"Hey, boy," he called to Jubal, "it's time you and your woman got your black asses over to the curing barn and started stacking the tobac racks."

He looked at Nina as if she was some brood mare. He gave Gilles a more cursory evaluation.

"Mr. Audry told me you'd be bringing in two more hands, but he didn't say nothing about them being time-servers and white."

"Mr. Josephs, sir," Jubal began. His tone of voice and even his gestures changed from a confident man with strong opinions to a subservient, timid, almost childlike creature. "Luck and me will be heading out just as soon as she comes back

168

from feeding old Edgar, sir. It won't do no good iffen we don't take good care of Massa's livestock."

Josephs was overseer to Audry's plantation. He had arrived only two weeks ago. His style was one of quick discipline and domination of his charges, but he had yet to figure out the gray-haired field boss. Audry was a hard man, but he had learned that the field boss's woman had been Audry's mammy and wet nurse. You had to watch out for these blacks who had special relationships with the planters. He had lost positions before because he had carelessly ignored ties almost as strong as blood.

He would never understand these rich folk. They kept blacks and treated them as property, as chattel, but should one of his class, hired help, try to get the most out of the lazy bastards, he could find himself riding down the road to the next plantation looking for a new job.

"You two, you're to follow Jubal and he'll show you how to do the work."

Nina and Gilles stared blankly at Joseph, until Jubal interrupted the silence.

"These two be foreigners. They speak some strange language. Don't know no English at all."

"I don't care what they talk so long as they work," the overseer responded. "You get all the hands up and out to work now."

Several of the inhabitants of the other cabins were outside already. Luck came down the path from the barn leading Edgar and his wagon. A huge broad-shouldered black man, even larger than Gilles, went up to her and kissed her on the cheek.

"Get yourself away from me, masher," Luck called out in mock panic. "You mind your manners or Jubal come looking for you."

"You line up Jubal and all of Jubal's kin in back of him and with my right hand tied to my left foot there won't be no one standing 'fore I finished with him."

"I know that 'cause the only weapon you need is your mouth. You got more wind come out of your mouth than comes out of a twister."

The black man laughed loudly and threw the tools he carried over his shoulder into the wagon.

"Gabriel, how many times do I have to tell you you don't need a hoe to stack tobacco," Josephs the overseer called out.

Gabriel suddenly looked lost and scratched his head. "I don't know, boss. I can't count much past five and I think you told me more times than that."

"Damn dumb nigger," Josephs cursed. "I swear Audry's got him the biggest collection of misfits in Virginia. A buck like Gabriel, you can teach him what a hoe is for on Monday and you got to reteach him on Tuesday, and sure enough he'll forget on Wednesday everything you taught him. Now he gets two time-servers that I can't even teach."

He walked away toward Gilles. "What lingo do you talk?" he asked.

"*Je ne comprends pas, monsieur,*" Gilles said, looking directly at the overseer.

"They's always complainin' about their pa," Jubal explained.

"Oh, shit, I got me a couple of mon-sewers," Josephs said, shaking his head. "How is anyone going to get through to them?"

"I'll talk to them," Luck offered, as she brought Edgar and the wagon to a halt before the doorway. "Me and the young miss gets along just fine."

Nina had turned her back on Josephs and began to empty the mugs of pot liquor back into the pot.

"You ain't got no time for housecleaning, little sister," Josephs called out to her. "You get your ass over to the curing shacks too."

Jubal looked at Luck with a twinkle in his eye. After years of living with him she knew he was about to begin a game he loved, a joust with an overseer. It gave Jubal more pleasure than almost anything else in his life.

"Now, Mr. Josephs, sir, I am thinking that the lady is big with child."

"A girl child," Luck chimed in.

Jubal gave her a quick look of disapproval and she shut up.

"I'm not sure," Jubal continued, "that Massa would want to risk losing the labor of this missy over the long haul, during planting season and packing, just so as to have an extra hand at easy work like stacking the racks."

"You trying to tell me how to run this plantation, field boss?"

"No, sir, I wouldn't even dream of doin' that. I be nothing but a dumb nigger."

"Just so long as you understand your place, boy."

"Yes, sir," said Jubal, "I sure understand my place. Why, Massa Audry said the same thing to me the day I made Lucy work in the field before you come when we was in-between overseers. He said to me, 'Jubal, you think a dumb nigger like you can run The Meadows better than me? You like to work Lucy to death and I paid good monies for that nigger. You nearly cost me a good field hand.' That was what he said to me, boss, and I sure learned from that."

Jubal stepped out of the doorway. He called out, then he reentered the house and deliberately took Nina by the hand and started to lead her to the others.

"Ah, the hell with it," Josephs said suddenly. "No sense in taking chances with the bitch. Let her stay behind."

"You sure about that?" Jubal said, looking in amazement at the overseer.

"I know what I'm doing," Josephs said angrily.

Jubal shook his head. "Yes, sir, Mr. Josephs, that's why you be the overseer."

Luck stepped behind Black Edgar so that Josephs would not see her smile.

The next day was a Sunday. Gilles and Nina had lost track of the days of the week and Nina awoke expecting to see Luck by the fireplace. But no one stirred in the cabin.

It was not until the sun was well up in the eastern sky that Nina heard noises from the other side of the blanket. She was embarrassed as soon as she recognized them. She had not thought that people as old as Jubal and Luck did such things. Certainly she could never picture her father and mother doing anything like that. She smiled when she remembered the first time she had realized that they must have "done it" at least twice to produce her and TiJoe.

Suddenly the memory of her brother overwhelmed her and she wept. She heard no more of the black couple's lovemaking.

Luck came into view fixing her hair beneath her kerchief. Nina raised herself from the mat, removing herself from under Gilles' heavily muscled arm.

"You awake, child? I hope Jubal and I didn't wake you up.

Sometimes I don't know what I am going to with that man. He wakes up all sweetness and full of vinegar."

Nina stared blankly at her.

Luck smiled at her. She made a circle with her index finger and thumb of her right hand and then stuck her left index finger through the circle several times. Nina grasped her meaning and blushed. Luck smiled.

"I don't hear no grunting or moans coming from your side of the blanket. I hope you and your man is not just being bashful. Folks your age should be having all the fun the good Lord intended for you. Now don't you worry none about hurting your baby. You got time enough before you have to stop."

Jubal got out of bed. He scratched his head and then his belly.

"Luck, honey, would you stop lecturing that girl. She don't know a word you're sayin'."

"She does," Luck said defiantly. "You men might not understand each other, but womens got extra sense."

As Jubal went outside to the common outhouse shared by the folks of the slave quarters, Gilles appeared from behind the blanket.

Luck stole a look in his direction. She nodded approvingly and poked Nina with her elbow.

"You got you a man, there," she smiled.

Nina looked about and saw Gilles and turned back in confusion. Then she realized that Luck was commenting on Gilles.

She blushed again.

"No need to be shy around me, girl. You won't find me a jealous friend. I got me a man too."

Jubal came in from outside. "You bragging about me again, woman?"

She smiled at him.

"I need some water for washing up. You got my best Sunday clothes ready?"

The whole slave quarters were dressed in their finest. Luck's ever-present red kerchief had been replaced by a black straw hat with a wide brim. Her homespun gray work dress gave way to a lacy white blouse and a black skirt. Over her shoulders she draped a red knitted shawl.

Jubal wore a black suit with a white shirt and a black string tie. Gabriel was dressed in his finest, as were all the men, women and children of the slave quarters. They wore a blaze of light colors mixed with a pandemonium of red. Many of the women carried parasols.

Nina and Gilles were drab in contrast. They had no good Sunday clothes to change into, but no hesitation was allowed by their mentors. No matter that they were Catholics. They were to go to the meeting. Luck produced another shawl for Nina. It was torn in one place and its color had long since faded from constant washing, but in a few places one could still find the patches of bright yellow the garment had once been.

Nothing Jubal owned would fit Gilles, but Gabriel did come up with an old gray jacket. Decked out with cast-offs from their new friends, the two Acadians joined the march up the wagon road toward the curing sheds and beyond them toward the woods that bordered the plantation fields.

In a cutover field a small platform had been set up. The slaves spread blankets on the ground and divided themselves up into family units. The morning was chilly still, and the children snuggled up closely to the warmth of their mothers.

When all were seated on the ground, a murmur of anticipation ran through the assembly. Jubal rose from his blanket and went to the front of the crowd. He stepped onto the stump of a great oak.

Nina leaned toward Gilles. "Is Zhubel a priest?" she asked.

Gilles shrugged his shoulders.

Jubal raised his hands high in the air for silence. "The spirit of the Lord is in this place," he called out.

A murmur of assent ran through the listeners.

"I come to talk to you today about heaven."

"Preach it, brother," a woman's voice called out.

Nina and Gilles looked about them. Every face stared up at the form of their friend, intent on missing not a word.

"Heaven," Jubal continued, "is a place where the souls of good folks receive their 'liverance."

"Give me that 'liverance," a male voice cried.

Gilles stared at him. He recognized him as one of the strongest of the field hands and one of the more silent.

"You gonna have that de-liverance," Jubal responded. As he spoke, his heavy accent became even more pronounced. Even if the Acadians had spoken English, they would have had difficulty understanding Jubal today.

"God made us all with souls. De trees all around us, dey got dem souls. You can hear 'em whispering to each other in de night when de wind slide easy through dem branches. 'Praise de Lawd,' dey whisper."

"Dem trees got sense," Luck called out to Jubal.

He smiled at his wife. "De ole possum dat live in de woods he got de soul too. I've been tryin' to trap him now for twenty years and all I gets is his children, his grandchildren, and his greats-grandchildren. No, I don't try trappin' him no more. His soul is goin' on to heaven and I trap him dere."

"Glad you didn't trap dat possum, old Jubal, dat ole bugger would make mighty tough eating."

"Dat's 'nother reason for not trappin'. I ain't no fool."

The whole congregation laughed at the preacher's joke, and Luck jabbed Gabriel with her elbow in appreciation.

Jubal waited until the laughter subsided and the congregation came back to order.

"And you and me, brother and sister, we got souls."

"Amen to dat," called out a chorus of voices.

"And when we dies, our souls live. De Lawd says so in his book. Do you believe it?"

The congregation roared back at Jubal. "I believes" pierced the air.

Nina was caught up in the sound. She did not know what was being said but it was joyful. She started to clap her hands with delight. At first, Gilles stared strangely at her. Then, realizing that she was happy, he smiled at her. He ignored Jubal for the moment and took pleasure in the obvious joy that was taking hold of Nina.

"Dat soul goin' to make it straight to the bosom of Abraham."

"What kind of bosom could Abraham have?" a very large and buxom woman called out to Jubal. "You send dem souls to Annie's bosom," she said, pointing to herself. "I show dem souls a real bosom—'magine bragging about some dried-up old man's bosom."

Again the congregation roared with laughter. Nina joined in.

"The bosom of Abraham, Sister Annie, is another way of 'scribin' heaven. And heaven is where we is all headin' for 'liverance. All you got to do to get there is to have faith in de Lawd and get yourself de baptism."

Hallelujahs rang out through the woods. "Do white folks get 'liverance?" a young child called out to Jubal.

"Some," he responded, after thinking for a moment. "But most folks who is white 'spects to find colored folk in heaven to wait on them and work with them. But there be no slaves in heaven."

The crowd roared its approval and a slow rhythmic clapping followed the shout.

"You gots to believe in Jesus," Jubal said. The cadence of his words matched the clapping of the crowd.

"Jesus loves you, Jesus 'livers your soul. Jesus carry you to heaven."

The clapping was louder now. The slave congregation began to sway with the rhythm of the clapping. Jubal's bass voice began a hum. Soon other voices picked it up. No words at first, only a humming. Then again it was Jubal. His voice was deep and seemed to come from deep within him. "Stealing away to Jesus."

The congregation joined with him for the next lines.

It seemed sad to Nina. She swayed with it, as did the others. She looked up at Gilles by her side. He seemed unmoved and merely sat there. So massive and so stolid. He did smile at her. She returned it. He loved her and he protected her and it was good to feel his arms encircle her and keep her from the horrors that seemed to lurk everywhere in their lives. But she could not love him back, and deep within herself she was afraid that in the long run she would hurt him deeply and bring harm to both of them.

The singing had stopped. Several of the slaves had climbed up onto the platform across a small clearing from the rough pulpit Jubal had used. They began to clap their hands more rapidly now. Gabriel produced a fiddle, which looked ridiculously tiny in his massive hands, but soon rollicking music, handclapping music, came pouring from it. The people on the platform began to dance.

"Watch your feet," Luck called out to the dancers on the platform. "You be sure no one crosses der legs. Dat be dancin' and we is good Baptists. We knows dancin' be a sin. No legs crossin', no dancin'. This is a good old-fashioned shoutin' time."

The dancers were moving rapidly now, and the music grew faster and more raucous. But true to Luck's admonition, not one leg crossed over another.

The dancers' pounding feet on the platform made an almost thunderous noise. The congregation kept time with the fiddle by clapping hands. The motion of the dancers became jerky and convulsed. Nina screamed in fright when one of them collapsed quivering onto the platform floor.

"Dat's the way, Sister Nina. You lets de spirit out," Jubal almost sang.

Another dancer had fallen in a frenzy on the platform. And soon all lay quivering on the ground. Some of the handclappers also seemed to go into trances.

Luck was swaying from right to left. If she leaned over any further she was doomed to fall to the ground. Gilles, who sat beside her, tried to steady her, but Jubal shoved his hand away. "Let her be with de Lawd," he shouted over the tumult of the crowd.

Suddenly the noise of a musket shot pierced through the din. The singing and shouting and handclapping ceased instantly, and all fell silent. For the first time since Jubal began to preach, the noises of a sunny day in the forest clearing could be heard.

Slowly Josephs the overseer rode into the clearing, his musket still smoking. His ever-present whip trailed behind the horse and dragged on the ground.

"Prayers are over," he said in a voice so low that only those closest to him could have heard him. When not everyone jumped to their feet to make their way out of the forest and back to their quarters, Josephs made his move and charged toward them. With a broad overhand swing, he slammed his whip into the back of a young woman who had been looking desperately for her dancer husband. She yelled in pain. The whip came slashing down again, this time wrapping about the waist of a little girl. The anguish that crossed her face caused Nina to rise to her feet in a panic. She raced toward the child and swept the girl up into her arms. The whip still clung to the whimpering, terrified child and Josephs began to yank on it, dragging Nina and the little girl toward him. Nina was frightened by Josephs as she had never been frightened by any other creature in her life. He was black-haired and white, like most of the men she had known in her life, but he was not like any Acadian man who cherished his family and his freedom. No Acadian would take a whip to a child. No Acadian would be part of a system that held people—good people like these—in bondage. She worked at the leather that bound the black child to the white man on the horse. She tore at it and finally pried it away. The child had a raised welt on her belly and back. Josephs grinned at Nina. But Gilles was quickly by her side. His huge arm quickly enveloped her in his embrace. The whimpering child was grabbed from Nina by her mother.

"Prayer meeting is all over," Josephs announced again, this time in a loud voice.

Nina and Gilles continued to stare at him. Josephs rode around them, still announcing the end of the service. "Tomorrow is a work day. You niggers get back to your quarters and get yourself some sleep. With all this ranting and raving and banging away up here, God knows there won't be many of you bucks who won't be making pickaninnies for old Massa tonight."

He laughed loudly.

Gilles pulled at Nina, and together they walked over to Jubal, who splashed some water on Luck's face to bring her from her trance. Some semblance of a line was formed and the slaves moved out of the clearing back down the road toward the quarters.

Josephs watched them march away. From out of the shadow of the woods he was joined by a second rider. In the dusk one could barely make out the darkened area of the patch on his shadowed face. "She's quite something," Audry said to the overseer.

Josephs merely nodded.

"Yes, we must look more closely at our little Frog."

CHAPTER NINE

The Meadows, November 1755

The days passed quickly for Gilles. He came home nightly from the curing sheds exhausted. He ate the dinner that Nina fixed for Jubal, Luck, and himself and fell asleep in the straw bed after smoking a pipe with Jubal on the bench outside the door.

Luck relished the luxury of not having to cook and rejected Gabriel's offer to relieve the field boss and his wife of their guests by sharing his cabin with them. She liked coming home to a hot meal with only dishes after dinner facing her. She had no desire to give up Nina. As long as she was allowed to spend her days in the cabin, Luck wanted Nina in her cabin.

But unlike those of Gilles, Nina's days passed slowly. She was not sure why she had been allowed to skip the manual labor, but she was grateful. She was afraid, however, that if she was seen by anyone, she might be put to work. So she busied herself as best she could with cooking and cleaning, but there was so little to do in the small cabin.

She passed a few days in this fashion until she could stand it no longer. One day, after the other three had left for work along with all the other inhabitants of the slave quarters, men, women and children, Nina poked her nose out of the cabin and inspected the little cluster of wooden huts. No sooner had she stepped outside than she nearly bumped into the leering face of Josephs. He held out a torn linen shirt.

"I thought since you ain't got no hard work to do, missy, you could take care of my needs."

Nina didn't understand Josephs's words, but his gesture was clear. She reached for the shirt and examined the rip. She stepped backward into the cabin. Josephs laughed and removed the whip from his shoulder and cracked it on the ground just for the fun of it. Nina cringed and dropped back farther into the gloomy shadows of the doorway. Josephs laughed again and turned his back on her. He remounted his horse, then turned back to Nina.

"I'll be back for the shirt tomorrow. You can demand your price then. I think you'll enjoy what I've got."

Nina sighed with relief when he left. She was angry with herself for being so timid. All the man had wanted was to have his shirt sewn. She made up her mind to explore the plantation and not be so frightened of its inhabitants.

Outside the air was heavy. The ground fog caused by the night chill had only recently burned off. Nina walked along the wagon tracks away from the slave quarters and up toward the marshes. The Rappahannock bent to the north here around the manor house. Nina was intrigued by the house. It sat like a plump, ugly turkey hen surrounded by the lushness of the poplar trees and green lawns. There was a horseman surrounded by baying hounds on the lawn farthest from Nina.

The sight of another human being, even a small figure off in the distance, reminded her of Josephs and frightened her again. Nina turned and walked back down the trail toward the slave quarters. She had done as much exploring as her nerves would allow.

Back at the cabin, she pulled the bench into the doorway so she could sit and enjoy the sunlight. She was still bone-weary from the long trip from Acadia. The tragedy surrounding the voyage and the overland trek had taken even more out of her. She needed time to think about her child. She cradled her belly in her arms. Everything had happened so fast, her night of love with Marcel and then his leaving.

Suddenly, directly in front of her, sitting astride his horse like some giant equestrian statue, was the man with the black patch and the sneering mouth. He slipped expertly from the saddle and walked toward her. Nina shrank back from him.

"Bon jour, madame," he said in a British-accented French.

Nina almost whispered her reply. Audry came closer to her. He placed one polished booted foot on the bench on which Nina sat.

"How is it, my pretty wench, that you are not off with the others making me richer?" he said.

Nina's voice had disappeared in fright.

"We'll have to see how Josephs explains that. Had I not seen you walking along the road I would never have known."

He dabbed at his mouth with a perfumed handkerchief. The scar on his lip made it difficult for him to speak without drooling slightly.

"You need not be frightened, my lovely."

Nina rose from the bench. He grabbed her arm, applying just enough pressure to impede her progress but not enough to draw her to him. She turned and looked at him. He was repulsive, yet he exuded confidence as no other male around her did.

"You know you belong to me?" he said to her in French.

"I belong to no one," she responded.

"Is that the case?" he responded. "I seem to remember a piece of paper signed by your lummox of a husband giving yourselves over to me for the next fourteen years. I paid a goodly piece of money for that paper."

"You have our labor, not us."

"I own your body, wench," he said and his sneer grew more pronounced. "I can crush your bull man with a whip and break him in two. If I can do that to him then surely I own his body and yours as well. If I can break a man with pain I can also bend a woman to my will."

Nina understood his meaning. "I am pregnant, monsieur," she said, a note of even greater fear creeping into her voice.

"Congratulations," he responded. He hesitated, as if expecting her to say something else. When she did not, he started to laugh.

"I hadn't expected to be the first you know, just the best. By the way, what is your name?"

"Nina."

"Ah, Nina, I had expected a more fanciful excuse. You disappoint me. You might have said that you suffered from the pox."

"What's the pox?"

He roared with laughter. "My dear, you are refreshing. Here I am proposing that we ride off to some secluded grove where I will ravish you and you respond with questions—questions that no proper lady would ask a gentleman. But then, you are no proper lady. You are my own bondswoman, a wench whose greatest good fortune would be to have me as a lover even for an afternoon."

He gradually drew her closer to him. At first she did not resist but, as he lowered his head to kiss her she began to panic and pull away, thrusting her hands against his chest. But he persisted. He yanked her arm and pulled her through the cabin door behind him. Then he shoved her onto the straw mat that she shared with Gilles.

The stacking was almost finished for the season. One more good day and part of a second would do it. Jubal gave the call to stop work for the day slightly early to reward his crew for a job well done.

Josephs rode his horse right into the huge curing shed.

"Did you give the signal to quit?" he yelled.

"No, sir," Jubal lied. "I thought you did."

"Well, I didn't. Get your niggers back to work."

Jubal hesitated just long enough to cause Josephs concern that he would not be obeyed. Then he turned to the one white man and twenty or so slaves in the curing shed and spoke out:

"You heard the man. We'se got more work to do."

"What's to do, Jubal?" Gabriel called out. "We stacked all the racks of the weed we have here. We have to send you and Black Edgar back for more."

Josephs unwound the whip from his arm, and Gabriel stopped in mid-sentence.

"What were you saying, Gabe? It is Gabe, ain't it?"

"Yes, sir, Mr. Josephs," Gabriel said softly.

"Well, Gabe, I give the orders around here and I don't expect any argument. Perhaps you need a little discipline. I think there has been too much nigger bossing around here and not enough overseeing. Jubal, you just go and string old Gabe against the tree trunk beyond the shed there."

"Mr. Josephs, sir," Jubal said, his eyes staring through the overseer, "this ain't necessary."

The whip seemed to take on a life of its own as it slashed through the air and cut through Jubal's shirt into the side of his throat. A welt appeared instantly on the black man's neck and a streak of blood dribbled down and disappeared under his shirt collar. There was a deadly silence in the shed. No one had ever struck Jubal before, certainly not since he had been named field boss. Even Josephs seemed startled by his own action. He slowly pulled the whip in and wound it up again. He turned the horse around, kicked it in the side, and rode briskly out of the shed.

Luck rushed to Jubal's side. She removed her red kerchief and began to dab at Jubal's wound.

"You not going to let him get away with taking a whip to you, are you?"

"For the moment," Jubal responded. "That's one mighty frightened overseer. He gives the boss nigger one swipe with his rib cracker and he plumb forgets the twenty-five or so he promised to Brother Gabriel. I think that's a fair trade."

"But you be the boss, Jubal," Gabriel spoke up. "I be mighty grateful to you, but it ain't right the overseer taking the whip to you. Massa Audry shouldn't ought to let that happen."

"Massa Audry is nothing but a shit-eater," Jubal said quickly.

"I knows that," Gabriel said. "But Josephs still shouldn't ought to hit you."

"Enough talk," Jubal said.

Once again he gave the signal to finish for the day, and this time the entire crew formed up behind Black Edgar.

Gilles stepped up beside Jubal. He did not know the words and so he tried to signal to Jubal his distress over the whiplash. They walked in silence down the slope to the slave quarters.

Luck led the mule and kept his head straight. Black Edgar wanted to turn around and begin his game of feints with his feet, but Luck would have none of it. She held his head straight and whispered into his ear. Finally the animal gave up thoughts of the game and moved ahead, slowly at first, but then more rapidly as the prospect of a barn and some oats loomed ahead of him.

Gilles stared down the red clay road toward the cabins, hoping to catch sight of Nina. Normally she waited for them at the cabin door. As he came closer to the cabin, Gilles became more and more nervous. About fifty yards away he broke from Jubal's side and ran past Luck and Black Edgar. The cabin door was wide open. He peered into the dark interior. He could see only the loaves of corn bread Nina had baked that morning.

He heard her moan and swung around toward the straw mat. He breathed out a sight of relief. She was napping. It was foolish of him to worry so. He walked toward her, then froze in place as her face came into view. It was swollen and bruised. Her left eye was almost completely shut and the blood that had trickled from the corner of her mouth had dried to her chin. Her shift sat obscenely atop the mound of her swollen belly.

Gilles could not bring himself to move toward her. He merely stared in shock. It was Luck who finally rushed to Nina's side.

"Jubal, get some water to clean this poor baby up!" she called out to her husband.

The black man went to the hearth and came back with a pitcher of cooking water. Luck picked up the linen shirt that lay on the floor beside Nina and dipped a corner of it into the water and began to dab at the most swollen areas on the child's face, all the while making a soothing sound in her throat. She glanced at the two men staring at her and carefully lowered Nina's dress to cover her.

It was that gesture that triggered in Gilles the significance of what was happening. His terror and shock gave way to rage. Nina had been raped.

"Let me see that," Jubal said, snatching the shirt from Luck's hand. "I know that shirt. Son of a bitch."

He turned to face Gilles, holding the evidence out in front of him.

"Josephs," he said through clenched teeth.

Gilles recognized the name and the shirt. He turned on his heel and went out the front door. He started out along the wagon road that Nina had followed that morning.

Jubal followed Gilles out of the house. He called out to Gabriel to follow him. The huge black man came to the door of his hut. He was stripped to the waist and had been washing his upper torso before making himself some dinner.

"What you callin' me for?" he yelled as Jubal ran past him following the Frenchman.

"It's that white nigger," Jubal said over his shoulder. "He's going after the overseer for taking his woman. I have to stop him but I don't think I can do it alone."

Gabriel grabbed his shirt from the hook behind the front door and began to walk quickly along the rutted wagon path behind Jubal. Once his arms were through the sleeves he began to trot to catch up to his friend.

The two black men trailed Gilles, who moved rapidly toward the green lawns of the mansion.

"I don't know how to persuade him that this ain't a good idea," Jubal said, his words coming in bursts. He was puffing from the briskness of his pursuit.

Gilles stopped when he reached the edge of the lawn. The trail turned toward the river at this point, and Gilles did not know which way to turn. Within him his rage still seethed. The only image in his mind was of Josephs straddling Nina's body while the girl screamed silently with no one to hear her pleas for help. He shook his head to rid it of the obscenity.

Three men rode across the lawn toward him. But he saw only one. His whip was still curled about his arm and shoulder.

Josephs kneed his horse ahead of Audry and his neighbor Col. George Wilson. These blacks were running all over the plantation. Audry would surely comment in his nastiest sneer just as soon as he caught up with him.

"You there, Frog. What the hell are you doing up here at the mansion? If you don't need your rest and supper I'll see to it that you have enough work to keep you from roaming all over like this."

He allowed the whip to slip from his shoulder and trail behind him on the ground. He rode straight at Gilles and slashed at him with the whip. But the whip was caught in midair near its base by the Acadian. Gilles yanked with all his strength. Josephs landed with a thud in the red dust of the road. He lay for a moment in pain, stunned by his fall. But he was given only a brief respite. Gilles stood over Josephs, hate distorting his face. He kicked with all of his might, smashing his hard leather shoes into the overseer's crotch. Josephs screamed in agony. Again Gilles kicked. He yelled in French at the contorted figure of the man on the ground. Over and over again he shouted and kicked and kicked. Several times his boot struck Josephs's face, turning it into a mass of blood.

"Stop him," shouted Colonel Wilson to Jubal and Gabriel as they came up behind Gilles. He was surprised that his neighbor Audry had said or done nothing yet to help his overseer.

Jubal and Gabriel looked at Gilles warily. Neither wanted to get in the way of the man's fury and neither had much desire to assist Josephs.

Wilson drew a dueling pistol from his saddlebag. The shot rang out. Gilles looked at the red blotch that burst forth from his shoulder with surprise.

Josephs was no longer moving. Wilson got off his horse. He pulled the twin of his first pistol from the other saddlebag and trained it on Gilles.

"I always feel safer riding the river road with these in my possession," he said by way of explanation to no one in particular. He bent down and put his ear to Josephs's chest. "He's alive," he remarked. "Audry, ride back to the house and get some assistance. You two," he said to the slaves, "hold onto this ruffian. He must not be allowed to get away. He's a madman. Audry, don't just sit there."

"Of course," Audry said finally, a bemused look still on his face. He turned his jumper about and started to canter up the lawn toward the manor house.

Wilson kept his pistol aimed at Gilles but there was no need to. The Frenchman stood drained of energy, staring at the quiet crumpled form of his victim.

"What got into the man that he would attack the overseer?" Wilson addressed Jubal.

"It's woman trouble, Massa Wilson," Jubal said in his most deferential tone. "Mr. Josephs here took his woman against her will, she being already big with child."

Wilson looked disgusted but said nothing in front of the slaves. Several house slaves dressed in livery came running down the lawn from the house. One of them carried some blankets. There was no sign of Audry.

When the slaves reached Wilson he directed them in making a stretcher out of the blankets. They lifted Josephs onto it. Blood trickled from his mouth onto the cream-colored woolen blanket.

"My good Jesus," said an elderly manservant who seemed in charge of the rescue contingent. "That blanket be ruined. Massa gonna have my skin."

"Steady," Wilson called out as he lowered Josephs down. A loan moan escaped from his lips. His breeches were covered with blood.

The house slaves walked carefully as they carried their burden up toward the great house.

"I wish Audry would return," Wilson muttered to himself. He turned to Jubal and Gabriel. "You two, is there any place your master uses as a jail on the plantation?"

"There's a smokehouse near the quarters, Massa Wilson."

"Take this poor ruffian there and lock him up. I'll tell your master. Remember, you two will be held responsible if he gets away. Get some one to fix his flesh wound."

"Yes, Massa Wilson," both men said simultaneously.

"What's going to happen to Jack here?" Jubal asked.

"I don't know," Wilson said. "That's up to Audry. It will depend, I expect, on what happens to Josephs. If he lives, Audry will probably take care of it himself, although I would think Jack will be lucky to be alive after the whipping he'll get. I know that's what I'd do if he were my man. But if Josephs dies—and I have every reason to think he will— then, boys, it will be in the hands of the county court and we'll have us a hanging."

Nina slept fitfully through the night. Luck sat beside her, changing the cool compresses on the girl's swollen eyes and lips. Luck never left her side, not even when Jubal and Gabriel returned with the news that they had locked Gilles in the smokehouse. The older woman put her head in her hands when she heard what Gilles had done. She reached for Nina's hand and took it to her breast.

"This poor child has just seen the beginning of her sorrows," she cried. Tears streamed down her face. "I 'spect that the girl child is going to come into this world with no pappy. Massa Audry ain't going to allow no life to poor Jack. He be a dead man."

Jubal looked at his wife, then turned away and stepped outside into the dusk. The sun set early now. He took his pipe from his pocket and stuffed it full of tobacco from last season's crop. That had been a good year. He walked back into the house to take a light from the fireplace. He cursed when he realized it was unlit. Then he stepped back outside again and placed the unlit pipe back into his pocket and sat on his bench. Gabriel walked over from his cabin and dropped down on the bench next to Jubal with a sigh. He was smoking.

"Give me a puff of that stuff," Jubal said.

"Ain't you got your own?" Gabriel mocked him.

"Don't tease me, nigger," Jubal said softly. "We got us a big problem."

Gabriel nodded.

"Massa Audry is going to take that fellow down with no more thought than he take down a tree that's been growing for a hundred years just because it blocks his view," Jubal said. "He don't care nothing for Jack 'cept that Jack cost him money. Like as not he won't want to see Jack die, but he sure will want him to suffer a piece before he puts him back to work. Massa Audry is one mean piece of trash when it comes to making you and me suffer, and we ain't done nothing like what Jack did."

"He had a right," Gabriel insisted.

"Where's your head at?" Jubal said looking at his friend in disbelief. "Jack is just like us. He's white in the skin but he's not free. He's in bondage, every bit as much as you and I be. And folks in bondage ain't got no rights."

"I heard that there was this Massa upriver and over toward Alexandria," Gabriel insisted, "that killed his slave for no good reason and the other Massas took him to court."

"And what did they give him? A fine? I'll bet that's what they did. He strings his nigger up to a tree and cut him up so bad he plumb goes and dies and the other white folks say now ain't that just a fine." Jubal laughed at his own pun.

But Gabriel just stared at him. "What's a fine?" he said finally.

"No mind." Jubal smiled sadly. "This is no fining matter we got on our own hands here."

He took another puff of Gabriel's pipe and blew the smoke out into the darkness. A few stars twinkled in the cool fall night air, but most were hidden by the clouds.

"Seems like a day of trouble is going to end in a night of storming," Gabriel offered.

"It's just the beginning of trouble, twenty-four hours a day," Jubal said, rising to his feet. He wanted to sit up with Luck and help her with Nina in case she needed him.

The heavens opened during the night and the rain pounded on the roof of Jubal and Luck's cabin. It found the several weaknesses in the structure and began an incessant dripping down onto the floorboards of the cabin, where it formed pools that seeped through to the ground below. The force of the rain hitting the roof created a thunderlike roar above their heads.

Luck did not leave Nina's side but drifted off to sleep in the straight-back chair next to the girl's straw bed. She sent Jubal to bed sometime past midnight, but he could not sleep with the pounding of the rain above his head.

It was a morning without a dawn. The pitch black of night gave way to a grayness that signified the arrival of the sun above the eastern horizon somewhere beyond the shrouds that enveloped them. The rains had not ceased.

Jubal lifted the oil paper that covered the window of his cabin. He saw smoke rising from chimneys but no other movement. Obviously no one was planning on going outside, much less working in this weather. With no overseer to challenge their unspoken declaration, the slaves would probably be able to take the day off.

Jubal and Luck spent the morning watching Nina. At midday she awoke from her stupor and Luck fed her some chicken broth. Shortly after that Jubal went to the smokehouse with some corn bread and broth. He found Gilles sitting on one of the shelves, his feet dangling just above the muddy floor of the cabin. He was wet through. The roof had leaked like a sieve during the height of the storm.

Gilles looked at Jubal quizzically. It was clear to the black man that he had many questions to ask about Nina and about his victim's condition, but not only was there a language barrier between them, Jubal had also received no word from the big house all day.

The field boss sat in silence while Gilles wolfed down his meal. When Gilles had finished, Jubal produced Gilles' pipe from his jacket. He took some lit tobacco from his own pipe and placed it in the Acadian's and then offered it to him. Gilles took the smoke deeply into his lungs and then breathed it out. It was good to taste tobacco. The one small comfort of this new life in a new land had been discovering the taste of Virginia tobacco.

Jubal rose. Jubal clapped Gilles on the shoulder, then stepped out into the light drizzle. He closed the smokehouse door and slipped the bar in place to lock it.

Luck was waiting for him in the cabin. She handed him a mug of coffee. Nina lay sleeping on her mat. Her facial swelling had gone down but the bruises had darkened.

"She told me what happened," Luck said.

"Go away, woman," Jubal said in annoyance. "She can't speak English."

"It wasn't Mr. Josephs who did this to her," Luck persisted. Now she had Jubal's full attention. "It was Massa."

"That wasn't the Massa's shirt we found in the cabin," Jubal protested.

"I don't pretend to know how that thing got here," Luck said shaking her head, "but that child pointed to her eye and she covered it with her hand and started weeping. When I understood to say the Massa's name that child got all in a terror and curled herself into a little ball to protect herself. That child was not raped by Mr. Josephs, though I don't suppose he would have minded being next in line. It was the Massa that did it to her."

Jubal listened quietly. He could believe it of Audry. He could believe anything of Audry.

"And we gots more problems," Luck continued. "Mr. Prissy Pants Rufus comes down here from the big house. He says the Massa wants to see you."

Jubal laughed. "Just imagine Rufus the house butler getting his feet all muddy on the road down here. Massa must have told him not to send anybody else." The full import of what he had just said finally dawned on Jubal and his laugh disappeared. He prepared to ruin his own shoes on the trek down the mud road trail to the lawn of the house.

Rufus greeted him at the kitchen door. Katie, his wife and the cook of the house, loomed large behind him. She was enormously fat. Normally she would not have even looked at Jubal. Not only did she consider field niggers, as she called them, beneath her, but there was also bad blood between Luck and herself. She had replaced Luck in the big house after the old master died and young Massa Audry took over. Luck had been his mammy, and a stern one, with the blessing of Massa Audry's parents. Her reward at his coming to his inheritance was a demotion. But Katie seemed relieved to see Jubal at the kitchen door, and now Jubal was convinced there was trouble. First Rufus had come to fetch him and now Katie was acknowledging his existence. Nothing like that had occurred since the Massa came from the cockfight up across the Potomac in Maryland. That night Katie had sent for Luck. It was the only time they had spoken since the mammy's dismissal. She had needed Luck's skills with herbs and medicines to save Audry's life. If he had died, Katie feared that they would all be sold off. Luck had pulled him through, but after that Audry had gone from wild to mean.

"Jubal." Katie took him by the arm. "It's Mr. Josephs. He ain't going to die. Massa brought Doctor Wilson, Massa Wilson's brother, to care for him. They stitched him up; they kept him alive."

"I helped clean him up down below," Rufus offered. "It wouldn't be no proper thing to let a woman do. I tell you, Jubal, there ain't much of him left down there. Just about enough to pee with, that's all."

"But he'll live?" Jubal questioned.

"That's what the doctor says. If no 'fection takes over. Iffen it does, Massa Audry will probably send for Luck hisself," Katie said.

Jubal looked at her quizzically. "What's getting into Massa? I never known him to be too concerned about the overseers or anyone other than himself."

"That's what troubles me," Rufus said. "He's been drinking now since the fight."

"'Keep the pig alive,' he's been yelling from his study, 'I'll knit him a pair of frog balls.' He knows full well that if Mr.

191

Josephs dies the sheriff will step in. But iffen he doesn't and Josephs don't press charges, it be a private matter here on the plantation. I'm afraid this old stink hole is about to have some punishment like we ain't never had before."

Jubal sat down at the kitchen table. Katie offered him several slices of cold ham. Jubal gulped them down greedily. Meat was a luxury in the slave quarters, if fairly common among the house slaves.

"Maybe we should arrange for that white man Jack to get away," Rufus suggested while hovering in the background behind Katie.

"They'd hunt him down. No place to go for the poor fellow. He don't even speak English. In the old days you could go over the mountains, especially if you was black. The Injuns would take you in. But since that Braddock fellow got himself killed the Injuns have been swarming around liftin' scalps, no mind if they white or black."

"It don't matter where he goes," Katie said. "Just so long as he isn't around here. Then the Massa will calm down. Lord knows he's bad enough in normal times, but when he's like this—" She need not finish her sentence. The two understood full well what she meant.

Jubal thought for some moments. "We can't just let him escape. You know the Massa just as good as me. He miss punishing Jack, he'll take it out on Gabriel and Luck and even you and Katie. And especially on me."

"Well, there's got to be another way," Katie implored. "I know the Massa too. There's no way it will stop with Jack."

Jubal decided to tell them the truth. Neither of them said a word when he told them it was their master who had raped the girl. Neither was surprised. Katie even suggested that Audry had planted Josephs's shirt to throw suspicion on the overseer. But Jubal doubted he even cared who was suspected.

Suddenly there was a crashing sound from the dining room. Then the door to the kitchen swung open. Audry stood in the doorway. He had left his jacket somewhere in the house and his white silk shirt was open all the way down his chest. But never before had Jubal seen him without his eye patch. The awful scar that ran from lip to nose began again just under the eye and tore through the empty socket and up across the brow.

"'Scuse me." Audry slurred his words. "I had no idea my slaves were entertaining in the kitchen." He held onto the door frame for support. An empty decanter was in his hand. "It seems I have run out of whiskey. Rufus, would you mind stirring your black ass and getting me some more?"

"Right away, Massa." Rufus pulled some keys out of his pocket and went to the cabinet. He pulled an earthenware jug from the closet and went over to Audry to take the decanter to fill it.

"No need," Audry said and pulled the jug from the black man's hand. "I'll just take the whole thing. That way you can go right on with your party without me disturbing you."

Audry stared at Jubal. His eye focused finally. "Is that you, Jubal?"

"Yes, Massa."

"How is our prisoner?"

"He's locked up in the smokehouse, like Massa Wilson said."

"Good. It seems our Mr. Josephs will live but I think he's used up his usefulness here as an overseer. He's probably used up his usefulness for anything worthwhile." He chuckled and took a swig of whiskey from the jug. Some trickled down his chin onto the lace collar of his shirt. "We'll be shipping Josephs out by the end of the week. He'll take a boat downriver. I don't know where he's from. Carolina man, I think. I suspect he'll end up back there. Can't have men like him around us, not after what he did to that girl. I don't mind black wenches fooling around with white men, but I don't approve of using force."

Jubal merely stared at Audry. Both Katie and Rusus looked down at their feet.

Audry's look was one of defiance. He dared Jubal to say what all four persons in the kitchen knew to be the truth, but nothing was said.

"Well, now we must punish the prisoner, mustn't we?"

"He had some reasons for attacking Mr. Josephs," Jubal offered.

"No slave has any reason for striking his master. None. Never." His voice rose into a high-pitched whine as he spoke.

"Jack ain't no slave," Jubal reminded his master.

"I own him," Audry screamed. "His soul is mine, his body

is mine to do with what I want. He thinks he can all but castrate my overseer just because the man had a little fun with his woman. I own the woman, too. I can do with her what I want anytime I want, and I will."

All three slaves avoided looking into Audry's face, but all three knew it was all but an open admission of the truth.

"I intend to make sure she gets nothing from that ox anymore." Audry turned from them, laughed another high-pitched laugh, and disappeared through the doorway back into the drawing room.

None of the slaves said anything for a moment.

"Maybe he'll sober up," Rufus said finally.

"I hope not," Jubal exclaimed. "You know he be worse sober than drunk. He only talks about things when he's in liquor, but when he sobers up he starts doing the thing he only talk about before."

"Maybe we can keep him drunk," Katie said. Her face broke into a smile for the first time. If Massa Audry got lying-down drunk for a week he'd leave her alone for a change.

"I know what he's hinting at," the sour-faced butler chimed in. "He was telling us Jack's lucky his woman is pregnant 'cause they won't be havin' no more children."

"He won't geld a white man," Jubal said.

"You heard him. I wouldn't put it past him to try. You remember what he did to Nathan. Lots of masters castrate, especially young men, to make an example to the others. Nathan didn't do nothin' wrong but he gelded him just the same."

"This ain't fit talk in front of Katie," Jubal said, wanting to change the subject. Katie's younger sister had been sold off the Audry plantation along with Nathan, and he could see the sadness in the cook's eyes. But Rufus was possessed by the idea.

"I can still remember that boy's scream, and I was up here in the big house and didn't have to view the punishment."

Jubal shook his head. He had been there. He would never forget. He was not going to allow Rufus to force him to relive it. He rose from the table and went to the kitchen door.

"I've got to get back to the quarters," he said.

"You can't go," Rufus complained. "The Massa sent me for you."

"I got a feelin' the Massa told me all he wanted to tell me."

Jubal walked across the lawn away from the mansion house. He turned back and looked at the great house at the top of the small rise overlooking the river. Its great windows looked like so many eyes. They stared down at him from a face of darkened brick. Even the chimneys that framed the face seemed to stand up like giant horns.

"That be the devil's own house," he muttered. He was not going to stand by, or even worse to hold down the victim as he had with Nathan. He had to stop Audry. No one was safe from him. Luck thrown out of her respected position, their own child sold upriver—all Audry's whim.

"Damn him," Jubal said aloud. "I'm goin' to stop him."

Josephs left The Meadows, as Audry had predicted, before the week was over. The rain stopped, but life did not return to normal on the plantation. Jubal took Gabriel and a small crew to the curing shed and finished the stacking, but that was all the work that was done. Gilles remained locked in the smokehouse. He was allowed out twice a day to relieve himself and stretch his legs, but he was not allowed to see Nina, who had not left Luck's cabin since the attack.

Jubal canceled religious services on Sunday morning. No one was much in the mood for a prayer meeting anyway. He spent Sunday sitting in his cabin with Luck and Nina. His silence disturbed Luck. She was used to Jubal's shouts and his loud laughter. When he grew quiet, it was because his troubles were deep. She cooked a possum that Gabriel had given them, along with the last of her collard greens from the garden. She was lucky they had lasted this long.

From past experience, Luck knew that Jubal was trying to make an important decision. He alone could make it. He was the field boss, the preacher, and the leader of his community.

Jubal went to the hearth and poured himself some hot water. He was a great believer in drinking a mug of hot water every day. He sipped on the mug absentmindedly. Then he slammed it down on the table.

"I got to be goin'," he said.

"Where?" Luck asked.

"I be headed over to Massa Wilson's. I'm going to ride the mule over there."

"This is no time for social calls, Jubal. You best stay at home."

Luck knew that Jubal was not contemplating a visit to relatives and friends. She dared not give voice to what she knew Jubal would be doing at Wilson's. To call on white authority to intervene in the business of one's own master was to risk everything they had. And what they had was already little enough.

"I be goin' anyways," Jubal responded.

Luck felt sorry for Gilles and Nina, but what had happened to them was no worse than what had happened to many black folk. Why should they risk all for these two? She rose from her chair and stood before the cabin door.

"What for you doin' this, Jubal? They is white folk. We don't even know them very well. Would they do anything for niggers like us?"

"I thought you liked them."

"I do, but not enough to see you hanging from a tree and to see your backbone laid open for all to see."

"I ain't doing it for them."

"Who then? Certainly not for us."

"I be doing it for Nathan. They took that boy's manhood, then they took his life. They sold Katie's sister someplace where some white man can paw her and where she'll have no family to fall back on, no one to kiss away the hurts. I be doing it for your own babe who they took from us 'spite the fact it took us ten years to make one and we ain't ever made another. They knew we'd be alone when we gets old with no child to give us comfort. I be doin' it for all of them."

Jubal's face contorted as he spoke. He tried to keep the tears from flowing, but without success. Luck's opposition melted with each new argument. She threw her arms around the man and kissed his face. His tears wet her face while mingling with her own.

Nina watched the two of them. She did not know what had happened between them but she suspected it had to do with Gilles and herself. Whatever it was it had frightened them, and her own fear deepened.

* * *

196

Jonas Audry rolled over in his bed. He cursed when he felt the bottle poke into the small of his back. He reached under himself and pulled it out of the covers and held it up in the air. His eye had not yet adjusted to the sunlight. The day had to be pretty far along. He would have to take a whip to Rufus for allowing him to oversleep. He had been trying to make church on these Sunday mornings. Perhaps the rector would say a good word for him with Wilson if he became a regular churchgoer once again. He had not attended regularly since his mother died five years ago. It was she who had insisted that he take communion. If he had shown even the slightest interest in education she would have sent him to college in England so that he could be confirmed by a bishop. There was no Anglican bishop in Virginia or, for that matter, anywhere in America, thank God.

But he had failed his first year at William and Mary and there was no more talk about an English education, and also no confirmation. But he needed a good word from Rector Blair. Wilson was the richest planter in King George County, and his only child was his daughter, Susan. What a catch she was! Unfortunately, this fact had been noted by every bachelor planter in the county. Even more unfortunately, Wilson looked at Jonas Audry with some reservations.

Audry raised the bottle to his lips and threw back his head. "Damn," he said aloud when the effort produced no rum. It had not been empty when he took it to bed with him. He rolled back again onto his side. It was only then that he realized that his bed linen and his nightshirt were soaked and that he reeked like a distillery.

He kicked off the down comforter and stepped out of the high bed to the floor. He staggered for one moment as his head began to pound. He applied pressure to his temples. Sometimes that made him feel better. He walked over to his bureau. There was a basin and a pitcher of water. He poured some of the liquid into the basin and then splashed it onto his face. He looked at himself in the round mirror above the bureau. He touched the scar. Nothing had been the same since that night, since the knife had slashed him.

She was a tavern wench. Without giving her a thought he had bedded her. He probably should have thought more when he discovered she was a virgin, but by then things had gone too far and he didn't want to stop, virgin or not. In fact, the discovery stimulated him all the more. He could never forget the fear that gripped him later when he looked up into the black beard and red burning eyes. The wench was gone but the bed was still warm where she lay. He was pinned down. His heart raced with the terror of a childhood nightmare. He tried to sit up, but his arms were held by pressure he could not see. He could feel the cold air and he shivered. He felt someone grab him roughly. He screamed in fear. A knife flashed briefly before his eyes; then there was a searing pain and blood. The fear turned to anguish. Blood was everywhere, filling his nostrils and his mouth. He felt the weight release him and the bearded face spoke to him.

"You're an ugly one now. That scar will guarantee that anyone who does it with you is a slut. Any normal wench will faint away at the sight of your ugliness. You'll still have the desire, you bastard, but you'll have to pay for your love from now on. No more pretty face to win the girls." Then he was gone.

That had been five years ago, shortly after his mother's death. The barber in Norfolk had stitched his face after removing his eye. Audry told everyone that he had been in a brawl over a gambling debt. But it was as the bearded one said it would be: he was unbelievably ugly. But the Beard had been wrong, too. He had not paid for his love these last five years. Not once. Nor did he wait to find out if the woman thought him desirable. He had simply taken what he wanted without asking.

Susan's return from Philadelphia eight months ago had changed some of that. She had spent a year away living with Wilson's sister and had come back a strikingly beautiful woman.

At first he had hesitated to approach her, but since they were neighbors it was not difficult to meet with her. Since that first encounter he was a constant suitor. He began to believe that she had some feeling for him. And why not? He could be truly charming if he wanted to be.

Then he had seen the French girl in Williamsburg. He had gone to all the trouble to arrange for this shipload with Cousin Hastings. He had meant it for profit. But then he saw her and profit gave way to lust. He had been sitting in his carriage with Wilson and his daughter. First there had been the uproar about his black servant, the troublemaker he had castrated. It was mortifying to have Ludlow step in, a man who despised him and had some influence with the Wilson family. But all that had faded before the sight of the brown-haired French beauty. It mattered little to him that she was pregnant or that her husband was the size of an ox. He even forgot about Susan, who was sitting across from him in the carriage. He didn't care; he had to have the French girl. Claiming that it was the man's obvious strength he bid for, he purchased Gilles' and Nina's contracts. And then he forced her. She had enjoyed it. He knew she had. They all did. At heart they were all sluts, and all the protests and the fighting were a sham—a sham to hide what they really were. Then Josephs, the fool, had taken the blame, and the vengeance of that ox had levelled the wrong man. No matter, the ox would be destroyed, just as the black buck Nathan had been after he tried to avenge Audry's affair with his cook's younger sister. He chuckled to himself when he thought of how he had taken care of the black man. Now it was the Frenchman's turn.

"Rufus," he called out. There was some scurrying in the hallway. He heard the patter of bare feet running on the hardwood floor outside the door. "Got his little spies on duty," Audry said to himself.

A few moments later he heard the sound of shoes. The door opened and the butler entered. Audry had stepped out of his nightshirt and was washing his arms and chest. He could see Rufus in the mirror. The man wrinkled up his nose as he entered the bedroom.

"It's only a little stale rum mixed with sweat and perhaps a fart or two," Audry joked.

The servant went to the window and opened it.

"Lay out some work clothes for me, Rufus."

The black man stiffened. The Massa only wore work clothes when he planned to enter the slave quarters to mete out discipline. Audry began stropping his razor on a wide strap of leather. The sound of it made Rufus shiver. It reminded him of what his master had in mind for the Frenchman.

"You shave me, Rufus," Audry commanded.

The black man finished laying out the clothes, then brought

a stool from across the room for Audry. Rufus mixed lather and applied it to the white man's face. There was several days' worth of beard, but the razor was very sharp. Rufus scraped the whiskers from his master's neck. Almost every time he performed this service he wondered what would happen if the razor should accidentally slip and sever a vital vein. But he really did not have to wonder. He had seen slaves hanged before for less.

Rufus completed the shave without a mishap. Audry quickly donned the old clothes.

"You run downstairs and tell all the house servants they are to go down to the quarters and witness punishment."

"Yes, Massa," Rufus said without looking at Audry. Then he turned toward the door to leave.

"Oh, and Rufus . . ."

"Yes, Massa."

"Make sure the large hunting knife is just as sharp as the razor."

Rufus merely stared at him.

"There is a certain Frenchman who will not bless you if you leave it dull. And, Rufus, make sure someone sets up a fire and iron to stop the bleeding. Don't want to lose a good field hand."

The slaves assembled outside Jubal's cabin. A large wooden table with four straps attached was set up. Most of the slaves stayed as far away from the table as possible. They had seen it used before on one of their own.

Audry arrived on horseback. He remained in the saddle and looked about for Jubal.

"Where's the field boss?" he called out.

There was no response.

"Luck, where are you, my old mammy?"

The black woman appeared at the door of her own cabin. She looked at her former charge and did not respond.

"Where's your man?" Audry asked.

"Out in the fields looking over what he's doing tomorrow."

"We have some harvesting to do this afternoon. You'd think the field boss would be right on top of it like the last time."

Luck did not respond.

"What about you, mammy? Aren't you going to watch?"

"I got's that man's wife in here. I thinks I better stay with her and keep her away from the devil's work that you be doing out there."

Several of the slaves gasped at her audacity.

"It's not the devil's work, woman. It is only justice. An eye for an eye."

Luck turned away in disgust. She looked at Nina, who stood horrified in the shadows of the house. What could have frightened her? She could not yet have learned of her husband's fate. And then Luck knew. She rushed to Nina's side and held onto her.

Gabriel went to the smokehouse. He carried a bottle of distilled liquor with him. It was the least he could do for the Frenchman. Gilles saw the glum look on Gabriel's face and instantly understood that the waiting was over. He would be punished. The bottle of rum was appreciated, even if it did mean his punishment would be painful. He had not expected anything else. It probably also meant that Josephs had not died. If he had, he expected he would be hanged, but probably not without a hearing. The English prided themselves on their system of justice.

He drank half the bottle in one gulp. It burned all the way down into his stomach. He offered the bottle to Gabriel. Gabriel took a swig and handed the rest back to Gilles. The Acadian saw Gabriel's hand shake. He was clearly frightened. That did nothing to steady Gilles' nerves. He took another enormous gulp.

Gabriel opened the door of the smokehouse and motioned to Gilles to step outside. Gilles was surprised to find all the slaves assembled. They were strangely silent, and men who had greeted him last week with open friendliness could not now bring themselves to look him in the face.

He walked back toward Jubal's cabin with Gabriel bringing up the rear. Audry was sitting atop his horse. He carried a pistol in his hand. He called out to Gabriel, and the black man and several others grabbed Gilles and twisted his arms behind his back. He was lifted bodily and lowered onto the wooden table. His wrists were strapped in place. When he felt his feet being strapped, too, Gilles became frightened and began to kick out. He caught one of the men and sent him flying away from the table. He felt the stinging sharpness of a blow, then remembered nothing.

Audry had dismounted and used the butt of his pistol on the Frenchman's head. The slaves quickly strapped his legs in place and then backed off. Audry was about to give his signal to awaken the prisoner and continue with the punishment when he heard the sound of hoofbeats. He turned to see his neighbor Colonel Wilson galloping at breakneck speed toward him.

"I command you to halt this sham, Audry," Wilson called from a distance.

Jonas stared at his neighbor in disbelief. As Wilson reined in his horse in front of Audry, the animal rose in the air on his hind legs.

"What is the meaning of this, Colonel?" Audry protested.

"I could ask you the same question."

"I'm disciplining my slave," Audry responded.

"Ah, yes, your favorite form of discipline."

"It is not an uncommon practice in Virginia," Audry said defensively.

"I regret that I must acknowledge the truth of your statement, but I must also point out to you that the man you wish to geld is not your slave. He is a white man, by God. It's bad enough that you mutilate your own slaves, but there are laws against this sort of thing."

"He mutilated my overseer every bit as much as I intend to mutilate him," Audry exclaimed loudly.

"Then have him arrested and bring him to court."

"It's a private matter. A matter of discipline here on my plantation. You have no right to interfere." Out of the corner of his eye Audry saw Black Edgar, the mule, with Jubal leading him, heading for the barn. So it was the field boss who had gone after help. Well, he would pay.

"I have every right, sir," Wilson replied. "If I hear of any harm coming to this man, I'll have you in court. And I would take it kindly, sir, if you would no longer pay court to my daughter. I will marry her to no one but a gentleman." He turned his horse and rode away.

Audry looked as if he had been slapped in the face. He watched the disappearing form almost in desperation.

"Release the Frog," he called out in a monotone. "And, Gabriel, see to it that Jubal takes his place in the smokehouse."

They worked it out together, the four of them in the smokehouse, while Gabriel stood guard outside. It was difficult for them to communicate, but after hours of trying, Luck and Jubal managed to convince Gilles and Nina that they had to run away. Audry would come out of his new stupor before long, and they could not afford to wait. They would leave that very night.

For Luck and Jubal it meant leaving the only home they had ever known. But Audry was insane, and they could no longer safely remain subject to his whim and his wrath. With Gabriel's help and with a collection of food taken up by Big Annie, Luck had loaded down Black Edgar with as many of their things as they could manage. They decided that they would pretend that Gilles and Nina were a young couple from New York settling in the valley of Virginia to the west. New York was as far away as either Luck or Jubal could imagine, unless Africa was farther away than New York. Most folks would understand why Gilles and Nina spoke gibberish if you told them they were from New York. Jubal and Luck were to be their slaves, and their slaves would do all the talking for them. They had not been able to explain much of their plans to Gilles and Nina, but the young couple did understand the urgency and the risks that Luck and Jubal were taking. Gilles was deeply grateful to them. Jubal had saved him from a pain from which he could never have recovered, and Luck was willing to give up everything she had ever known. He realized that she did it to protect Jubal, but Jubal would need no protection if he had not risked all for Gilles and Nina.

Nina had told him about Audry's attacking her. She seemed even more burdened and fearful now. He shook his head in dismay. She had every reason to be even more frightened. He had vowed to protect her and ever since that promise she had suffered one humiliation after another. The only consolation one could draw from all of their pain was that she clung even more to him now than before.

The Frenchman was sorry that Josephs had suffered for Audry's crime. He deeply wished he could settle the score with Jonas Audry. Perhaps in time.

Jubal signaled and Gabriel swung open the smokehouse door. The fugitives took off into the night. Luck held Black Edgar's bridle and followed Jubal down the road toward the great house. Gilles and Nina brought up the rear.

They had to make it to the road that ran along the river. They would follow it to the west. As they passed the house most of the giant eyes were darkened. There was a light on the second floor in the front. They knew it was Jonas Audry's room. But he would be oblivious to their escape. Not so Rufus and the other house slaves. Every black on the plantation knew the escape was in progress. All went about their business as usual, but all their thoughts and secret hopes went with those in flight. In the minds of all they were like the Holy Family fleeing into Egypt to escape the sword of the evil king.

The dirt road gave way to yellow gravel. Edgar's hooves striking ground sounded like an alarm to the fugitives. But they need not have feared. No unfriendly ears were listening for the sound.

The mule, angry to be taken from the comfort of the barn, bellowed once. Jubal would dearly have loved to whack the beast, but he dared not—not with Luck holding his nose. But again no enemy heard Edgar's call.

Another half mile and they would leave The Meadows and cross the line onto the Wilson plantation. After that they would pass the village of Port Royal on the other side of the river. Jubal knew a trail that passed Port Royal beyond view of any of the villagers and continued on to Fredricksburg. Beyond there it reached into the northwestern sources of the Rappahannock. There they would find freedom.

CHAPTER TEN

November 1755

Jubal opened his eyes before the sun rose. He had never been this far west. He had visited his son at Massa Washington's place near Alexandria on the Potomac, but that was several days to the north of where they now camped. Luck stirred in her sleep next to him. He looked at her face—a face that he had loved for so many years. There were some wrinkles there now in the corners of her eyes and around the mouth, and her hair had grayed considerably. On occasion they spoke harshly to each other, but it was a harshness born of confidence—a confidence that stemmed from years of living together and a confidence that no young lovers could ever possess. He looked over to where Gilles and Nina lay. Those two certainly lacked confidence in each other. Even in their sleep they made no contact.

The sun would be up shortly. He dared not light a fire. Audry must be looking for them now, three days out of Port Royal. He would probably strike out toward Alexandria, knowing that Jubal and Luck had family there. But when he did not discover their whereabouts he would backtrack and search along the river. They had avoided the villages and plantations along the river as best they could, but some had seen them. Two whites and two blacks traveling together with a mule would be a sight people would remember. Audry wouldn't rest until he brought them back to The Meadows. No planter, even a sane and kind one, could afford to allow his slaves to believe that escape was possible.

Gilles stirred and then sat up, resting on his elbow. "Monsieur Zhubel," he called out softly.

"It's time to rise," Jubal said and rose to his feet.

The mule was tethered to a tree several yards away. All the grass in the vicinity was gone now and he let his hunger be known by an angry bellow.

"Damn that Edgar. I believe he's got it in for me. Planning to tell the whole world where I be. Why, you evil-hearted bastard, Audry gets his hands on you and he'll skin you alive just for the fun of it."

"You leave that dumb creature be, Jubal," Luck said as she awoke.

"Dumb creature is right," Jubal complained. "I'll take him over closer to the riverbank. He can find some good grass there."

"Don't you go near him. All you do is rile him up."

She untethered the mule and stroked his nose. The animal grew silent and walked with Luck to the river's edge.

Nina, awakened by Edgar's noise, opened the leather saddlebag and took out corn bread and some cooked chicken, the last of their food. She parceled out a minimum to each of them, with extra portions for Gilles and Jubal, and then returned the rest to the saddlebag.

"We will need more food by tomorrow," she said worriedly to Gilles.

Luck returned from the river's edge where she had tethered Black Edgar and heard the exchange between the two Acadians.

"You be worried about our food supply. You just leave that up to Jubal. The man has a nose for food, and he is some kind of wizard when it comes to gettin' his hands on it."

Both Gilles and Nina smiled at her, not knowing what it was she talked to them about. But it never seemed to stop her. She seemed to think she knew exactly what they said and assumed that they could comprehend her.

The sky was growing lighter, but there were heavy clouds on the western horizon. It was time to be moving on. They ate their breakfast as they walked along the road. Within an hour Nina grew tired and Jubal hoisted her up onto Black Edgar's back. The mule snorted and complained about the extra burden and twisted his head around to see who it was that was responsible for it. Just before noon they reached the junction of the Hazel and the Rappahannock, and after that the road began to disappear. Soon it was reduced to a narrow path. They were moving beyond the normal roads of travel. The great Valley of Virginia, which lay beyond the Blue Ridge ahead of them, connected more easily with Baltimore and Philadelphia by the wagon roads running north and south than it did with Williamsburg and Tidewater Virginia to the east.

And in this valley most farmers worked their own fields without benefit of slaves. At least that was the word that spread from plantation to plantation—white folks farming without slaves. Jubal wanted to see for himself. True, there had been poor white farmers in the hinterland beyond the Rappahannock, but they were no-account poor trash scratching an existence from the soil. Their lives were barely as rich as the slaves'. But word had come to the shanties about rich white farms in the lush valleys to the west where men planted wheat, barley, and corn and not tobacco.

The clouds grew thicker and blacker in the west. Occasional streaks of lightning split the sky and the distant roll of thunder sounded like far-off heavenly cannon.

Luck pointed toward an old curing shed several hundred yards off the path. It leaned dangerously to the east like some sapling bent by constant blasts of wind. It had long been abandoned but it had a roof of sorts. She grabbed Edgar's reins and began to move off the path into the partially overgrown field.

The lightning cracked once again and the mule, terrified by the sound, nearly broke from Luck's grasp. But she held on. Gilles, fearful that the animal might bolt, lifted Nina lightly from its back and held her in his arms. He would have carried her the rest of the way just for the pleasure holding her body gave to him. Her legs strained to reach the ground and so he set her gently on her feet.

"I can walk," she shouted at him to be heard over the wind that raced through the leafless branches of the trees.

The shed had no door, only hinges where a door once existed.

They drove Edgar through the opening. Once inside, they saw that the gloom was pierced by daylight streaming through gaps in the roof. But the far corner of the shed was almost pitch-black. In that portion the roof was intact.

"We wait it out here," Jubal said to Luck.

She removed the bedding from the mule and spread the blankets and quilt onto the dirt floor.

The four fugitives then parceled out their lunch and remained huddled together while the storm raged about them. The wind blew fiercely through gaps in the walls but very little rain fell.

Jubal sat with his back to the wooden wall of the shed. It was as if he were lending his weight to keeping it upright against the gale that surrounded them. He smiled at his wife.

"I knows how Jonah felt in the belly of the fish," he said laughingly.

Gilles looked at Jubal with some concern. He feared that Jubal was speaking of Jonas Audry. He wished he could ask the black man if he had seen any signs of pursuit. He began to relax as Jubal continued to talk. It was clear that Jubal had let down his guard and was enjoying this unexpected respite in the middle of the day.

"I'm sure glad I feel like Jonah and not like Noah. Lawd, keep the rains away," he said, looking up at the hole in the roof.

"Much as I love your preaching, Jubal," Luck teased him, "please don't preach to me now."

"Woman," he said with mock indignation, "you don't want to hear the Gospel preached?"

"'Tain't Sunday and I don't got me going-to-meeting clothes on."

Jubal looked defeated. "I'm mighty glad the only ones to hear your disrespect for the preacher of the word is two heathens who wouldn't know the word even if de Lawd dropped it all around them like cow droppings in the barnyard."

Luck giggled at Jubal's analogy. "But they be no heathens, brother," she said to her husband. "They be Catholics."

"What's a Catholic?" he asked.

"Don't rightly know, 'cept I knew a nigger once who came from Maryland. His Massa baptized him a Catholic. He said that the Massa made him go every Sunday to a secret meeting. Nobody there talks but the preacher and he talks a language nobody can understand. And they eats the flesh and drinks some blood."

"I told you they be heathens 'less they come from Da Home. I heard my pappy talking about killing chickens and drinking the blood there."

"Look at that child," Luck said as she watched Nina's eyes close and her shoulders sag. "She be plumb tuckered out."

Nina started to fall backward. Startled, she sat bolt upright. Gilles tried to make her lean against his shoulder but she moved away. She would force herself to stay awake.

"I don't think these Catholics think too much about behaving like a man and a woman either," Jubal remarked as he watched the two Acadians.

"Hush," Luck said. "Those two be more private about things like that than we are."

"They don't know what I'm talking about," Jubal insisted. "Do you remember hearing any sounds from their side of the blanket?"

"The girl's with child," Luck protested.

"That never stopped us," Jubal laughed.

"Long as I've known you"—Luck blushed as she spoke—"you've never had no control over that tool of yours, preacher or no."

"But you've had control of it," he teased her.

"No more of that talk. You better off going back to preaching."

The winds died down as the storm passed overhead. Nina finally fell asleep, her head resting against the rough pine of the shed wall. Jubal and Luck lay down together and grew silent as they stared out of the gaps in the roof. The low bank of clouds seemed to weigh heavily upon them. Their darkest fears rose from the depths of their souls, and the specter of Jonas Audry haunted them.

Gilles' thoughts during these moments of quiet went back to the image of his mother and father. A few short months ago at the summer festival they had been in the prime of their powers, masters of their home, masters of their children, models for the whole of Port Hebert, and now they were gone. His mother dead, his father broken. How could a whole way of life have been so quickly destroyed? How could he and Nina now be fugitives from a monster and totally dependent on the good will of two black people who themselves were the property of that same monster? And how could it all have happened in such a short time?

The mule started to complain.

"Go feed that pest," Jubal said to his wife.

"I'm tired of looking after old Edgar. You go and take him back outside to graze. The storm's almost gone now."

Jubal sighed. He rose to his feet and clucked to the old mule.

"Here you go, you useless old piece of shit," he called out. "It's time to fill your sagging belly."

He never saw what hit him. The mule kicked out his hind legs and slashed Jubal in the chest. There was the cracking sound of bone splintering. Both Jubal and Edgar shrieked, Jubal in pain and Edgar in triumph.

As the black man crumbled to the floor, Gilles jumped to his feet and quickly pulled him out of range of Edgar's continued kicks.

Luck ran to control the braying animal. Nina awoke, suddenly alert. She cried out when she saw the blood trickle from the corner of Jubal's mouth.

"What's happened?" she called to Gilles.

"It's the mule. He finally got Zhubel. He let down his guard and the animal kicked him in the chest. Some ribs must be crushed. Why else would he bleed like that?"

"Oh, my God, how can we help him?"

Gilles opened Jubal's shirt. Huge bruises were already spreading across the brown skin of his chest. Luck rushed to his side after she had shoved, pushed, and kicked Edgar outside. She fell to her knees and scooped Jubal's head to her breast. He was unconscious.

"Listen to me, Jubal. You wake up now. Do you hear me? Oh, sweet Jesus, help your preacher man. Why did I make him go near that beast? They've always been hating one another."

She began to rock to and fro, keeping her husband's face nestled in her breasts.

Gilles took her by the shoulders and steadied her. If the man's ribs were broken he should lie still. That much he had learned from his mother the *traiteur*. Luck was crying. The tears streamed down her face.

Jubal's eyes fluttered open. "Well, I'll be damned," he said, gritting his teeth, "damn his ugly soul. He finally did it. He finally did me in."

"Lie still," Gilles said in French to his friend. Jubal lay quiet for some moments. Only the sound of Luck and Nina weeping broke the silence. He sighed and then closed his eyes again. Luck began to wail.

"Hush your face, woman," Jubal said in anger. "I ain't dead. Don't you start your weeping and shouting before my time has come. But I think my journey to 'liverance is just about over."

Gilles took the old gray jacket that Gabriel had given him for the prayer meeting and placed it under Jubal's head. The black man thanked him. Nina wiped the blood from his chin. He was no longer bleeding from the mouth. Luck sat beside him looking helpless.

Before long Jubal drifted off to sleep with Luck holding his hand in hers. She knew what Jubal meant about their journey being over. They could travel no longer. All they could do was sit in this shed and wait for Massa Audry to find them. It would kill Jubal if he were moved at this time. But she also knew that Gilles and Nina could go ahead. It would probably be fatal for both of them if they did not continue their flight. She stroked Jubal's forehead with her red kerchief and then spoke to Nina.

"Child, you gots to go on without us."

Nina stared at her.

"You can't wait here for the beast. No one knows better than you that my baby Jonas is a beast."

Still Nina did not respond.

"What's wrong with you, girl? We've understood each other up until now. Why are you suddenly becoming dense? You hear me. Answer me."

Finally Nina turned to Gilles, hoping he might have perceived some glimmer of meaning from the black woman's words.

"O Lawd," Luck prayed, "everything is just falling apart." She put her head down on the gray coat next to Jubal and began to weep silently.

Gilles and Nina watched her cry herself to sleep. Nina covered both of them with an extra blanket that the black couple had lent them when they first came to The Meadows.

"Is Zhubel going to live?" she asked Gilles.

"I'm not sure. Perhaps if he is allowed to rest here."

"But if we stay here *he* will find us and he'll kill you, Gilles, and to me he'll..." She could not complete her thought without the horror of that afternoon overwhelming her.

Gilles remained quiet a few more minutes. "I think we must leave here," he said finally.

"But you said Zhubel could not be moved."

"We have to leave them behind."

Nina sat back on her haunches. What Gilles suggested seemed like betrayal.

"Look, Nina," he continued, "if we remain here, Audry will catch all four of us. These two blacks have been with him a long time. Maybe he'll punish them, maybe he won't. But they are finished. They cannot continue the journey. If we stay behind, we both have a good idea of our fates. I think we should go on without Zhubel and Luck."

Nina looked at him dubiously.

Gilles continued. "We can leave them some food and blankets and the mule in case they need to move. Only Luck can control that beast anyway. If Zhubel gets better they can use the mule to get on with their escape."

"Can *we* make it?"

"We'll just keep heading west. Soon we'll come to where there is no slavery. That much I have understood from our friends. We will be safe there. Then we can plan to get back to French territory."

"Back to Acadia, to Port Hebert?"

"At least we can begin to think of how we can return," he responded.

"All right. Let's not wait any longer. If we travel by night

212

we won't have to meet with people and give ourselves away. There can't be too many French-speaking travelers in this part of Virginia, especially with a war going on between them and France. And by now word about us must have circulated in the countryside."

"Come." Gilles rose to his feet and offered Nina his hand.

She looked down upon the older couple wistfully. "I hate to leave them behind."

"They'll be all right," Gilles assured her. He gathered a few of their belongings and a small quantity of corn bread and two fried chicken legs.

"The rain has stopped. Let's get going before they awake."

"But we're deserting them and Zhubel is hurt."

"Nina, our lives are at stake!"

She nodded almost absentmindedly without being able to take her eyes from Luck and Jubal. Then slowly she stepped toward the doorless entryway of the shack. Gilles was already outside. Nina turned abruptly and joined him in the gathering dusk.

As soon as Nina was gone, Luck opened her eyes. The two children were on their way, for that she was grateful. She probably could have used their help with her injured husband, but she could never have asked them. The sacrifice they would have had to make was too great.

"Jubal," she whispered to her husband, "you awake?"

He grunted at her.

"Are you going to make it?"

"I ain't preached my last yet, Sister Luck," he said, still in pain. "And when I recovers we is going to have us a great big feast and the main course is going to be mule. Fried mule, boiled mule, broiled mule, and even baked mule pie." He laughed but it hurt too much. The laughter gave way to coughing.

"Hush, my lover," Luck cooed in his ear. "Don't you lose no more strength. You and I has got a long way to go yet."

They followed the river closely through the night. Its twists and turns added extra miles to their journey toward the mountains, but its slow rippling sound was sweet to the ears of the two strangers stumbling along in the black darkness. The stars blinked in the cold frosty fall air. There was no

213

moon, and the darkness of the sky made the pinpricks of light all the brighter. Gilles and Nina clung to each other. Gilles studied the river embankment to avoid falling, while Nina held onto his arm. She turned her head back frequently, expecting at any moment to hear the sounds of pursuit, the baying of hounds and the shouts of men. But there was no sound other than the soft swish of the river current as it swirled past muddy embankments.

They walked for hours in silence. Nina struggled to keep the pace set by Gilles. She knew it was important to put as much distance as possible between themselves and Jubal and Luck before the two slaves were discovered. And they would be discovered. She did not know what would happen to them, but her instincts told her it would not be as bad as what would happen to Gilles and herself if they were apprehended by Audry. She shuddered when she thought of him, his clammy hands touching her.

"What's wrong?" Gilles asked. "Are you cold?"

"No," she answered. "Where will the river take us?"

After some moments of silence he responded. "To the mountains and then the Great Valley where there are no slaves."

They had come several miles before the sky lightened in the east. They did not notice it. Their eyes were riveted in front of them, toward the west, toward freedom.

It was not until the sun was already above the eastern horizon that they actually saw the mountains ahead of them, to the right and the left. Directly in front of them there was no black mass on the horizon. The river had led them to the Chester Gap.

Shortly after that the river itself disappeared into several tiny streams. Gilles quickened their pace. With no stream to follow, his course led directly to the gap between the hills, and they made rapid progress. Before lunchtime and after two brief rests they were west of the hills and into the valley of the Shenandoah River. They came to the south fork of that stream and followed its course northward.

The sun warmed the chill air, and by midafternoon both Gilles and Nina were sweating. The man could tell by the stiffness in his own legs that the hours of trudging had probably overtaxed the woman's strength. Only a few days before she had been beaten and badly abused, and in only a few weeks it would be her time to deliver. Yet she had not complained.

The Shenandoah broadened as a branch joined it from the west. It would be difficult for them to cross. Whatever shelter they found would have to be found on the east bank unless they discovered an easy ford or, less likely, a boat.

Gilles' love for Nina was augmented by a growing admiration for her strength and courage. He could not have known that Nina had grown numb hours before. She placed one foot ahead of the other only by instinct now. Earlier she had forced herself by sheer willpower, commanding her legs to push forward. Now her mind was blank. If Gilles had thought to speak to her she could not have responded.

They followed no path, only the riverbank. Nina went first. She pushed aside the branches of the bushes. Earlier she had held them so that they did not snap back at Gilles. Now she no longer cared and he was beyond noticing. Her feet no longer pained her, although blisters had formed and broken earlier, leaving her linen stockings fetid and damp and her skin raw and swollen. She wasn't sure she'd be able to walk the next day. But Gilles had staked all on reaching the eastern portion of the valley in a single last march, and they had made it.

It was Gilles who called a halt. The muscles in his calf had cramped and he could move no further. His legs gave out and crumpled under him.

"Nina," he called out to her. She walked several more paces forward. "Nina," he shouted again.

She turned and the look of surprise finally broke the blank expression of her face.

"I'm done for," Gilles sighed. "Come help me over to the river. We'll make a camp."

She offered her arm to help him rise again. The agony showed on his face as he tried to straighten his legs. He leaned heavily on her and once again streaks of pain rose from the soles of her feet up into her legs. They reached the bank of the Shenandoah and collapsed at the river's edge.

"Rub my legs. My God, how they hurt," Gilles complained.

Nina tried to knead the knotted muscles back to normal, with little success. But the pain lessened and Gilles himself

was able to take over from her. Nina removed one of her
beaten up leather shoes. Her gray-white stocking was covered with a wet brown stain. She gasped as she tried to peel
the stocking off of her foot. As she did she opened sores, and
fresh red blood began to flow freely. Gilles' eyes widened
with disbelief. He took her into his arms and held onto her.

"My love," he whispered, "how you have suffered."

She started to weep with pain.

"Come," he said to her, "let me help you with the other
shoe."

"Gently," she admonished him as he slipped the second
shoe off of her foot. The second stocking was stained the same
color. He removed it carefully. The pain was so great that she
began to cry again.

Gilles then undid his own shoes and stockings. His feet
were blistered too, but none of the blisters had broken. Both
of them put their feet into the cool waters of the river.

Nina gasped at first but as the coolness enveloped her sores
it numbed the pain and took the heat from them. Her tears
stopped and she began to relax. As she did she began to
notice the aching muscles, muscles that had numbed miles
back down the path and that rest had brought back to life.

"Tonight will be cold. Even though we are in a valley, we
are at a high elevation and the air will be cold once the sun
disappears," Gilles told her. "We'll need a fire. We'll warm
our chicken and we'll warm our bodies."

"Won't it make it easier for...him...to find us?" she
asked. The terror that Audry raised in her made it impossible
for her to use his name.

"We've come a long way today," he responded. "If Audry
has caught our scent, Jubal and Luck will be his first discovery.
It is a discovery that will delay him. If I know our friends,
they will try to throw him off the trail. We deserve a hot meal
and a warm sleep."

Gilles alone was able to regain his feet and look for
firewood. He soon had a blaze under way. Nina found a short
branch and thrust the end of it through the two chicken legs.
She placed the broken pieces of corn bread on a stone near
the flames. Before long they had warmed and eaten their
dinner.

The sun set behind Massanutten Mountain to the west and

darkness descended quickly. The flames of the fire illuminated the area several feet around them, but then all was blackness. The pain in their feet had lessened. But it was clear to both, without their having to communicate, that neither was in condition to continue the journey the next day. But they were too tired to care. Warmed by the heat of the fire both of them fell into a sleep of exhaustion.

CHAPTER ELEVEN

Blue Ridge Mountains, November and December 1755

The darkness enveloped him. He was lost somewhere between consciousness and sleep when he felt a pressure in his temples and a painful pounding in his head. More and more the pressure became concentrated on his forehead. It was as if someone were pressing a metal rod downward into his head. And then suddenly he was awake. Someone was pressing the muzzle of a musket on his forehead.

"Don't move a muscle," a voice said in a strangely accented English.

Gilles needed no translation. He swallowed hard to little effect. His throat was completely dry.

"Who are you and what are you doing setting fire to my woods?" the presence looming above him demanded.

"Je ne parle pas anglais," Gilles said forcefully.

"A Frenchy. Jeremy, these people are French."

"What are they doing here?" another voice said.

Gilles' captor suddenly switched to French. "What are subjects of His Most Christian Majesty doing in the middle of bloody German George's western valley?" The French had a peculiar accent but it nevertheless warmed Gilles' heart,

219

especially since it included a derogatory mention of the English king. His mind ran ahead. Could they possibly have stumbled into a French war party come on a raid in the heart of Virginia? He tried to look over at Nina but the musket barrel bore down harder into his forehead.

"Don't make any false moves, Frenchy."

Gilles' hopes sank. The constant reference to him as "Frenchy" clearly indicated that his captors were not French. But who were they? He decided he had nothing to lose.

"Monsieur," he addressed the form that loomed above him beyond the length of the musket barrel. "We are French people from Acadia and have been transplanted against our wills to Virginia. We are peaceful farmers, and all we desire is help to get back to our homes."

"Jeremy," the voice said in English, "the ox here says they are 'Cadians. I've heard what the bloody English have done to these people. I think they'll be a wee bit harmless." He reverted to French. "You. I'm going to let you stand up now. Don't try anything foolish. If you're telling me the truth we may share a common enemy and the good Lord may have brought you to a place where you can be helped. You heard me now. Stand up slowly."

Gilles felt the pressure of the gun lessening. He had no intention of attempting any tricks. He just hoped the trigger finger of his captor was as steady as his voice. He barely noticed the pinpoints of pain that burst on his feet when he rose.

His eyes adjusted now. He looked at the figure in front of him. The man was grotesque. His belly protruded from the bottom of the breastbone to the beltline. But Gilles' eyes continued downward, amazed by the garment the man wore. It was a skirt in plaid that hung down to his knees. Gilles' gaze then went to the man's jovial round face, with its multiple chins and eyes that seemed to twinkle amid all that flesh.

"What's the matter with you? You've never seen a true son of St. Andrew before?"

Gilles had no idea what the man was talking about. He looked over at Nina. Her face was twisted in shock at being awakened with a gun pointed at her.

"Who are you?" Gilles finally asked.

"I just told you. My name is Duncan McGriff. All this farmland along the south fork is mine, purchased from Virginians who got it all from the Stuarts and therefore got it honestly. Even if the Hanoverian pig who sits on the British throne claims jurisdiction over us all, we all know who the true king of the Scots is. He lives in your motherland and he is treated with as much kindness as you shall be in my home."

McGriff had four young men with him as well as an older man, whom he addressed as Jeremy. This last was a short man with thick steel-gray hair and very little to say, which was just as well because McGriff rarely shut up.

McGriff led the party along the path beside the river for about a quarter of a mile. Then he struck a course away from the stream. Within a few minutes they emerged from the woods onto a dirt road. The moon came from behind clouds and illuminated the rolling hills all about them. There were fields of cornstalks, silent and ghostly. A slight breeze sent a rustling through the dead leaves of the already harvested plants. Farther along the road the stalks had been cut down and staked in bundles to prepare the fields for next spring's planting. The country sloped gently upward toward the Blue Ridge, which Nina and Gilles had crossed earlier in the day. They crossed one knoll and the road bent to the left. Before them, bathed in moonlight, was a two-storey log house. Beyond it was a large barn and silo. Split rail fences surrounded the house lot, with stone fences dividing pasture land from corn, wheat, and barley acreage, which lay in square patterns up the slope toward the high ridge and down away from the house.

The road ran right up to the front gate, where it stopped abruptly. There was nothing beyond McGriff's property except open pasture and the high rounded humps of the Blue Ridge.

They walked single file with McGriff leading the way. He carried his musket carelessly over his shoulder, and his bald head shone in the moonlight.

Nina's spirits had lifted sharply. Her feet still hurt and the abrupt awakening had terrified her. Yet when they came upon the farmhouse, the setting seemed so familiar and so comforting. The only thing lacking was the smell of the salt water breeze and the sound of the surf beyond the salt marsh.

The door swung open, and the glow from the fireplace within flooded the front yard. A young girl of about eighteen stepped into the yard.

"Is that you, McGriff?" she called out.

"None other," he responded with a laugh. "Do you have left any of that fine leg of mutton you served up for supper last night?"

"You must be joshing me, McGriff. With all of you men to feed how could a single leg survive supper? Perhaps a hindquarter would do. Or maybe a leg of the ram himself, then maybe I'd have me some leftovers."

"You're a beautiful woman, Lucy, but you don't know how to answer a man's questions with a simple aye or nay."

He opened the gate for Gilles and Nina.

"This young maid with the rambling tongue is my own dear wife, Lucy McGriff," he said in French.

Gilles looked at the bald-headed little man in the skirt in surprise. He was at least fifty years old. At first Gilles thought he had misheard and that she was his daughter, but when the Scot reached over and threw his arms around the girl and pulled her to him he knew he had heard right.

"And these, my friends, with the exception of the weasel who calls himself Jeremy, are my sons, Angus, Charles, Andrew, and Robbie, my baby."

Nina looked totally confused and decided that the Scot's strange French accent was beyond comprehension. McGriff saw the look of confusion and started to laugh.

"Mrs. McGriff has not found the secret of perpetual youth, lass," he said to Nina. "She would have had to give birth to three of the four lads before she herself appeared in this world if she was to be the boys' mother. Why, Angus is near thirty himself and almost old enough to father my Lucy. Certainly when I was twelve I was up to it." He laughed loudly at his own joke.

Angus walked past him into the house.

"The first Mrs. McGriff gave birth to all four of the boys. Jeremy Campbell is my first wife's brother," the father continued, ignoring the son's rudeness. "A spot of tea would help all of us chase the night chill from our bones, lass," he said to his wife.

"The water is on the fire already," she responded.

THE ACADIANS

"Come into my house, my friends," he said ushering the two Acadians ahead of him into the warmth of the cabin.

The house was a large one, constructed of rough logs with mud patching the space between them. But most of the walls were covered with woolen tartans, military instruments, ancient blunderbusses, pikes and swords, and even an old crossbow, along with several muskets of modern European manufacture.

The furniture was old and European-made. The floor was totally covered with woolen carpets except for a raised stone platform in front of the hearth.

McGriff collapsed into a heavily upholstered chair and looked about the cozy room with obvious pride.

"Sit down," he said to Gilles and Nina. They took chairs closer to the fire. "We hauled all this stuff across the sea to Philadelphia and then down the road into the valley by wagon. Lads," he called to his sons, "take yourself some tea and then off to bed with you. It's near two in the morning and you'll have to be up with the sun for your chores."

Angus was already sipping from the mug that Lucy had set out for him. Andrew and Robbie, the youngest, climbed the steep wooden stairway to the second floor. Their footsteps could be heard on the board ceiling above the main floor. Charles joined his uncle and his brother sipping tea in front of the hearth.

"Am I ever going to learn about these two?" Lucy said, carrying tea and slices of warm bread.

"They're refugees from the English and therefore friends of mine, as they would have been of your father, my friend MacDonald, who fell at Culloden when the English scum slaughtered the flower of the highlands. I vowed to him that I would care for you and for all victims of English tyranny. It is that vow that makes me take these two wanderers into my home."

"Where do they come from? They didna pop out of the blue," Lucy said.

"They're French, 'Cadians, Canadians, something like that. They're from the northern islands where more and more of our people, I'm told, are settling. The English have even had the audacity to name one of the islands New Scotland, as if there was something wrong with the old one."

"McGriff," Lucy laughed, "you chide me for my tongue. There is not a night that comes without your tongue crying out for rest. I hear it every night as I lie on my pillow. A wee squeal comes out of your mouth so low you could hardly notice it and it says, Lucy, my darling, get McGriff to shut up."

The older man merely smiled.

Nina and Gilles had not understood their repartee. They sat sipping the tea and wolfing down the bread.

"Perhaps you care for something stronger," McGriff addressed Gilles. "I have a bit of barley brew that I make here on the farm. It will curl the hair on your chest."

Gilles smiled. "I'd like that," he said.

"I don't know about the curling," Nina said shyly, "but a little bit in the tea would be appreciated."

"Aye," McGriff laughed, "she's a lass after me own heart."

He went to a great oak cabinet and pulled down an earthenware jug. He poured a small amount of its contents into Nina's mug and refilled Gilles' empty tea mug with the whiskey. He did the same for himself.

Gilles took a gulp and held it in his mouth. He allowed the brew to slip slowly down his throat. He was glad he had taken the cautious way. It burned a path all the way to his stomach. Nina started coughing as soon as she took her next sip of tea.

"Glad you appreciate it," Duncan McGriff said to her, smiling.

"Now, you two, tell me what you are doing lighting fires on my land in the middle of the night."

Gilles recounted their story. McGriff hissed when he came to the part about Audry's attack on Nina. "His name sounds English and his behavior is certainly English," he said angrily.

Gilles said little about Jubal and Luck, not knowing if McGriff's Highland hospitality extended to friends of black slaves.

McGriff was silent for some moments after Gilles had finished. "The man owned your contract?"

Gilles did not know how to respond. But it was Nina who answered him.

"We were taken from our homes, monsieur, against our will. My father attempted to escape and the English pigs hanged him. They shot my little brother and Gilles' mother.

They forced us from our homes and loaded us into ships and set us ashore in this horrible place where they treat people worse than cattle. Yes, Gilles signed the paper, but he did it so that they would not put me on a platform in public view and strip me for the lechers and then sell me to one of them. He tried to protect me when Audry—" She hesitated to say what it was that Audry had done to her. "When he did what he did to me. But Gilles thought it was the overseer and he nearly killed him. We had to run away."

"Child, calm yourself. Lucy," Duncan called to his wife, "see if you can help her."

Lucy sat on the floor by Nina's chair and took her hands into her own. "Now, now, a woman in your condition should not be crying like that. An old witch at Castle Grapian in the Highlands told me that a pregnant woman who cries too much will have a bairn with the colic."

Nina stopped crying, not because of the witch but because of the soothing touch and obvious concern of the girl who was no older than she was but whose actions seemed so motherly. It was a gesture she would have expected from Maman Adele, if not from Dette Babineau.

"We'll find a place for you to sleep tonight. Jeremy," McGriff called to his brother-in-law, "would you give over your room to these strangers? They need a good night's sleep."

The slight gray-haired man agreed, but without much enthusiasm. His voice was thin and whiney. "I'll have to sleep with the boys in the large room upstairs, and I don't mind telling you that it is no joy to listen to their snoring."

"Why, Uncle," Charles laughed, "it was mutton we ate tonight and you ate more than any skinny man ought to be able to eat. It's not your snores that I worry about, it's your farts."

Angus was sipping his tea as his brother spoke. Charles's comments caught him unawares and his burst of laughter sent tea spraying in all directions.

"Don't disrespect your uncle, boys," Duncan said, trying to keep from laughing but his eyes betraying him. He turned to look at the Acadians. "Friends, you'll have a warm bed for the night and some hot food in the morning. I'll take care of you until you feel well enough to travel. Where will you be heading?"

Gilles shook his head. "Eventually we want to go home, but our first plan was to get away from the plantations with slaves. We wanted to make it to the valley."

"That part of your journey is over," Duncan interrupted him. "Getting home will be more difficult."

"Is there a French fort nearby?"

Duncan smiled. "Braddock was crushed on the Monongahela, but his conquerors have not yet come this far south. The closest French post will be at the forks of the Ohio beyond Fort Cumberland and the Potomac. But even so, that fort is in the middle of the wilderness south of the lakes, a good thousand miles from the French settlements."

Nina was crushed by his words. She had no idea where this valley was but she had had no idea it was so far away from her home. How ironic, she thought, that this house had first reminded her of the farm at Port Hebert.

"But that's a worry for tomorrow. Tonight, what's left of it, is for sleeping," McGriff said.

He rose from his chair and walked across the room to the hearth. There was a door on either side of the stone chimney. "This room here belongs to Lucy and me," he said, smiling at his wife. He pointed to the door on the right. "This other is normally Jeremy's, but tonight, my friends, consider it your own."

It was a small room. The single bed was placed close to the back side of the chimney for warmth. There was a wooden clothes tree in the corner on which hung various breeches and shirts, and there was a large seaman's chest at the foot of the bed. There was not much room for any other furniture.

McGriff placed a candle holder on a small niche in the stone wall. "I'll leave you two," he said to them. "We'll talk more in the morning." He turned and closed the door behind him.

Gilles and Nina looked at each other. They were both exhausted beyond anything either of them could remember. Nina sat on the bed. It would hold two people snuggled closely together. She slipped her shoes off her swollen feet and grimaced. She reached behind her head to undo the buttons on her homespun dress.

"Let me help you," Gilles offered.

He slowly undid the buttons, sitting beside her on the bed. He removed his shoes and stockings and then his breeches.

Nina started to laugh silently when she saw the condition of his undergarment. It had been worn and washed and worn and washed so often that almost nothing about it was intact. Gilles laughed along with her. He neatly folded his clothes and placed them atop the seaman's chest, except for his shirt. He folded it in two and made it into a pillow for his head.

There was a small rug on the board floor. Nina pulled one of the two thin blankets from the bed and handed it to him. Then she pulled her dress over her head and placed it on top of Gilles' garments on the seaman's chest. Her feet throbbed when she lifted them off the floor. Very gingerly she raised the remaining blanket and slipped her feet down under the covers. She rearranged her shift, which bunched up about her waist, and pulled it back down below her knees. Then she placed her head on the pillow.

She heard Gilles yawn on the floor below her. He turned once to get more comfortable. A few minutes later he turned onto his other side.

"Gilles?" she said softly.

"What?"

"Come up with me," she said, her back turned to him.

Gilles looked at her back for a few seconds. It was an offer he had waited for for so long. He rose to his feet and placed his blanket on the bed, covering Nina's body with it. Then he slipped under the covers next to her. The heated stones of the chimney along with the whiskey and the tea had warmed Nina's body. Gilles could feel the heat coming from her. His groin fit next to her buttocks, quickly arousing him. He reached around her and placed his hand on her breast. He could feel the rise and fall of her breathing. She had fallen asleep. His first reaction was one of hurt, but then again he realized that she was exhausted. Once again he would have to satisfy himself. It did not take long. He pulled away the remnants of his undergarments and cleaned himself with them. He dropped them on the floor next to the bed.

Nina had not been asleep at all. She had only taken pity on Gilles because he was sleeping on the floor. She had not intended the invitation as Gilles had understood it. His arousal had frightened her, and the only course of action she could think of was to pretend sleep. Since Marcel she had known no man except Audry. His violation made her even more determined to keep herself from any man until Marcel came for her.

Gilles' actions had embarrassed her, yet she could not stop him. She was grateful when he finished and fell asleep. She remained awake for a few more minutes. Gilles turned once and she felt his back against her own. It was a position with which she felt more comfortable. She relaxed and finally drifted off.

Gilles struck a bargain with Duncan McGriff: he and Nina would stay for the winter. Gilles was to help Jeremy and McGriff's sons to harvest the pumpkins and Indian squash and to stack the last of their hay in the barns. Nina was to help Lucy with light work around the house.

The two Acadians were enormously relieved. Nina would be giving birth sometime before Christmas and did not want to be alone in the wilderness when the baby came. True, Lucy was only a girl herself, with no experience when it came to childbirth, but Duncan assured the whole household that he had been present at the birth of all four of his sons. Although his beloved first wife had died giving birth to Robbie, he knew he could have done nothing to stop the hemorrhage that had taken her from him. He would help Nina deliver her child. He and Lucy together.

Jeremy had his room returned to him after he protested to Duncan. Instead Lucy hung a blanket dividing the upstairs sleeping quarters. There were no more beds available but none of the McGriff boys slept in beds. They simply threw straw-filled mattresses on the board floor. They made a similar mattress for Gilles and Nina. The sleeping arrangements worked out well.

McGriff took no part in the management of the crops of the farm. He left that to Jeremy, assisted by Angus. Duncan alone took care of the livestock, the three plow horses, a milk cow and a herd of prized sheep. The ram he had hauled all the way from Scotland. He had purchased the first two ewes in Germantown, outside Philadelphia. He had bought two more from neighbors in the valley and all had lambed several times since they had come to this farm. Gilles was happy to work with McGriff's sons. He did not like sheep. Their stench was truly offensive, he thought, not clean like that of a horse or a cow.

One week after his arrival he found himself atop the hay wagon forking hay Into the loft of the barn. It was the last wagonload. The rest of last summer's hay crop had been stored away for the winter months.

The afternoon sun was hot for late November. Gilles was sweating badly and he did not wish to ruin his shirt. He took it off and hung it across the side posts of the wagon. He loved this type of work, and he threw forkload after forkload of hay into the open loft door until Andrew McGriff stuck his head out to see what kind of infernal pitching machine had been brought in to torment him.

"Whoa," the Scotsman yelled.

The Frenchman smiled and stuck his fork into the hay. He ran his hand across his sweaty chest and wiped it off on his breeches.

He heard the horsemen before he could see them. There was a large party coming up the road toward the farmhouse. Gilles called to Andrew to alert him.

The lead horseman was riding a large bay horse. Gilles did not recognize him, but he had no trouble whatever identifying the chestnut jumper that was second to appear at the top of the rise. Audry's horse was instantly recognizable. The rage that Gilles had leveled wrongly at Josephs was still within him. He clutched the pitchfork so tightly that his knuckles went white with the pressure. Six more riders followed Audry. One of them was Colonel Wilson, Audry's neighbor, and another was Dr. Wilson, the colonel's brother.

Audry spotted Gilles standing atop the hay wagon.

"There's the scoundrel," he called out to the others. He kicked his horse viciously and it bolted forward at breakneck speed toward the barn. The others followed Audry's lead.

Andrew McGriff picked the musket up off the loft floor. His father had insisted that all the boys carry arms ever since the word came of the defeat of the British army on the Monongahela last summer. He was sure Indians would penetrate even this far east in search of scalps after tasting British blood in the wilderness.

Andrew took one look at Gilles' face and fired the musket into the air. Audry drew his pistol and fired it at the two men. The planter was well beyond pistol range, but the spent ball struck Andrew in the thigh. It penetrated his muscle and went no further. The farmer looked down at the fast-growing stain on the leg of his breeches and yelled out in shock.

"Get down," he called out to Gilles. But the Acadian's anger boiled over. He leapt down from the hay wagon, holding the pitchfork in front of him like a spear. Audry came directly at him, intent on forcing the chestnut into him and bowling him over. The horse's eyes seemed to glare at Gilles.

At the last second Gilles stepped aside and plunged his fork into the animal's side with all his might. The animal screamed in pain and collapsed in a heap, throwing Audry to the ground. The handle of the fork had snapped and Gilles' arm still shook, but he recovered quickly. The animal lay dead and motionless. The fork had pierced its heart.

Audry was trying to get to his feet. Gilles moved toward his tormentor, the stump of the pitchfork still in his hand. Audry raised his arm to ward off the blow, but before Gilles could swing, a second man wrapped his arms about Gilles. But the man had underestimated the Acadian's strength. Gilles expanded his chest and easily broke the man's grasp. He faced Audry again. The planter was standing unsteadily on his feet. Gilles started to move toward him, but Audry turned his back and began to run. Gilles followed, but before he could take three steps he was tackled from behind. He fell on his face with a heavy thud. Two more men jumped from their horses and pinned him down. Still the Acadian rose to his hands and knees and tossed the two newcomers off his back. He swung backwards with the stick and caught one of the men across the bridge of the nose. Blood gushed down his attacker's face. Gilles staggered to his feet. Four more horses charged at him. One clipped him on the hip and swung him around. He fell to his knees again. He dodged away from the next closest charge.

He turned to face them as they wheeled their horses about to come at him again. He was breathing heavily, his chest rising and falling rapidly. His sweaty shoulders and back and chest were now covered with grime. He tried to see where Audry had run to, but the sweat ran down into his eyes, partially blinding him.

"That will be enough brawling," the voice of Duncan McGriff rang out. Gilles turned to see McGriff, Jeremy, Angus, and Charles, each carrying a musket. They came from different directions in response to Andrew's signal. By prearrangement Robbie had gone to the house to protect his stepmother.

The man with the smashed nose rose to his feet and tried to speak, but the blood poured into his mouth and he choked on it. One of the mounted men rode his horse toward the older Scotsman.

"My name, sir, is Colonel George Wilson. I have a plantation in King George County on the Rappahannock. The gentleman bleeding so profusely is the sheriff of that county and he possesses a warrant for the apprehension of that ruffian." He pointed to Gilles.

"Does he now?" said McGriff. He turned to Gilles and quickly translated Wilson's comments into French.

Gilles had a sinking feeling in the pit of his stomach. He was prepared to fight a dozen men, but contracts and warrants were beyond him. He assumed they were beyond McGriff as well.

"This man Hebert has already given crippling injury to Mr. Audry's overseer, one Mr. Josephs. He has inspired two of Mr. Audry's best-treated slaves to run away. Fortunately, they have been recovered. But they were severely punished because of this man's bad example. He has now injured the sheriff. He must be returned to King George and brought to trial."

"We're not in King George County here. Your warrant has no effect in the valley."

Audry came out from behind some bushes next to the barn.

"I beg to differ with you, sir. This is still the Royal Colony of Virginia, and His Majesty's authority as seen in his warrants issued by courts of a county have jurisdiction everywhere in Virginia."

Wilson looked over at Audry with some disdain. He found

the man despicable. But justice and the law required that he join in bringing Gilles Hebert before the bar.

"The only word that counts here on this farm is mine," said McGriff. "You'll not be taking the Frenchman back with you. He's under my jurisdiction. Now which one of you bastards shot my son?"

Wilson's face flushed with anger. "If injury to the lad is what is causing you to be so stubborn and, I don't mind saying it, insolent, be assured that Mr. Audry fired in response to your son's shooting at us."

"Balls," McGriff shouted. "He fired in the air as a signal."

"An honest mistake," Audry said.

"That honest mistake could have cost the lad his leg if you had been closer."

Audry merely shrugged. "I want my property," he said finally.

"In this valley, and especially on this farm, people are not property."

Gilles was angry, but at the same time he was wary about the dialogue, which continued in a language he could not understand. He could take it no longer.

"Audry is the man who raped my Nina. He intended to castrate me. He is a liar and a molester of innocent women, a monster beyond belief."

McGriff smiled and translated every one of Gilles' words into English.

"He lies," Audry said softly.

Again McGriff translated.

"Ask Nina," Gilles responded quickly.

"He says ask the girl."

"She'd say anything to protect her husband," Wilson objected.

McGriff raised his hand to Wilson for silence. "I've heard enough. I believe the Frenchman. I'd believe any Frenchman's word ahead of an Englishman's."

"Sir," Wilson protested loudly, "I am a gentleman."

McGriff looked him over carefully. "I suspect you are," he responded. "It's the other one," he said, pointing to Jonas Audry, "that I don't trust. I think this fellow's just about what Gilles said he is, a liar and a rapist. Now get the hell off my land!"

Audry's face was almost purple with rage. "What about my

horse? He was the best goddamned jumper in the county. And this scum has gone and killed him."

"And what about the sheriff's face?" Wilson protested. "This can't go unpunished."

McGriff ignored him. Instead he raised his musket. His sons followed his lead and raised theirs as well. With muskets pointed at them from all sides, the sheriff's posse was helpless. Wilson rode over to where Audry stood. He offered him his arm. The planter swung up into the saddle behind his neighbor. Another man removed Audry's saddle from his dead horse and placed it precariously between the neck of his own horse and his own saddle. The sheriff remounted, but one of his deputies took his horse's reins and led him away. Audry stared at Gilles and then at McGriff.

"You'll pay," he said with a sneer.

Wilson urged his horse forward and the posse disappeared down the road.

Jeremy climbed up into the hay wagon and reached up to help his nephew down from his perch in the hayloft. Andrew waved his uncle's hand away. Instead he stood up and followed the disappearing horsemen with his eyes. Once they went from his view, he reached for Jeremy's hand. He grimaced with pain when he landed on the soft hay of the wagon.

Jeremy grabbed him under the chest and slid the boy over the side of the wagon into Gilles' arms. Andrew started to walk, and blood flowed freely from his wound.

"Sit down, you jughead," his father commanded.

Lucy and Nina, followed closely by Robbie, came running from the house. Lucy carried water and some clean cloths, and Nina had the good sense to bring the bottle of McGriff's brew.

Nina was relieved to see Gilles standing and unhurt. He was filthy but he was whole. The sight of Audry riding by the house, even in defeat, had sent chills of terror through her body. She went to Gilles and placed her arm gently about his waist. He looked at her and smiled.

"Don't touch me, I'll get you filthy," he warned her. But the touch of him was reassuring to her, especially when she saw Andrew sitting on the ground, his father leaning over him.

Jeremy handed Duncan his knife.

"Not yet," McGriff said in annoyance. "Before I can remove the ball he'll have to take his bloody breeches off."

The whole family, with the exception of Jeremy, started to laugh. Their father's curse was in fact no curse at all but an accurate description of Andrew's pants.

"McGriff," Jeremy said in annoyance, "cut the cloth with the knife."

"And ruin a good pair of breeches?" McGriff objected. "What do you take me for? I am not made of money, and even though a good pair of breeches are not as comfortable as a good kilt, they are nonetheless not to be ruined lightly."

"It's men like you, McGriff, that give our race a bad name for stinginess."

"If being thrifty is to have a bad name, well then call me Beelzebub and be done with it."

While the two men were arguing, Andrew undid the top button of his breeches. Lucy gave them a good yank and pulled them down to his knees, revealing a flesh wound about an inch deep in his thigh. Nina looked the other way in embarrassment, but Lucy paid no attention whatever to her stepson's nakedness. She held up her hand for Nina to give her the bottle of whiskey. Nina, her back turned to Lucy, did not see the gesture.

"Nina," Lucy yelled, "give me the damned bottle."

Nina turned at her name and handed the bottle to the girl.

"It's not proper," Jeremy complained.

Lucy ignored him. "Take a swig," she said to Andrew. He did as he was told. Then she poured some of the whiskey over the blade of the knife and more of it into the wound itself. He gasped at the sting of the alcohol.

"Now brace yourself," the girl ordered. Andrew tried but he was not prepared for the fiery pain that accompanied the probing of the knife. He yelled in anguish.

McGriff held his son's hand, but his older brother, the dour-faced Angus, broke out laughing. "Our little Andy got himself a pinprick."

"Shut up," Lucy said.

Andrew gritted his teeth and complained no more, not even when Lucy dug the blade beneath the lead ball and literally popped it out of the hole. The blood bubbled up.

Lucy stemmed it by placing a cloth over the hole. She waited until the flow had lessened.

"Brace again," she said and without hesitation poured more whiskey into the open wound.

This time Andrew would not give his older brother the satisfaction. He did not cry out.

"That's a brave lad," McGriff said. "Bind the wound, lass, and let's take our Andrew home. I believe he needs the rest of the day free from work. But I'll be expecting you to be helping Gilles in the hayloft tomorrow."

They decided to celebrate the victory of the battle of the hayloft that very night. Charles and Robbie butchered the carcass of Audry's horse. McGriff called it the spoils of war. He ordered some of the meat smoked and some pickled to preserve it for the coming winter. It was appropriate, he said, that Gilles and Nina should provide food for the long winter ahead. Although they had come empty-handed, their pursuers had provided a good portion of next winter's meat. That night they would eat the best part of the horse. It was to be washed down with some homemade beer and some beans baked in molasses with salt pork and cornmeal bread, along with the ever-present McGriff brew.

Lucy cooked but Nina insisted on helping. When Lucy put heart, liver, and lung of the horse into a large pot, Nina was sure it was some strange Scottish ritual to appease the spirit of the horse. Therefore, when Lucy left the house to go back to the site of the butchering, Nina took the pot to empty it in the garbage bins where food for McGriff's old haggard sheepdog was stored.

"Where are you taking that, girl?" McGriff asked from the corner of the living room where he sat drinking with his wounded son.

"To empty it."

"To what?"

"To feed it to the dog," she continued.

"My good lass," McGriff protested, "you're not going to feed food fit for a king to a mutt, a mangy flea-bitten mutt at that. It's for us, girl."

Nina's eyes widened. Then she realized that McGriff was teasing her. She started to laugh and walked again toward the door.

"The girl thinks I'm pulling her leg," he said to Gilles in French. He translated the English expression and produced only a dumb look on Gilles' face.

"Save me from the lack of wit of the two of you." He rose to his feet and intercepted Nina. He took the pot from her and returned it to the table.

"I wasn't jesting, lass. When my Lucy's finished it will be a feast worth remembering."

Lucy entered the house just at that moment. Her dress was spotted with blood and she carried a washed but still bloodied trophy, a large portion of the horse's cleaned-out stomach.

Nina gagged and had to run from the house. Even Gilles went white and felt queasy.

Lucy dropped the stomach bag on her table. She took suet from around the animal's kidneys and dropped it into the pot. She opened a large tin above the table and removed some onions she had stored there. She chopped them finely and dropped them into the pot. She added some water and salt and finally a mugful of coarse cornmeal. She stirred and mashed it with a pestle. When it was the proper consistency, she filled the stomach bag with the mixture and lowered it gently into a large cauldron of boiling water that bubbled over the fire in the hearth.

Nina did not return until Lucy had finished. Even then the smell of the cooking haggis nearly drove her back outside. McGriff laughed at both Nina and Gilles. The rest of the family, including the butchers, were drawn back into the house by the scent coming from the boiling pot.

Lucy drove Charles and Robbie back out of the house and ordered them to strip off their fouled clothes and go down to the stream to wash themselves. Before long, the family sitting in the cabin heard whoops of joy as the two young men wrestled and splashed each other in the stream.

And still the haggis boiled on. Finally, after several hours of stewing, it was pronounced ready. Lucy pulled the contents out of the water. The insides of the stomach bag had been reduced to the consistency of a pudding. Lucy passed out steaming plates of haggis, which gave off the same peculiar odor that had seeped into the entire house during the course of the cooking. McGriff and Jeremy wolfed down the contents of their plates. The four McGriff boys ate with relish. Lucy satisfied herself with some bread and fresh milk.

"Lass," McGriff said, holding his stomach after his third plateful, "I've tasted calf's haggis and sheep's haggis, but never have I tasted a better dish than what you've made from the Englishman's steed. Indeed, the fact that it was an Englishman's horse makes it all the more delicious."

"Aye," the usually silent Angus joined in. "It was a feast."

The others grunted approval, all except Jeremy. He disapproved of too much praise going to Lucy. He regarded flattery of the second Mrs. McGriff as an implied criticism of the first, and he would not tolerate criticism of his dead sister, the boys' mother.

"It's not a proper haggis," Jeremy said finally.

McGriff stared at him openmouthed. "I've never tasted a better one," he responded.

"I didn't say it was not tasty," Jeremy continued, "I said it was not a proper haggis."

"And what's the difference?"

"You don't make haggis from a horse," he responded.

"Balls," McGriff uttered his favorite exclamation. "I just ate me a horse haggis."

"But it's still not proper."

McGriff grew red in the face. "I know what you're up to, Jeremy Campbell. You can't stand the thought of me marrying a MacDonald after the death of your sister. I know your game."

"I was discussing haggis," Jeremy persisted.

"I'm not going to spend another night listening to you refight the Campbell–MacDonald thing again," Angus complained bitterly.

"You have your uncle's disposition, lad, and although I have to put up with him for my dear dead wife's sake, I don't have to put up with much sass from you."

Angus looked away from his father angrily.

"Have some of the haggis," McGriff said to Gilles. "And you, lass," he addressed Nina, "you haven't touched a thing."

Lucy could tell by McGriff's gestures that he was trying to force the dish on his guests. She herself could not abide the stuff.

"The lass helped me with the cooking," she interceded. "It

always kills my appetite. Nina should have some bread and milk with me." She motioned to Nina to join her at the hearth. At least she could be spared. Her bull of a husband would have to fend for himself.

Gilles resisted McGriff with all his will. No one was going to make him eat what to him looked like pure offal. Finally McGriff grew tired of trying. He rose from his chair and stretched.

"It is time for my evening walk," he said. "Who'll be joining me?"

All the boys groaned except for Andrew, who sat grinning at the others. For a change he would not have to go. McGriff frequently insisted that his sons and his dog accompany him on his walks. After a hard day's labor it was an unappealing task for them.

"You'll get constipated like your uncle if you don't stretch your bowels after eating," he insisted, patting his rotund belly. He turned to Gilles. "How about a walk?"

"Fine," Gilles said.

"A volunteer! Damn my soul, it's been a while since anyone volunteered. The hell with the rest of you. I'll go with my friend Hebert. May the bowels of the rest of you shrivel like pricks on a cold night."

Jeremy clucked. "That's no way to be talking in front of ladies," he protested to Duncan.

"One didn't understand a word I said and the other has heard me say just about everything at least once. A second time around can't do any more harm."

"Cumberland," McGriff called his dog. The black mutt crawled from underneath the bed in McGriff's bedroom. It scratched some mange spots and finally entered the living room. "There you be, you piece of walking mange, you trough for fleas. Now doesn't he remind you of His Royal Highness, the Duke of Cumberland? Look at the fat of him. Doesn't he remind you of German George's obscene son?"

McGriff loved to abuse his dog verbally. But the dog took any attention from its master as praise and came over to McGriff wagging his tail. "And you are as dumb as His Royal Highness, no doubt about it." The dog's tail banged again and again against McGriff's leg.

"Come," McGriff said to Gilles. The two men went to the door.

"Your musket," Lucy called out.

McGriff waved the thought away.

"Father," Robbie cautioned the old man, "are the rules only for us?"

McGriff walked over to his youngest and ruffled his black curly hair. "No, lad. Get me my weapon."

Robbie jumped up and ran to the gun rack. He loaded a musket for his father and one for Gilles. Each took a weapon from the boy and stepped out into the chilly air.

The night was particularly bright and the road was easy to follow all the way to the woods. The fields of harvested corn and squash that bordered the road were bathed in a silver light.

McGriff set a brisk pace and before long he and Gilles were breathing heavily. Their warm breaths appeared as steam in the cold air.

"You disappoint me, Gilles," Duncan said loudly. "I've always viewed the French as adventurous when it comes to some delicacy. I learned to appreciate frog's legs and snails in France. I would have thought that a haggis would be a challenge."

Gilles smiled. "We are not that adventurous in Port Hebert. We eat mostly fish and corn and milk. Every once in a while we have some beef or possum."

They walked on in silence. McGriff stopped at the top of the rise and turned to look back at his farm. He rested his musket against his leg and placed his hand on his hip. He quieted the dog when it growled at some forest sound.

"It's a good feeling," he said to Gilles.

The Acadian looked at him quizzically.

"I mean, it's good to work on the land with your own hands, to carve a farm out of the wilderness. I am an orderly man, Gilles. I hate the wilderness. I hate to see wild things sapping the nourishment from the rich soil. It's why I love this valley. Someday it will be green with the fruits of man's labor from the Potomac in the north to south of Massanutten Mountain and on both sides of that ridge. It'll be a beautiful sight to behold!"

Gilles stood next to McGriff and allowed his eyes to wander

across the moon-drenched landscape. Off in the distance he could see the smoke of the McGriff chimney rising dull gray into the silvery night. He was sure the smell of the haggis still clung to the smoke.

"I know what you mean," Gilles said finally. "In Acadia it is the sea, not the wilderness, that we fight. We drag our living from it and we reclaim farmland from it with dikes and weirs and trenches. We must always be alert because the sea is a relentless enemy. It never stops working against us, undermining within hours the work just completed."

"It's the same with the wilderness," said McGriff. "We fight a battle with weeds and then second-growth forests. The wilderness reclaims its acres just like the sea in your home."

The two men smiled at each other. The Frenchman and the Scot had a common understanding—a link that tied them together.

"You have a pipe?" McGriff asked.

Gilles nodded.

"Have some of my tobacco." He handed Gilles a leather pouch. Gilles filled his own pipe.

"Here," McGriff said, "fill mine while I look for my flint and taper."

Gilles filled the Scotsman's pipe for him.

"Damn," McGriff cursed as he dropped the flint. Gilles bent down quickly to retrieve it for him. The silence of night was shattered by the roar of a musket. McGriff's hands flew to his chest and he gave out a tiny whimper before falling. Cumberland let loose with a wild howl.

Gilles turned to face the direction of the musket report, his own weapon at the ready. He saw a shadow move across the bushes at the edge of the woods. He raised his musket and fired. He saw nothing more. He picked up McGriff's loaded gun. He could not follow the assailant and leave the older man alone. Next he heard the sound of horses' hooves. Then he saw the horse and rider dash across the open field for the cover of the woods. Gilles raised the gun and fired, but the range was too great for a musket. He missed. But he had no doubt about the identity of the assassin. It was Jonas Audry.

The whole McGriff family raced out of the house, muskets in hand.

"*Ici,*" Gilles called out.

They ran in the direction of his voice.

Gilles bent down and put his head to McGriff's chest. His breathing was raspy and there was a gurgling sound in his throat.

Lucy fell to her knees beside her husband. "McGriff, you old warhorse," she cried, "don't go dying on me. Listen to me."

He opened his eyes. "I'll not be dying if there's any more haggis left," he said. There was still a twinkle in his eye but his face had suddenly become drawn and haggard.

"Then it will be the rest of us who will die," she said in mock resignation. "I don't think the smell of haggis cooking is half so bad as the smell of haggis recooking."

Jeremy and Robbie ran back to the house to put together a stretcher to bear McGriff back to his home.

Nina clasped Gilles' hand.

"It was meant for me," Gilles said angrily. "It was that bastard Audry. He aimed for my back. I bent to pick up the flint just as he fired and he hit Monsieur McGriff instead. Damn him to hell. This good man struck down."

"Why is it," Nina cried, "that since Port Hebert every good person who touches us is made to suffer?"

Angus interrupted them. He spoke no French and his frustration was obvious.

"Who did this? Who? Who?" he repeated.

"You sound like a bloody owl," McGriff said weakly. Then he switched to French. "Did you see who shot me, lad?" he asked Gilles.

"Oui, it was that bastard Audry. He rode off through the woods toward the river."

McGriff translated Gilles' words.

Angus said nothing. He merely nodded to Charles.

Andrew spoke out. "Me too, Angus, I can ride. My leg is not that bad."

"There are only plow horses, and those 'gentlemen'," Angus pronounced the word with a sneer, "have fine mounts. They're probably far away by now. But we can't just let them ride off after having shot a McGriff."

Charles left the group when Jeremy and Robbie returned. They had brought Lucy McGriff's comforter from the couple's bed. They put the old man in the middle and slowly carried him down the slope. At the house they were met by Charles, riding a large gray gelding and leading its twin and a smaller, though still sturdy, black mare.

Angus and Andrew carried their father to the bed, then both young men reemerged from the house and quickly mounted the horses.

"Should we take the Frenchman?" Charles asked.

"To what purpose?" Angus asked.

"To identify the scum."

"I'll never forget what he looks like," Angus responded. "We don't need Hebert."

"But you need me," Robbie protested from the doorway. His eyes were red from crying.

"Go in and wipe your nose, laddie," Angus said cruelly.

"Don't talk to the boy that way," Jeremy said from behind Robbie. "And one of you will have to make room for me."

Angus spoke for the others. "We shall not. Robbie is too young. When we find Audry what we'll do to him will not be a fit sight for a boy's eyes. And you, Jeremy, you should stay because you're not a blood McGriff."

Jeremy's anger overflowed. "I'm not any kind of a McGriff, you bloody idiot, but I am the brother of the woman who gave you birth, and don't you forget it."

Angus pulled the reins and swung away from his uncle. Charles and Andrew followed suit. Soon all three were cantering up the slope away from the house. Jeremy placed his arm around Robbie's neck and they returned to the house.

McGriff lay in his great bed, brought all the way from his home in the Highlands. He was deathly pale and his lips were blue. Lucy had removed his shirt to get a look at the wound. The ball had entered his chest on the right side and had not reemerged. Gilles sat at the foot of the bed. Nina was at the hearth heating water with which to wash McGriff.

The old man was awake. "Prop me up, lass," he called to Lucy. "I have a bit of a problem breathing."

Lucy grabbed a large down-filled pillow from her side of the bed and placed it under her husband's head and shoulders.

"Where are my boys?" he asked, his eyes darting about the candlelit room.

"I'm here, father," Robbie said stepping out of the shadows.

"Where are your brothers, lad?"

"They went looking for the man who did this to you."

"Jeremy?" McGriff saw his brother-in-law standing behind his son. "You didn't go with them?"

"It was Angus, Duncan. The lad is surly at best. He told me I was no blood McGriff and had no business avenging McGriff blood. You should have taken a stick to that one a lot more often when he was a wee lad, Duncan."

"He wasn't always so sour. It was his mother's death that turned him."

"You're being polite, Duncan. It was your marrying me that soured him," Lucy protested.

Jeremy signaled Lucy with his eyes to get off the topic. She looked away from Jeremy and from Duncan. She rose from the bed. "Robbie, go outside and give us a warning if your brothers return," she ordered the boy.

He left the bedroom, grabbed a musket leaning against the door, and departed.

Lucy took Jeremy aside. "I'm afraid of those Virginians," she said to him. "They are a wicked crowd. They ride like the wind and they shoot without thinking. They are too damned confident. They give orders as men born to give orders and without any fear of being disobeyed. So if you cross them they can't handle it. They turn to violence."

Jeremy said nothing at first. He just watched Duncan. "Don't underestimate a Scot."

"How could I? I'm one myself."

"And so are Angus and Charlie and Andrew. We have a doggedness to our nature, lass. We don't give up easy."

Gilles replaced Lucy at Duncan's head.

"Ah, my Acadian friend," he said. The pain of his wound began to rack him. He gasped.

"Can I do anything for you?" Gilles whispered to him.

"Never fear, lad," Duncan smiled. "I'll not die on you and leave you without anyone but your lass to talk to."

Gilles smiled. "I'm gratified," he said. "And I feel guilty. That ball was meant for me."

"And you should feel guilty." He grimaced as another wave of pain hit him.

Again the night's silence was shattered by the report of a musket.

"Robbie!" Lucy called out with concern.

Jeremy started for the door. Gilles allowed McGriff's head to sink back down into the pillow, then grabbed his musket and raced out of the house after Jeremy Campbell. He saw the other man run up the road and then stand still. At the top of the rise five horsemen came trotting forward. Behind them, waving his musket, was the youngest McGriff boy.

"They're back," Robbie shouted.

Duncan's three older sons were accompanied by two of the Virginians.

Gilles caught up with Jeremy and joined the Scot in leveling his musket at the two newcomers. He would take no chances, given what had happened to McGriff, but the three sons of the wounded man did not seem to regard the other two men as prisoners.

Gilles recognized one of the men as Audry's neighbor, Colonel Wilson. The horsemen slipped past them on the road and made for the front of the house. They were tying their mounts to the shrubs that grew in front of the cabin when Gilles and Jeremy finally caught up with them.

"This fellow here and his brother were camped on the south fork," Angus related to his uncle. "The one here is a doctor. He agreed to come back with us and take a look at father."

Colonel Wilson looked at Jeremy. "I assume you are in charge here during the incapacity of the other gentleman."

Jeremy looked at Angus as if he expected an argument from him. When he saw the defiance in the young man's eyes, he simply ignored Wilson's question.

"I want you to know," Wilson continued, "that my brother volunteered to return with these boys and that I decided to come with him. We are not prisoners of any kind."

Jeremy nodded his understanding.

"The young man there," Wilson said, pointing to Angus, "told us what happened. He says Hebert believes that Audry is responsible. I am afraid I must conclude, as you have, that it was he who did this cowardly thing. He slipped away from our camp. He has not returned. He has no alibi, and there is no one else who would have had any reason to do this." Wilson shook his head as he spoke. "He was always a wild lad. But the gambling brawl and his loss seem to have warped him."

Dr. Wilson stepped past his brother and entered the house. Lucy showed him into the bedroom. He sat on the bed and pulled away the covers and the bandage that Lucy had placed on Duncan's chest. He poked at the wound, causing McGriff to gasp in pain. He reached behind the wounded man's back to see if he could discern the exit wound, but there was none. He frowned but tried to hide his concern from Lucy. He turned to Nina, who stood in the doorway watching.

"Get some water," he ordered.

The girl did not move.

"What's the matter with you, child," he yelled. "I've got to do some probing and I need some boiling water. I do nothing without boiling water. I use nothing unless I boil it first. And I am one hell of a fine physician despite what my colleagues say about my theories."

"She doesn't speak English," Lucy interjected.

"Oh, so this is one of the runaways we were chasing. It doesn't matter. Someone get me boiling water."

Lucy showed Nina the iron kettle in which she kept water and gestured for her to fetch some more. Nina nodded and left the house.

The men had reentered the living room. Dr. Wilson joined them.

"Set up a table out here," he ordered. "I think I might have to operate to get that ball out of him."

"Can you do that?" Angus questioned him.

"Can you pass wind?" the doctor responded in disgust. "Of course I can do that. I wouldn't have said I was going to do it if I couldn't."

The young men flashed an angry look at the doctor. "I asked you a civil question, Englishman. I expect a civil response."

"You insolent pup," Wilson flashed back.

Angus made a move toward the doctor but Jeremy stepped in his way. "What's the matter with you, lad? This man is here to help your father and you're going to brawl with him?"

Angus made no further move toward the doctor. He turned instead and slammed his fist on the table.

Charles and Andrew brought the oak table from next to the hearth into the center of the room. It was a drop-leaf table with curved legs and was large enough with the leaves raised to accommodate eight persons. Tonight it would serve a different purpose.

Nina struggled with the heavy pot. When she drew open the door, Gilles grabbed the pot from her hand and carried it to the hearth.

"That's it," exclaimed Dr. Wilson. "Now—" He never finished the idea. Nina grabbed her stomach in pain as if someone had punched her.

"What is it?" Gilles called to her.

"I need to lie down," she gasped.

He rushed to her side and started to lead her to the loft stairs and their bed.

"Don't be silly," Jeremy insisted. "Take her to my bedroom." He shook his head when he realized that Gilles had not understood him and was already leading Nina up the stairs.

"Gilles," he called out.

Once he had the Frenchman's attention he pointed to the door to his own room. Gilles smiled and led Nina back down and into Jeremy's room, where he helped her stretch out.

"What's wrong with the lass?" Charles asked.

"Are you blind?" Dr. Wilson said. "She's going to have a baby. But that can wait. Having babies is mostly about waiting. First we must do our best to save the lord of this manor."

The house was quiet again at last. McGriff lay sleeping in his great bed. He was dressed in a clean white nightshirt. The corners were pulled snugly over the bed, leaving a giant lump created by his belly. His head was propped on pillows. Lucy slept upright in the chair across the room. The tiny flickering of a candle on the bureau cast an enormous shadow on the far walls of the room, like a shaded reflection of a giant blaze. McGriff breathed evenly.

Gilles tiptoed to the open door and peered inside. He could not help contrast the peace of that scene with the barbaric chaos on the table only hours before. McGriff, filled with cupful after cupful of whiskey, was carried naked from his bedroom and placed on the table. He sang raucous songs dating from his schooldays at old Edinburgh.

"Lay him on his stomach," Dr. Wilson ordered.

"He's shot in the chest," his brother, Colonel Wilson, complained.

"Oh, no, not from you too? Suddenly you become a physician. Wasn't it bad enough our dear father, by the laws of primogeniture, gave the entire estate to you, leaving me in the cold? Now you want to take my profession from me as well."

"Brother," Wilson said finally, "all I said was he was shot in the chest."

"And the ball did not emerge. It seems to have severed no vital arteries or veins. There is little or no internal bleeding. His color is good. But if you look at his back you'll see a bruise growing. I expect the ball almost penetrated and that I can reach it by going in from there."

"You'll have a damnably hard time getting McGriff on his stomach," Jeremy interjected. "It protrudes too much."

"I'm not trying to arrange the most comfortable position, just the most effective one so that I can get to his back. Now, Frenchy," he called to Gilles, "get me that water."

Nina cried out in anguish in the bedroom just at that moment, and Gilles looked first at Dr. Wilson and then at McGriff. He wanted the doctor to go to Nina, yet he knew McGriff's surgery could not be postponed.

"Pay no attention to that girl," Dr. Wilson ordered. "She ought to have more self-discipline. Must be that only French women carry on that way. You'd never hear an English lady yelling like that."

McGriff lifted his head from the table. "I don't know whosh you are, you bloody bastard," he said drunkenly, "but you don't know what the hell you're talking about. There ain't no such thing as an English lady."

Dr. Wilson pushed McGriff's head face down again. "Shut your face. And watch who you insult. It's hardly wise to give injury to the man who is about to stick his knives into you."

"Up yours," McGriff laughed.

Wilson looked around for his water bearer. "Damn him," he cursed. "The Frenchman has gone in to look on his wife."

McGriff's screams soon drowned out Nina's. He was held down by his sons. Lucy or Jeremy took turns holding his head and trying to comfort him.

"Don't allow those legs to move," Dr. Wilson screamed at Robbie. "If I slip, your father is a dead man."

The boy gulped. His arms stiffened their hold on his father's bare calf and thigh. His hands were shaking with the responsibility but Wilson did not notice it. The doctor cut deeper and probed with his fingers into the hole he had made in McGriff's back. Blood poured from his back onto the table and spilled over the edge.

Then it was all over. Dr. Wilson's finger touched the lead ball. He forced it to the surface with his index finger and picked it out of the wound. He let out a whoop of joy. Now he was sure McGriff would live. He poured whiskey into the wound, but there was no sound from his patient. He had fainted earlier.

Dr. Wilson announced to the sons that the father would live, although he expressed the usual caveat about infectious vapors in the air undoing all his good work.

"One other thing," Dr. Wilson said. "He'll probably never walk again, but I hope he'll have the use of his arms."

The sons stared at him in disbelief.

"The ball was right next to the spine. If it did any damage to the cord, and I think it has, there will be paralysis."

Lucy stifled a cry by shoving her hand into her mouth.

"He would have been better off dead," Angus said with surprisingly little emotion in his voice for him. "Why didn't you tell us that might be the outcome?"

"My job is healing, not killing," the doctor responded.

His brother, the colonel, had watched the drama helplessly as an observer. He stepped forward. "My brother used his skills to save your father's life. You should be grateful."

Lucy gained control of herself. She took the doctor's arm. "We are grateful, doctor."

Again Nina yelled in anguish.

"Now you must attend to your other patient." Lucy led him toward Jeremy's bedroom.

"I hope you're more successful with the wench than you were with my father," Angus muttered. "Who knows, maybe in there you can leave two persons paralyzed, mother and little one."

Charles, Andrew, and Robbie had become equally angry

with the thought of a Duncan McGriff confined to a chair or worse for the rest of his life.

Dr. Wilson ignored the boys, although the colonel stared at them warily. He would have preferred to leave before these wild men sought revenge on both of them. But it was impossible to drag his brother from a patient, and now he had gone off to deliver a child.

Wilson examined Nina quickly. "She's coming along nicely," he said to Gilles. He remembered then that the man spoke no English. So he flashed him a smile.

Gilles smiled back, quietly relieved that the doctor did not think Nina's suffering so great that he couldn't still manage a smile.

"Hot water," Wilson called back into the living room. But all the McGriffs were busy carrying Duncan back to his bed. Finally, Colonel Wilson came into the room with a steaming pot. He looked sternly at Gilles. He thought the Frenchman should occupy a cell in the basement jail at King George County courthouse. After watching the suffering of Duncan McGriff and feeling the tensions and animosities displayed toward him by the McGriff family, he was also certain that Jonas Audry should occupy the second cell.

The doctor rinsed his hands in hot water. Nina's pains were coming rapidly now. There were no complications. The baby's head would be born shortly.

"Oh, do shut up," he said to her when she cried out in anguish. "Bear down," he shouted at her, more to get through to her and to drown out the sound of her own screams.

"Damn, she won't understand."

She had stopped yelling and was now merely whimpering.

"Young lady," he snapped his fingers before her eyes, "when the pains come bear down!" He tried to imitate what bearing down meant.

Colonel Wilson started to laugh. "By God, brother, you look more like a constipated old man making his toilet than anything else." His remarks seemed to release his own tensions and he started to howl and slap his hands on his thighs.

Gilles held Nina's shoulders and head in his lap. He resented the presence of the Virginia colonel almost as much as he was grateful for the presence of the colonel's brother.

He wished the doctor would do something to lessen Nina's pain.

"It's going to be all right," he whispered in her ear. "The doctor is here."

The pains were building again. He could feel it in the way she gripped his fingers. The look in her eyes was one of desperation. He didn't know if she could take any more pain. Again Dr. Wilson shouted at Nina and strained. This time Gilles understood.

"Nina," he said loudly to draw her attention from the pain, "the doctor wants you to bear down. Press."

She tried. She grabbed him even more tightly.

"That's it, girl. Finally I got through," Wilson called out.

Nina started to scream again and Wilson bent down to assess the progress.

"Less voice and more effort up there." This time he addressed his comments to Gilles.

The Frenchman could not understand. "Keep bearing down."

But Nina had given up. The contraction consumed her and she was actually quivering in pain. Finally it began to subside again. She opened her eyes and stared directly into Gilles' face.

"I'm dying," she said as her whole body shuddered.

"Nonsense." He kissed her cheek. "Try to bear down like the doctor said. Scream if it helps, but don't give in to the pain."

He could see the terror as another contraction began.

"Oh, no," she cried out, "I can't stand any more."

"Bear down," Wilson yelled.

Gilles squeezed her hand this time before her grip tightened, just to let her know he was there and he was with her.

"*O mon Dieu,*" Nina prayed. Her body arched as the pain racked her, and she pushed downward with all her strength.

"That's it," Wilson shouted, "I can see the head. Keep it up."

Nina exhaled and screamed all in one breath. "Mar-cel-ll, help me," she called out in desperation.

"There we go, almost have it. Keep it up." He turned to Lucy, who had entered the room as it was clear the baby was about to be born. "Girl, get me cloths, a basin, and some warm water. We're about to have a new life enter the world."

His tone was excited. One could never have expected that he had delivered hundreds of babies. No matter, to Dr. Wilson each one was exciting.

Gilles sat stunned. He relaxed his grip on Nina's hand. She called out again, this time using her mother's name.

"Here we go," Wilson called out. "There's the shoulder. Now let's see what we have here. By God, it's a little wench. May she be as pretty as her mother and as faithful as her father."

Nina was drenched in sweat. The pain still persisted, but it was of less intensity. It continued until the afterbirth was expelled. Finally she looked up at Gilles and smiled. She did not notice the distant look that crept into his eyes.

Lucy wrapped the baby with some clean white cloth after she had washed it. She placed the child in Nina's arms. The baby's face was red. Her reddish brown hair was still wet and looked darker than it was. Nina cooed to the child. The other members of the household crowded into Jeremy's little room to wish the French girl and her husband good luck.

The two Wilsons left the room and stepped out into the main room of the house. The doctor ducked into the master bedroom and checked his other patient.

"Let's get out while we can," the colonel whispered.

"Why should we? If we leave now we'll have to camp out on the hard ground. These people owe me a meal and a good bed."

"Those young ruffians are angry about their father. A tidewater man shot him, and a tidewater man opens him up and leaves him a cripple."

Dr. Wilson looked at his brother in amazement. "You don't believe it was my operation that crippled him, do you?"

"What difference does it make what I think? It is what these damned barbarian Scots think."

"Well, I won't have it," the doctor said, pulling himself up in indignation.

"Don't be an ass. Let's go," the colonel urged. "The horses are just outside the house."

"No! I won't leave with such a misunderstanding blotting my reputation." He strode past his brother and reentered the room where everyone crowded about Nina to get a look at the child.

"Ladies and gentlemen," he called out over the din in the room. There was a quick silence. "It has come to my attention that some of you hold me responsible for the condition of Mr. McGriff, who, by the way, is sleeping comfortably, if alone, in the next room. I protest the concept vigorously. Your father, young men, was rendered a cripple by a lead ball that damaged his spine. His ability to move would have been impaired whether or not I operated. That, I believe, is a certainty. What is also a certainty is that if I had not operated your father would have died in excruciating pain within a fortnight. I expect to be thanked for keeping him alive. I will accept nothing less."

Lucy placed her hand on Wilson's arm. "I am aware of what you did for McGriff and I acknowledge it. What can I give you in the way of payment?"

"Nothing but my intact reputation and a meal and a bed for the night. My brother, the illustrious militia colonel, seems intent in sleeping in the damp bog called 'our camp' back by the river. He may return to that pest hole if he wishes. I expect a bed."

Jeremy Campbell followed Lucy to the doctor's side and one by one the sons of Duncan McGriff offered their apologies to Wilson—all except Angus, who left the bedroom without a word.

"What's troubling him?" Dr. Wilson asked, following Angus with his eyes.

"He's just Angus," Jeremy said.

"Well, I'd keep an eye on him and my back to the wall with him around. He's trouble. Now what did you have for dinner tonight that we can warm over for my supper?"

Wilson should have guessed something was up when everyone in the room but the two who spoke just French began to laugh and poke at each other.

That had been hours before. Now the house was quiet. Upstairs Jeremy and the McGriff boys and the doctor and Colonel Wilson snored away. Gilles could not help but smile when he heard the cacophony of snorts and whistles that floated down to him on the main floor. He looked away from McGriff and Lucy and opened the door to the room where Nina slept. Next to her in a tiny wooden cradle that Jeremy dragged from the barn lay his daughter and his niece—Adele Hebert. The cradle had been Robbie's, Jeremy had noted, as he teased the large-boned youngster about having been small enough once to fit in it.

Nina lay sleeping. She looked cool and fresh. Lucy had washed her and given her a clean nightgown. She had nursed her child. No milk had come yet, but the doctor said to do it anyway to toughen up her nipples.

Gilles recalled the bittersweet moment when Nina told him her choice of the name of the child.

"It's Adele, after your mother," Nina said to him.

Gilles had nodded and said nothing. If she thought she fooled him then she must think him very dense indeed. It was Marcel's mother's name as well.

CHAPTER TWELVE

Virginia, January 1756

Marcel walked along York Street. He was dressed in a homespun coat and breeches he had purchased in Halifax. Atop his head was a poor man's version of Benoit's three-cornered hat. He patted his coat pocket just to make sure the paper was still there. It was a precious document. It identified him as a truly sworn subject of King George from his province of Nova Scotia. With England and France fighting and a declaration of war expected at any time, such a document could prove invaluable in the midst of Virginia.

It had taken Marcel weeks to recover from the losses at Port Hebert. Losing both of his parents almost simultaneously had shattered him. Yet he had tasks to perform. He asked Benoit and Old Gums to take care of little Lucien while he went looking for the survivors. Benoit attempted to talk him out of it. He grieved for Marcel. In so short a time the boy he had taken with him into the woods had aged into an angry young man. He had liked the boy better but no one could undo what was already done. He took the child from Marcel. He would winter on the St. John again with the woman and the child and would be there next spring when Marcel came looking for them.

Marcel hated to leave his son, little Lucien. After all, he did not even know if Helene, Gilles, or Nina were alive. Lucien was his living flesh and blood. He was tempted to stay behind to make his peace with Governor Lawrence and Audry Hastings, who was now one of the largest landowners in the Fundy area. Yet he found it unacceptable to rent his own father's land from Hastings. Moreover, he would not be able to live with himself if he did not do what he knew his father would have expected of him, what every Acadian would have expected from every other Acadian. He had a responsibility to reunite his family. He would look until he either found his brother and sister or until all traces of them had vanished. And he would find Babin's daughter; that was an urge that went beyond even blood ties. And so he kissed the brown-skinned lad good-bye. The boy would barely notice his departure. He had eyes only for Old Gums and in reality only for Old Gums' nourishing teats.

Marcel had gone first to Halifax. He found the records of all the ships that had sailed for Virginia. There were four of them and all had landed at Yorktown and had consigned their captives to the markets at Williamsburg. Marcel used some of his money to buy his clothes and to purchase his passage to Boston. From the Yankee capital he sailed on to Virginia. In Yorktown he had found a wagoneer going to Williamsburg and he hitched a ride.

His walk through the capital continued. He crossed the Exchange and walked up Blair Street until he entered the area immediately before the House of Burgesses. Rows of taverns lined the street here. Farther down there was a military magazine on the market square.

Now his task would begin. First, he had to find someone who could speak French. But that could take hours or maybe days. How would Benoit solve the problem? The idea struck Marcel like a flash of inspiration. It was precisely what his friend would have done.

The marketplace was busy. White women, dressed in drab homespun, shopped at the various stalls along with black slaves who were dressed in calico, or whatever red and yellow cloths they could find. Some fruit and vegetable stalls were still selling squash and pumpkins but at this time of year there was little else to be had. The fresh vegetables had been replaced by candles and soaps. Some stalls sold perfumed scents and firewood for winter.

Marcel walked to the middle of the square.

"Je ne parle pas anglais," he shouted loudly. *"Parlez vous français?"*

The first passerby stared at him as if he were insane. Some children stopped their game and ran to watch the man who made such strange sounds. Between shouts Marcel looked at each member of the little crowd and asked the same question. It was usually enough to chase the adults away. The children merely stared at him or lost interest and went back to their game.

After a half hour, someone reported him to the constable for disturbing the peace of the village. As the constable approached, the crowd grew larger.

"What's all this commotion?" the constable called out. Then he caught sight of the young Frenchman.

"Je ne parle pas anglais," Marcel addressed him.

"What's this nonsense? What are you saying to me?"

Marcel repeated his disclaimer.

"I think I'd better take you in so that we can begin to find out what is going on here," the constable said, taking Marcel by the arm.

The Frenchman did not resist. He went with the constable. The crowd of about thirty, mostly children, went along. The little posse passed down Duke of Gloucester Street to the palace green and then they turned right. Ahead of them was the red brick governor's palace and to their right a wooden building that served as the town hall.

"All you brats, scatter," the constable yelled as they came to the hall. "This is Crown business. Go back and play."

The constable, holding tight to Marcel's arm, led him into the hall and down a flight of steps. He opened a door and shoved Marcel forward, slamming the door behind him. Then he slid back a tiny panel in the door.

"You take me for a dummy, don't you, Frenchy?" he said through the panel. "I know French when I hear it and I know the French are our enemies. You can just cool your heels in there until the justice of the peace arrives. He speaks your language. And let me tell you, if you are some kind of spy, you'll find out that we know how to hang in this country."

The constable then slammed the panel shut and returned upstairs fully convinced that he had apprehended the first in a series of spies France had sent into the heart of the colony to further exploit the defeat of the British army in the west.

Marcel was beginning to have second thoughts about the "Benoit method" as he paced the tiny holding cell. Had he come all this way from Beauséjour just to end up in a Virginia jail? In his despair, his determination to find his family grew. They were all he had left. The whole village had been destroyed. If he could free even two or three of the persons he loved, maybe they could return and begin anew. Marcel realized that it was ironic that it was he who now thought this way. When Port Hebert was all he had to look forward to, he had rebelled and fled to the woods. But bringing his father to the ruins had changed all that. It was as if the dying father's love for all that had been lost had been transferred to him. He wanted his sister and brother and Nina to join him and Benoit and Lucien to begin Port Hebert all over again. He slumped to the floor and waited.

He did not know how long he remained there. The panel on the door was pushed back at least twice and an eye peered at him. He presumed it was the ever-vigilant constable. There was only one window in the room. It was closed and barred. The light became more golden as the afternoon wore on.

Marcel had drifted off into a troubled doze when the door's bolt was thrown and the door itself squeaked open. He awoke just as a black-coated man in a three-cornered hat and a wig entered the cell. He was followed by the constable.

"Here is Lawyer Pike. He speaks your language," the constable said.

Then the lawyer spoke. Some of his words were familiar to Marcel but he could make no sense whatsoever out of the totality. He repeated that he spoke no English and needed to find a French speaker. The man in black seemed to grow agitated and spoke even more rapidly. It finally dawned on Marcel that he was trying to speak French. While the man knew some French words he had no idea how to pronounce them. Marcel grew even more depressed. His task seemed hopeless. If this was Williamsburg's French speaker then he would never learn anything here. His two visitors grew even more indignant with his silence. Finally they turned and left the cell, slamming the door behind them.

Night fell. Marcel tried to make himself as comfortable as possible. He curled up in the corner and tried to sleep, but the floor was hard and his mind was troubled. Even worse, he desperately needed to relieve his bladder. Sometime after midnight the cell door opened and a tray of food was slipped in on the floor, along with a blanket and a pillow. The plate contained cold potatoes and a good-sized mug of beer. Marcel drank the beer quickly and put the empty mug to good use. He wondered if unconsumed food and drink were the property of the constable. He hoped so.

The potatoes were bland, but he was hungry and he downed them quickly. He spread the blanket in the corner and lay down on half of it. The other half he folded over himself. The pillow was what put him to sleep. Its softness enveloped his aching head. In the middle of the wilderness he had slept with just a folded blanket for his head. Before many minutes had passed he was snoring quietly.

When he awoke in the morning the tray of food was gone. He chuckled aloud. But very little else that morning was amusing. His muscles ached from the hard floor. Even the earth was softer, he decided. His beard was several days old and he wanted to shave. His mouth tasted foul, and he was in need of a clean shirt, or at least an opportunity to wash his current one and himself. Not that he smelled any worse than these Virginians.

His captors seemed in no rush to communicate with him. It was not until almost noon that the constable reopened the cell door. He peered in and then opened it.

"Come out. Today you get your hearing. You're a lucky one. The justice of the peace speaks your language." He placed manacles on Marcel's wrists and ankles. Marcel protested the absurdity of the constable's action, but to no effect. He was led upstairs to a courtroom jammed with spectators. The citizens of Williamsburg loved a good trial. The trial of a suspected spy with the prospect of a good hanging at the end of it had brought spectators early and left standing room only by ten o'clock.

Mr. Ludlow waited until the prisoner shuffled into the room and was placed in the prisoner's dock before he entered.

Everyone was called upon to rise for the justice of the peace. Ludlow sat down, followed by the whole courtroom except for Marcel. The first words out of Ludlow's mouth disappointed the spectators.

"You are aware, I am sure, Mr. Constable and Lawyer Pike, that this is an informal hearing to determine if we have cause to send this man to trial."

"Does that mean there ain't going to be a hanging?" someone called out.

Ludlow rapped his gavel down for order. "They'll be no hanging, Jedediah," Ludlow said to a chorus of moans. Then he turned to Marcel and spoke to him in fluent French.

Marcel was taken by surprise. His face broke into a smile at the sound of his own language.

"Mr. Judge," Marcel said, "you don't know how glad I am to speak to someone in my own tongue. None of these people could understand me."

"You must understand, Monsieur..."

"Hebert," Marcel interrupted.

"Monsieur Hebert, that I don't take the charge of spying seriously. Spies don't announce their presence in our country. But our two countries are at war, and here in Virginia feelings are running high after the slaughter of General Braddock's force of regulars and Virginia militia by you French and your Indian allies. There are some here who have lost relatives in that battle, sir. Why did you risk coming here so publicly?"

"I am a British subject, sir, and I have the papers to prove it." He reached into his coat and took out the official document from the governor's office in Halifax.

Ludlow turned to Pike. "Bring that paper to me."

Pike looked at Marcel suspiciously, then took the document and handed it to the justice.

Ludlow looked at it carefully. "Constable, did you search the prisoner?" he asked.

The constable hesitated a moment.

"Well?" Ludlow asked.

"Of course, sir."

"I suggest that you are lying, since if you had searched him you would have read the document which Mr. Hebert has given me, and you would have found evidence that Mr. Hebert is a legal subject of His Majesty and a resident of

260

Nova Scotia. Given his inability to speak English he took the precaution to have such a document on his person just in case he ran into fools and bigots on his journey. Now we know we have no fools or bigots in Williamsburg. Lawyer Pike, you, of course, questioned Monsieur Hebert."

Pike's expression sagged. He knew that once Ludlow stopped referring to the man in the dock as the prisoner and began to use his name, he was about to set him free.

"I questioned him, sir. He refused to respond."

"You spoke to him in French?"

"Of course, sir."

"Now I understand," said Ludlow. He switched to French. "Monsieur Hebert, please accept the apologies of the court. You have been wrongly retained by a pair of complete dolts." He changed back to English. "Monsieur Hebert," he said in a loud voice to the whole courtroom, "is to be released at once."

Then he addressed Marcel again. "Please join me at the Raleigh Tavern on Duke of Gloucester for some wine and perhaps a good bird. Of course you will be my guest."

There was a fire burning in the hearth. The afternoon was chilly. The sun had disappeared shortly after the trial was over and rain had started to fall.

The innkeeper served partridge, well seasoned and stuffed with chestnuts and dried fruit. Then he brought the men a port that was almost forty years old. The pipes were taken from the rack and filled with fine-cut Virginia tobacco. Marcel could hardly believe how content he felt. Last night cold potatoes and a hard wood floor, tonight a feast fit for a king with a down-filled mattress in one of the bedrooms upstairs waiting for him, courtesy of Justice Ludlow.

Marcel had objected at first. He could pay.

"Nonsense," said Ludlow. "What kind of people would you think we were after the way Pike and his idiot friend treated you? A northern visitor to Virginia must be introduced to southern hospitality."

Despite the generosity, Marcel detected a certain condenscension in Ludlow's behavior. He ignored it. Instead he leaned back in his chair and enjoyed his pipe and his wine.

"What is the purpose of your visit to Virginia, Monsieur Hebert?" Ludlow asked, blowing smoke into the air.

"I seek my family, sir."

"Here?"

"Yes, sir. My family were among the deportees from Acadia who came through Williamsburg last fall. I am looking for my sister, Helene Hebert, and my brother, Gilles."

"Gilles Hebert. Oh my. Yes, the name is familiar to me. He has become notorious. But the woman with him was not his sister, if I recall, but his wife."

"Why do you say my brother has become notorious? Has he done something wrong, monsieur?"

"I suppose I must come right out with it. Your brother arrived with his wife, a pretty girl with light brown hair, a lovely complexion, and very pregnant."

Marcel knew immediately that he had found the trail of Nina Babineau as well.

"Well," Ludlow went on, "they were both sold as indentured laborers to Mr. Jonas Audry of Port Royal in King George County."

"How do I find this Mr. Audry?" Marcel asked.

"That's the problem. They've run away. Your brother did terrible injury to Mr. Audry's overseer. He's a man, I'm told, of terrible temper and violent actions."

Marcel smiled. Yes, gentle Gilles has a temper.

"I'm afraid," Ludlow continued, "that he and the girl have become fugitives from justice."

"No hint of their whereabouts?"

"Perhaps Audry knows. Nothing more is known here in Williamsburg."

Marcel rose from his chair and put the pipe down on the table. He drank the last of his port wine in a gulp. "I thank you, sir, for your generosity and hospitality It reminds me of the generosity and hospitality of my own people until they were so gravely injured."

"The result of their own fickleness, wouldn't you say? If they had sworn allegiance as you did, nothing like this would have happened?"

"You're correct," Marcel said to Ludlow, "unless, of course, it had been France who won the war."

Ludlow saw only jest in Marcel's words. He began to

laugh. "Oh, that is a good one, sir. Yes, I see your point. Then perhaps it would have been you who had been transported by the French."

"Good evening, sir." Marcel dismissed himself. "I must arrange to travel to the Audry plantation."

"I'll arrange a horse for you."

Marcel took coins from his money belt by reaching up under his jacket and shirt. He placed them on the table in front of him.

Ludlow picked one up. "This ought to do it. You will be returning, of course. Otherwise the price would be much higher."

"I'll be coming back," he lied. If Gilles was a fugitive, then there was no possibility of their returning via Williamsburg.

It was midnight and the slaves in the kitchen wanted to go to bed. To hell with them, Jonas Audry thought as he sat eating his dinner and getting steadily drunker despite the food. He had three bottles of New England rum sitting on the buffet, and one and a half were already empty. He was only half finished. The door to the kitchen opened and Rufus stuck his head inside.

"Massa, you sure you wants a roast leg of mutton?"

"That's what I want!"

"We ain't got none."

"I still want some."

"We ain't butchered no sheep since the spring, Massa. No way meat's going to keep that long. It's too late to go to Massa Wilson's to see if he gots any."

"That's your problem. I don't get lamb, you get a thrashing."

Rufus retreated into the kitchen and Audry laughed loudly. He loved to pose these dilemmas to his slaves. They were brilliant in working out solutions and he delighted in seeing how they got around the problem. If they failed, he had the pleasure of meting out the punishment.

He had never done more to Rufus than box his ears. He wondered how a soft house slave would bear up under the lash. Probably he would break with three strokes. They were not tough like the field hands, or the field boss, for that matter. Field bosses were tough. He recalled what he had done to Jubal. The man had never cried out. He was remarkable. He had broken both the man's legs. The pain must have been excruciating, yet he survived the punishment and the shock that set in afterwards despite his broken ribs. Now he hobbled about the plantation on crutches, a field boss no more. Useless, in fact. Audry had stopped issuing any rations to either Jubal or Luck. They would have to live off what they grew and the charity of others. It was a cardinal rule of his for a well-run plantation. No work, no food.

Breaking the legs of a runaway was a harsh punishment, but no one had taken him to task for it. Nor had anyone complained when he manacled Luck's legs. It was hard to run away when your legs were shackled together. Word spread among the slaves from plantation to plantation about his "abuse" of his own mammy. But she had tried to run away. She would try no more.

No, there was no criticism of his treatment of the blacks. Yet he was ostracized by the white community. None of the planters invited him to any social gatherings. He had not heard from the Wilsons since their return from the valley. So what if he shot the Scottish bastard? The man was sheltering the French runaways, and unlawfully at that. Strange that no one in King George County seemed upset that the law of the colony had been set aside and the sheriff assaulted. They seemed to care only about what he did. They spread rumors that he had raped the girl, as if every planter, at one time or another, had not had his way with a wench against her will. And in this case the girl had no will. He owned her. Besides, people were taking the word of the wench and her illiterate husband against his. That was mortally insulting. He was a gentleman, after all.

He took another swig of rum directly from the bottle. Perhaps he should ride over to Wilson's and demand to see Susan. He had not spoken to her since that day in Williamsburg when he purchased his two problems. He was sure she would understand why he did what he did. If only he could speak to her. He took the bottle of rum and drained it.

"Rufus," he called out.

The black man came to the door.

"Saddle me a horse. I'm going courting." He stood up from the table and collapsed into a heap on the floor.

"Going courting," Rufus said with disdain, "you ain't going

anywhere but bed, you ugly bastard. And by morning you ain't going to remember you wanted leg of lamb in the wintertime. That's how I solves most of the troubles you gives me, Massa Shit. I just let you drink them away for me."

He picked Jonas up under the arms and hauled him out of the room and up to his bed.

Katie entered the room just as Rufus left. She had to clean up the mess. This happened every night now, ever since he returned home ahead of the posse that went looking for Jubal and Luck.

"Lawd be praised," she said when she noticed that Audry had failed to eat one leg and one wing of the chicken. In the old days that would have been dinner for Katie and maybe some for Rufus if he spied it. But now it went directly to the quarters for Jubal and Luck. Those two had never eaten better. She attributed Jubal's recovery to the food from the kitchen. "Just as good as the Massa," she said aloud, but no one was ever going to make a field hand of Jubal no more. His legs were gone but he sure still was a powerful preacher.

There was a commotion in the kitchen. She had left Rose alone in the kitchen. That child sure wanted to be a cook and replace Katie someday in the kitchen, but she was as clumsy as the old mule they kept in the quarters.

She pushed open the door and found Rose sitting in front of Gabriel, the new field boss. And he was reaching where he hadn't ought to be reaching.

"You piece of trash," Katie yelled at Rose. "You try to turn my kitchen into a cat house."

"I told Gabe you wasn't in any bed, Katie, but he just insists on pawing me."

"You want to paw that girl, you best jump over the broom handle together and then you can paw nice and legal-like in the eyes of the Lawd. It ain't doin' you no good, Gabriel, to be living in that cabin alone."

Gabriel just laughed and backed away from Rose. He had known Katie was not in bed, not with the kitchen a mess. Katie never went to bed with her job undone no matter what the hour. But he was the field boss now and entitled to some privileges.

"I dropped by," he said, "to let you uppity house niggers know that we gots us another visitor in the quarters. French fellow, like the last one. Jubal suspects they be brothers or some close relative from the looks of him. Seems he rode right by the big house. He didn't come to see Massa Audry. He came looking for that fellow Jack and that girl. Thought you ought to know that here. Jubal thinks we shouldn't tell Massa about this fella, seeing that Massa is plumb crazy and all."

"Pawing a girl seems to suit you, Gabriel. You just said more in one time than I ever heard from you before. What is more, you made sense. God knows what will be happening to you when you get beyond pawing."

Gabriel laughed and patted Katie's ample rump.

Rufus returned to the kitchen smelling of rum and vomit. When Gabriel told him of Jubal's message, he slumped into the chair by the kitchen table.

"Seems like trouble ain't never going to stop," he said, looking up at Katie. "Those foreign folks brought misery to this plantation. Can't say I'd be happy to see another one of them. That man upstairs has got a devil in him and these 'dentured folks seem to stir it up."

First thing every morning since he had returned, Jubal went out to the barn and fed Edgar. And this morning was no exception. He first offered to feed the beast because he knew how difficult it was for Luck to walk about to the barn with chains on her legs. Initially, Edgar had shown his traditional hostility and attempted a few kicks at Jubal, but the black man ignored him and fed him generously. Now Jubal spent his first hours of the day talking to his old enemy.

"Can't stay too long today, you old bastard," he said, with more affection than hostility. "There be trouble brewing at the old Stink Hole once again. Got another one of those French fellows, Cadians, I think they call themselves. Well, this Cajun fellow he be related to Jack, the other one. If he finds out what happened to the last one that come here I don't think he be staying too long."

Edgar snorted and continued to munch on his hay.

Jubal rose from the stool on which he sat. He picked up the crutches that Abel the carpenter had made for him. He placed them under his arms and swung his all but useless legs forward. He could move quite fast if he had to, and this morning there was a chill in the air. He looked up into the gray sky with its low-flying clouds. "There might even be a bit of snow in those clouds," he speculated. Snow or not, his flimsy shirt and pants let enough of the wind through to his skin to get him moving fast across the barnyard to his cabin. He opened the door to find Luck standing at the hearth cooking some breakfast. He was glad to see that their neighbors supplied them more than usual. It was shameful enough to have to take charity from his friends. At least their generosity spared him the shame of not having enough for a guest.

Marcel sat at Luck's wobbly table and was amazed by the warmth and hospitality of the two infirm and abused slaves. He was glad for Gilles and Nina that they had encountered them as protectors, although from all he could gather their encounter had brought much grief to the slaves. He could not believe that the woman had been chained for months. The scabs at the top and the bottom of the manacles were, however, ample proof of her suffering. He wished he could communicate better with them.

The Frenchman ate the corn bread they placed in front of him. It did not taste much different from the corn bread his mother used to serve at Port Hebert.

"Jubal, what we going to do with this Frenchman?"

"We should send him west where he can find those other two."

"I heard Massa Wilson say they was with a Massa Griff, but that disturbed me. Way folks always talk there be no slaves in the valley, and if there be no slaves there be no need for Massas. Why they got this Massa Griff?" She reached down and touched his hand. "If we had only made it."

"Wouldn't do no good if there be Massas up there. What's the use? There be no 'liverance for black folk in the world. We won't get none till we be with Jesus."

Gabriel came to the door. He was the new field boss but he still deferred to Jubal in all decisions.

"A message came down from the big house from Rufus. The Massa is awake and asking questions. What do we do?"

"Do what comes natural to you and Rufus. Play dumb. I think we ought to send this French fellow over to Massa Wilson. Perhaps he can send him to the right place."

Suddenly Gabriel swung away from the door. He had been pulled back. Jonas Audry stepped into Luck's cabin. He was only slightly disheveled. His whiskers had not been shaved in days, but he no longer reeked of rum.

"You darkies are such children and you take me for one too. Who are you, sir?" Audry said pointing to Marcel. "And why have you snuck into my plantation and visited my niggers without my permission?"

Marcel rose. *"Je m'appelle Marcel Hebert."*

Audry's good eye widened at the sound of the name Hebert.

"Gilles Hebert?"

"Mon frère."

Audry hesitated a moment.

"Massa Audry." Jubal tried to distract him.

"Shut up, nigger," Audry shouted at him. "Brother?"

By now Marcel was wary of the white man. His tone of voice in speaking to the blacks betrayed his true intentions.

"Oui, brothair," Marcel replied.

"What a mistake. How could you allow a brother of Gilles Hebert to stay in the slave quarters? You must come with me up to the house. Gabriel, get my horse. Mr. Hebert and I will ride back to the house together."

"You don't have to put on no show," Jubal spat out. "He don't understand any English."

"Watch your mouth, Jubal. You're lucky all I did was have your legs broken. I could have done worse."

"How?" the black man said boldly. Luck squeezed his hand and forced him to stop.

"Don't tempt me. You'll not like the results." He dabbed his chin with his handkerchief. He walked toward Marcel.

"Come back to the house. We must talk about your brother's whereabouts," he said in very poor French.

Marcel went reluctantly. His horse was saddled and ready to ride. Audry mounted and Marcel followed suit. The Virginian was a magnificent rider. He gave his horse his head and the animal charged across the fields and over the fence. Marcel's past experience had been with plow horses when he was a boy. He saw Audry waiting for him on the road. He rode more cautiously, following the road as it turned up toward the mansion.

Audry seemed to be smiling at him as he approached him but it was hard to tell with this man. The scar distorted his face. Was the expression a smile or a sneer of contempt?

Audry remained by Marcel's side as they completed the rest of the short ride to the house. A gray-haired black man in livery took the reins from both of them.

"Rufus," Audry said to the man, "I want a good country breakfast for both of us, eggs, bacon, sausage, some johnny cake, and some good honey and fresh butter, and above all some good tea."

"Yes, Massa," Rufus said, "it will be just as soon as I can get Katie out of her bed."

"What is she doing in bed? Do I have to watch out for every one of you?"

"You ate late last night, Massa. She was up until two in the morning cleaning up."

Audry smiled at Rufus. "Tell her to get her fat black ass out of bed or I'll stick a hot poker up it," he said softly.

But Rufus had no doubt his master would try it if provoked. As soon as the two whites stepped into the foyer he raced to the house slaves' sleeping quarters on the third floor of the house to arouse the cook.

Audry gave Marcel a tour of the house. The furnishings were lavish. Marcel had never seen anything like it in his life. He gazed in awe at the crystal chandeliers in the giant drawing room, which also served as a ballroom for The Meadows although there had been no balls and no one had danced at The Meadows since Audry's mother had died.

Audry amused himself showing this country bumpkin about the house. He was slightly better dressed but no better educated than his brother. He was even more amused to watch the fool eat his breakfast. He obviously had never seen such a meal before. Nor did he know what to do with the knife and fork. He followed every move Jonas made. Just for a joke Jonas stuck his sausage with his knife, raised it to his mouth, and ate it from the knife. He had to struggle to keep from laughing aloud when Marcel very solemnly proceeded to eat his sausage in exactly the same manner.

Marcel stiffened in anger and instantly realized he was being toyed with when Audry stirred his tea with the handle of his knife. Audry ignored him and went right on with his meal.

After eating, Audry took Marcel upstairs and showed him his bedroom. It was on the side of the house away from the river. His room looked out onto the fields, which now were void of any crop but in spring were green with tobacco. Beyond the fields he could see the smoke of the slave quarters. Audry indicated that he could wash up and rest if he wanted. Marcel stood by the closed window. Audry closed the door behind him. Marcel swung around in apprehension when he heard the lock click and the man laugh insanely on the other side of the door.

"Now I'll get word to that bastard McGriff to tell old Gilles that his brother Marcel is waiting for him at The Meadows. He'd better get there quick if he wants to save his brother from what I had intended for him. Oh yes, and he'd better bring the girl."

Marcel heard the Englishman laughing and talking to himself. He was now convinced that the man was crazy. He sat down on the bed and checked that his hunting knife was still in place. Then he cursed himself for walking right into the spider's web. He should have done it Benoit's way and simply stuck a knife into Audry's belly, giving an extra twist for the sake of all those to whom he had brought pain—especially the two blacks in the cabin. But this wasn't the wilderness of Acadia. If he tried it Benoit's way he would find himself dangling at the end of a rope.

Audry was busy all afternoon. He ordered all the slaves to remain in their quarters while he personally inspected each shanty. He reminded Jubal as he left his cabin that he was taking Black Edgar from the barn and bringing him to the big house.

"If you want to trot over to Massa Wilson's on your own," he laughed, "you feel free to go." Then he returned to his house and his rum.

Jubal sat by the hearth warming his legs. The cold hurt them so much. The pain would shoot up to his hips. He loved to bake them in front of the fire. Luck sat rubbing her legs. The manacles gave her almost as much grief as the mended bones gave to Jubal.

"What you thinking about, old man?" Luck asked.

"I'm thinking about how glad I am that I found you back those many years ago."

"What do you mean you found me! I had my eyes on you well before you ever knew I was around. I saw you working in the tobac fields. You was topping that day. Lawd, it was hot and you was stripped to the waist. Your muscles was something to behold and I been beholding them all the years since."

Jubal smiled at her and tapped her hand. "It be coming to a close soon."

"What you talking about?" she asked.

"The white man, Jack's brother, coming here. I feel it. It's going to be the end of things."

"You and your feeling. Just like you had a feeling we was going to be free in the valley where they had no slaves and no masters."

"I was wrong then."

"What makes you think you feel right now?"

"I don't know. It's a special African feeling like my pappy old me about in Da Home."

Luck shivered. She did not like it when he spoke of Da Home.

Gabriel came into their cabin without knocking.

"Good evening, Gabriel," Jubal greeted him.

"It ain't going to be good, Jubal."

The older man looked at him quizzically.

"It's Audry. He sent orders down to bring out the table with the straps, the punishment table."

Jubal's whole body stiffened. He had been stretched on that table some months before. He could remember the feeling of the rough boards under his skin. Then the blinding pain.

"What's he planning?"

"He's screaming up at the big house. Rufus was afraid to leave. He sent my Rose."

Luck's eyebrows rose at Gabriel's admission of his relationship with Katie's apprentice.

"He's shouting," Gabriel continued, "that he's going to finish the job he started on the Frenchman at last."

"It's not even the same Frenchman. He's got no cause to harm this fellow," Luck protested.

271

"We going to have to go to Massa Wilson again."

"Now I know what he meant." Jubal smiled sadly.

"The man's crazy, Jubal. What are we going to do?" Gabriel asked.

"We're going to stop him. We can't go to Massa Wilson. There isn't time to walk there. Even if Massa Wilson did stop the punishment for the white man, that bastard Audry would break someone else's legs or cut off someone else's black balls. I promised myself something back in Nathan's time when I held that boy down while Audry unmanned him. I promised myself then, I promised that boy on my soul, that it would not happen again. I am a preacher. I believe in Jesus and his message of goodness, but Jesus never knew Jonas Audry. If he did he would abandon the Sermon on the Mount; he would have thought more about the law as Moses gives it, an eye for an eye. There ain't going to be no punishment. I'm going to avenge that boy."

"I'm with you," Gabriel said.

"No. It has to be just me alone. If anyone else is involved they'll kill all of you."

"Jubal," Luck called to him, "ain't no life living without you. I'm coming with you."

Jubal looked at her. She was old now and hobbled. So many years together. He did not want to be separated from her either in life or in death. He held out his hand to her.

"Come to me, old woman," he said. "Four legs is better than two."

He threw down one of his crutches and leaned on his hobbled wife. Together they started down the road to the big house.

Audry sat in his dining room. He called to Rufus. There was no response. "Damn his ass," Audry cursed. On the table there was a little dinner bell his mother had always used. He picked it up and used it. Still no response.

He rose, knocking his fine glass full of rum onto the lace tablecloth. "Shit," he said. He walked across the room into the kitchen. The fire was burning. Someone had recently put more kindling on it. There were potatoes warming and a wild duck in the oven. Yet the kitchen was completely empty.

"Katie," he called out. He opened the door to the butler's

pantry, fully expecting to find Rufus there. It was empty. "What is that new wench's name?" he said to himself. But he could not remember it. He returned to the empty kitchen. "Rufus," he called again. No answer. He went upstairs from room to room, calling out. "Where the hell are they all?"

Audry began to panic. Except for the Frenchman locked in his bedroom, he was alone in the house. He had never been alone in the house before. He climbed the stairs to the third floor. He had not been up there since he was a boy when his mammy, Luck, took him to the household slaves' quarters. The distinction between the painted and papered walls and damask-draped windows of the second floor and the damp and musty-smelling third floor was striking. But in one aspect they were the same. They were both devoid of inhabitants.

He hailed anyone and no one in particular on the landing between the floors. Then he searched the servants' quarters room by room. One room actually smelled of tobacco smoke and there were hot ashes in the clay dish near the straw mat that served as a bed. In another room there was a rocking chair, which he could have sworn was still rocking gently when he entered the room.

He returned to the second floor. He called again. His voice seemed to echo through the empty corridors. He returned down the grand staircase to the foyer. Standing just inside the great doors were Jubal and Luck.

Audry was relieved to see someone. "My, we're getting bold," he said to the two old people. "Niggers are not allowed in the front door." He came down the remaining stairs.

Jubal merely stared at his master. Luck walked away from the two men.

"Wasn't it enough I broke your two legs for running away, old man? Maybe I should take the knife to you."

"Like the poor white trash did to you?"

"What are you talking about?" His hand shot to his face to adjust his patch. "I received my wound at the hands of a gentleman in a gambling disagreement."

"You got yourself cut up for sleeping with a tavern wench. Her father did it to you," Luck corrected him.

"Shut up, you bitch," Audry screamed at her. "You lie."

"What I say be the truth," Luck insisted. "I got the story from your mother."

"And every slave on this plantation knows the true story from Luck and me," Jubal added.

"Goddamn you, goddamn you both," Audry yelled. Spittle shot from his mouth and dripped down his chin. But this time in his rage he did not go for his handkerchief. He moved toward Jubal. He reached out to grab the black man by his shirt, but he was not fast enough. Jubal swung his crutch with all of his might. It crashed into the side of Audry's head and knocked off his patch.

Luck screamed.

Upstairs there was the sound of a door cracking. A few moments later Marcel came tearing down the stairs to the foyer. He saw Audry lying on the floor. His knees were drawn up into his belly and he was groaning. Jubal looked down at him without pity and without fear, even though by striking his master he had condemned himself to death. Luck was sobbing in the corner of the white marble entryway.

Jubal took Marcel by the hand. "You best be out of here," he said urgently. "Jack Hebert be at Massa Griff's in the west. You go there. Massa Griff, Massa Griff in the west. You hear me?"

Marcel repeated, "Massa Griff—*ouest*."

Luck called out and Marcel turned. Audry was on his feet. He had picked up a chair, a fragile decorative Louis XIV sitting chair. Almost in one action Marcel removed his knife from his belt and threw it. It struck Jonas with a sickening thud in the chest. He was dead as he hit the floor. His body quivered a few times, then lay motionless.

Luck hobbled to where he lay. She looked down at him, tears streaming from her eyes. No matter what he had done to her she could only remember now the little boy she carried around on her hip. "Poor Massa, poor Massa" was all she could say.

There were some shouts outside the house. The doors burst open and a mass of black people poured through. Jubal raised his hand to try to stop them.

"You keep away from here. I don't want all of you to be punished for this. Now it is only me. Jubal is responsible. I got to take on the punishment for this."

Gabriel pulled him outside. Marcel did the same to Luck. Rufus ran past them, his face in ecstasy. In his hand he carried a torch. Others joined him—field hands and house slaves, all with torches. Suddenly flames started to leap in the windows of the first floor. The same happened just as suddenly on the second. Curtains were ablaze, flames shooting up from the windows to the carved white wooden ceilings. Someone threw a chair through one of the giant windows of the first floor. Flames shot out into the night. Suddenly windows began to break all over the house. Cool air rushed into the house through the windows and turned the building into an inferno. Flames shot hundreds of feet into the night sky.

All the slaves had fled the house now. They backed away onto the green lawn to escape the heat. They had cheered as they torched the house but now they grew silent and watched. The only sound was the cracking flame and the crash of timbers as the floors gave way and came hurtling down on the debris below, sending sparks even higher into the night.

Gabriel produced Marcel's horse and held it steady while Marcel climbed into the saddle. He looked to the black faces crowded around him. He wondered what would become of them. As if reading his mind Jubal reassured the Frenchman.

"You be on your way to Massa Griff out west in the valley. The other planters, they hate Massa Audry. They'll call this an accident. You be off now."

Jubal slapped the rump of the horse and the slaves backed away from it as it began to kick and prance. Marcel had little choice but to leave. He gave his horse his head and started down the road toward the Rappahannock and the west.

The slaves watched until he disappeared into the dark. Gabriel walked over to Jubal, who stood with his arm around Luck.

"What do we do now?"

Jubal looked solemnly at his friend. "Let's us all go to the prayer meetin' place in the woods."

The slaves followed the orders of their preacher. They got into a long line and began to move forward. They walked slowly to accommodate Jubal and Luck. Someone started humming, and soon all of them broke into a song of sorrow. Luck looked up at Jubal as they passed the slave quarters.

"You don't believe they're going to think that was an accident."

Jubal shook his head sadly. "Massa Wilson and the others will be here before long. It's best we be at the prayer meetin' place when they come."

Duncan McGriff looked out over his pasture land. It was covered with a fine powdery snow. Lucy bundled him up and his sons carried his chair outside onto the porch every morning as long as the sun was shining. Lucy believed that the sun could cure almost anything, summer or winter. McGriff did not believe it. He knew he would never move again. From the neck down he was dead. It was a shame the Englishman's ball had not cut his spine and killed him. Or better yet, he should have been cut down on the field of Culloden, as so many of the friends of his younger days had.

Now all he could hope for was that Jeremy would screw up his courage and put an end to Duncan McGriff. McGriff had asked him to do it. Nay, begged him. But the perversity of the Campbells was in him, and Jeremy refused him. It still angered McGriff. He had taken the little weasel into his own home out of pity for his loneliness. And for all his bitching Jeremy loved the McGriff boys like his own sons. Yet he would not do their father the one favor he asked in return. If he was afraid of losing the love of the sons by killing the father, who would know? Duncan didn't demand a dramatic ending. No bullet in the brain was required. Just a little something in the soup or a pillow over his face while he slept helpless in his bed.

But release he must have. He could not continue to be fed, cleaned when he messed himself, and washed. He had no manhood left. It would be better for all if Jeremy screwed up his courage. After all, Lucy deserved a man in her bed. Before long she would succumb. He knew it. He hated it but he could not fault her. Since the day he brought her home from the MacDonald's he had known that Angus's anger was only partly because she replaced the mother he loved. Angus was also humiliated and ashamed that he lusted after his father's wife. He flailed out at her and everyone else. Someday they would come together. He would know it when it happened. It would be when they stopped fighting one another. In his heart he would die a little more. And the two young ones would destroy themselves with guilt. The other boys would never accept Angus and Lucy. Not while Duncan lived. Probably not after he died, but more easily if he was gone.

The sun shone on his face. He thought again of Gilles, Nina, and tiny Adele. Had they fled McGriff because of the ambush, or because they were afraid to bring more anguish to their protectors? More likely, they left because Audry was still trying to lure him back to King George County with the crazy story of holding another Frenchman captive. It was true that there had been no mention of leaving until that message had come. Then suddenly Gilles had panicked. He was truly terrified of the man's insanity. If Gilles' relatives and friends had not been killed in the expulsion then surely he might have been lured back into the trap. But they left just as soon as they could with no real good-byes, a strained leaving made no easier by Angus's anger at the Frenchman for bringing Audry into their lives in the first place.

He had given Gilles specific instructions on how to find Fort Cumberland—damn that name, a flea-bitten pestilence hole for sure or nothing could be described by a name again. From there he was on his own. He was determined to make it to the French fort at the forks of the Ohio. It was a dangerous mission. The Indians of those northern regions had been on the rampage since last summer. But maybe French people would be safe. Once at the fort Gilles told him he was determined to find a way home. God help him. He would never do it in winter. He was told that it was so cold in the north that the great inland seas froze solid, cutting off all contact with the rest of the world. He had advised the lad that if he wanted a home within the dominions of King Louis of France he should descend the Ohio to the great river of the west and seek the French colony of Louisiana to the south. But Gilles had not given him any hint of his plans beyond the forks of the Ohio.

Duncan regretted that he never got a chance to say good-bye to Nina or the beautiful child, but they left in the early morning well before he was taken from his bed to the porch. Only Angus had seen them off with a good riddance.

The sun prevented him from seeing the rider until he was

almost directly in front of him. He squinted to get a better view. He gasped. So there was a brother after all, smaller and darker but every bit a brother in feature.

"*Bon jour,*" Duncan greeted him.

Marcel felt overwhelmingly defeated—to have come all this way and to have missed Gilles and Nina Babineau by less than a week. Why had they gone? The Scotsman thought that they did not wish to be a burden to the McGriffs. But up to that point they had already been a burden and it didn't seem to bother them. McGriff seemed to know more but he was not talking.

It was hard to fault him, however, or any of his family. They had suffered much because of the Heberts, and except for the oldest son and the whiney brother-in-law, they were extraordinarily hospitable.

The snows came to the valley the very night Marcel arrived, further frustrating him. McGriff warned him it would get worse the farther north he went. He only hoped, and Marcel's hopes joined him, that Gilles and his family had made it safely to the French fort.

The whole family sat up well beyond their normal bedtime to hear Marcel's story, which McGriff translated into English. They warmed to him, even Angus and Jeremy, when he related Jonas Audry's death to them. He did not trust any of them enough to admit his own guilt, but McGriff understood the meaning of his silences almost as much as he understood his words, and he conveyed both meanings to his audience.

They drank McGriff's home barley brew until very late. For the first time since his wounding, McGriff seemed to enjoy himself, and with his lightened mood the old joy seemed to return to all. Jeremy passed out and had to be carried to his bed. All the boys except Angus climbed up into the loft and joked with each other until a succession of snorts and snores indicated that all had fallen off. Lucy fell asleep with her head resting on McGriff's lap.

"What will you be doing now?" McGriff asked Marcel as Angus passed Marcel the last drink left in the jug.

The Acadian was close to losing control. He knew deep within him that if he took this last drink he would go over the edge. He shook his head to Angus. The young man downed the liquor himself.

McGriff roared. "Where the hell are your manners, you brooding billy goat? Your father should have had that drink."

Lucy was awakened by his outburst. She saw anger in Angus's eyes and she signaled him quietly to hold it in.

McGriff's heart sank. It had gone that far already.

"It's time you got to bed. Angus, help me with him," Lucy said.

They lifted his chair. Marcel rose unsteadily to help them.

"No need," said McGriff sadly. "Hebert," he called as the two carried him across the room, "what will you do?"

"Go home," Marcel said. "Gilles and Nina are on their way. Someday we will come together. I have a son. I want to see him again. After that I have one more promise to keep, a second one I made to my father. I will go looking for my sister. I had hoped she would be with Gilles, but now I must begin anew."

"Good," McGriff said. "You'll find a mat upstairs and I hope you snore. If you do you're in good company. If you don't, I hope you are a sound sleeper. And Hebert"—this time he called from within his bedroom—"it is always good to fulfill the trust a father places in you."

Part Three

CAJUNS

CHAPTER THIRTEEN

Louisiana, Summer 1763

Helene opened her blouse at the neck to permit the faint whisper of a breeze to cool her. She wiped her forehead with her arm and tried to brush her damp curls off of her face. Finally she pulled her honey-blond hair back and tied it in a club with a small piece of green ribbon.

She was miserably hot. For the past three years, ever since Lionel had lost his ship in a storm off the Florida Keys, she and her man and several of his crew had lived at Bayou Mazant—in the cypress swamps. The men spent their time hunting, fishing, trapping, and taking their wares to market. Helene, on the other hand, had spent most of the last three years cooking, sewing, and serving for the whole group. Today it was cooking. The men would be returning from the traplines in an hour or two and they would want their dinner.

Helene had learned to treat their palates. Everything she did she did right, and cooking was no exception. The heat from the low charcoal fire was contributing to her discomfort. She always cooked outside unless it rained. It kept the heat out of the cabin.

She slapped a mosquito that was feasting on her perspiration-soaked neck. She stirred the rich brown sauce in her iron pot. She had been cooking it for over an hour. She had to be careful that it did not burn. Stirring was the secret. The mix of lard and flour to make the brown sauce was something Maman Adele had taught her. Lionel had added the spices to her recipe, hot peppers and sassafras.

Helene added okra and onions and potatoes when she could get them. Once all the ingredients steeped together for long enough, she would add whatever meat or fish was available—crawfish or shrimp and oysters, and a bit of sausage—all of that went into the gumbo also.

She heard Lionel's call from deep within the swamp. He and the others would be here soon. She quickly threw in the remaining ingredients and stirred some more. She raised the pot higher over the burning coals. Now she could leave it. She retired to the dark interior of of her home.

It was a bit cooler in the log house. Its primitive exterior did not do justice to the inside of the dwelling. Lionel's booty filled the interior and decorated and covered the roughness of the logs. The mahogany table was covered by fine Chinese lace. It was set for two with gold tableware and the finest Japanese porcelain ware. Heavy cut-crystal wine goblets reflected the light from the gold candelabra that graced the middle of the table. The rest of the main room was decorated with equal luxury. A thick blue rug of interchanging circular designs covered the floor. Helene loved the feel of it when she sank her bare feet into its pile. She made everyone who entered the cabin take off their shoes before they were allowed to step on her prize rug.

She regretted the soft yellow silk covering of her chairs and loveseat. They clashed badly with the blue of the carpet. But she could hardly condemn Lionel for attacking a ship carrying lemon-colored furniture instead of seizing ships whose cargo matched the decor of her cabin. She could hardly condemn him, but she did nevertheless. Despite the color, she loved the loveseat and chairs. She delighted in running her hand across the smooth silk.

Her bedroom was done in mauve. The spread on her bed matched the curtains on her windows. The walls were covered with silk screens from the Orient. She allowed Lionel to turn his own bedroom into a replica of his cabin on the ship they had sailed in together.

But none of this finery satisfied her as much as the gold pieces she hid under the loose stone in the fireplace. It comforted her to count those coins, but the very counting was a source of disquiet. Provisions had to be purchased, salt, flour, sugar, and rice. The cache of gold coins was declining. She drove Lionel and his workers all the harder to replenish them, but she was not succeeding. The first skins they trapped and cured were not bringing enough in the New Orleans market to cover all of their expenses. She had thought to cut expenses by letting go some of Lionel's surviving crewmen. They cost more to feed than they brought in. She knew more about trapping from listening to Marcel than they would ever know, and Lionel was not much better than his crew. But when she spoke of it, Lionel flew into a rage. He grew so angry she thought he would hit her. She backed down quickly and took a few more gold pieces out of their hiding place to cover expenses. She told herself that the hard times were a result of the way and the uncertainty of the future of the colony of Louisiana.

The war had gone badly for France. She had lost not only Acadia with the capture of the fortress of Louisbourg by the English general, Amherst, but now Quebec and, even Montreal had fallen. The vast French empire in North America, a network of waterways guarded at the narrows by forts, had lost the key narrows. The bottleneck of the system had been corked by the English victories. Only the Mississippi, with its bottleneck at New Orleans, lay open to France.

Helene looked over the table. She wanted a good meal for Lionel. She had to convince him of the scheme that she had formulated right here at her dining table as she listened to Lionel's friends, the privateer captains who worked out of Bayou Mazant. New Orleans, she had decided, was the spot to be in. It alone had access to the interior—to forts like St. Louis, Detroit, and Fort Miami. The empire of New France would be sustained through Louisiana. The captains had said so, and Helene wanted to be a part of the effort. Her desire stemmed not from any love of France but from her knowledge that whoever purchased goods from the privateer captains could become very wealthy by serving as a middleman to the French army, as well as to civilians in Detroit and the Illinois country and beyond. And Helene had developed a sincere love of money.

They would be here at any moment. She went into the bedroom and quickly stripped off her work dress. She poured water into a basin on the bureau. She washed herself carefully. She turned to look into the full mirror on the back of the wooden door. Her figure was still shapely. She had become pregnant twice since living with Lionel and both times she had had early miscarriages. She was secretly satisfied. She wanted no little ones. She was not meant to be a mother. Besides, little ones ruined figures and she would allow nothing to ruin hers. Her breasts were firm and stood high. No sign of sagging there. She turned to get a profile of her stomach. It was flat, with just a slight bulge at her lower belly.

She went to her dresser. Her best perfume was old but still pungent. She dabbed a little behind each ear and in each armpit. She looked again in the mirror. She smiled at herself and then placed the stopper of the perfume bottle against the fine gold hair that began just below her navel and then fanned out into a V. He would like that, she thought. She wanted to please him tonight.

She put on a new shift, and over that she placed a white linen dress with a low-cut bodice. She began to brush her hair. It was still damp at the temples, but as the brush ran through the gold strands, the lighter streaks bleached by the sun became highlighted. Her face was an even better feature than her breasts, she thought, and she thought very highly indeed of her breasts.

She heard him hail her. She put the brush down and took one last look in the mirror. She smiled at what she saw.

Lionel came into the house carrying the iron pot filled with tonight's gumbo. His hair had grayed slightly at the temples and small wrinkles had appeared at the corners of his eyes, but life as a trapper suited him. Anything physical suited him—although, of all things, he most loved the sea, and having no ship had caused him much pain.

Helene waited at the doorway of her room for Lionel to come to her. He set the iron pot on the workbench by the hearth. He came toward her and enveloped her in his arms.

He loved the smell of her hair. The perfume clung to her. He took a deep breath to inhale her beauty. He could never get over it. The spell she had over him was complete. When he was away for even a brief moment she dominated his thoughts. Even as he worked the traplines with his men, his thoughts were that each animal killed was another skin and each skin brought him closer to the wealth Helene wanted and needed.

She pushed him away. He smelled of trap scent and sweat.

"Go wash," she ordered.

"I'd rather eat," he said, glancing at the steaming gumbo. "We can't let it get cold."

"It will keep," she said, wrinkling up her nose at him.

Lionel relented. He would not wash, but he would go for a swim in the bayou's cool waters. He removed his gray shirt. His hairy chest was covered with dirt streaked by rivulets of sweat.

"No wonder you stink—you're filthy."

"Nothing wrong with the good honest dirt or sweat, especially when earned trying to make my love happy.".

"If you want to make me happy," she countered, "take me to New Orleans."

He stiffened. "We've been through all of that too many times, Helene," he said. "I'd die in the city."

"That's what you said after you lost your ship and you had to become a trapper. But you didn't."

He stepped out of his pants. His upper torso was browned by the sun but his belly, thighs, and buttocks were fish-belly white. He dropped the pants on the floor and walked out of the house toward the bayou.

Helene picked up his pants from the floor. They too were filthy. She found his shirt where he dropped it and placed it with her own laundry. She would have to do the wash tomorrow.

She followed him outside. He had already dived into the water and was splashing around like a porpoise. She was tempted to join him to escape the heat of the afternoon, but she rejected the notion.

"Lionel," she called. Just then he dived beneath the surface and exposed his rump to her. He was deliberately trying to annoy her. She waited. He did not resurface.

"Lionel," she called out in alarm. "Where are you?"

Still the waters were unmoved by anything other than the ripples from the breeze.

"Lionel," she screamed.

"Yes," he said from behind her.

She jumped from fright.

He had swum underwater across to a tiny point of land and climbed into a clump of trees. Unseen, he had come around the water's edge and up behind her.

"You bastard," she said, sobbing.

He reached out to take her into his arms, but again she pushed him away. He was all wet. He bowed to her. He looked so ridiculous being gallant without a stitch of clothing that she started to laugh and cry at the same time.

"You bastard, you frightened me."

"I just wanted you to feel what it would be like for you without me. Take me to the city and you can magnify that feeling one hundredfold. Just let me work the line until I get enough money for a new ship."

"Lionel," she said in exasperation, "the war with England is almost over and France has lost badly. Even Spain coming in on our side has not altered things, except that now England beats our Spanish cousins."

"Maybe they're your cousins, my lovely," he said, raising an eyebrow with mock disdain, "but I'd never admit to any relationship with the Dons."

"I don't care whose cousins they are," Helene retorted. "The fact is that England has won, and there won't be any more privateers. I'm not going to spend my life cooking gumbo over an open fire in the middle of a goddamned swamp for you and your bloody friends."

Lionel looked offended by her outburst.

"It won't be long now," he said. "You were happy with me at sea."

"And I was glad when you left me ashore on the last trip."

"You were pregnant. I couldn't take you."

"And you didn't hear me complain. Love, I'm trying to tell you that I am not pregnant now, and your goal of saving our money to get another ship is precisely that—your goal, not mine."

"What else can I do?" he responded defensively. "I'm a sailor. A sailor goes to sea."

"Become more. Become a merchant. Start selling your own goods. Prosper in peace as well as in war."

"There's always a war."

"Not this time. France has been beaten so badly it may take a generation for her to recover. We may have a long wait here in the swamp."

"When did you start to become an expert on Europe's politics, my little Acadian wench? What was the name of that cosmopolitan little city-state you deserted to come frolicking with me?"

"Don't joke about Port Hebert," she said angrily.

"You don't talk any more about going back there, do you?"

She remained silent.

"What's the matter?"

She looked away from him. "You reminded me of something sad, that's all."

He instantly regretted his remark. "I'm sorry," he said and placed his arms around her. This time she did not resist.

"I miss them less and less," she said, looking up into his handsome face. "They fade away on me and that frightens me. Sometimes I can't remember the sound of my father's voice. At first I used to hear him calling me at night in my dreams. Once I sat bolt upright in our cot. You asked me what was wrong. I didn't say. Well, I heard him. I even saw him. He beckoned me with his hand to come with him. Then he disappeared. He has not come back. Now if he were to call me again, I doubt if I'd recognize the sound. And I don't remember Gilles' face. I stay awake trying to recall it. All I can think of is his huge body. But no image comes to me when I think of him. Just size."

"You told me once he had a blackened tooth."

"You're right, I remember that now. I had even forgotten that. Strange that I can remember every detail about Marcel but not Gilles."

"If you should leave me, would I be a Marcel or a Gilles?" he teased.

"You've a handsome face."

"*Merci.*" He smiled at her.

"Even if the rest of you is eminently forgettable."

He grabbed her hand and thrust it between his legs. "Tell me that's forgettable."

"Oh, *mon Dieu*," she mocked, "it's like a sausage."

Lionel almost purred with pleasure.

"Yes, like a sausage," she continued, "and always with the sausage the smallest is the sweetest."

"Bitch," he said, laughing, "keep rubbing like that and it will turn sour all of its own accord."

Helene pulled away from him at last, leaving him awkwardly exposed.

"The men will come by shortly from their cabin for their supper."

"We have time," he said placing his hand on her semiexposed breast.

"The gumbo will get cold."

"Did you burn the *roux*, the brown sauce?"

"No, it's perfect."

"Then you can't ruin the gumbo. You can reheat it. It will taste even better reheated as long as the sauce is as perfect as you claim."

"It is," she said, gasping as he placed his mouth on the soft white skin of her bosom.

She stepped toward the cabin. "Let's go inside," she said.

"No," he insisted, "I want you right here." He reached behind her and began to undo the buttons of her dress. He opened his mouth and sought hers. She responded. Their tongues touched. It was almost as if a spark passed between them. Her whole mouth seemed to come alive as his tongue and hers entwined passionately. His hands stopped working on the buttons as he concentrated more and more on the kiss. He pushed his tongue forward beyond hers and thrust it toward her throat again and again.

Afterwards she lay with him resting on top of her. He was heavy, but she loved the feeling of his strength pressing down on her. She moved her hands slowly across the muscles of his sweaty back and down lower to his buttocks. He was half asleep, luxuriating in the doldrums that come after the heightening of all the senses and the explosion of pleasure that climaxes it. She saw the men come to the front of the cabin and knock on the front door. When they saw the two of them lying where they had fallen at the edge of the bayou, they stood with their hands in their pockets looking in the opposite direction.

Helene raised her hand and placed it on the back of Lionel's neck. She whispered in his ear. "That was good, eh?"

He groaned with pleasure.

"Lionel?"

"What?" he sighed.

"At least take me for a visit to New Orleans. I'm dying of loneliness here. I would like to see what the women are wearing and what I can buy in the shops."

"A visit?"

"Just a few days."

"A visit wouldn't be so bad," he rationalized. He hated to disappoint her, and they could use the opportunity to sell their furs. "All right," he said finally.

She squeezed him tightly.

"You do that again," he laughed, "and we'll start in all over again."

"Not in front of the children," she joked.

"What do you mean?" Lionel pulled away from her. He blushed when he saw his fellow trappers congregating only a few hundred feet away by his cabin. "Why didn't you tell me they were there? Did they see anything?" He covered his sex with his hand.

Helene started to laugh. He behaved as if the trappers had never seen him naked before. In truth, they lived, slept, bathed, and trapped together for days on end. When she laughed, he gave her a dirty look.

"Lovemaking is a private thing," he said angrily. "It is not to be performed like an act on a stage. It was not meant for an audience."

"Rest easy," she continued to laugh. "No one saw the least little thing."

He was too relieved by her words to pick up on the double meaning.

"Why did you let me think they had?" he said still shaken.

"To get even with your disappearing act earlier," she responded as she slipped back into her dress. She rose to her feet. "You can walk behind me into the house. I have to reheat the gumbo." She started to laugh again.

The first thing that struck Helene about the city was the smells. Some were offensive, like the stench of so many unwashed bodies coming together in the cathedral square or chamber pots dumped out into the dirty streets from two-storey wood-frame houses that lined the regular grid of streets along the high riverbank of the Mississippi. But these were overcome by others, like the fresh clean smell of the muddy river as it twisted and bent in its tortuous path to the delta and the Gulf of Mexico beyond. But more pungent was the aroma of the flowering trees that blossomed in the courtyards of the private houses. Sweet olive, magnolia, and honeysuckle combined to perfume the heavy water-laden air that enveloped them.

They walked along Rue St. Philippe toward the river. It had been a long time since Robichaud had been in the town and Helene had never been there. Lionel remembered a tavern—an inn on the corner of Chartres Street and St. Philippe. The proprietor was Gaston Landry, who had sailed with him against the English. As they walked along the street, Lionel pushed ahead. He was weighted down by a backpack of furs. Two of his trapping crew carried a similar load. The other two waited back at the canoe with two more packs. If Lionel was successful, word would be sent for them to join him.

Helene could not resist staring at the sights of the village. The square in front of the cathedral was crowded with stalls. The cries of the vendors advertised their wares: fresh fruit and incredible varieties of catfish from the bayous along with shellfish and shrimp from the gulf. One stall was maintained by a small man dressed in black clerical garb. Helene thought he would be selling crucifixes or holy pictures. Instead he had green and yellow sticks cut in six-inch lengths. There was a crowd of people in front of his stall. A few spoke with the accent of her homeland, but most spoke with the clipped, crisp accent of the Louisiana Creole. These people had come directly from France or the West Indies. Some in the crowd were extremely well dressed, but there were also some black slaves crowding with others to see what the cleric sold.

Helene lost sight of Lionel. She did not care. She knew the address he was searching for. She would catch up.

Someone called out to Brother Bernard and the man in black smiled and bowed to the audience.

"Please don't push," he called out. "There's enough for all."

"What is it?" Helene asked no one in particular.

"Ah, mademoiselle wastes no time in amenities." He addressed her directly. "Her lack of subtlety is worthy of the founder of my order, St. Ignatius. He had the bluntness of a soldier, as does this fair maid."

"Watch out when a Jesuit priest flatters," said one of the Creoles with sarcasm dripping in his voice.

The Jesuit ignored the sarcasm. "No priest, I'm only a humble illiterate Brother."

"Watch out when a Jesuit pleads inability," said the same Creole.

The Brother continued to ignore him. Instead he picked up one of the sticks. "This, my friend, is sugar cane. It's progenitors were imported here from the West Indies by the Reverend Fathers when they began their plantation just outside the city limits. We have succeeded in raising this cane ourselves. The Fathers think it the crop of the future for this colony."

"Bah," another Creole voice uttered in disgust. "Novelty. You priests play with novelties. We have our indigo plantations. They prosper. What do we need with your cane, priest?"

Brother Bernard ignored his continued elevation to holy orders. "This cane," he said, waving a stick in the air, "has produced most of the wealth of the West Indies. Islands like Cuba and Puerto Rico have given more wealth to Spain through sugar than all the silver mines in Mexico since the days of the conquistadores. Santa Domingo is worth more to France than Canada, Acadia, and Louisiana combined. Louisiana could become another Santo Domingo—something Acadia and Canada can never be."

"Are you sure Acadia and Canada are still French?" said a sharp-faced little man with an Acadian accent. His voice made Helen homesick. "The last we heard, an English general sat behind the walls of Quebec."

"As they have before," the Jesuit reported. "It's always the same. Someone wants an island in the Caribbean more than they want Canada, so an exchange is made."

"Not this time" said the Creole who had attacked the Brother earlier. "France has no victories in India or the West Indies or in Europe to bail her out this time. We are lucky we are so far removed from the English. Otherwise they would never have left us alone here in Louisiana."

"Let us not forget about my sugar cane," Bernard repeated.

"Stuff it," the Creole said, walking away.

"It won't grow there," another advocate of indigo claimed.

"It will grow here in Louisiana," Brother Bernard said, holding up his hands to the sky for his God or at least St. Ignatius to witness the shortsightedness of some of the farmers.

"It won't grow without slaves," said the little Acadian. "The Spanish disease—slavery."

The Jesuit smiled. "I thought the Spanish disease was one that persons of my profession, if they remained true to their vows, had no reason to fear or occasion to catch."

"How do you plant it?" Helene asked.

"Again the fair maid cuts through the verbiage and asks the direct question. That answer, my lady, is given only after the payment of a fee and the purchase of a seed crop from my Order."

"The money-grubbing priests are at it again," said another Creole. "We'll put an end to you Jesuits once and for all." Someone shoved Bernard. The little man grabbed up his collection of cane and stuck it into a carpetbag. He had no intention of remaining at his post if he was to be physically abused.

The spectators lost interest and began to stroll away looking for greater amusement and better bargains. All but Helene. She stood watching the Brother.

"How much would it cost me to find out?" she asked.

The Brother looked over her country dress. "More than you have, mademoiselle."

He had been worried by the ferocity of the crowd's criticism. Under his breath he cursed the rector and the other priests who sent him out to do the selling amid such hostility. He continued to ignore Helene. Once his bag was completely packed he took off without looking at her again.

"Little bastard," she muttered. "He suffers from the priest's disease. He ignores women, sources of temptation, every one of us."

She continued down Rue St. Philippe. She knew she had found the tavern by the noise outside. She opened the high wooden gate and entered the small courtyard. It was filled with men smoking, drinking, and playing cards. Some of the noise lessened as many of the gamblers looked up openmouthed at the beautiful young girl entering this male lair on her own.

Helene felt instantly uncomfortable and regretted not having tagged along behind Lionel. She resented the stares of the men.

Lionel came out of the taproom into the courtyard. When he saw Helene standing alone, he quickly went toward her. There were several mock groans of disappointment when the men saw him step to her side and take her arm. The groans and several whistles dispelled her tension and she started to laugh. She curtsied to the group and the men started to cheer. Now it was Lionel who became tense. He rushed Helene through the courtyard and through the double wooden doors of the taproom.

"What were you trying to do in there?" he asked her, his annoyance obvious. "Why didn't you keep up with me?"

Helene ignored him. After the initial feeling of awkwardness she had enjoyed their open acknowledgment of her beauty.

She walked around the taproom. It was a large building made of wooden beams and mud. The mud was mixed with Spanish moss from the bayous and with horsehair to make a hard structural material when it dried. There were wooden tables and benches in the taproom, but the room itself was rarely used except on rainy winter days. Half the room had a high ceiling while the second half was covered by a gallery with four or five doors leading to private rooms. The gallery was reached by a wooden stairway built into the wall to Helene's left.

Lionel had piled his furs and skins on the taproom bar. The room smelled musty and close from the lack of fresh air. The aroma of the recently cured furs did not help.

Lionel stepped behind the bar. He pulled a bottle of West Indian rum from the shelf and poured himself a generous drink. He offered the glass to Helene. She shook her head. She hated the taste of hard liquor and she hated it when Lionel drank.

"Can I rely on you to stay out of trouble while I speak to Gaston?"

"You mean look like an old hag for other men but remain a raving beauty for you?"

"That's it," Lionel retorted.

She smiled.

The door to the back room opened and a rotund man squeezed himself sideways through it. He was enormously fat. His legs were so large that his thighs rubbed together when he walked, producing a kind of slow shuffle. His middle hung over his belt and was so large that he could not button the last two buttons of his shirt. He had no neck at all, simply rows of fat that made his head seem ludicrously small sitting atop such a frame.

"Gaston?" Lionel could barely recognize his old crewman.

"Captain Robichaud." Landry smiled and shuffled toward Lionel. He grabbed Lionel's hand in his pudgy fingers and shook it vigorously. His eyes darted over toward Helene.

"Oh, that's right. You had left my galley before I met Helene. This is my . . ." Lionel stammered, not sure what to call Helene.

"I'm his concubine, Helene Hebert," she interrupted him.

Again Lionel gave her an annoyed look. "This is my old cook, Gaston Landry."

"And a fine cook I am," Landry joked, patting his enormous middle. "My problem is that most of the food I cook never gets out of the kitchen." His laugh was more a high-pitched squeal.

Lionel joined in the laugh. "I could never sign you on now the way you look. I am afraid that if you moved from one side of the galley to the other you'd capsize my ship."

Gaston stopped his squeal and looked at his former captain angrily. It was clear that he had taken offense at Robichaud's remarks. But his attention was drawn to the furs piled on the bar.

"What have we here?" he remarked as he shuffled over toward them.

"Half my season's work," Lionel said. "I have an equal amount back in my dugout outside the city."

Gaston poked through the furs. He wrinkled his nose and turned to Lionel. "I can give you half a year's provisions for these and the rest of the lot, if they are of the same quality."

Lionel's whole body stiffened and his eyes flashed with anger. "A half year? It took me a whole year to trap them. I expected a year's provisions plus some cash to get me started toward a new ship. How can I even go back and trap with only a half year's provisions?"

Gaston's eyes, set deeply in his face, twinkled. "Surely it wouldn't help if you brought me along as your cook. I'd eat up everything you had in a month." Then he grew more serious. "Captain Robichaud, I'd like to help you. Go back to the sea. Do something you do well. You may trap animals, but their skins are not cured well. They'll not bring the price they might otherwise have commanded."

Lionel's anger left him. His shoulders sagged. He pulled out one of the taproom's wooden benches and sat down heavily on it.

"For old times' sake, Gaston, can't you give me a full year's provisions so that I can try again?"

"No," Helene interrupted, "we'll take a half year. If you give us the cash equivalent."

Lionel stared at her in amazement.

"Cash?" Gaston pulled at one of his numerous chins. "That may take some doing."

"Why?" she asked.

"It's hard to come by cash. France has rarely allowed us to keep much of it in the colony with all the laws on trade."

"Nonsense," Helene objected. "There's been a war going on for more than seven years. There's been smuggling. I usually find that fat men are hoarders, hoarders of cash as well."

Again Landry looked offended. Helene quickly perceived the key to him. Only he could joke about his size. Let anybody else do it and they became his enemy.

"What the hell do you think you're doing?" Lionel protested to both of them but primarily to Helene. "I don't want cash, not unless it's cash to buy a ship."

Gaston Landry shot his heavy arm up in the air to beseech the gods. "Cash to buy a ship! There aren't enough decent furs here to pay for a dugout canoe."

Lionel started to pick up his furs. "Let's get out of here, Helene. I should have known better than to trust a fat cook."

"Lionel," Helene ordered sharply, "watch your tongue. We have no need to insult Gaston. Besides" she said, placing her arm on his enormous shoulders, "I think he's cute."

Lionel continued to pack the furs. In his haste, he knocked

some off the bar and had to bend down and pick them up off the floor. "I'll be back at the canoe," he said angrily. "As soon as you finish fondling the slob I'd be obliged if you would join me." He stormed out of the taproom and into the courtyard.

Gaston looked at Helene slyly. "Is there any chance of your fondling me?"

"No," she said bluntly.

"As I thought," he said, sighing. "No harm done in asking."

"None whatsoever," she said. "Any chance of getting the cash?"

"No," he said equally bluntly. "Not from me."

"Who would have the money?" she asked.

Gaston pulled on another chin. "Only the Jesuits," he responded.

Helene immediately thought of the Brother she had met only an hour before. "Where can they be found?"

"Better to ask where they can't be found," he said with disdain.

"I gather you have no use for the priests."

"It's not priests," he said with some fervor. "I am a Catholic and a good one." He thought for a moment. "I probably would not be so good, however, if my girth"—he patted his belly—"didn't get in the way." He laughed. But then his mind jumped back to the Jesuits. "It's those devils, the Jesuits, with their schemes and their tricks for getting money that I have no use for."

"What tricks?" she asked.

Gaston thought again. "Well, everyone knows about their forgiving unforgivable sins for a fee."

"How fortunate for the sinner," Helene responded.

"I suppose so," Gaston said, still trying to come up with a heinous Jesuit deed. "They run a plantation with slaves— black men whom they work very hard, raising that sickly sugar cane."

"No one else has plantations with slaves around New Orleans?"

"Of course they do. But priests shouldn't."

"They must be very successful planters."

"They are," Gaston responded. "Everyone knows that. You just have to ride past their fields to see what a crop they've raised. And since they have their own connections with others in the Order in France, they make a handsome profit."

"And they are despised," she added.

"Roundly!"

She was about to make a pun on his choice of words, but remembering his sensitivity she refrained. It was almost as if he perceived her restraint. He relaxed and spoke more confidentially to her.

"Hatred of the Jesuits grows daily. I don't believe they will be able to remain in this city or the colony for many more days. So if I were looking for their money I would do it sooner rather than later."

Helene patted the fat man's plump cheek. He blushed.

"I shall be back," she said and started to follow the line of retreat Lionel had taken.

"Where are you going? I haven't told you how to get to their plantation."

"I'll be back," she said. "First I want to see a man about some sugar cane."

Helene saw no sign of Lionel. She had expected him to wait for her somewhere outside the taproom. A few of the men called to her as she made her way through the tables of the courtyard, but no one did anything more.

She stepped onto Chartres Street and looked both ways. Still no sign of him. "Just as well," she said. She retraced her steps back along Chartres Street until she emerged into the market square. It was quieter now. Only a few still hawked their wares to a diminished crowd of potential buyers.

There was no sign of Brother Bernard. Where would she find him? The church stood open. So did a small wine shop across the square. She chose the wine shop and she chose correctly. He was seated by himself at a small round wooden table, sampling wares and complaining aloud about what the proprietor charged him. Not like in the old days when the shopkeeper tried to show his love of his Creator by giving a little wine gratis to those who served, weighed down by poverty, chastity, and obedience. His carpetbag filled with cane sticks was by his feet.

Helene sat down at his table. He looked up at her in surprise. Helene thought it best not to try any path but a direct one.

"I need money," she said. "And I've been told the Jesuits are the only people in town who have what I need."

The Brother looked at her sharply. "What are you selling?" he asked. "Usually young women like yourself who have a need for Caesar's things have the, shall we say, the assets to raise it without too much trouble, even in a holy city like this one."

"You are a dirty old man," she said to him.

"I'm not so old," he responded. "And besides, child, I have a vow of chastity. You have nothing to fear from me. Now, why do you need money?"

"Because I am tired of living in a log house in the bayou."

"I can appreciate that," he interjected.

"And I want to be rich, so rich that I will never have to work again. So rich that no one will ever think he can use me again. So rich that I can build a home that no one can take away from me—ever."

"Why do you tell me these things?"

"Because you have access to the money that I need."

He smiled at her. "Now, seriously this time, child. What are you selling?"

"Furs and prime hides," she said. "Some of the best hides you've ever laid your eyes on."

Bernard leaned back in the chair, lifting the front two legs off the floor.

"My child," he said in his best clerical tone, "who the hell needs furs? Reverend Father Rector has been, shall we say, liquidating the assets of our Order in New Orleans. The feelings against us here have been whipped up. We may have to leave at a moment's notice. What would we do with furs?"

"But someone has got to buy them," she insisted.

"Try one of the local merchants, or trade them."

"I have tried."

"Who?"

"Gaston Landry, who owns the tavern on Chartres Street."

"I know him." Bernard said. He spat on the floor of the shop as he spoke and rubbed the spittle into the floorboards with the sole of his shoe. "He's a pig with no appreciation for men of the cloth."

"He also has no money."

"Oh, he has money. I'm sure a thorough search of his sty

would discover an old satchel filled with Spanish coins. He deals frequently with the Florida officials. He knows well how things are going."

"What do you mean?"

"The war, my lovely, the war is lost. France has been humiliated. Once we were the world's greatest power; once we threatened to become the universal monarchy feared by all Europe, controllers of the balance of power. That was in the days of King Louis XIV of happy memory. But now in the reign of his successor we are prostrated at the feet of the English lion and his Prussian cur of an ally. Spain too has been crushed. But our king, it seems, has despaired of empires. The rumor is that, as price for entering the war against England, Spain is to receive His Most Christian Majesty's colony of Louisiana. Gaston Landry is already in the pay of our new masters."

Fear clutched at Helene. She pictured the arrival once again of foreign troops bearing papers for her to sign, oaths of allegiance to a new foreign king, and finally expulsion.

"Not again," she said aloud.

Bernard put his hand on hers. "Acadian, eh, my lovely one? I feel for you. Yes, it could begin all over again for you."

Helene stiffened. "My word, sir, was a vow and not an expression of fear."

"What is your name?" Bernard asked.

"Helene Hebert."

"Helene," he said, "it is difficult enough to keep vows over which one has some small measure of control. I certainly should know something about that." But he sensed something in her. She had backbone, this one did. He suspected that she would not take vows easily, not like some, including himself. When she took a vow, not even the Archangel Michael or Jesus Christ or Father Rector himself could make her break it.

"If you want your money, my child, go back to Gaston Landry and get it from him."

Helene was discouraged. She did not think anyone could get Gaston to give money for Lionel's semiputrid skins. He was too shrewd a dealer for that. She had hoped that the Jesuit would be more gullible. The image of the cabin in the bayou loomed up before her. She grew even more determined.

She would not go back to Mazant. There was a place for her here. She was sure of it. All she had to do was find it.

She did not go back to Lionel Robichaud's camp at the foot of the ramparts. Instead she returned to Landry and rented a room off the gallery. Landry demanded payment in advance but relented finally when Helene promised him that Lionel was working on a deal with the Jesuits. It was a lie, of course. She suspected he knew it was.

The room he gave her was almost bare. There was a small cot and a plain square table with two chairs. There were no curtains and no rugs. She sent word to Lionel that she was back in Landry's tavern. She expected him to come to her but she had no idea what she would do once he arrived. All she knew was that she was not going back to the bayou. She was in the city to stay.

The night was a stormy one. The rains came in off the Gulf of Mexico and fell in torrents. High winds accompanied the rain. Helene lay on her cot alone. A single candle flickered in the room. Lionel had not come. The shutters on her windows had come loose and banged against the mud wall of the tavern with each new blast of wind. Lightning cast weird shadows onto the bare walls opposite the cot. Helene was frightened. She had not been alone since Lionel took her from Captain Rofheart's cabin eight years earlier. She loved Lionel. Why was she defying him? Compared to being alone in this cell, the cabin at Mazant, so warm and filled with their things, seemed no longer to be such a purgatory. The shutter finally tore off its hinges and fell with a clatter to the courtyard below.

She heard footsteps on the stairs leading to the gallery. They were too light to be Landry's. Her heart leapt. Maybe it was Lionel. She listened carefully. The steps advanced along the gallery. They stopped in front of her door. A lightning flash filled the room with its blue-white light and several seconds later the thunder clashed. Helene's eyes were riveted on the door. There was a knocking. Her heart soared no longer. Lionel would not have knocked. She would be lucky if he didn't tear the door off its hinges in his anger with her.

She rose from her cot. She had gone to bed in her skirt and blouse since she had nothing else with her. She crossed the room and opened the door. She stifled a scream with her hand when the dark form in the doorway was illuminated by another flash of blue-white lightning. He was a hunchback beggar. His clothes were filthy and torn and there were scabs on his face.

"Alms?" he said to her. "Something for the poor for the love of St. Francis?"

Helene recovered. "I've nothing," she said and started to close the door.

The beggar's arm shot out quickly and slammed the door back against the inside wall.

Helene grew angry. Why didn't Landry protect his guests from this sort of riffraff. She opened her mouth to call for her landlord. God only knew what the fat man could do about this intrusion.

"Don't call out." The beggar's voice had changed. Helene recognized instantly the voice of Brother Bernard, the Jesuit.

"What are you—?" she started to question him.

"Quick, let me in," he interrupted her. He did not wait for her to respond but pushed past her and slammed the door behind him. He went to one of the chairs and collapsed. He was breathing heavily.

"That was close," he said finally.

"What in God's name are you doing here? And what is the meaning of the disguise?" she asked him.

Bernard's composure was returning. "I thought it was rather clever of me, given what I was carrying, mademoiselle. You asked for hard coin. *Voilà*." He took off his jacket. His hump had been created by his ever-present carpetbag. He opened the bag and dumped its contents onto the table. Hundreds of gold coins slid onto the wood. Some rolled off the edge of the table and struck the floor with a clatter.

Helene stood openmouthed.

"The least you could say is thank you," said Bernard.

Helene looked at him but still no sound emerged.

"The explanation is simple, my lady fair," he said. "We have been liquidating for some time. Tonight in the refectory the Very Reverend Father Rector announced that he had received word from the governor that we have been expelled from the colony of Louisiana. We were to forfeit our holdings to the vicar general, who represents the bishop of Quebec, and we are to be on the next ship back to France. Father Rector told us to be ready to go tomorrow morning."

Still Helene looked at him in wonderment.

"Don't look like that, child. I don't want to go back to France to live in some awful house of probation. Father Rector said we leave tomorrow. Well, Brother Bernard has already been obedient, extra obedient. I decided to leave a little earlier and with the house treasury."

"You stole it?"

"That's a harsh way to put it," Bernard said, clicking his tongue against the roof of his mouth, a mocking sound of feigned displeasure. "Let us say I put these funds into my care for the duration."

"Duration of what?"

"Until the Order is restored here in Louisiana."

Helene sat in the chair opposite Bernard and began to stack the coins in neat piles.

"They are fun to play with," he said to her.

Helene stopped stacking. "Why did you come to me?"

"An accident, my lovely. How was I to know that Father Rector would decide to enter the vault tonight just after I had emptied it. I thought I'd have at least ten hours' head start." He paused. "You know, it just dawned on me . . ." He shook his head. "No, it's not possible. You don't suppose he came into the vault so that he might take off with the money?" He shook his head a second time. "No," he muttered, "I must stop judging people by my own standards."

"You haven't answered my question," Helene interrupted him.

"Right," he said. "Well, they fanned out all over the city looking for me. They were everywhere. One patrol of two priests and two Brothers actually stopped me. If they had searched me I would have been done for, but as it was I got a sou from one along with a swift kick in the butt from another. But I had strained my luck and I knew it. I had to find some place to spend the night. I found myself on Chartres Street and I thought of you. That fat goat downstairs pointed out your room to me when I said I bore a message about the furs. He thought it would be a great joke to have a beggar enter your room while you—"

The door to the room burst open. Bernard lunged forward

and began to sweep his gold into his bag with a great yelp of surprise.

Helene looked up from the table to see an angry Lionel standing in the doorway. Helene went to him. She grabbed his arm and pulled him into the room, closing the door behind him. He pushed her away. His face was contorted with rage. She thought he was going to hit her, but he was distracted by the gleam of the money on the table.

Bernard swept as much of it as possible into the bag, but several coins had eluded him.

"What the hell is going on here?" Lionel said to Helene. "Who is this beggar?"

"He's not what he appears to be," she shot back.

"Not from the gleam of his gold," Robichaud added.

"Lionel, I want you to meet—I'm sorry but I don't remember your name."

"Good. Now if only Father Rector would forget it."

"He's a Jesuit," Helene said excitedly.

"Or *was* a Jesuit," Bernard added.

"A priest? What the hell do we want with a priest?"

"I was just hearing her confession. Bless you, my daughter," Bernard said, making a quick sign of the cross and moving toward the door.

"Stop him, Lionel," Helene called out.

The captain's muscular arm shot out and grabbed the Brother by the collar. He was thrown back into a chair.

"Open his bag," Helene ordered.

Lionel grabbed the bag from Bernard. The Jesuit tried to keep it from him, but Robichaud nearly tore Bernard's arm from the socket when he twisted the carpetbag from his grasp.

Lionel could only whistle in surprise when he opened it. There was more money than he had ever seen in one place.

"He stole it from the Jesuits," Helene offered.

"I resent that, mademoiselle," Bernard said pompously. "I have placed the funds in safekeeping."

"He stole it," Helene asserted again.

Bernard remained silent.

"What do we do with it?" Lionel asked.

"*You* do nothing with *my* money," Bernard said angrily.

"Shut up," Helene said with equal vehemence. "One more

shout from you and I'll throw you out into the street and into the clutches of the priests."

Bernard became silent at her threat.

"I'll tell what we do, my friends. We form a partnership," Helene said.

"That's better," said Bernard.

Helene sat again in the chair. Her mind raced ahead. Everything was open to her now. The Jesuit money was the answer to all her prayers. All she had to do was keep the Fathers from finding out she had it. After that she would use it to make them all rich. She and Lionel, and even Brother Bernard, would be safe at last.

CHAPTER FOURTEEN

New Orleans, 1764

Helene lost no time in putting her plans into action. At first Lionel tried to dominate the partnership, but he made little headway with either Bernard or Helene and even less with Gaston Landry, whom Helene insisted on bringing into their group. Lionel soon became frustrated and silent.

Helene purchased a large, comfortable four-poster bed and set it up where her cot had been. She persuaded Lionel to send for their rugs and other furniture from the cabin at Mazant. They fought bitterly over the decision, but Helene refused to return to the bayou. Although he threatened and sputtered, Lionel finally acknowledged that he could not live without her and consented to life in New Orleans.

She could not sleep at night. Her mind seemed to work overtime on the schemes she formulated. She sent Bernard—now thoroughly forgetful of all of his vows, not just his vow of poverty—to purchase the Jesuit plantation at auction. It was not safe for him to appear in public. All the members of the Society of Jesus had been ordered out of the colony. If he were discovered he could be deported. But Bernard was a master of disguises.

Bernard was delighted to buy the Jesuit property with their

own money. When Helene assigned him the task of running the plantation and supervising its sugar crops he became ecstatic—to run the plantation where once Father Rector reigned supreme.

Soon the cane tilled by the labor of black slaves filled every acre. Helene agonized over the purchase of slaves. She did not like the concept. Since she herself was determined to be free, she found it difficult to enslave other human beings. But she wanted to make the plantation work and she accepted Bernard's arguments that it could only be done by slave labor. Someday she would set all her slaves free. She vowed it to herself.

Helene came to a quick understanding with Gaston. The tavern was to be remodeled. The courtyard was planted with flowering perfumed trees and shrubs. Gardenias, Helene's favorite flower, were placed everywhere. The wooden tables were replaced with wrought-iron furniture that was painted white. Every night lanterns were placed in the trees to give the courtyard a festive mood and to invite the players to the game.

The men of New Orleans flocked to Landry's. They crowded the courtyard tables, playing the card game of five-card trumps. It was a tense and quiet game until someone was left without a trick and lost the pot. Then the entire courtyard would erupt in derisive laughter as the loser stuffed the pot with cash for the next hand.

Gaston would then shuffle out of the taproom followed by three young men carrying trays of beer mugs and whiskey for the players. There were no women in the courtyard. They could be found only indoors in the taproom and upstairs in the gallery rooms. All except the room reserved for Lionel and Helene.

The taproom was converted from the drab wooden beams of mud and moss stucco of Gaston's tenure to a garish room of gilt paint and red velvet. In the middle of the ceiling, a crystal chandelier with thirty candles burned every night. The girls Gaston picked came in all sizes and shades. Some were Creoles, some had clear African ancestry, while others would have fit comfortably in an Indian warrior's lodge.

Helene had only one rule. Gaston could not hire an Acadian girl. As Gaston said in his clipped Creole accent, "Cajun girls need not apply."

Lionel was not at ease with any of it. He protested the spending of each and every gold coin, but Helene and her two other partners overruled him each time. Now most of the money was gone, invested in the plantation and the tavern. With each passing day Robichaud became more depressed and more morose. Helene tried to relieve the tension between them at night in the large bed. She wore the most expensive perfumes available in the town and donned the finest lace nightgowns, but it had little effect on him. She soon suspected that he preferred her in pants and blouse on a quarterdeck or in a homespun dress smelling mildly of sweat and of the spices of the gumbo pot.

Still she lay awake at night. She tried to push the rejection from her mind. She had reason to be proud. The investment in Gaston's tavern was already paying dividends. The gambling revenue, so much of every pot, went to the house. In addition, they charged higher prices for drinks. Together, they had already recovered the cost of the redecoration of the structure. But the real profit was the girls. They were well paid, but what they brought in far outstripped their wages. Men from the city were joined by indigo planters from the outskirts of town as habitues of "Gaston's place," as the bawdy house came to be known. No longer were Gaston's courtyard and taproom the hangout of the rowdy unwashed day-laborers of the town. Now the men came dressed in the latest styles from Paris and Madrid. Shortly after Gaston's place opened with its new furnishings, the peace accord with England was signed, ceding New France and Acadia to England. To no one's surprise France in turn ceded Louisiana to Spain. Spanish influences were now everywhere in New Orleans.

Profits were rolling in. In a few short months Bernard would be ready to cut his first cane crop since taking over the "Domaine Hebert," as Helene called the old Jesuit plantation. Bernard warned her how tricky it would be to choose just the right moment to pick the sugar. Cut it too soon or too late and profits plummeted. Bernard was a scoundrel to be watched, but he was a clever one and damned useful.

If only Helene could figure a use for the hundred and

seventy pounds of bone and muscle that lay snoring next to her. She loved him and wanted him with her, next to her during the day and in bed at night. But she knew she was destroying him. He could never run a plantation as Bernard did. She had tried to dress him like a gentleman and replace the slovenly Gaston with the handsome Lionel as host of Gaston's place. He had lasted one night. He got drunk and refused to come to bed, swearing that no woman would turn him into a pimp.

She despaired of finding anything for Lionel to do in New Orleans. She knew there was only one thing that would make him happy. She was just unwilling to pay the price. It was not the money. Ships were expensive, but they too could return a profit. No, it was the thought of life without him that kept her from choosing that course for him. Gaston had told her, however, of a small sloop under construction at Mobile. With the war's end, the owners wanted to unload it. But she said nothing to Lionel. Give him a ship and he would be gone for months at a time. He would not be lying snugly next to her, his warm rump comforting hers by its very presence. There must be something he could do in New Orleans. She yawned. She would sleep. She would have to do something about Lionel tomorrow.

She did nothing. The months went by and the returns grew greater and greater. The cane was cut. Bernard complained bitterly that he had waited too long. It was all his fault, he said, but the yield would be poor. Helene went over the accounts herself and found the false entries. Bernard had recorded the yield from only half the acreage of the plantation. Even the most disastrous season could not produce so low a yield.

Helene confronted the ex-Jesuit Brother with his deceit. He confessed his error and pleaded with Helene to have mercy on him. He promised it would never happen again. Helene knew how to evaluate his promises. His capitulation was too quick and the scheme to cheat her too obvious. It was a cover for an even bigger but much more subtle thievery. Of that she was certain, but she could not figure it out. It would bear close scrutiny. With the fall and winter rains, the gambling moved indoors from the courtyard. Helene found an Acadian fiddle player desperately in need of work. She hired him to fill the old taproom, now called the salon, with joyous music.

The Creoles had never heard the jiglike tunes of Acadia, but before long they too were tapping their toes. But the Acadian fiddler player disappeared shortly after Christmas. He left no word other than the briefest notes: "Can't take no more. Going home."

For one brief moment Helene envied his decision. But she had no time to look back. Instead she hired a black fiddler. His music was slower and sadder with some strange rhythms, but the Creoles seemed to like it, and after a while even her Acadian listeners were tapping their toes.

In January Helene began to relax. The fall cane had been planted; the crop had been killed off by the chill of winter but the sucker roots were snugly underground just waiting for the warm rains of early spring to take advantage of the mulch provided by the winter kill-off.

Bernard had given her his revised accounting that very afternoon. It was clear they had made a handsome profit. Lionel was away at Bayou Mizant supervising the transport of some more of their personal things to New Orleans. Helene stayed in her bedroom. She never went downstairs to the salon when it was in operation because it made her feel like a madam, or worse, someone might mistake her for one of "the girls."

She studied Bernard's figures and compared them with the new growing pile of coins that she kept locked in the heavy oak wardrobe. They had turned an important corner. Now both of their ventures were making a profit. But Bernard had disturbed her with a request for more land if the profits of the plantation were to be increased. Sugar cane must be planted in new fields in the fall while the old fields were being harvested.

There was a soft knock on her door. It was Gaston. His timid rap differed greatly from the bold pounding of Bernard. Lionel did not bother to knock at all.

"Come in, Gaston," Helene called out.

The fat man entered. He was breathing heavily from the climb upstairs. He was followed into the room by a young man.

The newcomer was dressed in a dark blue suit of the finest

European cloth. His stock was of lace. He wore his own powdered hair pulled back and tied neatly. He was thin. His legs had little shape and his chest was narrow, yet his face was extraordinarily handsome. His complexion, even in midwinter, was affected by the sun, giving him a ruddy color and a robust look despite his frail body. His eyes were green and his nose was aristocratically straight and thin.

"We have a problem with this young gentleman, mademoiselle," Gaston said, ushering the problem into the room.

"Oh, what could that be?"

The young man bowed deeply to Helene. His courtly manners were impeccable, even if she did note a slight exaggeration in them. She watched him carefully for any sign of mockery.

"Mademoiselle, my name is Robert Parlange." He said no more. It was as if he assumed that was sufficient to dispel the problem.

"Yes?" Helene said. "Is that a problem?"

Robert suddenly looked confused. "N-no," he stuttered, "but—but—you know by my name that I am a gentleman and therefore there is no problem."

Helene looked at Gaston for an explanation.

"Monsieur Parlange has been gambling with us for several months now. He has had, shall we say, a streak of bad luck. The other gentlemen don't seem to mind that he has not paid them. It is part of their code. He is, after all, one of them, a gentleman. And gentlemen pay their debts—sometimes later rather than sooner. But as you know, mademoiselle, a portion of each pot comes to the house, and I'm afraid Monsieur Parlange now owes us a considerable number of levies; more than we can ignore."

"I'm good for the money," Robert interrupted. "And I resent your attitude. If you were a gentleman I would call you out."

"But alas," Helene's tone dripped sarcasm, "neither Gaston nor I am a gentleman."

"Mademoiselle," Gaston sniffed with feigned insult, "you may make that claim for yourself without aspersions inflicted on your good name but I . . ."

Robert interrupted. "I resent this conversation bitterly," he

312

said. "I can in conscience no longer frequent this—this establishment."

"That was precisely what I was going to suggest to you, monsieur," Helene remarked. "Now what arrangements can you make to pay us what you owe?"

Parlange looked away from her. "I am temporarily embarrassed."

"Do you support yourself?" she asked.

"That, mademoiselle, is none of your business."

"No," Gaston responded, "I've checked up on him. He's the only son of Monsieur Etienne Parlange, the owner of a very large indigo plantation that adjoins our sugar holding. The old man controls the purse."

"I will not listen to this fat pig discussing my family's private concerns," Robert said angrily.

Gaston gave Parlange a withering look. "This fat pig pays his bills."

"Gaston," Helene interrupted, "I hear shouting in the kitchen. There must be some kind of crisis. Would you look into it?"

"We have no one in the kitchen. Since the girls and the cards came, no one eats anymore."

"Nonetheless, I believe we have a crisis down there."

Gaston resented her attempts to be rid of him, but he shuffled his way to the door. As he opened it and stepped into the corridor, he could not resist the temptation to make one more retort. "Given the young gentleman's habits, I'll remain outside in case you need me."

The look of anger that crossed Parlange's face finally frightened him and he scurried away with a quickness that belied his size.

Parlange was tempted to go after him and place his foot squarely in the middle of his fat rump, but to do so would probably offend this woman, and he had no desire to offend her. He had never seen anyone so beautiful in all his life. Certainly no woman in all New Orleans could compare with her. The candles reflected their light off her golden hair. Her complexion was flawless and her eyes were striking. Her gown was low-cut to reveal her full breasts and deep cleavage. He tried to imagine what her breasts must look like fully exposed. His anger gave way completely to a new interest.

"Monsieur Parlange," Helene addressed him much more formally and politely than she had when they first met, "I hope you will forgive my associate's impertinence. I respect your rank and family name. Let us postpone the question of paying any debts for the time being. Please feel free to grace this house with your presence whenever you decide to. The pleasure is ours."

Robert's anger was entirely gone now. He beamed with pleasure. Her compliments were appropriate, he thought. Given the beastliness of Gaston, the proprietor, he had never hoped to find that the man's partner was such a lady—well, not really a lady, but no doubt a gorgeously beautiful and obviously intelligent and sensitive woman.

"Mademoiselle, you enchant me." He picked up her hand and kissed it.

"And you, sir, charm me."

"How is it," Robert asked, "that I have never before laid eyes on one so beautiful? Surely you must just have arrived in New Orleans. I pride myself on knowing every beautiful woman in the city. How can it be that I lay eyes on its most beautiful woman only now?"

"I rarely go out," Helene said truthfully.

"We must change that. I invite you to ride with me in my carriage tomorrow. I'll take you out of the city to my plantation. Then you will confirm for yourself that you have made the right decision tonight in overruling your . . . associate."

"I have no doubt of it," Helene laughed, "but I really don't think I could accept your offer."

"Nonsense, it would be fun. We could have a picnic. I know a spot overlooking a bend in the river. Please, you break my heart. Accept my offer."

"Not tomorrow."

"When?"

Helene thought for a moment. Her ideas were quickly falling into place. "Next Sunday."

"You force me to wait a whole five days before I have the pleasure of your company, mademoiselle?"

"Good things are worth waiting for, monsieur." Helene flirted.

"I am your slave." He bowed again to her. "My carriage loaded with the most exquisite delicacies will be standing in the front of this establishment right after Mass at the Cathedral—about noon shall we say?"

"No," Helene shook her head.

Robert seemed confused. "You've changed your mind?"

"Of course not," she laughed, "it's just I want your carriage waiting for me at the side door of this establishment on St. Philippe Street."

"Again your wish shall be obeyed." He raised her hand to his lips and kissed it for the second time.

She found his manners exaggerated but still she enjoyed them.

"Until next Sunday," he said and backed toward the door.

After he had left, Helene sat at her desk smiling. There was no doubt in her mind that the man was a profligate and a fool, but he was a charming fool. The door to the room was pushed open again and Lionel staggered through it. He had been drinking again and reeked of brandy.

"Who was that pup who went prancing down the hall swinging his hips like the Queen of the May?" His words were slurred and Helene had some difficulty understanding him.

"Just a young planter's son having some difficulty with his gambling debts."

"I hope you showed him no mercy," Lionel said as he collapsed on their bed. "Let me know if he doesn't pay up. I'll personally kick him in the balls—that is, if he has any."

Helene went to the bed and sat on the edge. Lionel shifted over to make room for her. She began to unbutton his shirt. He started to laugh as her fingers touched his ribs.

"Don't do that," he said drunkenly. "I'm ticklish."

She smiled at him. She reached down and pulled off his shoes and stockings. His feet were dirty. She reached for the top button of his breeches, but again his body convulsed as if she were tickling him. She decided to let him keep his breeches on.

"Lionel," she said as she played with the black hair on his chest.

"I'll kick him in the balls for you," he repeated.

"Lionel, listen to me," she said.

"I always listen to you," he said argumentatively. "I'm living in this goddamned town, am I not? Of course, *living* is not the right word; *rotting* would be a better word. Yes, I'm rotting in this goddamned town, am I not?"

"I know," she said softly. "That's why we must do something for you."

"I know what you can do for me," he laughed. "You can get out of your dress." He looked up at her. "You're only partially in it anyway. Then you can let me get my hands on those two beautiful . . ." He raised his head to put his face in the region he described, but he grew too dizzy and his head fell back onto the pillow.

"Remind me not to drink so much in the future," he said. "I can't even pick the forbidden fruit, must less eat it."

She picked up his hand and placed it on her breast.

"Ah," he sighed. "I die in peace."

"Don't you dare," she admonished him. "Now that you have taken my innocence from me, the least that you can do is make me enjoy it."

He tried to focus his eyes on her. "I can't," he said miserably. "It's sometimes difficult now when I'm sober."

She knew that would be his response. "Lionel."

"Go away," he said. "Let me sleep."

"No, I need to talk to you."

"Not now, I'm drunk," he responded.

"Yes, now. I've learned about a ship—a small one, mind you, but still a ship—under construction in Mobile. With the profits from this place and the plantation I think we can buy it and open the third branch of our enterprise, the shipping branch."

Lionel's eyes shot open. He wondered at first if he had heard her correctly. Again he tried to sit up. This time with some success.

"You want me to run it?"

"I want you to supervise the construction of that ship and I want you to take it to sea."

He threw himself back down onto the pillow and let out a whoop of joy. "A ship, a goddamned ship. We can all sail all over the gulf and the Caribbean," he laughed.

"Not we, Lionel," she insisted. "I've got to run this business from New Orleans."

That sobered him a bit. "But that would mean we wouldn't be together. Ah, come on, Helene, you love the sea. And we've been together on land or sea since that first day we met. It will be like it used to be."

"It will still be. The ship is a small one, Lionel. The voyages can't be all over the seven seas, just from here to Mobile or to Pensacola in Florida. They say Spain will cede Florida to England. We could begin to smuggle sugar into the English colonies or even indigo or brandy or rum, especially rum and molasses from our cane. You'll be in port frequently. We'll barely miss each other."

At first Lionel looked at her quizzically. There was something wrong but his uneasiness was dispelled by the thought of his own ship. He fell off into a deep sleep.

Helene sat watching him sleep for a long time. Guilt almost overwhelmed her. She reached over and touched his cheek. She was deliberately deceiving him to remove him from her. She loved him. She had no doubt of that. But she intended to pursue Robert Parlange, and for her to do that Lionel had to be out of the way. Oh, God, if only he did not trust her so much, she would not feel so bad. At least he would have his ship. She hoped it would offer him some consolation from the grief she knew she was about to bring to him.

They rode in the open carriage along the high bank of the river. Helene was dressed in a pale yellow lace gown with a matching wide-brimmed hat and parasol. Gaston had searched for the material in every mercer's shop in the town, and the dressmaker had worked every night to finish it on time. On Friday night Helene was convinced it would never be finished and had frantically searched her wardrobe for something suitable. Her temper flared again and again all day Saturday.

Lionel had left for Mobile on Friday. Up to that point she had held herself in check, not wishing to alarm him, but once Robichaud left, restraints were abandoned. Everyone felt the lash of her tongue, including Bernard, who made the mistake of paying a social call on Saturday afternoon. But most of all she attacked Gaston. She called him a stupid oaf, a lazy son of a sea cook, a molester of little girls. He took it all. Gaston knew she was really in control of herself despite all of her histrionics. Never, not once, did she mention anything to do with his weight.

The carriage ride was glorious. While they were still within the city limits, strollers along the river route stopped dead in their tracks. The young couple, she in pale yellow and Robert in light blue, were strikingly beautiful to behold. Many knew Parlange and nodded in his direction. Soon the gossips were whispering about the girl. Who was she? And how beautiful she was.

But now they were beyond the eyes of the snoops. They followed the dirt road leading from the city out toward the Parlange indigo plantation and Helene's sugar fields as well.

Robert's horse knew the route well and needed little direction from Robert. Instead Robert stared at Helene. He feasted on her beauty. Helene was happy. The dress proved smashing and she gloried in the whispered attentions she had attracted. Now she even felt spellbound by Robert's flattery.

The road curved and then swung to the left and entered the Parlange property. The house stood at the end of a broad avenue. It was surrounded by giant trees that dripped Spanish moss. There was something ephemeral and airy about it, as if the summer breezes could pass right through the house. It was wooden, painted white, but on all four sides and on both storeys an open gallery supported by white pillars ran about it. A set of white wooden stairs descended to the lawn from the second floor gallery. Robert's family occupied the second floor, which caught more breezes. The stairway, therefore, was the main entry to the house.

The front yard was surrounded by a low white picket fence, and off to the west there was a white wooden swing. To the right, surrounded by and almost lost in the moss of the trees, there was a white wooden summer house—almost a miniature version of the main structure.

Robert brought the carriage to a halt. "There it is," he said, "the ancestral seat of the Parlange dynasty."

"You make it sound like some ancient European barony," Helene joked. "How many generations of Parlanges have dwelt here?"

"On this land? Three. My grandfather came with Bienville. In this house, two. My father built this house."

He sat looking at it for some minutes in silence. The sun's rays cut through the trees and struck the shingled roof, creating a halolike effect.

Robert clucked to his horse. The confused beast moved reluctantly away from the direction of his stall and back along the road toward the river again.

They came finally to a break in the shrubs along the embankment. Here they could see the sweep of the Mississippi. Robert climbed down from the carriage and spread a blanket upon the ground. He assisted Helene as she stepped down. He placed a plump feather pillow on the blanket for her to sit on. Then he pulled the food basket from the front seat where Gaston had placed it. She had not trusted Robert to remember to bring the food and she had been right.

Gaston had packed a cold stuffed squab for each of them, along with a long, freshly baked loaf of white bread. There were freshly cooked shrimp with hot pepper sauce. The sauce burned their mouths, so they stuffed them with the bread, which was difficult to do when they were laughing. Gaston had supplied them with a superior bottle of French white wine, which they consumed quickly and which was the main reason they were laughing.

They sat overlooking the river for the whole of the afternoon. The sun sank in the sky: its light struck the waters of the Mississippi and turned them silver. The sky took on rich hues of orange and red mixed with purple and rose. Robert leaned over to Helene and kissed her on the lips. It was an innocent, closed-mouth kiss. Helene responded to it by pressing her lips more firmly into his.

Robert pulled away and took her hand in his. They sat for some moments in silence. Finally Robert turned to her.

"Helene, I would very much like you to spend the night with me. I have a room I use on Toulouse Street in the city."

"No," Helene said. She had been prepared for this, but she had not expected it to come in this form. She had fully expected that a slap would be necessary. Robert was making it easy. "I may run a whorehouse, Robert, but I am not that sort of woman."

The young man blushed. "I was not suggesting that you were," he stammered. "I just want to make love to you."

"Just once, tonight?"

"Of course not. Many times—on many nights."

"You want me to become your mistress?"

Robert looked confused at first, but as he grew accustomed to the idea he began to like it more and more.

"Yes," he said, nodding his head firmly. "Yes, I want you to be my mistress."

Helene rose to her feet. "I want you to take me home, Robert."

Again the young man grew addled. "What have I said?" he asked.

"Nothing." Helene turned to him and walked over to the carriage.

He sat dumbly watching after her.

She waited by the carriage steps and turned to him. "Do you intend to help me up or must I climb unassisted?"

Robert jumped to his feet and rushed to her side. He was struck by the perfume of sweet flowers as he stood next to her. He could not take his eyes from her face except to steal a glance downward at the top of her breasts, which were revealed by the cut of her lace gown.

By God, how he wanted her. Yet somehow he had offended her. He helped her into the carriage. She sat there looking straight ahead. He raced around to his side and climbed into the seat beside her.

"Helene, forgive me," he pleaded. "I simply cannot abide your ire."

Helene relented and looked him full in the face. He was shocked to see that her eyes were brimming with unshed tears.

"My God, what have I done to you?" he said, taking her hands in his. "You expected more from me, didn't you?"

She turned from him and stared back at the now darkened Mississippi. The western sky still had a blue tint of daylight to it even though the sun had fallen below the horizon.

"I did not have the right to expect marriage. I am a nobody, a poor girl from Acadia, a woman of business, a madam.'"

Robert could not stand to hear her speak in this manner. Again he grabbed her hand. "Don't speak like that. You had every right to expect. I know what happened to the Acadians. By now the whole world knows. You were brutalized, forced to survive any way you could." He placed his hand under her chin, forcing her to look into his eyes. "You have every right to expect more from me, just as I had every right to expect more from me." He reached over and kissed her lips again. This time his lips parted and he wet her lips with his tongue. Helene responded by parting her lips slightly.

Robert pulled his face away and lowered it into the nape of her neck. He was intoxicated with her, her skin, the perfume of her hair, the perfect lines of her long neck, and those breasts, always those breasts.

Helene sat with her hands gently touching his chest, just enough pressure to arouse him all the more but in perfect position to fend him off if he went too far. But he did not. He pulled away again and rearranged his clothes to try to hide his arousal from her. At last he clucked to the horse. Night was on them and he must return her to her quarters before anyone began to talk about her.

They had one more lingering kiss at the side door at St. Philippe Street, then she slipped inside the house. Singing and fiddle playing came from the salon. She slipped into the kitchen to find Gaston. He stood in front of the giant iron stove, blocking it from the view of anyone entering the room. He turned as she entered. She tossed her parasol and her hat into the air and threw back her head and howled with laughter. She did a little pirouette into Gaston's chubby embrace.

"I did it, Gaston. I played the virgin and he fell for it. Me, little Helene, raped at eighteen by a pirate, concubine to a sea captain for a decade, madam of a whorehouse, and I played a virgin."

"Superb" was all that Gaston said to her. But it was enough of a compliment.

"I need a bottle of wine in my room tonight. It will be hard to get to sleep."

Gaston smiled. "Especially since virgins must sleep alone."

Again she laughed.

Robert sent a note three days later inviting her to attend the Parlange annual ball in two weeks' time. Once again the mercers' shops were ransacked for the right material, this time a silver-blue silk. A wigmaker, the only one in New Orleans, was brought in. He protested that he was too busy making up wigs for proper ladies and gentlemen. Bernard was brought in by Gaston and the wigmaker changed his tune once his purse was filled. Bernard complained about the bribe. He did not see how her glorification and rise among the social elite of New Orleans helped their enterprises. He was shocked, then amused by her response.

"Parlange land, my dear Jesuit."

He cringed at the use of that name and raised his fingers to his lips to admonish her lest anyone hear. He wanted no ties to his former allegiance.

"Parlange lands, Bernard," she repeated, "border our sugar land. Are you not always complaining how we don't have the extra land to plant? Well, there's your answer."

"But how will you get hold of it?" Then Bernard's face broke into a sly smile. "You little vixen, you. You plan to marry that lad, don't you?"

Helene smiled smugly.

"But how? How will you get that young man to the altar? His family is old New Orleans, third generation. They'll never allow it."

"Money," she said. "There are Robert's debts, not only to us but to all the card players in the courtyard and the salon."

"But that will not be enough." Bernard said, shaking his head. "These young cocks will fight each other at the drop of a card, but when threatened by the outside—and you, my dear, are very much the outside—they close ranks. They'll never agree to call in his debts if you try to use that device."

"But there's more!" Helene said, smiling. "Monsieur Parlange Senior has money problems."

"Now that is more promising," Bernard agreed. "What kind and how large?"

"The old mansion is mortgaged to the hilt to lenders in France."

"Very promising indeed. They'll show no mercy."

"In addition," Helene continued, "the new Spanish regulations cutting off trade with all but Spain will finish the indigo. No more government subsidies from Paris; no more profits from indigo. Parlange Senior is about to lose his claim to gentleman status—his estate."

Bernard sipped the wine she had poured for him. "Felicitations," he said. "I believe you may succeed after all. Don't forget, though, that you'll have to bring a large dowry and have the means to control it if you're going to bail out the family. And you mustn't forget either that your plans could be disrupted by one sour note, although I am sure the gentleman would bash me in the mouth if he heard me refer to him in that manner."

"Lionel is in Mobile."

"Forever?" Bernard asked sarcastically.

"For long enough."

Bernard shook his head. "I hope you know what you are doing."

"It's for all of us, including Lionel. It doesn't mean we will stop being lovers."

"Oh my, tell that to Robert!"

"Why does he have to know?"

Bernard threw his hands in the air.

"You underestimate me, Bernard. I am clever enough to have both husband and lover."

"I have no doubt you are, but are you clever enough to keep both husband and lover from knowing about each other? Usually the lover is aware of the existence of the husband. In this case it would be dangerous if either one were to discover the existence of the other."

"I will tell Lionel."

"Please, not while I am around."

Robert sent his carriage, driven by a black slave in livery, to pick up Helene—again at the side entrance. Helene was splendid in her new gown, which was hooped at the bottom and draped with layers of almost sheer silk. Her wig sat high on her head and was decorated with a garland of tiny fake violets.

Bernard and Gaston waved good-bye to her at the side door.

Helene was gratified by the way things had gone. Bernard and Gaston had managed once again to get her ready. Robert, whom she had taken to calling Bobby in private, sent flowers every day to her in her room at the tavern. Even Lionel cooperated. She had lived in dread that he would come sailing up the Mississippi at the last moment and ruin everything. Instead she had received a note proclaiming profuse love and the need of another week's outfitting. Everything had fallen into place for her.

Slaves, similar in dress to her driver, waited at the picket fence outside the Parlange house to help arrivals from their carriages. Carrying torches, they led the guests up the white wooden steps to the second floor. Helene's heart was beating rapidly when she stepped down from Robert's carriage. She had hoped he would be waiting for her, but he was nowhere in sight. She followed the torchbearer, holding her skirt up slightly. She knew that no one at this ball would be more beautiful than she, but still her entrance was supposed to be perfect. It would not be if Bobby was not there to take her arm.

Then suddenly he was there. He was dressed in the uniform of a captain of the local militia. Most of the men were in military uniform, despite the fact that the war had ended the year before. They wore them as an act of defiance against their new masters, the Spanish. They were Frenchmen and they would wear a Frenchman's uniform. There was little risk in doing so since no Spanish official had yet entered the colony to take possession.

Helene smiled at Robert. He wore a white powdered wig and on his uniform he wore the family honors, ribbons and medals won in Europe and in North America. The first Parlange had come to New Orleans with the explorer Iberville and his brother, Bienville, on their expedition from Canada.

A small string orchestra played a minuet. The men and women danced to it. The gowns of the women were a flash of color, as were the uniforms of the men. Helene gasped at the beauty of the drawing room, which had been stripped of furniture for the occasion. It was surrounded on three sides by windows. Above there were two giant crystal chandeliers whose lights were reflected in the darkened windows. The effect was one of sparkling light.

Many heads turned to see who it was that the Parlange heir led into the room. It was the mystery woman once again: the same one he had been seen with in his carriage. Some claimed she was a Creole woman of blood from Martinique. Others said her hair was blond and fair and that such a claim for her was ridiculous. Tonight she wore a wig, so it was impossible to tell who was right.

Robert led Helene directly to where his parents were seated. The elder Parlange was a short man. He wore his own white hair and had a large white handlebar moustache. He was dressed in a black velvet coat with white breeches. He resembled Robert not at all.

Not so Eugenie Parlange, Robert's mother. Her hair was hidden beneath her wig also, but her green eyes and straight nose marked her easily as Robert's parent.

"Mama." Robert spoke to his mother first: "May I present to you Mademoiselle Helene Hebert."

Helene curtsied to the older woman.

"*Enchantée*," Eugenie said through her nose.

"Papa."

The older man bowed from the waist, then he took Helene by the hand as she curtsied to him. "My child," he greeted her, "you must tell me all about yourself. Robert has not stopped talking about you for weeks, yet he really could tell so little."

She smiled at Robert. It pleased her to know that she was frequently in his mind and on his tongue.

"But pay no attention to the curiosity of an old man. You children be off and dance. We can talk later."

Robert took Helene's hand and led her to the floor. Helene had dreaded this part. She was sure that all Bernard's coaching would come to no useful end. She felt as if someone had bolted her knees together whenever she tried to do the formal dances. Prior to the ex-Jesuit's teaching she had danced only to the jigs of Acadia.

She stood at the head of the line. The music struck up again and men and women on the dance floor went quickly into motion. The swish of velvets and silks of the women's dresses all but drowned out the music. Helene dipped her knees in time with the rhythm as Robert bowed to her. "Well, here we go," she said under her breath.

She danced awkwardly at first but soon the rhythm came to her and she began to relax. Robert smiled at her when they came together in the line of dancers. It was clear to everyone with eyes that he adored her.

The older women who sat about the edges of the dance floor began a steady whisper. No one in the room knew who the gorgeous creature was. Someone announced that she was the niece of one of the Jesuits recently expelled. With her noble beauty only one Jesuit came to mind; Father Rector was known to be the third son of a count. She was of noble blood. Bernard had gone to great lengths to plant that story. He would have loved to hear it repeated as solemn truth on the Parlange drawing room floor. Direct inquiries by the bluntest of guests brought only the frustrating truth that her name was Helene Hebert and that she was a recent arrival in New Orleans.

Helene danced twice with Robert. Her third dance was with a young man slightly younger than Robert, who had himself only just turned twenty-one. He introduced himself as Guy duPont. Helene recognized the name and almost froze. He was in even greater debt to the salon than Robert had been when Gaston tried to cut off his credit.

She wondered if this frequenter of her establishment had caught sight of her there. But he clearly failed to recognize her. He treated her as the greatest lady he had ever encountered. He fell all over himself trying to impress her with his brilliant manners. He was such a boy, she thought. Robert might be only a year older but he was so much more mature.

Guy led Helene to a table where a white wine from France was being served, along with delicately spiced fish, shrimp, lobster, and oysters.

Robert left his partner in a fashion that could only be described as rude. He intercepted Guy and Helene on their way to the refreshments.

"Guy, my friend," Robert clapped him on the shoulder, "I keep stepping on Marie Jeannette's toes. Please make my excuses to her. Besides, she pines for you, not for me."

Guy's face was easily read. The disappointment was clear, yet he had been calling on Marie Jeannette for the last two months, and her father, Monsieur Vinay, was watching. If he left the girl alone to follow Robert and Helene, he could forget any thought of marriage and the Vinay dowry. He might even have to worry about the Vinay brothers and an insult to the family name. He reluctantly turned his back on Robert. Robert could afford to be rude to Marie Jeannette with a woman like Mademoiselle Hebert on his arm. Guy saw Marie looking with downcast eyes. God, she was plain, but she smiled when she saw him coming. From the corner of his eye he saw Monsieur Vinay nod to his mother. He sighed.

"You're hungry?" Robert said to Helene.

"Not really."

"There is a chance for us to step outside briefly before anyone notices we're gone."

He grabbed a glass of wine for himself and one for her. They slipped behind the refreshment table. Robert nodded to the slave in livery. He opened the door that led out to the gallery.

Helene was grateful for the breeze that moved the tiny glass chimes hanging from the gallery roof. The scent of the gardenia bushes weighed heavily in the air.

"Don't you love that aroma?" she said, raising her face to the breeze.

"My mother does," he said. "She had them planted."

She turned to face him, her back leaning against the white railing. He approached her and offered her a glass of wine.

She shook her head but he insisted. "Just this one," he said. Helene took the crystal goblet in both hands and raised it to her lips and sipped.

"To us," Robert toasted and allowed the wine to fill his mouth. He leaned over toward her and kissed her on the mouth. He tasted of the wine. As if to challenge her, Robert pushed his body forward toward her. With the railing behind her, she could not retreat. But this was not the time to retreat. He put his glass on the flat top of the white railing. She followed suit, then placed both of her hands around his neck. He leaned down to her and they kissed again, this time with far greater passion. Their bodies seemed to melt into each other. Helene could feel him thrusting toward her. She pulled her mouth away and whispered into his ear, "Let's not go so far that we can't turn back."

"I don't want to turn back," he insisted.

"But I will not go beyond this."

He pulled away angrily from her. "Then what the hell do you want?"

She turned her back on him and looked out into the night toward the white painted swing in the summer house. "I didn't think you'd have to ask," she said. Then she broke away from the railing. "I'm sorry," she said with tears streaming down her face. "I presume too much."

She turned to race past him, but he raised his arm and pulled her to his chest.

"Forgive me, Helene. The last thing I want to do is to make you unhappy."

Helene rested her head on his shoulder.

"Spend the night," he whispered to her.

Her body stiffened.

He laughed. "I don't mean that. I mean spend the night at Parlange House. You'll have your own bedroom next to my mother's. I want to speak to my father tonight and I want you to be available."

He could not see the smile that broke across her face.

Helene sat at the dressing table in the bedroom that Eugenie Parlange had assigned to her. She noted that it was as far removed from Robert's as the house would allow. It was in the back overlooking acre after acre of indigo fields. She had removed her wig with the assistance of the slave girl, but she did not remove her dress. Instead she made the girl assist her with her own hair. She swept it off her neck and up on top of her head. She knew her long neck was one of her best features and this hairdo accentuated its length.

The wall mirror she stared at was framed by hand-carved wooden roses. They were frosted white and were bordered by a line of etched leaves on each side of the mirror. She looked carefully at her eyes. The makeup was there but not enough to notice, just enough to highlight. She leaned back to get a view of her whole face. It was good enough. She would need all her beauty and all her wits this night.

There was a rap at the door. The black girl opened it. Robert seemed surprised to find that Helene was not alone.

"I thought you might have retired for the evening already. It was my father who suggested I see if you were still awake. Nell," he addressed the slave, "you may go to sleep now."

The girl curtsied and ran out of the room.

"Father wanted to know if you would join us for a brandy."

Helene rose from the dressing table. "What kind of gentleman invites a lady for a late night drink?" she teased.

He looked at her with concern, afraid she might refuse him.

"How could I refuse two such handsome gentlemen?" she said finally. "Lead away, Bobby."

As they walked down the long corridor from the back of the house to the library, Robert took her by the arm and spoke softly to her.

"I've told him I wish to marry you."

Helene looked up at him in surprise.

"Yes, marry you. I don't want you to be my mistress or my concubine or any of those other things you speak of when you mock my intentions."

She flashed him her warmest smile.

"But, Helene, he has asked so many questions. He asks who is your guardian, what kind of dowry do you have, who are you? I can't answer most of them."

"I'll answer them for you," she said.

They came to the double white oak doors of the library. Robert knocked. His father called out to them to enter. Monsieur Parlange was sitting at a small mahogany leather-topped writing desk.

"Ah, mademoiselle," he said, rising to his feet and quickly tapping out the light of his thin cigar. "Please take the seat opposite mine."

Helene curtsied. "It was not necessary for you to stop smoking, monsieur," she said politely. "I rather like the smell of a good cigar."

"In itself, mademoiselle, that might be reason enough to choose you as a wife."

She laughed.

"Would you like a brandy?"

"I would," Robert interjected.

"I would prefer it if you left us, my son," the elder Parlange said.

Robert stiffened. "Am I to be dismissed like a child while my father discusses my intentions with my future wife?"

"Bobby," Helene interrupted him, "I think a quiet conversation with your father is precisely what I need right now to help me make up my mind as to whether or not I wish to accept your generous offer."

Robert looked at her with shock. "But you always said . . ."

She interrupted him. "I always said I would accept nothing less. I did not ever say that I would accept you if you offered."

"But—but—" he stammered.

"Robert," Parlange Senior interrupted, "do as the lady says."

Robert looked from his father to Helene. Both stared at him in anticipation.

"Damn," he said finally and left the library in anger.

"Forgive my son, mademoiselle."

"He had every reason to be annoyed with us, Monsieur Parlange."

"Etienne, please, or Papa if you prefer."

"You tease me," she responded.

"A brandy?" he offered.

"No, I don't really like to drink."

"Then let us cut through the formalities, mademoiselle. My son has told me very little about you, but I have my sources. When rumors began to fly that Robert and the beautiful mystery woman were seen together I made certain discreet inquiries."

"And you learned that I live in a certain house of ill repute in New Orleans and I am reputed to be the part owner."

He seemed surprised by her bluntness.

"I thought you would try to evade such a question."

"Hardly," she responded. "I am part owner of the gambling and prostitution establishment on Chartres Street in the city. In addition, I am part owner of the plantation next to yours, the old Jesuit place, and I have just begun a new venture in shipping and I expect soon to have a fleet of merchant ships operating out of the Port of New Orleans."

"You are enterprising, mademoiselle. But what makes you think you would be a suitable wife for my son? Do you love him?"

Helene had not expected that question. She hesitated for a moment.

"No," Etienne Parlange stopped her, "don't answer that."

Yet she was aware that he interpreted her hesitation in a negative manner.

"Did you love your wife when you married her, monsieur?"

"*Touché.*" He laughed. "But she loved me."

"Bobby loves me."

"It's best when at least one of the partners does," he said. "Robert has a distinguished family name to offer you, as well as his social position and this estate."

"Which is deeply in debt," she interrupted.

"Ah, I see that you have made discreet inquiries as well." Helene smiled at him.

"What do you want of him?" Etienne finally asked.

"I want the name and I want the social position."

"And what have you to offer us?"

"Money! I will bail you out of your debts here and in France. I will put the Parlange plantation back on a paying basis, and I will also, of course, cancel Bobby's debt."

The old man took a long sip of his brandy. "If I were truly a gentleman," he said finally, "I would turn you down cold and forbid my son ever to set eyes on you again."

Helene knew she had won. "You accept the offer then?"

"Of course. I always knew I would."

He rose from his chair and walked to the window looking out on the gallery. He stared for some time into the darkness. "I love this house and this plantation, Helene. Excuse me, may I call you Helene, since you will be becoming my daughter?" He said this last turning in her direction.

She nodded.

"And I love this way of life," he continued. "I was mortally afraid that Robert would never really know it as I have known it. I was even afraid that I would lose it for myself and for Eugenie. I was prepared to put a bullet in my brain before facing that, you know. Now I shall not have to."

Helene could not help herself. She was contemptuous of the sentiment that the loss of status should produce suicide, especially after all she had endured without once thinking of taking her own life. Still she could not help but admire his devotion to his family and his land. The Acadian in her could understand that.

"Well, daughter," he said, returning to his desk, "what shall we tell nosy New Orleans about you?"

"As little as possible, Father," she joked.

"Indeed you're right. We will simply deny none of the stories circulating about you. I do not much care for the Martinique story but I do enjoy the one about the Jesuits.

But neither of us should tell Eugenie about any of these arrangements. She must remain mistress of her own house."

"Agreed," Helene said. "Bobby and I will take rooms in the city."

He rose again and walked to where she sat. He kissed her hand and she took the liberty of hugging him.

"My son has exquisite taste in women," he said to her, returning her embrace.

She curtsied to him and left the room.

He watched her leave and stood still until the heavy oak doors to the library were closed. He barely moved his lips when he muttered the word "slut."

The small coastal trader was tied up at the wharf along Rue de la Quai. It had made the difficult journey upriver from the delta with relative ease. Lionel Robichaud knew the lower Mississippi almost as well as he knew the bayous to the south and west. He was a good navigator. The ship was trim and handled well. Despite its low tonnage, he would have dared to take it anywhere in the world.

He sent word to Chartres Street that he had arrived. He wanted Helene to join him in his tiny cabin for the night for old time's sake. He had ordered Gaston to send along a full dinner of seafood and a bottle of good wine. They would eat on deck. He asked Gaston for food enough for his four men as well. It would do no harm at all for the captain and his lady to put on a good feast for the crew the first night in home port.

After two hours without a reply he began to curse the little black boy he had sent on the errand. Finally he saw her approaching. She wore a white dress and her hair hung loosely about her shoulders. He preferred it when she piled it high on her head. He waved to her and called to his first mate to have his crew ready to meet his partner in the ownership of this vessel.

The three other men lined up at the entryway. They were all fishermen from the Mobile region looking for the excitement of travel to New Orleans and other spots on the gulf. Perhaps the law in Mobile was searching for one or two, but not very hard. The officials of the town would be satisfied just to know that they had departed.

Lionel rushed to Helene and swept her into his arms. He

kissed her warmly on the mouth and she responded to him. He put her down.

"There she is," he said, pointing proudly to his new love. "She's small but she's a beauty. You can't imagine how she handles. Even with headwinds most of the way she just cut through the waves on each tack."

Helene smiled. She thought the vessel terribly small compared to Lionel's ship from his privateering days. But she was happy for him. There was no smell of rum, no smell of the musty mildewed parts of town about him. He looked alive again.

"Come on board." He led her up through the entry onto the deck. The mate made a slight bow of acknowledgment to the ship's masters and owners. Helene smiled at him and won his heart.

"Come with me," Lionel said, pulling her by the hand and taking her down the single step to the low wood-beamed cave he called a stern cabin. It had room for a small cot and a small table with two chairs, although the latter were missing, having been set up on deck for their meal.

"You're happy," she stated.

"Yes," he said, flopping onto the cot and patting the spot where he wanted her to sit.

She complied.

"It's like coming back to life, getting away from the stench of the swamps and the aroma of improperly cured pelts."

"You admit that now?"

He laughed.

"But most of all it was the feel of the sea spray and a good breeze filling the sails. It made a man of me again." Then in a lower tone he said, "And I'd like an opportunity right now to demonstrate what I mean." He reached up and touched her thigh.

Helene did not move toward him.

"What's the matter?" he said. "Find someone new while I was gone?"

She did not dare look at him. Did he know something or was he merely teasing? She decided to confront him directly.

"Worse," she said. "I got married."

He threw back his head and started to laugh. "You're such a joker, Helene."

"I'm not joking," she said. It was the slight tremor in her voice that finally convinced him that she was not teasing. He sat bolt upright on the cot.

"What the bloody hell do you mean?" he said, grabbing her by the shoulders. "Who?"

"I am Madame Robert Parlange as of last Sunday, a private wedding at the Lady Chapel of the Cathedral. My father-in-law was able to get the banns waived."

"Parlange, Parlange?" he said almost as if in a trance.

"You remember, the boy with the gambling debt who walked like the 'Queen of the May.'"

Lionel smacked her squarely in the face, knocking her off the cot and onto the floor. She sat there dazed. The angry red outline of his hand was imprinted on her white cheek. Tears came to her eyes.

"You whore!" he shouted. "You couldn't keep true for three weeks. I'm gone less than a month and you can't keep your hands off some faggot's crotch."

Helene stood up. The cabin ceiling was so low that she had to crouch. "There was very little sexual about it. It was business," she said defensively. "I suppose you want me to believe that your prick was ever true to me during those three weeks."

Lionel went red. "No, I wasn't true to you. I fucked every whore in Mobile and in every town along the Gulf Coast until I reached here."

Helene started to laugh. Mobile was one hundred and fifty miles from New Orleans with almost no intervening villages, and the port of Mobile would consider itself lucky if it could enumerate more than three ladies of the night. It was Lionel's pride speaking now. His face was red with rage.

"What could you be thinking of?"

Helene was only now recovering from the blow to her face. "I'll tell you what I was thinking, you stupid son of a bitch. I was thinking of getting more sugar land and more profit and bigger ships for you so that you could stick your fat ass behind a wheel and navigate a ship, which is the only thing you can do without messing it up."

He looked at her. Tiny twinges of guilt for having struck her were gnawing at him. He was still enraged, but he was sorry he had hit her.

"Why marriage?" he asked almost plaintively. "I don't understand how you expect to make things better for you and me by marrying this young shit. That's going to take a lot of explaining."

"Nothing changes between you and me," she asserted.

"Really? What does Parlange say about this?"

"He doesn't have to know."

"I'm not taking sloppy seconds to no planter's pretty-boy son."

Helene reacted as if Lionel had slapped her a second time. She turned to leave the cabin. Lionel jumped up and cracked his head on one of the overhanging beams. He saw stars and fell to his knees. He had cut his scalp, and blood quickly soaked his hair and began to dribble down his forehead. He sat down in a daze.

Helene heard the thud and saw him fall. She stopped to see if he was all right and then made a small cry of concern when she saw the blood. She returned to his side. She saw a dirty towel he had hung near his washstand. She grabbed it and pressed it against the cut in his head.

He lay back, his head still bleeding. "I'm sorry I hit you," he said to her.

She said nothing.

"Will you forgive me?"

"No," she said.

He grimaced.

"Don't take it so hard, Lionel. I'm not giving you up either. It's just that I'll never forgive you for striking me. If I do, you may get it into your head that you can do it a second time or any number of times when the mood takes you."

"Damn it, woman," he said, pressing the towel more firmly against his own head. "You betrayed me."

"Rubbish. I made us richer, all of us—you, me, Bernard, Gaston."

"You're sleeping with another man!"

"Why not? He's my husband. Besides, it is he who should be complaining about my sleeping with you."

He looked at her in surprise. "You still intend to?" he said softly.

"Didn't you think I would?"

"But you're a newlywed."

"So is Robert," she said, "and honestly, Lionel," she said as she flopped to her knees beside the cot, "he doesn't know what to do and he's, well, smaller than you. And he doesn't do the things you do."

"What things?" he teased.

She leaned over him and kissed him openmouthed. Their tongues intertwined and played against each other. "You know," she said as she pulled away from him, "the naughty things that you do."

"I thought I messed up everything except a ship."

"I was angry with you. I'm not anymore."

She opened his shirt.

"I'm helpless," he said squirming his body from side to side on the cot. "My hands are above my head keeping my scalp and for all I know my skull together."

She leaned over him and began to nip at his chest, causing his nipples to become taut.

"That's one of *my* tricks," he said.

"I know," she responded. "Robert doesn't know about nipples." She opened the top button of his breeches and traced a line along his stomach with her tongue until she came to his navel. She drove her tongue into it and he squirmed even more.

"I suppose Robert doesn't know about belly buttons either."

"Not a thing," she said.

She reached down even further. She could feel the warmth of him along with the musky odor. She did not need to tell him that straight, old-fashioned Robert would know nothing about what she now did to him.

CHAPTER FIFTEEN

Port Hebert, 1766

Nine houses had been restored already and Marcel and Benoit were hard at work on a tenth. The Hebert residence was as close to the original as they could make it. The chimney was narrower, but they hadn't been able to spend too much time on it last fall. The weather had grown colder and the chimney had to remain smaller if they were to be able to light a fire to keep themselves warm. He built the foyer, completing it just before the storms came.

But even before the storms came, the British came from Fort Cumberland and demanded Marcel remove himself or be arrested. There was no room for Acadians in this land any longer. It delighted him to show Major Hastings his oath of allegiance. In turn, Hastings delighted in showing Hebert his deed signed by the governor acknowledging Audry Hastings as rightful owner of the lands along Chignecto Bay. Marcel would have to pay rent—a steep rent—if he wished to remain in residence. It angered Hebert beyond any other anger he had ever known, but he surrendered the last of his gold coins to Hastings in order to stay on his father's own land. Benoit left with the first dusting of snow, taking Old Gums with him. A lasting relationship had developed between the two of them over the years. At first Marcel had thought of Gums simply as a substitute mother for Lucien. The first night on the Saint John, when he had rejoined his friends after the frustrating trip to Virginia, she put little Lucien to bed and then waddled across the campfire to the other side and joined Benoit in his bedroll. Marcel had teased the Penobscot the next morning about losing his freedom and was surprised to hear his friend extol the virtues of women without teeth. It had embarrassed even him.

That had been ten years ago. Every spring Benoit came to Port Hebert after depositing his furs at Fort Cumberland, as they now called old Fort Beauséjour. He spent the summer helping Marcel rebuild, slowly but surely. Each year the town grew as more and more Acadians returned. So far none of the original inhabitants of Port Hebert had come back, but the very existence of a French village attracted those who heard of it. Every year Marcel had brought in one or two more families. Some had to live together for a season, but each spring a new building was begun. Gradually, some were able to help Marcel with the rents—yet every spring Marcel was forced to borrow money from Benoit to pay to Hastings.

Until Lucien was completely weaned and trained, the boy returned to Benoit's traplines with Benoit and Gums, but when he was four, Marcel insisted that his son spend the winter with him. Gums had cried and carried on, as had Lucien, but both of them recovered. The boy thrived with his father, although every spring he waited impatiently for his best friends, Benoit and Old Gums, to return to the village.

That had been eight years ago, and the boy grew tall, very tall for a twelve-year-old. He already had a dark line of hair on his upper lip. His hair was black, the same color as his father's but without any wave.

Marcel made up his mind that this spring he would have to lecture the boy on the facts of life. He told Benoit of his intention and listened in horror as his friend outlined the plan for Lucien's "first time." Benoit swore he had located the old hag, now obviously much older, who had given Marcel his one and only dose of clap. He thought it would be appropriate to allow Lucien to have the same woman.

"Who knows," Benoit had reminisced, "perhaps the boy will get his first dose from the same woman who gave it to the father." The squaw was at Cumberland, a day's journey away. Benoit wondered if Lucien was capable of it yet.

Marcel knew the man so well he forbade Benoit to go near the boy until he had explained things to him. The father-and-son talk was a disappointment to Marcel. He discovered that the lad knew everything. It seemed that Old Gums had instructed him on the birds and the bees from the time he was a toddler, and there was nothing he did not know.

Marcel abandoned the hard work of fatherhood for the relative ease of house construction with a sense of relief. As in most things he did, Benoit was a wizard with hammer and saw. He taught Lucien, who soon outstripped Marcel with tools. But neither Benoit nor Lucien could compete with Marcel when it came to the number of hours worked and his devotion to the rebuilding of his father's town. He was fanatical about the restoration. It was as if each house he finished brought him closer to restoring the land of the Acadians. And each house put him further in debt to the hated Englishman.

This spring had been scorching hot. The sun beat down on them mercilessly. Marcel stripped to the waist daily as he climbed the ladders to finish roofs or fix mortar to hold the stone chimneys in place. His torso was burned at first, but then turned a dark brown.

Some of the new Port Hebert men had revitalized the project of working on the sea dikes. They did not yet attempt to reclaim more salt marsh from the gray Fundy, but at least they had started to restore the dikes and levees that the old-timers had constructed.

At night Marcel sat in his chair by the hearth in his house. He had built furniture that reminded him of the things that Maman Adele had loved so much. He smoked his pipe and listened to Benoit tell outrageous lies to his openmouthed, trusting Lucien. Then he would chase the boy into the loft upstairs, smoke another pipe, and say good night to Benoit and Old Gums. He shared the loft with Lucien to allow his friends the privacy of the downstairs bed.

Benoit worried about Marcel's celibacy. One day, as they shingled a roof together, he offered to share his squaw with him. "It wouldn't be so bad," he argued with a disbelieving Marcel. "You could have her three nights and I could have her on three other nights."

"And on the seventh night she rests?" Marcel joked.

"If that's what she wants, we can give her the night off," Benoit continued, missing Marcel's joke altogether. "But she rarely wants time off from sex. To tell you the truth," Benoit said wistfully, "you'd be doing me a big favor if you took her off my hands." He laughed. "If it was only my hands she was after."

Marcel laughed loudly. "I'm sorry, Benoit. She's all yours."

"It's just not right," Benoit continued as his hammer struck in rapid succession and made firm a row of shingles. "A man your age. How old are you now, boy?"

"Twenty-nine."

"My God, you're well past your prime. You're hurting your internal organs, to say nothing of your external organs. I assume you beat your wick a great deal."

Marcel merely smirked. "Benoit, my friend, don't worry about my organs or my sex life."

"You can't say that to me. I got that tool working for you the first time. I have a responsibility."

"Benoit, it was hardly the first time it worked."

"Pissing don't count."

"I wasn't referring to pissing."

"There you go again, describing a whole life of self-pollution." Marcel laughed. "Benoit, I have this theory."

Benoit's interest was immediately riveted. He had a love of theories.

"It's about the *last* time. It must be the best. I am searching for the person who will be my partner the *last* time I have sex."

Benoit pulled at the three-day growth of whiskers on his face. "Now that's damned interesting," he said. "You're looking for the girl who will be the last."

"And once I find her she'll be the last."

"There were times I thought you pined away for that girl from Port Hebert."

Marcel grew somber and his mood changed.

"I guess I should not have spoken of her to you," Benoit commented.

"I am sorry, my friend," Marcel apologized, "but that was very painful and it was a long time ago."

"Pain is near the surface with you always, my friend."

"Ten years ago, when I lost Nina in the wilderness of Virginia, I hoped she and my brother would return here. Since they haven't, I can only assume that they perished."

"Why do you think that? Many Acadians settled elsewhere. Some in St. Pierre off Newfoundland and others in Santo Domingo and even more in Louisiana. Why couldn't they have gone to one of those places?"

"Because Gilles, my brother, was Lucien Hebert's son, in some ways much more like him than I was. If he was alive he would be here."

"People change, Marcel. Things happen to them. Who could have predicted how the unhappy runaway that I befriended would someday so value the home he fled that he would return here and live like a monk?"

Marcel chuckled again. "Always you return to my sex life."

"Was the girl Nina your ideal last one?"

Marcel grew serious. "I think I could have been happy with her." He shrugged his shoulders. "But it wasn't to be. I think she fell in love with my brother. Maybe she and Gilles knew some happiness together. I hope so. But their disappearance wasn't my only loss."

Benoit had heard the story of Helene before but there was no turning Marcel off once he started. "I promised old Lucien," he said sadly, "that I'd find my brother and my sister. I tried every ship's list on the Atlantic Coast until I found the ship of Captain Rofheart of Boston bound for Charleston, South Carolina. Helene was on that ship. It was the saddest day of my life, even worse than losing Gilles and Nina, to discover that Rofheart's ship had never arrived. It was listed as lost at sea. Helene—so beautiful, so young—lost at sea. At least Gilles and Nina had each other to cling to, but Helene was alone when the end came. I think I would rather die almost anyplace else but at sea."

"Strange sentiment for an Acadian. You live your lives either on it or surrounded by it."

The shingles were finished. Benoit leapt down from the ladder, skipping the last few rungs. He too was bare-chested.

His skin, naturally several shades darker than Marcel's, looked almost like that of a black man.

"This is warmer than I can ever remember in the spring," Marcel said as he joined his friend on the ground.

"Is it warm enough for a dip in the River Hebert?" Benoit asked.

"It is never warm enough for that." Marcel laughed. "But let's do it anyway."

They walked slowly, as men are prone to do after a day's work.

"Lucien," Marcel called out as he passed his own house, "Benoit and I are going for a swim. Join us."

The boy's head popped out of the window. "Rescue me," he shouted. "Old Gums is heating water for a bath." His head suddenly disappeared as if his feet had been cut out from under him, which was precisely what had happened to him.

They heard a shout in Indian language. Marcel could tell by the cracked voice that it was his son and not the Indian woman who reverted to that language.

"What did he say?" Marcel asked Benoit.

"You wouldn't want to know," Benoit responded.

"I'm his father."

"That's why you don't want to know."

"Benoit!"

"All right. He said, 'May you have ground glass in your vagina and may the next man you sleep with lose much blood inside of you' or something to that effect."

Marcel waited for more noise from the house. "Why doesn't Old Gums beat the shit out of him?"

"Because she's a Micmac and he spoke Penobscot."

"A language he did not learn from Old Gums."

Benoit looked away as if by his not facing Marcel the guilt would somehow or other miss its mark.

Lucien, dressed only in short breeches, came running out of the house. When he joined the two men, Marcel grabbed the boy by his ears. "You speak like that to Gums once more, you little brat, and I'll kick your butt from here to the Bay of Fundy."

Lucien gave Benoit a wicked look. Only the Penobscot could have betrayed the meaning of his curse to his father.

But Marcel was not really angry with the lad. They walked

through the town to the river. There was a small open fishing boat docked at the riverfront. It belonged to a newcomer to Port Hebert. He had lived in Grand Pre in the old days, the major Acadian town before the deportation, now a ghost town of rubble and burnt-out dwellings.

Once they passed the boat they would be beyond the view of any of the citizens of the village. Lucien ran ahead, opening his breeches. They began to slide down his backside as he ran. He almost tripped as the pants fell to his knees. The boy was free of them in another three steps. He took a running leap headfirst into the river.

Marcel laughed. It was an endless source of wonderment to him that the boy could leap into the numbing waters of the river without a second thought, but put him in a tub of warm water with a bar of brown soap and he screamed as if someone was extracting his fingernails after having first roasted his tongue over a slow-burning fire.

Marcel reached the spot where Lucien cavorted. The boy shouted great war whoops to reduce the agony of the chill and to try to get his breath back.

Benoit had also stepped out of his breeches. He put his foot in the river and removed it. "It's warmed up," he commented.

Marcel stripped off his garments. He did not approve of the slow immersion technique. He dived into the water like his son. The chill stabbed at him. He surfaced and yelped, then turned around to see Benoit take several steps backward from the river.

"Come on in, you old chicken," Marcel called.

Benoit stood naked except for his feathered hat, but Lucien's and Marcel's reactions were enough for him. He was already slipping his pants back on. The thought of Lucien's unused bath water was becoming more attractive to him than the River Hebert.

Suddenly he looked toward the slight turn the river made on its way to the salt marshes and the bay beyond.

"A boat's coming this way," Benoit called.

Marcel came up the bank dripping freezing river water. He was delighted to have an excuse to quit, but a boat normally meant Hastings coming to demand money. And that depressed him at the same time.

Benoit stared at him. "No wonder you have no need for sex. You have no sex organs."

"Shut up," Marcel responded. "No one would have anything left on the outside after jumping into that water. I swear my balls are still on their way up into my belly trying to get warm again."

He was now back in his breeches. "Lucien," he called, "get dressed. Someone is coming."

"I don't want to," the boy responded. "They're probably men, and if they aren't, I can stay under the water."

"God knows how," Marcel said to Benoit.

The boy did a handstand on the muddy bottom, exposing the whole lower half of his body above the water level.

"That's it," Marcel said angrily. He waited until Lucien resurfaced before calling his name once more. "You little savage, get your ass out of the water or I swear I'll come in after you."

Lucien doubted his father's threat, but nevertheless started to return to the riverbank.

"Move," Marcel yelled again. The boat was now in sight. Marcel grabbed his son and stood between him and the oncoming rowboat while the boy put his pants back on.

They were not all men. Four men rowed, but there were two passengers and one of them was a woman, who carried a parasol. She looked vaguely familiar to Marcel.

"Yoo-hoo!" the woman called out to them from the back of the boat. "You men there, come help me out of this craft." She spoke with the accent of Acadia, and the tone of her voice helped Marcel to place her. It was Odette Babineau—Dette—Nina's mother.

But she was a Dette that none of her friends could have recognized. Her hair was the same color but her face had aged a great deal. Marcel helped her out of the boat onto the bank. But it was neither her face nor her hair that would have disguised her. It was her clothes. She was dressed in a heavy violet brocaded material. The skirt was full and the bodice low-cut. The only concession she made to the heat of the day was her parasol. The outfit she wore was extremely expensive.

"Roger," she called to the elegantly dressed man who warily attempted to leave the boat without falling. "Don't be such a silly ass, Roger. There's nothing to leaving a rowboat. I've done it all my life. Young man," she said to Marcel, "who are you?"

"Dette," Marcel called her by her nickname.

Her eyes widened in surprise. She had not been called that in years. "You know me?"

"I am Marcel Hebert, Lucien and Adele's son."

She screeched with joy and threw her arms about him, smothering him in her ample bosom. She reeked of old sweat disguised by heavy perfume. Her eyes looked beyond him to the ten restored houses standing all alone where so many had once stood.

"Where's the rest of the town? The church? My God, there's nothing left." Tears flowed down her cheeks.

Marcel turned to Benoit and Lucien, who stood shyly behind Marcel's friend.

"You must meet my friend. This is Benoit, whom I have known since I was not much older than this boy. And this is my son, Lucien Hebert."

She ignored Benoit. "Such a pretty boy. But he looks more like your Maman Adele than he does his namesake. And your wife?"

"Dead," he responded. There was no sense going beyond that explanation. "Lucien, Benoit, this is Madam Odette Babineau, a neighbor and a citizen of Port Hebert."

"No, it's not Babineau any longer. It's Madame Bégin." She took hold of the arm of the small gentleman who came up behind her. "This is my husband, Roger Bégin." The man bowed to both Marcel and Benoit.

Marcel, who had extended his hand to Roger, pulled it back rather sheepishly. Benoit curtsied. Dette ignored all this and walked to the dirt road that led to the remnants of the town.

"My God, it's hotter here, Roger, than in Cape François."

"But without the yellow fever, my love," he responded.

"We came here, Marcel, to escape the heat of the summer in our home in Santo Domingo. The fever rages there. I have been after Roger for years to take me here."

"We welcome you."

"Marcel," she said, ignoring Roger, "take me to your home. And you, Lucien," she said, turning to the boy, "you

345

must tell me all about yourself. Oh my, he so reminds me of my little TiJoe. Marcel, before we go to your house, you must take me to my little boy's grave. I must see where my TiJoe is buried. Oh, my goodness," she continued, "I have Maman Adele's grandson right in front of me. Roger, my medicine, I think I'm going to faint. It is all too much."

Roger Bégin rushed to Dette's side. He took a small bottle from his coat pocket, opened it, and placed it under his wife's nose. She inhaled deeply and recovered almost instantly from her swoon. She started down the dirt road, sweeping Lucien ahead of her and almost bowling Benoit over.

Marcel followed with Roger. "Have you been married long, monsieur?" Marcel asked politely.

The man sighed. "Very long," he responded. "Almost five years. My first wife died of the fever in Santo Domingo. I have a sugar plantation there. My three daughters were motherless for four years until I met Odette."

"How fortunate that Madame Babineau was an experienced mother."

"Yes, she is experienced. Unfortunately, my daughters have little appreciation for her experience."

"Madame Dette," Marcel called to her as she came even with the small fenced-in yard. "Here's the graveyard."

Dette rushed up to the fence. She saw a grave marked by small wild violets.

"There it is," she exclaimed. "Oh, I could never forget this spot. Here is where my baby lies. Oh, my child, my little TiJoe, torn from my breasts and murdered." She started to weep loudly.

Marcel did not have the heart to tell her that she wept over his parents' grave. The Babineau plot was to the right and unmarked. He did not fail to notice that she made no mention of her former husband, Babin, who shared the grave with her son. He thought that it must be her concern for her new husband's sensibilities.

Roger was by her side once again, medicine bottle in hand. Dette took another sniff. It seemed to energize her. She turned away from the graveyard. "Marcel, the house, where is it?"

He pointed to the mud-and-timber structure on the left-hand side of the road. Dette grabbed Lucien's hand and charged ahead, all thoughts of little TiJoe vanished. She pushed her way through the outer door of the foyer.

"Oh my," she said, "I have forgotten how quaint these houses are and how small they are." She opened the inner door and and started to enter, but blocking her path was Old Gums. Dette took one look and began to scream at the top of her lungs. She grabbed her hair and raced into the yard howling, "Hostiles," at the top of her lungs.

Roger panicked and froze when Gums stepped out into the yard following Dette. The poor Indian was totally confused by the French woman's behavior.

"Relax, Dette," Marcel shouted at her. "This is only Benoit's wife, a Micmac woman, very friendly to whites, especially French people."

Dette glanced behind her with considerable trepidation. She tried to regain her composure.

Benoit took Old Gums by the arm. "Nothing to be afraid of here," he said. He placed his arms around the ample frame of Old Gums and gave her a sloppy kiss on her large nose.

Gums gave him her gap-toothed smile.

"What's for dinner tonight?" he asked her.

"Fish stew," said the Micmac.

"Gums," he asked her, "have you enough food for two more people for dinner?"

"There's always more for guests," she responded to him in French.

They sat up late eating and drinking. Dette was the first of the old Port Hebert residents, besides Marcel, to return to the old site. Marcel introduced her to all the new neighbors. They played some fiddle music and they sang together until midnight when all the other guests went home.

Benoit and Gums agreed to join Marcel and Lucien in the loft and leave the bed to their guests, Dette and Roger.

Dette had misgivings about sleeping in a stranger's bed, especially when one of the strangers was an uncivilized savage. She was mortally afraid of picking up some form of bug or vermin. She would have been mortally offended if she had understood Gums' complaint to Benoit about surrendering her bed to someone who smelled so bad.

Marcel stayed up with Dette and Roger for a few more

hours. He invited them to join their community. He could tell they were having some difficulty keeping straight faces at the suggestion. Dette Babineau had come a long way since the days of the deportation. They began to reminisce, leaving Roger to his own thoughts.

"It was so awful, Marcel. You remember how they came and rounded up all the men?"

"I was not here, Dette."

Her face turned suddenly hard. "Oh yes, I remember. It was you after all who left my poor Nina in the condition she was in."

Marcel smiled again. "You confuse me again, madame. That was my brother Gilles."

"Gilles, shit," she said loudly, causing Roger to blink out of his reverie and then blush. "Nina said it was you and no one else. She was not a liar. Do you deny that you could have been the father of her child?"

Marcel was flustered for a second. The thoughts of his torn breeches and the tender moment atop this very woman's own bed came flooding back to him.

"But—but—Gilles could have been also."

"Are you suggesting that my sweet Nina, who is probably dead and gone forever, was a whore like your sister? She told me it was you and only you. She never let Gilles near her. Your mother knew it, your father knew it, even that miserable son of a bitch Babin knew it."

Again Roger blinked at the mention of his predecessor's name.

Marcel was confused. He was shocked to discover that he may, in fact, have been Nina's true love, and to hear his sister's name mentioned, especially in an uncomplimentary fashion.

"What do you know about Helene?" he demanded.

"Aha, what don't I know about her?"

Marcel's heart was pounding. He had given up all hope of ever hearing about his sister again. "Where is she?"

"With that diseased greaseball Lionel Robichaud, I'm sure," she responded.

"Tell me everything you know," he commanded in great excitement. "I thought her ship sank at sea."

"It did sink," Dette said. "We never made it to the

Carolinas. The captain of that first ship, he was a madman. He raped your sister."

Marcel swallowed hard.

"The girl came back to the hold bleeding and bruised. All our hearts went out to her. She had cured some of us. You know, she is a *traiteur* like your mother. She discovered her talents aboard the cargo ship. Then he sent for her again, the scum Rofheart. We all would have hidden her, but the bitch went freely on her own to his arms. She never came back to the hold. We saw her on deck sunning her filthy body, eating while the rest of us starved. We were headed for the auction block when a storm hit us. We ran aground and were rescued by a French ship, a privateer. We hanged that scum. You know, I'll never forget it. He died laughing."

"What happened to Helene?" Marcel asked nervously.

"She hopped from one captain's bed to another. It made no difference to her so long as her needs were met. This new man Robichaud brought us all to the West Indies islands, all but your sister. He promised us New Orleans—but went to Santo Dimingo instead, chasing a juicy English merchant ship. He dumped us unceremoniously at Cape François. God knows how we suffered, while Helene lived in luxury."

Marcel sat silently for some moments after Odette had finished her story. "Where is she now?" he asked finally.

"On her back with her legs spread, I suppose, or burning in hell if she got her just reward," Dette responded.

"You don't know where this Captain Robichaud is today?" She shook her head.

Roger spoke for the first time. Before the war, monsieur, Captain Robichaud carried sugar from Cape François and Port au Prince to France, but he also sailed from the gulf ports."

"That's it," Dette interrupted. "He probably took her to Louisiana. I'll bet that is where she is. I hope they both rot from a crotch fungus."

Marcel needed time to think. Helene was alive. That fact, mixed with the news that Nina might have loved him after all, was almost too much to absorb all at once. Dette continued to speak, however, filling him in on the details of her life.

"Helene had it easy, the bitch." She seemed to forget completely about the fact that the man she spoke to was

Helene's brother. "Oh, it was easy for her. She did nothing to help me. I stood up for her when the others wanted to hang her. She openly admitted she was Rofheart's whore. No self-respecting Acadian woman could stand by her after that. And then she took to Robichaud's cabin. It was a disgrace. *She* was a disgrace. I even told her so. And how did she reward me? When we came to Cape François and that pig Robichaud ordered everyone off his ship, I begged her to let me stay on. I was her mother's best friend. Her brother had fathered my grandchild. I begged. Did she listen to me? No. I found myself on the docks with all the others, not a sou to my name. We had to take a dole from the French authorities there."

She rambled on. Marcel could not get her voice out of his brain. As long as she continued to speak he could not think about what to do next.

"But I survived despite those two, Helene and her captain. I did those things I knew how to do best. I cooked. I took care of children. Babin always said I was the best cook in Port Hebert and my children were the best behaved in the village."

Marcel smiled. He would say nothing to her about TiJoe. It was amazing how time altered memory.

"Then Monsieur Bégin invited me into his house to care for his motherless little ones and we fell in love."

She looked over at her snoring Roger. A look of amazement crossed her face when she realized he had slept through her account of her trials and later courtship. She poked him hard in the ribs. He looked about, startled at the strangeness of his surroundings.

"Roger, did I waken you?" she asked. "I was just telling Marcel that you had agreed to build a monument at the gravesite of my little TiJoe. We were told that people were back at Port Hebert and we could get workmen to do it for us. We never suspected we would find friends who could do it for us. Oh, we will pay. Roger, give Marcel the money."

Obediently, Monsieur Bégin reached into his coat pocket and removed a leather pouch. He handed it to Marcel. "There should be more than enough in there for a good stone," Bégin said.

Marcel opened the pouch. It was filled with Spanish gold

coins. There was enough for five stones, he thought, but he kept quiet.

"I'll take care of it," he offered.

"Oh, yes. Isn't it wonderful, Roger, that someone who actually knew my TiJoe will be able to look after him even after we return home."

"You're not coming to live at Port Hebert?"

Dette looked at him as if he were insane. "My goodness, no." She laughed. "That was fine for one part of my life, but Roger and I will be returning to Cape François as soon as the fever season is over."

"Will you return?"

She looked startled. "I suppose not, not now that we know you are here."

She turned to Roger for confirmation, but he had already returned to his snoring.

Dette continued with her life story in Santo Domingo, but Marcel now made only a pretext of listening. He was beginning to doze off himself. The money would come in handy. He would build a monument to TiJoe. He would fulfill her request but he would also build another sort of monument to all of them—TiJoe, Babin, Old Lucien, Maman Adele, to all the Acadians. He would use the money to build more houses for returning Acadians. He smiled. It struck him that some of the money would help to meet Hastings's incessant demands for rent as well.

Marcel rose to his feet. He had to get to bed. "Excuse me, Dette, I don't mean to be rude. But I'm exhausted. I must sleep." She looked at him in surprise but said nothing. He climbed off the steps to the loft. His mind raced ahead. Louisiana was terribly far away and he was devoted to rebuilding this village and taking care of his son. He couldn't go so far just on the belief of this man Roger, whom he did not know, and the malicious gossip of a spiteful old woman. But he had promised his father to find Helene and bring her home. And if only half of what Dette said was true, then Helene had suffered much, much more than any of them.

He thought of Nina and Gilles. Perhaps he should have told Dette that he thought Nina had perished. The woman deserved bad news since she herself seemed to thrive on it. But what she had told him about Nina had shaken him. He needed time to think. He did not wish to talk of Nina Babineau with anyone, not even her own mother.

Marcel looked about the darkened loft. Benoit and Gums stirred yet continued to snore. Their arms were wrapped about each other and they were scantily dressed. He hoped they had had the good sense not to do anything in front of Lucien, but knowing Benoit it would not surprise him if his friend had deliberately awakened Lucien so that he might observe.

Marcel climbed onto the mat that his son occupied. He had to move the boy over to make room for himself. He lay down without taking off any of his clothes. His mind raced wildly. Nina Babineau, pregnant with his child. He shook his head, trying to dispel the guilt he felt. How she must have felt when she discovered she carried a baby and had no way to get in touch with him. Had he known, he would have returned. Even if she had been transported by then, he would have followed her into the wilderness beyond McGriff's place. Nothing would have stopped him. But he had been sure she was safe with the man she loved, the father of her child.

He remembered that McGriff had told him that Nina had had a daughter, his daughter. He wished now he had gone on looking for them. Now it was too late. But he had news now of Helene. He had to look for her. Benoit and Gums would take care of the boy and his friend would continue the restoration and till the house garden for the winter's food supply of potatoes while he went off. He knew he would go. He could not betray his last promise to his father.

CHAPTER SIXTEEN

Bayou LaFourche, 1768

The clump of oak trees shaded the house on hot summer afternoons. The house itself was built of sawed boards painted white and raised off the soggy earth by wooden posts driven deeply into the ground. When the floods came in the spring and forced the waters of the bayou over the levee, the family had a few hours' notice, at least, before water lapped at the front door and seeped up through the floorboards. The roof was sharply pitched. That was the way roofs were made in Acadia, and Gilles Hebert knew no other way to build a roof. The stairway to the attic area ran on the outside of the house from the raised front porch up to the finished attic. In the cooler seasons, little Adele loved to sleep up there alone with her pet raccoon, but in summer, even with the shade of the oaks, no one could tolerate the heat that built up in the roof rafters. Inside, the house was divided into main room, kitchen, and bedroom. It was the front porch that the family occupied most of all. There was an overstuffed couch against the front wall on the left, under the eaves created by the roof. On the right there was a table and three chairs. Most often the family ate here.

Gilles cast his fine net out into the waters of the bayou. He allowed it to settle slightly, then he watched it sink to the bottom. The water was clear and he could see the bait of possum meat that he had tied to the center of the net sway with the current. All he had to do now was be patient. He did not have long to wait. The crawfish were motivated by curiosity and hunger. Before long three large ones were nibbling at the possum meat. Jacques pulled the corners up, trapping his prey. He pulled the net out of the water and emptied its contents into a jug. He counted six crawfish. That was enough for this evening's meal, he thought, along with rice, tomatoes, and hot pepper sauce.

He was sweating heavily from the waist up. The perspiration flowed down his chest and his sides. He looked down at himself. He could see a little gray in his chest hair, and there was a little bulge of flesh all about his waist where the top of his breeches pressed into the skin.

"Getting a little fat, Gilles," he said aloud to himself. "A little fat and a little old. Thirty-two in fact." He plucked one gray hair from his chest and grimaced at the sharpness of the pain.

He decided to cool off. He left his already soaked breeches on and dived headfirst into the languid waters of the bayou. He remained underwater for as long as he possibly could and then broke the surface. He turned over on his back and looked up into the hot summer sky.

He heard her call to him from the porch. He turned back onto his stomach and swam with a slow, strong, steady stroke back to the riverbank. He picked up their dinner and walked back to the house.

He loved this place and had never regretted coming here. He had cleared the woods along the bayou and constructed the house with his own hands. The boards for the house had come from the sawmill on the "German Coast" along the Mississippi where settlers had migrated from Germany. It was a fine strong house built in the sturdy Acadian tradition. One didn't need houses here that could stand the cold Arctic wind, but this one had withstood some storms from the gulf that would have awed the fishermen of Port Hebert.

At first he thought frequently about Port Hebert. Nina talked about it continuously from the time he made up his mind at Fort Duquesne to go south rather than north over the lakes to Canada. He told her it was because the lands in the north were alive with warring Indians and English troops and that the English had promised to murder any Acadian returning home. It was a lie, but she had believed him. More than that, he told her that an English army approached them at the forks of the Ohio River and that the French garrison would surrender if the English lay siege. Though he had not known it then, he later was turned into a prophet by subsequent events. Their only course, he had convinced her, was to retreat down the Ohio where it joined the Mississippi and then to travel that giant muddy stream until they came to French land. That was twelve years ago. He regretted not a single lie. He had gained much by his lies. He had a daughter. Even if she was really his niece, she was a daughter to him. At twelve she promised to surpass her mother in beauty. They shared the same hair color, the same eye color, and the same smile. But little Adele adored her papa. At first he thought Nina would insist that Adele call him something else, but she had not and he was immeasurably grateful.

It was, in fact, the beginning of a growing acceptance of him. She was thousands of miles away from their home, and she had only the child and him to tie her to Acadia. She had not mentioned Marcel in years. Her blind faith that he would come for her died years ago and was replaced by a contentment with him, Gilles.

They never made love. At first it drove him to distraction to sleep by her side and never lay a hand on her. But he knew that if he did she would take the child and leave him. He satisfied himself as best he could. As he grew older that no longer seemed so difficult. There were other things—clearing the land, building the house—that came first. Although they lived in isolation here at Bayou LaFourche, there were fellow Acadians nearby. The village of Thibodoux to the north of them on the bayou was prospering. He went there with Nina and Adele on Satudays to barter for necessary provisions and in the evening to dance occasionally—although he was still horrible at it. He would never forget the night at the fête in Port Hebert when he had refused to dance and Marcel had cut in. He mentioned it to Nina as he tried to do in Thibodoux what he refused to do at Port Hebert. He never mentioned it again. Her mood had turned almost instantly black and it had not improved for days.

Also in Thibodoux he met with the other men who made up the militia of LaFourche. Some thought it silly to keep the company together now that the war with England had come to an end, but the rumors of the Spanish takeover had proven not to be false. Last year the new Spanish governor of Louisiana, Antonio deUlloa, arrived with a garrison to man the barracks in the city of New Orleans. The bayou company had received secret word from former regimental leaders among the Creole planters to keep training in anticipation of an uprising to restore French control.

Nina was standing on the front porch. Her homespun dress was covered with a white apron. Her dress was stained with sweat at the armpits and at the bodice. She had become heavier and thicker through the middle since the birth of Adele, and her breasts were larger from nursing the child and, he guessed, just from getting older. Her hair still had a tint of reddish gold in it, however, and her fuller face was even more beautiful.

Adele sat at the table, knife and fork already in hand, awaiting the arrival of the crawfish. Nina had wisely lit her fire out of doors in front of the porch. The minute she saw Gilles coming she stepped down to the fire and began to stir anew.

"Papa," Adele called to him, "hurry up. I'm hungry. Mama has the *roux* ready. Hurry with the crawfish and let's get going."

Nina smiled at Adele's impatience. Gilles walked to her side and kissed her on the cheek. She smiled at him also. She stirred the rice that was cooking over the same fire as the brown sauce.

Gilles was soon busy cleaning the shellfish. The yellow crawfish fat was dumped into the sauce, where it joined Nina's favorite mixture of sauteed onions, celery, pepper, and garlic. Then she dumped in some of the season's first tomatoes from her garden.

Gilles was impatient to drop the crawfish tails into the cauldron but Nina stopped him.

"Wait until it's ready," she chided. "You're as impatient as the child."

The pot cooked for ten more minutes. Finally Nina gave

the signal and Gilles dropped the meaty part of his catch into it. They would not take long to cook.

Nina parceled out three plates of boiled rice from the pot and then placed the crawfish *étouffée* on top of the rice. Jacques carried the plates to the table on the porch. Nina removed her pot from the fire and joined the family, carrying her own dinner. ·

Adele smacked her lips and began to wolf down her food.

"Slow down," Nina scolded her irritably.

Adele paid no attention to her mother. Nina was hot and had little patience with the girl. "Gilles," she said, "make her behave and eat like a proper young lady and not like her pet raccoon."

Gilles looked over at Adele. There was a twinkle in his eye that the girl knew well. It said, "Do what your mother asks and we'll have more fun later on." Adele put her fork down on the plate and began to chew the food systematically. Her new obedience seemed to make Nina even more irritable.

"Gilles, she's mocking me," Nina complained.

The man looked sternly at the little girl, and Adele again picked up her fork and started once again to shove her food into her mouth.

Nina dropped her fork onto her plate.

"Adele," Gilles said, "take your plate over to the loveseat and eat there."

The girl rose without saying a word and did as she was told.

"I can't handle her," Nina complained after Adele departed. "She's so defiant and so wild." In her own mind she added, "Just like her father, irresponsible and unthinking."

"She'll learn," Gilles assured her.

Nina looked away out across the yard toward the bayou. She hated it when Gilles tried to soothe her nerves and told her whatever he thought she wanted to hear.

"You look warm," he said to her after they had finished eating. "Why don't you and Adele go down to the bayou for a swim? I'll clean up here." She looked at him. She was sorry whenever she was cross and irritable with him. He was a good man. He loved her. Of that she was sure. She had hurt him, hurt him in a way for which she could never make amends. She had denied him herself, the one thing he desired above all else. At this stage even she did not know why. Marcel had faded in her memory. Perhaps she avoided Gilles now out of habit. She did not know how to approach him and offer him what he wanted, and it had been years since he last entreated her. Maybe he didn't care anymore either. She rose wearily from the table and called to her daughter.

"Adele, how about a swim?"

The girl jumped from the couch and raced into the house to find something suitable for swimming.

Both Gilles and Nina started in fright when they heard the report of the musket. It was a friendly warning, however. Someone was coming down the bayou toward their house and signaled their coming in advance.

There were four of them, militiamen from the bayou at Thibodoux.

Gilles grabbed his musket from the rack in the house and met them at the landing.

"What brings you this far south?" he asked the leader, Corporal LeBlanc.

"We need you, Sergeant Hebert. There is trouble brewing in the city. Colonel Vernay and Lieutenant duPont, his son-in-law, have summoned us to New Orleans. The time to strike is at hand."

"When do we leave?" he asked.

"The company will await you at Thibodoux at noon tomorrow."

"You'll await me?" Gilles said with some confusion.

"Yes, Lieutenant Fôret has broken his leg. You have been elected to replace him. We'll have you confirmed as our commander by the colonel just as soon as we get to New Orleans."

Gilles nodded solemnly. He had some misgivings. He did not think of himself as a leader. He remembered with some bitterness the way Port Hebert people had turned to him after his father died. He had failed. He did not know even what it was they had wanted of him. He wondered if it would be any different this time. He concluded that it would. He was older now, and this time he had men like Colonel Vernay and Major Parlange to turn to.

Nina had already entered the house to pack his things. Adele cavorted in the bayou and splashed the militiamen as their boat passed her, heading south to more isolated farms to spread the news.

"Adele," Gilles called to her, "your mother will not be joining you. You've had enough now. Out of the water."

As usual the girl obeyed him. If it had been Nina who called to her, there would have been an argument.

Gilles entered the house. The rooms were dark. The sun was now low in the evening sky. Nina had packed his carpetbag with clothes, razor, and razor strop. She put in a good-sized piece of yellow soap.

She said nothing to him, and he was relieved she did not try to argue him out of going. He sat in their bedroom and watched her. Then he became confused. She went to the wooden dresser he had constructed for them and began to place some of her own clothes in the carpetbag as well.

"What are you doing?"

"If you think I'm going to remain behind in this swamp alone without you then you don't know me very well."

"But it could be dangerous. Besides, you will have to bring Adele along as well."

"She'll love the city. So might I if I could only see it. Our trek to town will not be as dangerous as our flight from The Meadows to McGriff's or our journey from Fort Cumberland to the Ohio."

Gilles knew there would be no changing her mind. He had seen that set look before. Long ago he had given up trying to change her mind once she became that determined. He worried about the reputation of women who followed their men into battle. Then he chuckled. There was not much chance of a battle. The Spanish had a small army, but it would never stand up to Frenchmen fighting for their land. No one was going to drive him away again or take from him what was rightfully his. He had been driven from Acadia, but he would never leave Louisiana.

CHAPTER SEVENTEEN

New Orleans, 1768

Helene had not had time to count her coins. She had counted them weekly since that night Bernard had dumped them on the table at Gaston's. There were many more of them now, but many more of her assets were tied up in the two plantations. Bernard ran the sugar plantation and mill. She now made almost as much money from the molasses and rum as he did from the sugar itself. Monsieur Parlange had insisted on running his own estate. It limped along showing no profit, but at least it wasn't in the red anymore either, thanks to Helene's smuggling abilities. If it hadn't been for her, the Parlange indigo would never have found its way into the European cloth markets in the Lowlands. Lionel's new brig, as sleek a vessel as ever sailed and capable of giving slip to any revenue cutter anywhere in the world, was the key to that success. But the only really profitable part of the Parlange plantation was the acreage that Helene forced from Etienne Parlange and gave to Bernard for sugar planting.

Gaston also flourished. The salon and the courtyard were filled with gentlemen every night. When Helene moved out of her room, Gaston had filled it almost immediately with another girl. Business was so good that the fat man introduced a new system, two girls to a room. While one was at work, her roommate was down on the floor helping the gentlemen with the card games and plying them with more of Gaston's whiskey. They would also accept whiskey at top prices from the gamblers, but most often all the girls got was tea.

Gaston persuaded Helene to finance a second establishment on Rue de la Quai. The rooms were smaller and the prices lower and more often than not the men were rougher— sailors from the docks—but what it lacked in quality it made up for in quantity.

Helene had taken over Robert's room on Toulouse Street as her office. There was also a small back room, which she converted into a bedroom. She placed her heavy-piled rug in the bedroom and her yellow silk chair and lounge in the outer office. She now had them both with her and they no longer clashed.

The bed was large enough for two, but Robert rarely stayed in the city any longer. He spent most of his time out plotting with his Creole friends. She always knew what he was up to—thanks to Bernard. The ex-Jesuit had many contacts, one of whom had infiltrated the militia movement. She knew that Vernay and Guy duPont, the boy with the horseface wife, Vernay's daughter, were planning to assassinate Governor de Ulloa and then appeal to France for reannexation and the lifting of the Spanish yoke from Louisiana.

Helene fanned herself with a small white fan decorated with tiny embroidered rosebuds. It was her favorite, and she had many. In the city in the summer one could barely survive without a fan. She smiled at the naïveté of her father-in-law and her husband. They were in the thick of the plot. Whatever they told her was passed on to Gaston, who passed it on to the governor. So far she had protected Robert and his father. She was sure she could continue to do so even after the Spanish arrested all the Creole leaders in the town.

Robert had returned to the plantation yesterday. She would be alone again tonight. Lionel was in Mobile arranging to have his small ship refitted. So far she had kept him in the dark concerning her arrangements with the Spanish. He was not very shrewd politically and would probably protest to her about her lack of patriotism.

Patriotism was not the issue with Helene. It was all business. The Creoles represented the old order of French mercantilism and elite control. Under them, Helene could never have risen to the top. The Parlanges and Vernays would run Louisiana as lords, just as their counterparts had run Canada until the English took over. Their pretensions were based on those of the nobility of France.

The Spanish were just as pretentious but they were incredibly corrupt, even by Helene's standards. With them she would increase her holdings immeasurably. If the Creoles overcame de Ulloa, the horizons were limited, and no one was going to limit her horizons.

There was a soft tapping at the door. She was puzzled. It was late, well past midnight. She rose from her desk and went to the door and stared openmouthed. She recognized him instantly. He was older and more heavyset, but otherwise unchanged.

"Marcel," she cried out and rushed into his arms.

He held onto her as tightly as he could, fearing that if he let go she would disappear for another decade. She cried openly, her tears wetting his white shirt.

"Little sister" was all he could say over and over again. He had found her. His promise to his father was at least partially fulfilled.

Finally she pulled him from the doorway into her office. She made him sit on the silk couch next to her.

"How did you find me?" she asked.

He smiled.

She started to cry again. His smile was the same and it flooded her mind with memories of Papa Lucien and Maman Adele and Port Hebert.

"It was not easy," he said to her once her tears stopped again. "I had given up when I found they had listed you on a ship that was lost at sea."

"We were rescued."

"I know," he said laughing.

She looked at him quizzically.

"Odette Babineau Bégin, as she is now called, returned to Port Hebert from the West Indies."

"You're living in Acadia at Port Hebert? I thought the English would stop us from returning."

"They have let some back."

"Dette, eh?" Helene looked sheepishly at her big brother. "I'll bet she had some tales to tell about me."

"A few."

"Well, most of what she had told you is true. And whatever she made up I've done since we dropped the bitch off in Santo Domingo."

Marcel chuckled nervously, but he was not terribly interested in what she said. He wanted only to look at her. She was even more beautiful than he remembered.

"I want you to come back to Port Hebert with me," he said. "I'm rebuilding. Benoit, Lucien, and I have ten houses already constructed."

"Benoit, Lucien?" she questioned.

"Benoit is a half-breed friend of mine. I used to trap with him when I was a boy. Lucien—well, Lucien is my son."

"You found Nina Baineau, then?"

"No," he said sadly. "You knew about her and me too?"

"She told me when she first became pregnant. I remember feeling so proud of my big brother. I was sure you would be returning and there would be a wedding. How different it all was. But you say you did not find her."

"She went off with Gilles. I traced them to Virginia and followed. I missed them. But I did learn she had a daughter and she named her Adele."

Tears came to Helene's eyes again, and she had to look away from him.

"I only just learned from Dette that the child was mine. I always thought it was Gilles'."

Helene said nothing. He did not explain Lucien to her and she made no more inquiries of him. But she shook her head sadly. "I can't go back with you, Marcel. My life is here."

"But I promised Papa that I'd look for you and bring you home."

"It's too late, years too late. I have a new life and a husband. I am Madame Robert Parlange, the wife of a planter."

"I know. I've found no one who knew about Helene Hebert. But when I described you, everyone recognized Helene Parlange, the beautiful wife of the richest man in New Orleans."

"Is that what they say?" She laughed. "If they only knew. Robert is a dolt."

He looked at her in surprise.

"Oh, I know how that sounds, but when I found him he and his whole family were up to their asses in debt."

Again he looked at her in surprise.

"I can read your face, just as I could with Papa. You don't like my language. But I'm not going to hide anything from you, brother. I've had to fight to survive. I've had to be tough and I am tough. I own businesses that make money. I hire men and I fire men and I buy and sell slaves. I hire whores and I fire them. If anyone reneges on a debt, my collectors go out and break their fingers. Not the gentlemen, of course, only the common folk."

"How can you do all those things?"

"How can I do them?" Helene said angrily. "How could I avoid them? I have had to take care of *me*." She tapped her chest lightly with her fist. "Where was my papa and my big strong brothers when that pig Rofheart threw me on my back, spread my legs, and taught me the meaning of 'love'?"

"That's not fair," Marcel said softly.

"Of course it's not, but neither is it fair for you to expect me to be the same sweet girl you knew back in Port Hebert. It is one of the reasons I'll never go back. You never can, you know, not when you've experienced what I have."

Helene rose and went to the cabinet across the room. She took down two glasses and filled them with whiskey. She offered one to Marcel. He took it from her. She took a long drink from her own glass. "You should write me off, Marcel. Go find Nina Babineau. Maybe she has not changed as much as I have. Maybe you can bring her back to Acadia and start your life again."

"I don't think she is alive, or Gilles either. They would surely have returned to Port Hebert if they were."

Helene smiled sadly. "I'm still amazed, Marcel, that it is you who has become Papa's heir, the rebel tamed."

Suddenly she stopped speaking. She turned to the cabinet and opened a drawer. She removed a yellowed and crumpled piece of paper. "You should have this since you are the heir of Lucien Hebert."

Marcel took it from her. There was faded brown scribbling

on one side. She saw his consternation. "Turn it over," she ordered.

He did as she said. The French script seemed familiar. His eyes widened as he read it. Then his face broke into an enormous grin. It was a signed letter from Hastings granting Port Hebert to the heirs of Lucien Hebert. He did not know how it would hold up in a Halifax court, but he certainly intended to test it.

"How did you get this?"

"Don't ask," she interrupted him.

His face darkened. "This pig Hastings is now the greatest landowner and the greatest oppressor of our people in all of Acadia. I hope you did not give him what I think he would have demanded for this."

"He, and perhaps only he, got nothing," she said laughing.

There was a timid rap at the door.

"Gaston?" Helene called out. The door opened and the largest, most obese man Marcel had ever seen filled the doorframe. He was breathing heavily and perspiring.

"Gaston, my friend, either you must lose some weight or I must get rooms on the first floor. What's wrong?" She said this last with some anxiety. He had not noticed her reference to his obesity. He looked panic-stricken. His breath came in gasps. "It's Vernay, your father-in-law, and Robert. They've entered the city with an army, all the militia from the bayous. The uprising for France is taking place. It has started before we thought it would. Bernard came in from the plantation. Some had been there looking for the Jesuit. He escaped dressed as a nun. He's at my place now."

"The bloody fools. They'll all hang for this. King Louis is not going to go back on his gift to his Spanish cousins." Then she offered her friend the rest of her drink. "Come, Gaston, sit and rest."

"I can't," he whined. "They'll be looking for me. I must hide. They know I am in the pay of the Spanish."

"Where's the governor?" Helene asked.

"He has barricaded himself in the barracks on Rue de la Quai."

"He is safe enough there. He has a strong position. No militia can drive him out." Helene thought for a moment. "I think we had all better go there. If it was only Robert I wouldn't worry, but his father is much smarter. He knows of my connection with Gaston and he knows I am here."

"He does indeed." Etienne Parlange stood in the doorway. Behind him was a troop of militiamen.

Marcel stepped in front of Helene.

"Daughter, who is this man?"

"My brother."

"I am Marcel Hebert, monsieur."

"I didn't know you had family here. No matter. You will go with my men into protective custody. My daughter-in-law means very much to me and the welfare of my son and his wife is foremost in my mind this evening. But I have other duties. Corporal, take Madame Parlange and her brother downstairs and give them to the care of one of my officers. I have some questions to ask of this fat pimp, and it may take me and my men some time to get the answers."

The corporal led Helene and Marcel into the street. There was shouting coming from Royal Street. They could hear men running. Occasionally a musket report would echo from some part of the town. There were no signs of Spanish troops, only the French militia.

"Place your hands behind your back, monsieur," the corporal said to Marcel.

"I'll be damned if I will."

The butt of the musket cracked into Marcel's back directly between the shoulder blades, sending him sprawling on the ground. His hands were grabbed while he lay there stunned. They were quickly tied behind his back.

"I'm Helene Parlange, Captain Robert Parlange's wife. This man is my brother. You will pay for your mistreatment of him."

"Sorry, lady," was all the corporal would say. "*Major* Parlange said protective custody, and my orders on protective custody are to tie them up so that they can't use the hands."

"Do you intend to tie me up as well?"

He blushed. "Only if you make me."

Helene decided to remain quiet.

The corporal hustled Marcel to his feet and prodded him forward with his musket. They moved quickly down Toulouse Street until they came to Chartres Street. There troops of militia moved in different directions. Most headed toward

Rue de la Quai and Barracks Street, where the governor and his garrison were barricaded.

A grim reminder of the militia's serious intent hung from a cooper's sign on the corner. The man was very small and light. The fragile sign had been strong enough to support his weight. His neck was canted at a grotesque angle and his tongue protruded. The front of his breeches were stained where he had wet himself before the chair supporting him had been pulled away. Around his neck was a sign: "Traitor."

They stopped in front of Helene's salon, which had been taken over for the headquarters of the militia. The corporal waved them into the courtyard. It was jammed with militiamen, most of them officers. Helene saw Robert almost immediately. She called to him. He looked sheepishly in her direction. Helene had to stifle a scream with her hand when muskets fired on command from the courtyard next door. Summary executions were being carried out by firing squads.

Robert joined his wife. "Helene, I am sorry you were mixed up in this, but Father has discovered everything. He knows about my debts, about this house, about everything. He was enraged."

"Bullshit," Helene swore. "He always knew. You fool, it was all part of our deal to get the Parlange plantation out of debt and get me my sugar lands. Did you find my plantation manager here?"

"There was no one here but the girls. And also, can you imagine, there was a nun in the house. The girls had let her into the kitchen for some food. Imagine that, a nun in a whorehouse. We have kept her locked in the kitchen."

Helene smiled. Bernard at least was free. "What of the girls upstairs?"

"They remain there. Ah... entertaining the officers."

"Well, Robert," Helene spoke, "what do you intend to do with me?"

"Father says we must have an annulment."

Helene laughed. She had meant what was he going to do about her standing in front of him, a prisoner under protective custody. Obviously his planning was far more long-range.

"Incidentally, Robert, this is your about to be ex-brother-in-law, Marcel Hebert."

Robert looked embarrassed. He offered his hand to Marcel and then withdrew it when he realized that Marcel's hands were tied behind his back. Instead he bowed.

"*Enchanté, monsieur.*"

"*Moi aussi, monsieur,*" Marcel said sarcastically. "Helene, where did you find such a simpleton to marry?"

Robert turned red with anger and walked away from them.

Helene looked at Marcel. "I'm not sure we should have antagonized him, brother. We might have need of him to get ourselves out of here."

The corporal appeared.

"Prisoners are to be held in the kitchen."

They entered the salon, which was a shambles. Officers and men mingled. Muddy boots had rested on red velvet furniture, and chairs and tables had been overturned. And the rich red wool carpet was stained beyond repair with mud.

The kitchen was also crowded with soldiers. There were also a number of civilians with their hands tied behind them like Marcel's. Over in the corner near the stove a nun crouched on the floor, eating a bowl of rice with hot pepper sauce. Helene guided Marcel over to where Bernard sat. She flopped down on the floor and made room for Marcel to sit next to her.

"Don't you think this is a bit obvious?" the nun said to her. "Suppose someone suspects me?"

"Good sister," Helene responded, "if you were under the slightest suspicion you'd be halfway to Mexico City by now."

Bernard laughed softly. "But we were betrayed, Helene. By the way, who is your new companion? And does Lionel know?"

"It's my brother, Marcel Hebert, whom I have not seen for over a decade and who chose tonight to come calling."

"Superb timing, monsieur," Bernard laughed softly.

Marcel was only just realizing this nun was a man. He recalled the fat man's remark about the ex-Jesuit in disguise.

"So you are the Jesuit?"

"Jesus," Bernard nearly leapt off the floor at Marcel's remark, "words like that can get you shot around here."

A heavyset man with two days' growth of beard entered the kitchen. "Private," he called out. The guard who leaned against the back door of the kitchen, a musket cradled in his arms, looked lazily at the newcomer.

"The lieutenant wants you immediately." The private pushed himself away from the door with his foot and ambled out of the kitchen.

"I suppose that door is locked?" Marcel asked.

Bernard looked at him in disbelief. "Are you sure this is your brother, Helene?"

"You know I've never hit a nun before," Marcel said, "but there could be a first time."

"Behave, gentlemen, both of you. Yes, Marcel, it is locked."

"Where is the key?"

Again Bernard groaned. "The private shoved it up my ass. I can't reach it. Maybe you can get it for me."

"With my foot, and it will come out of your mouth," Marcel said angrily.

"Shut up!" said Helene. "Marcel has a point. Gaston used to keep an extra one on a hook behind the stove." She reached over beyond Bernard to feel for the key. It was not there.

"Do you think I would overlook such a thing?" Bernard scolded Helene.

"Reverend Sister."

Bernard was startled by the musket that prodded him as much as by the voice of the returned private. "The lieutenant wants you. Come with me."

Helene felt cold. Had Bernard's disguise failed him for this once? Marcel, too, tensed. The muskets next door fired again. He was becoming very frightened.

Bernard rose to his feet and shuffled off behind the private.

Marcel looked at Helene. His throat was dry and he had to swallow several times before he could find his voice.

"What are our chances of getting out of here?"

"They'll let you go," Helene said, although she was not at all sure that this was the case. "And they'll not kill me. I fear for Bernard if they discover him."

"If we get out of here you should come home. Your husband has disavowed you and his family are obviously hostile."

"My husband has good reason to be hostile."

"Why? What have you done?"

"Someday I'll tell you," she said, laughing, "but there is another gentleman Robert will have to contend with if he harms me in any way."

Bernard came back into the room accompanied by the private. Helene breathed a sigh of relief. His disguise was still intact.

"You there," the private said. "The two of you there by the stove, on your feet. Come on, sister." He reached into his pocket and pulled out the key to the kitchen door. Then he cut the rope in Marcel's hands.

The muskets crashed again in the open courtyard. The private swung the door open. Helene did not know whether this was the way to the firing squad or whether they were being released.

"All of you go straight home now," the private said. "Here are your passes from the lieutenant."

Marcel took one of the pieces of paper, as did Helene. Bernard already had his. They stepped into the alley and the door slammed behind them. They were in total darkness.

Bernard started to laugh nervously. Only seconds ago he had been sure that he would be taken out and shot. Instead he found himself released. It made no more sense than his original detention, but in a revolution it was much easier to be detained than to be released.

"Let's not stand here," Marcel said. "Let's go some place where we will be safe."

"Where?" Helene thought aloud. "Toulouse Street is out."

"We must get to where the Spanish are barricaded," Bernard said. "It's on the river. The easiest way in and out of New Orleans is always the river."

The three of them walked quickly out of the alley to Chartres Street. The body still swung from the cooper's sign. They passed through the street until they came to Bourbon Street. Here everything was dark and quiet. The houses were shuttered and silent. The sound of shoes on the pavement echoed through the cavelike darkness of the abandoned street.

Bernard raised his hand and halted them. They crept closer to the shadows of the house. They heard musketry off in the distance and closer at hand the clunk of iron wheels.

Helene walked up to the street sign on the building. They were at the corner of Bourbon and St. Philippe. Torches cast shadows on the building as militiamen with muskets flung over their shoulders came ambling along the street. They had been drinking and they called obscenely to each other and up at the shuttered windows of the houses. "Come and get it, girls," one militiaman called out. "Hot sausage ready and waiting."

Helene held her breath and clutched Marcel's arm. He stared directly at the soldiers and without thinking he patted her hand. She looked down at the dark object in his left hand. It was a hunting knife of prodigious length. She realized he must have had it on him all along. The amateurishness of the militia had led them to arrest a man without going through the formality of searching for concealed weapons. She could feel from the steellike tension in his muscles that if they were discovered several militiamen would not make it back to their bayous.

The soldiers went past them without seeing the fugitives. The cart was now even with them. There was something grotesque in it. It shook like jelly with each bounce of the wheels on the cobblestones. The torchlight finally fell on the contents. Helene sucked in her breath with a sharp noise. The tiny head bounced unsupported off the end of the cart. He was naked and his enormous belly had been ripped open, exposing his pink bloated innards. The cart dripped blood onto the street behind it as it passed.

"Oh, my poor Gaston." Helene began to weep. Marcel gripped her and Bernard clapped his hand across her mouth. She sagged at the knees and Marcel had to hold her up. The gruesome torchlight parade continued on down St. Philippe. If it continued in that direction it would soon be passing the side entrance to Gaston's place.

Helene fought the urge to vomit. Her whole body had broken into a cold sweat.

"Courage, little sister," Marcel whispered to her.

Bernard again led the way. They crossed St. Philippe and continued down Bourbon Street. It was deathly quiet again. They crossed several more streets until they reached Barracks Street. There were more patrols there. They were close to the barracks where the governor had barricaded himself. The three fugitives huddled again in the shadows of a building.

"How do we get through their lines?" Marcel asked.

Bernard patted his wimple. "I always knew being a nun was tougher than being a Brother," he said, "but I didn't know that it was the habit that made it tougher. Damn thing cuts into you. If you're game, you'll do it my way. We'll just be brazen and walk right through their lines."

Helene was dubious, but she had no suggestion of her own and she was still reeling from the sight she had just seen back down the street.

Marcel agreed to go along with it but his knife would be ever at the ready.

Bernard stepped piously into Barracks Street, his eyes again cast down to his feet. Marcel and Helene followed him. At the end of the street the military barracks loomed dark, but with occasional flickers of light behind its barred windows clearly indicating that it was not abandoned. They were halfway down Barracks Street toward the quai when a soldier stepped from the gloom and challenged them.

"Halt. Sister? What are you doing out on a night like this?" He grew more alert when he saw Marcel and Helene.

"We have a pass," Helene said and passed her paper to the man. As she looked at him she realized he was only a boy. Helene put her hand on Marcel. She could feel the cold steel blade hidden in the sleeve of his jacket. She put pressure on his hand to signal him to hold back. He was only a boy; he could hardly be shaving yet.

The boy took Helene's paper over to the opposite side of the street. He knocked on a door; it opened and an officer stepped out. The boy spoke to him and the officer reentered the building. A few seconds later the door opened again and the officer stepped out on the street.

"Madame Parlange?"

Helene recognized Guy duPont immediately.

"Marcel, we are done for. He knows me," she whispered.

"Run for it," Marcel shouted.

Bernard needed no further urging. He threw off his veil and started to run toward the barracks. He tripped on the long white cincture but he kept to his feet and continued to run. DuPont made a grab for Helene but he never reached her. Marcel stepped between them and sank his knife to the hilt in the young man's belly. DuPont screeched in agony. The young soldier raised his musket to fire but Marcel kicked the barrel up into the air. The gun went off harmlessly but alerted both French and Spanish to trouble in the street.

Marcel pulled his knife out of duPont. Guy fell to his knees, his hands holding his belly.

Marcel grabbed Helene's arm and started to pull her along the street. He called out in French for the barracks door to be opened. When nothing happened Bernard screamed in high-pitched but fluent Spanish that the French were trying to rape the Sisters.

The corporal of the guard behind the doors did not wait to check with an officer. He could believe it of the French. He blessed himself. The Virgin would reward him for the deed. He raised the heavy oak bar and opened the door. Three people stumbled through just as the French muskets crashed, sending lead balls into the stucco and wood.

The corporal slammed the door shut and barred it. He stood in disbelief at what he had allowed in: a beautiful fair-haired woman, a young man, and what looked like a man posing as a nun. She had no veil and her hair was short, but he had heard that the Sisters shaved their hair off when they entered the order. The captain came out of his quarters. He was disheveled and dressed only in his undergarments. He apologized when he saw Helene, but he went white when he saw the nun.

"Forgive me, Reverend Sister." He started to flee back into the room, but stopped dead in his tracks when a low masculine voice called out, "Think nothing of it, Captain."

The three fugitives were taken immediately to Governor deUlloa as soon as their identities were discovered.

The governor had set up headquarters in the military commandant's suite. He was a large man who looked slovenly despite the resplendent uniform and decorations.

"Madame Parlange," he greeted her, "I'm delighted you made it to safety and distressed that you *had* to make it to safety." His French was heavily accented but understandable. "And I am distressed that your husband and father-in-law would attempt to harm you. It is despicable."

"They are fools, Your Excellency. They have placed themselves in open rebellion against the king of Spain. The Acadians in the crowd should have known better. They did the same thing once before against the English, and look what happened to them."

"But it seems they have outmaneuvered us," said the governor.

"For the time being, Your Excellency. For the time being."

"I hope you're right," he said.

Helene stood between the governor and the other members of her party. "Excuse my rudeness, Your Excellency. This is my brother, Marcel Hebert, from Acadia."

"I'm charmed to meet any relative of this great and noble lady." He bowed toward Marcel. The Frenchman acknowledged the bow in return.

"You know," said deUlloa, "your sister is one of the few pragmatists I have found among the French. She works to strengthen our rule in this colony, and we, shall we say, look the other way at some of her business practices."

The governor sat down once more. Muskets barked from inside and outside the barracks. The governor's face went gray when he heard them. If this was the man who led the side Helene had chosen, Marcel had great doubts about her judgment.

Bernard coughed.

"Oh, yes." Helene acknowledged him. "You know my man, Bernard."

"Oh, yes, the Jesuit."

"Tabernac," Bernard cursed. "Is there no one who doesn't know?"

DeUlloa questioned them carefully about their escape. The story of Gaston's death seemed to affect him deeply. "A tragedy," he said. "He was a strange man but a devoted friend of Spain."

"For the right price," Bernard said softly so that the governor could not hear.

"Madame," the Spaniard said to Helene, "I understand everything that you relate to me except your escape from the rebel headquarters. How was that achieved?"

"The passes. The passes did it," said Helene.

"But why?" deUlloa asked. "Why did you get them? Let me see them."

"DuPont took mine," Helene said with some pain at the fate of her husband's friend.

"Here's mine," Marcel said. He took the paper that he had folded and stuffed in his pocket. He opened it. As he read his face went white. He handed it to Helene. It read simply, "God be with you. Gilles Hebert."

Morning came to New Orleans but did not bring an end to the chaos. There were some fires raging in the city but the fire brigade did not respond to the call. Behind the barricades of the military barracks a sentry kept a careful watch on the activities on Barracks Street and beyond.

Marcel stretched as he awoke. He had found a spot on the floor in the enlisted men's area of the barracks. His muscles ached and he was stiff all over. He and Helene had sat up late into the night talking. At first they could not believe that Gilles had seen them. Why had he not identified himself? Why had he not tried to communicate except through the message on the passes? They had speculated about what had happened to him. Helene guessed that he was living in the Acadian communities in one of the bayous and had come to the city with the militia forces. Whatever the truth was, both of them knew that their lost brother was found within hours of Marcel and Helene finding each other. The dispersal carried out at Port Hebert in the midst of one war was reversed in New Orleans in the midst of another.

Marcel rose from the hardwood floor. He had a throbbing pain in his right hip. He must have pulled a muscle in the running last night. He needed some soap and water, some fresh clothes. All his belongings were back at the tiny inn on Dauphine Street where he had been staying while he searched for Helene. They could stay there. He had no intention of trying to retrieve them.

He walked down the corridor after several enlisted men. A back door to the barracks led to a heavily guarded military wharf. Soldiers were going out on the wharf and pissing into the river. It was a risky business. It was even riskier to lower your breeches to complete other necessities. That was a target the French snipers could not resist.

Marcel went outside and urinated as quickly as nature would allow. He was fortunate that the French concentrated their marksmanship on a fat Spanish sergeant who was obviously constipated and very vulnerable.

As Marcel buttoned up and turned toward the safety of the barracks, several of the Spanish soldiers began yelling and pointing toward the river. A sleek brig was approaching the barracks wharf. A cannon belched from the bow of the ship. It was not fired in anger since no ball had been loaded. It was a signal. Marcel searched in vain for an ensign indicating whose side the captain of the ship was on. It was clear, however, that its arrival would tip the scale in favor of one side or another.

Marcel reentered the barracks and practically plowed into Helene and Bernard, accompanied by Governor deUlloa.

"Whose ship is it?" Helene asked. No one seemed to know, but Bernard squeezed past Marcel out the door onto the wharf.

A sniper fired at him. The range was too great and he was in no danger. He took only a quick look and ducked back inside again behind the safety of stone and stucco. He danced a little jig of joy before Helene.

"It's Lionel. Robichaud has returned."

Helene clapped her hands. "He has a cannon—a bow chaser, he calls it—and he knows how to use it. We are saved, Your Excellency."

Antonio deUlloa was not sure. In fact, he had all but made up his mind to surrender his little fort to the rebels. He had even sent out feelers for a possible truce. The arrival of the brig changed his plans, not because he could turn the tide and chase the French militia from the streets and their fortified positions, but because now if a truce was arranged he would have the means to escape this pestilential French pisspot.

"Have Captain Robichaud report to me," deUlloa said to Helene, "just as soon as you say your greetings to him. Bernard, do you speak Spanish?" he asked the ex-Jesuit in that language.

"*Si*," Bernard responded.

"Then come with me. I think I shall need you."

Helene waited patiently by the back door. She held onto Marcel and winced every time someone fired a musket at the brig. No one was prepared for the roar of the cannon, this time in anger.

Lionel had loaded his bow chaser with grapeshot and fired

point blank into the French position. The small lead balls wreaked havoc. Smoke rose from the overturned bales of hay that the militia had used for protection. After the echo of the cannon shot dissipated, it was followed by the screams and moans of the wounded.

Helene felt relieved that Lionel had fired the gun. Now it was clear that he must join the Spanish. She had not been sure whom he would support once the chips were on the table. She was not even sure it was a conscious decision on his part. More likely he responded in anger against those who fied at his ship. But by one cannon shot he had demonstrated that the militia's position was untenable. There were no muskets fired at Lionel as he walked boldly across the wharf from the brig to the barracks.

Helene awaited him as he stepped through the doorway. He smiled when he saw her. She ran to him and he wrapped his arms about her.

"I was worried when I heard about the rebellion, my love, but I should not have concerned myself. There never will be a day when you don't emerge on top. I knew that I would find you in the one safe place for a Spanish sympathizer."

"Robert's father would have had me shot."

"If I were Robert's father I would have you shot. Come to think of it, if I were Robert's father I would have Robert shot. Then I would put a bullet in my brain just to make sure I sired no one else." He laughed loudly at his own joke.

"My brothers saved me," Helene said, grabbing the silent Marcel and pulling him closer to her. "This is my brother Marcel Hebert."

Marcel nodded. He looked somewhat confused. He had met her husband. This was clearly not her husband, although she behaved far more intimately with this man than she had with Parlange.

Robichaud extended his hand to Marcel. Marcel grabbed it and was pleased with the friendliness and warmth of the other man.

"Glad to meet a member of this lady's family. By God, you must be a strong-willed bunch, judging by the members I've met."

"I suspect we are." Marcel laughed. "But there is another one of us in town as well."

378

Helene recounted the past twelve hours for Lionel—their capture, their escape, and their retreat to the barracks. She cried when she told him of Gaston's fate.

Lionel swore when he heard. He would have a score to settle with both Parlanges, father and son. No one tortured and killed one of his men without answering to him for it.

He held·her closely.

"Oh, Lionel, it's good to be with you."

"You missed me, eh?"

"Missed isn't the right word. When I saw the brig I knew I never wanted to be without you again."

"Enough to come sailing with me again as we did in the old days?"

"No," she responded, "I was thinking that you should give up the sea."

They both looked at each other and started to laugh.

Bernard now returned to the corridor where his friends still congregated. Lionel saw him and laughed a bit more. "Here is one scoundrel I was sure would survive. Poor Gaston, if only he had been able to move a little faster. He had enough of the scoundrel in him to have allowed him to survive as well. But Bernard, he will survive forever."

Bernard did not laugh. He looked quite confused.

"The Spanish are giving up," he said. "They plan to arrange a truce and then to slip away on Captain Robichaud's boat."

Lionel looked at Bernard, not believing what he heard. "What kind of trick are they playing? They've won this thing. I'll blow the bastards right off the levee. How can they give up? I don't believe you." Lionel grew more angry as he spoke.

Helene watched Bernard carefully. There was much about him that bore watching. She had never really trusted him and she would not begin now.

"I am to serve as translator. DeUlloa meets with Vernay and Parlange almost immediately."

"But why?" Lionel was shouting now. "We'll lose everything!" he said excitedly to Helene.

She nodded, still watching Bernard. He looked away.

"Not everything, I suspect," she said.

"What's to salvage?"

"Oh, nothing," she addressed Lionel directly now. "We have the new brig, the new coastal vessel, and the best seamen on the Gulf Coast to handle them. I think we'll do all right." Her words soothed him and he grew quiet.

"Monsieur Bernard," Marcel spoke, "would you do my sister and me a favor?"

"If I can."

"Could you persuade His Excellency to allow both of us to join the truce party, and could you request that the governor insist that the French party include Lieutenant Gilles Hebert?"

"Again, I will try," Bernard said after Helene nodded yes to him.

DeUlloa had refused to allow Helene to attend the parley. He was very close to panic. The closer they came to the hour of departure, the more desperately he wished to keep the French in the dark about his plans to flee. The presence of the female might alert them and make them more suspicious. He would have preferred to leave the brother behind, but Robichaud started to make angry noises and he needed Robichaud desperately.

They met in the same house where Guy duPont had been stationed when he had intercepted Helene and Marcel and met his fate. DeUlloa was splendid in his dress uniform. They marched out of the barracks with a guard of six soldiers, their muskets pointed downward toward the ground. The governor followed the soldiers, and behind him came Bernard and finally Marcel.

Colonel Vernay, a black armband displayed prominently on his uniform, met them in the street. Behind him were Major Parlange and his son, Robert.

"Your Excellency," Vernay greeted the governor and bowed.

"Vernay, I must know the meaning of this outrage against His Most Catholic Majesty of Spain and your king."

"I am doing my duty, sir, by His Most Christian Majesty of France and my king."

"Louis of France surrendered this colony freely to Spain. You are not only in rebellion against Spain, you even defy the wishes of the monarch whom you claim to support."

"We hope to persuade our king to change his mind."

Marcel had little patience with the give and take between

the officials. His eyes searched everywhere for the sight of his brother. Finally he nudged Bernard. "Didn't you ask?"

The ex-Jesuit was busy following the debate as it went on in French just in case deUlloa decided to switch to Spanish for the record. He ignored Marcel.

But Marcel caught sight of Robert Parlange. Robert signaled to him to come toward the house off to the side through a small alley. Marcel moved into the alley without arousing anyone's interest. Parlange met him at the door.

"Monsieur Hebert." He bowed to Marcel. Hebert nodded back. "This has been very difficult to arrange. The lieutenant was nervous at first and you are rumored to be the assassin of Captain duPont, my friend."

"Unsupportable gossip," Marcel lied.

"I'm sure of it," Robert responded. "Come with me." They ducked back out into the alley behind Barracks Street and walked several blocks until they came to Bourbon Street.

"Here," Parlange said, "be quick. You must go back with deUlloa."

He opened the door of a small house. Marcel felt the knife in his sleeve. He was tense and he was prepared for anything.

The room was dark. The shutters were closed, allowing no sun to enter. Parlange closed the door and remained outside. Marcel waited for his eyes to adjust to the darkness. He saw a large form across the room.

"Gilles," he whispered. The form came closer to him. When it was several feet from him Marcel recognized him. He stepped forward and threw his arms around his brother. The other man sobbed and they held each other tightly. Gilles stepped back from Marcel finally.

"When I saw you a prisoner with Helene, I could not believe my eyes. My little brother and little sister sitting there right in the next room."

"You saved our lives," Marcel said. "Why did you not greet us and let us know you were there?"

"I was afraid of drawing attention to you," Gilles lied rather lamely. In fact, he was sure when Marcel appeared in front of him that his life was drawing to a close. He had hoped that by setting Marcel free he would be free of him forever.

"When you insisted on seeing me," Gilles went on," I

believed it was all over. I tried to avoid this meeting but I couldn't bring myself to lie anymore."

"But why would you do that?"

"You have come for her, haven't you?"

Marcel was puzzled at first. Finally it dawned on him. "You mean Nina?"

Gilles nodded, but in the dark Marcel could not see him. After some awkward moments of silence Gilles said, "Of course."

"Is she here?"

The older brother choked back a sob. He walked to the far side of the room and opened an inside door. Marcel walked to the door and stepped through. He recognized her instantly. She was slightly heavier but, if possible, even more beautiful than before. Next to her was a little girl. She was very much like her mother.

"Marcel," Nina said softly.

He went to her and hugged her. He could feel the tension in her body. She did not pull away from him but neither did she fold herself into him. For several moments neither of them could say anything. They merely held each other. The barriers of miles traveled and time passed were evident to both of them.

"I'm sorry," he whispered into her ear finally, "I never knew until it was too late." Then he released her to look into her face. She was dry-eyed and unsmiling. He dried the tears from his own face with the back of his hand.

"Nina, please tell me that you forgive me."

"There is nothing to forgive," she said finally. "It was no fault of yours."

"I was callous. I should have thought less of my fight with Gilles and fear of Papa and more of how you would feel."

"Yes, you were callous," she agreed, "and young and handsome. You were such a beautiful boy, Marcel. But it would have made no difference if you had stayed. We were caught up in events. We might have been separated anyway, and that would have been even more unbearable."

"I would have stayed with you."

"Would you have? Did you have the enduring kind of love I have had from Gilles despite all the horrors we went through? I'm not sure."

She saw the hurt in Marcel's face and she regretted the words. He might now be as strong as his brother, but he had not been so strong then. She searched for Gilles with her eyes but he had remained in the shadows of the darkened room, perhaps not able to bring himself to watch this reunion. Her heart went out to him at last.

"I want you to meet Adele."

"Adele, this is your papa's brother, your uncle Marcel."

The girl looked up at him calmly: "You're handsomer than papa," she announced.

"That's what all the girls used to say," he said softly.

Nina put her arms around Adele. "We live at Bayou LaFourche. It is a small house. Gilles built it himself. He built an attic for Adele and her raccoon. The weather is pleasant there except for the summer. We swim, we fish. It is a good life and Gilles is a good man." The words seemed to pour out of her. She was close to hysteria.

"Do you think ever of returning to Acadia?"

"I did once," she said, "but no more. My home is on the bayou with Gilles. I could never go back."

She looked up and saw him finally, standing in the doorway. She walked quickly to his side. He placed his arm about her waist and she clung to him as she had from the day when all their lives had been torn apart, the day when the English ships arrived.

Marcel knelt down and took Adele in his arms. He kissed her on the cheek and she kissed him back. She was as much his daughter as Lucien was his son, but he knew he would never hold her again, and he did not really want to let her go.

Finally Nina grew alarmed. She called Adele to her. The girl pulled away from Marcel and joined Nina and Gilles.

Marcel rose to his feet. He looked longingly at this woman he had loved—and at the child their love had produced. He still loved her. He wanted her with all his heart. He kissed Nina on the cheek and clapped his brother on the shoulder. He had fulfilled his promise to his father and he had found both Helene and Gilles, but he knew he would return to Port Hebert alone and in sorrow.

"Good-bye," he said softly and then fled the house into the alley without looking back.

Gilles' grip on Nina had been tight. He had feared she

would run after Marcel, but she had not moved. When she did, it was toward him rather than away from him.

"Let's go home to the bayou," she said to him.

The cloud lifted from Gilles. For the first time in eleven years he thought that maybe she would not leave him. In itself the removal of that burden would make this day the happiest one of his life.

The brig coasted with the flow of the river toward the delta. The garrison was jammed on the deck, and there was no room left in any of the cabins below deck.

Just before they reached the open sea the little ship encountered a Spanish warship, a frigate of fifty guns. DeUlloa and his men arranged a transfer. The captain of the frigate wanted to return to New Orleans, but the governor, who outranked him, would not hear of it. He would not return and face the French wildmen unless he had regiments of regulars under his command. He ordered the captain of the frigate to sail across the Gulf of Mexico to Vera Cruz and safety.

Bernard decided to go with deUlloa. He came to Lionel's cabin to say good-bye. Helene sat at Lionel's desk. The captain was on deck helping with the transfer to the frigate.

"I'll be going now," Bernard said.

Helene rose from the desk, walked over to him, and kissed him on the cheek.

"We met as paupers," she said, "and we leave each other with most of what we earned lost."

"Not quite," Bernard said. "In the hold you will find I have left behind one of my sea chests. I think you will be pleasantly surprised by its contents."

"I don't think I'll be surprised," Helene said, smiling. "I've already examined its contents."

Bernard laughed. "You know the two of us deserve each other. We are both scoundrels."

"How did you do it?" she asked.

"I am the best sugar man in America. There was never a season when I missed the right time to cut cane."

"And there was never a season when you did not claim to have missed the right time."

"Precisely. You can earn much by understating your yield."

384

"And you've been cheating me all these years."

"It was for a good cause. Besides I am refunding half of what I took from you."

"But why, Bernard? Why did you cheat me?"

"You've never guessed?"

"No."

Her answer pleased him. *"Ad majorem Dei gloriam,"* he responded as he stepped from the cabin.

She never did understand his meaning.

The brig sailed out into the gulf heading for Mobile. Helene had decided to make that town her headquarters until she could go back to New Orleans.

Lionel entered the tiny cabin. His mate had the wheel now and would be in charge for another four hours. Helene sat up in the cot.

"Is there room in that thing for more than one person?"

"No, not side by side," she responded with a sly little laugh.

"All the better," he said.

NOTE

In 1769 General Alexander O'Reilly, an Irish mercenary in the service of Spain, arrived in New Orleans along with a large Spanish relief army. He invited every officer in the French militia to a large truce parley. During the course of that negotiation he arrested all of them and had them executed. Only one officer escaped, a Lt. Gilles Hebert of Bayou LaFourche. Rumor had it that he received advanced warning of O'Reilly's intentions from a mysterious woman with high connections in the Spanish service.

THE END

ABOUT THE AUTHOR

ROBERT E. WALL was born in Brooklyn, New York, in 1937. He received his education at American schools—B.A. at Holy Cross College, Worcester, Massachusetts, and an M.A. and Ph.D. in History from Yale University. He has taught history at Duke University and Michigan State University. In 1970 Wall moved his family to Canada where he became chairman of the History Department and, later, Provost of the Faculty of Arts & Sciences at Montreal's Concordia University. In 1976 he became a Canadian citizen.

Robert Wall draws on his love for Canada and his native United States in creating THE ACADIANS. It is a saga of a people torn from their roots in Canada and transported against their wills to a new home. It illustrates the process by which Acadians are transformed into the Louisiana Cajuns. It involves the history of the two nations—Canada and the United States. Wall perceives the histories of his adopted land and the land of his birth as deeply entwined. Influenced by the writings of such figures as Kenneth Roberts, he seeks to teach those histories through the historical novel. Wall is author of the six-volume series, THE CANADIANS, which includes "Blackrobe," "Bloodbrothers," "Birthright," "Patriots," "Inheritors" and "Dominion."

Wall is married and has five children. He is currently the Acting Vice-President for Academic Affairs at Fairleigh Dickinson University in New Jersey.

ABOUT THE AUTHOR

**BLACKROBE
BLOODBROTHERS
BIRTHRIGHT
PATRIOTS
THE INHERITORS
DOMINION**

and now

BROTHERHOOD

Book Seven of The Canadians
by
Robert E. Wall

*Here is an excerpt from the seventh novel
in this compelling historical saga.*

Craig stepped out of the bathtub and grabbed for the soft towel that was draped across the sink. The greatest wonder of coming to live East and into the Brants' home was the indoor plumbing, hot water at your disposal. As a boy he bathed frequently in the lake and in the rivers in the summer. He loved to swim and cavort in the waters. Both his parents would join him and after a while it was Craig and Beth and David, his tag-along little brother, who would splash and swim but the luxury of a hot bath, even in the dead of winter, was unknown to him until now. Now he bathed as often as he could. It did not bother him that the servants had complained to Willy and would no longer heat his water for him. The Chinaman needed a good yank of his braid, but no matter he heated his own water. He liked doing things for himself anyway.

God, the air was cold. He had goose bumps all over himself and he was all shriveled up. He pulled the towel closer about his naked shoulders and chest and stood there shivering. No, this would never do. He pulled the towel away and began to rub his stomach, legs and backside vigorously with it. He could feel the blood returning to his skin and with it a rush of warmth. He wrapped the towel about his middle and stepped out of the bathroom and into his bedroom. There was a soft knock on his door. He grabbed the old bathrobe which Michael had given to him and wrapped it around himself.

"Who is it?" he asked.

The door opened and Meg slipped in.

"I didn't say for you to come in, I'm not properly dressed."

"Oh shoot, Craig, I'll bet you aren't such a prude back home."

"My mother would respect my privacy and has done so ever since I became a man."

"Well, you're hardly naked except for your feet and yes, it is true you have very attractive feet."

Without thinking Craig looked down at his toes.

"Oh my goodness, cousin, you are such a simpleton."

He blushed. "Did you come here to admire my feet?"

She laughed. "Touché," she said. "No, I want to come with you to the Irish workers' meeting."

He grinned at her and turned his back on her. "There are no women allowed."

"I suspected as much and have anticipated that unenlightened attitude. You'll lend me some of your clothes."

"I really should take you, you know. It would do you some good to rub elbows with real people. It might teach you more about life than all the books in your fancy library."

"Since when have you turned anti-intellectual?"

"I haven't. I just know there is more to be learned than can be found in books."

"Like what?" she questioned.

"Like knowing where to find the herds and how to cut up a calf or a cow for the tenderest meat or how to skin an antelope or when to cut the wheat to avoid a killer frost."

"I don't need to know any of those things. They are of little use to me here in Halifax."

"Which is why, as soon as I can get my full of book learning, it's back to Manitoba for me. But you need knowledge here in Halifax too. Men who take their living from the sea need to know too."

"Well, how will I ever know, if I am kept locked up in this house without ever having any real experiences?"

"No, you can't come with me."

"Damn," she said stamping her foot, "why not?"

"I've told you why. Besides I could not do so without betraying the trust of Uncle Michael and Aunt Willy. Now get out of here so that I can get dressed. You're going to make me late for my meeting."

"I hope you're good and late, Craig Miller," Meg said petulantly. She turned and ran from the room.

Craig smiled. He liked her very much. She was immature and insolent but that was because she had been so protected in this household. He wondered how any of them, Michael, Willy or Meg, could survive without their luxuries in this civilized town. Well, far be it for him to condemn them. He had gotten used to those baths and indoor plumbing and he had gotten used to them very quickly.

He pulled on his pants and tucked the tail of a clean shirt into his breeches. He would need only his light jacket since the evening was mild. He saved the shoes for last. How he had hated wearing them at first, so hard and unbending when compared to Indian moccasins. He still hated them but by now he was used to them.

He trotted down the stairs two at a time. He stuck his head into the the parlor, and found his uncle reading. He could hear his aunt conversing, shouting really, with Chou in the kitchen.

"I'll be leaving now, Uncle Michael."

"Take care," Brant responded without looking up from his text.

"Where's Meg?" Craig asked.

Brant looked up over the top of his spectacles. "She says she's tired and she's not joining me tonight for our evening declaration of war and she's off to an early bed."

Craig smiled. "Well, good luck in case she changes her mind."

Michael gave him a look of mock hurt. "Young man, I'll have you know I've taught that girl everything she knows and I can still hold my own with her."

"I'm glad you can. It will be a long time before I can."

"Nonsense, can't let the women bully you my boy. You must put them in their place which is properly the kitchen."

"I heard you," Willy said as she came out of the kitchen. Michael rolled his eyes upward.

"And dammit you may be right especially if the book is Chinese. Michael, you must go out there and speak with that man. He's brought a monkey into the house. He got it off a sailor down at the docks. When I yelled at him that I would have no pets, he just smiled. 'No pet, missy,' he said. 'You eat, make good supper'."

Michael blanched. "God knows what we've been eating!"

Craig decided that it was time to depart. He could shock them with stories of fighting with his brother for raw buffalo intestines and raw liver but he saw no point of further shocking their sensibilities. He stepped out the front door and walked down the hill toward the harbor. MacSorley's was around the corner near the docks. Craig could see other men moving along the street in the same general direction. There would be a large crowd at the tavern tonight. He turned the corner and entered MacSorley's alley. The tavern was at the end of a narrow street. It actually was on pilings over the water. The front door had panels of cheap stained glass. It was difficult to tell what was drawn on the glass because it was covered with the grime of the waterfront and years of neglect. All that Craig could identify looked like a bow with many strings, a clumsy thing he thought. He had no prior experience or knowledge of a harp.

The taproom smelled of whiskey, stale whiskey. It was lighted by oil lamps and some candles on the tables. He had guessed right about the crowd. There was barely room to move. He worked his way into the crowd and found himself leaning against the bar.

"What will it be for you, chap?" He was addressed by a large woman from behind the bar. He could barely see her in the gloom but his first impression of largeness was correct. She must have stood just under six feet tall. She was taller than his own 5' 9". Her arms rivaled the small kegs of whiskey which were piled behind her on the bar and her bosoms protruded over the bar itself. Her face was round and made even rounder by the close-cropped man's haircut she wore.

"What's your pleasure, boy?"

Craig pointed at himself.

The woman's eyes rolled up toward the ceiling in exasperation. "What are you drinking?" she said sighing.

"Nothing."

"Oh yes you are or it's out you go. I love the cause but I love Bella MacSorley better. You come to a meeting in my tavern, you drink."

"Well, in that case I'll have a mug of ale," Craig said to the proprietor.

"That's more like it." She drew ale from the tap and slapped a pewter mug down on the bar. The foam started to run over the side. She stuck her finger into the ale. "You don't mind, do you? That finger ain't been any place it shouldn't have been and I've misplaced my sponge."

Craig was not too certain of her assurances. The woman was a mess. Huge soil stains spread from her armpits down the side of her blouse and almost reached her waist and she stank badly. Yet there was something about her that appealed to him. He couldn't place it. There was something familiar. He smiled at her.

"Wipe that shit-eating grin off your face," she said angrily.

He did as she demanded.

Yet she continued to stare at him. "Why did you smile at me?" she said finally. "No one smiles at me. Are you trying to make a pass at me?"

He almost bent in two with laughter.

"Why, you little pecker. I suspect that's exactly what you've got. You think that's funny?"

She reached across the bar and grabbed him by his brown locks. "Why, I could take everything you've got and still have to ask you if you were in yet."

"I wasn't laughing at you. Ouch, let go," he laughed.

She did as he demanded.

"Are you always so affectionate with new customers?" he asked.

"Only with shit-eating grinners."

"I wasn't making fun of you," he said. "It's just that I finally remembered who you reminded me of."

"Who?"

"My grandmother."

Again the barrel-like arm shot forward far faster than its size and girth should allow and her fingers entwined in his hair. His head was moving toward the bar for a good slam when he stiffened his neck and shoulder muscles and braced his arms on the bar bringing her motion to a sudden halt.

"No insult intended again," he said laughing.

She was more impressed with the strength of his muscles than with his words.

"Most young cubs come in here all puffed up and that's all they are—hot air. When did you get muscles like that from? You must be a dock worker. But if you were I'd know you."

"I got my muscles from honest enough hard work harvesting wheat and hay, paddling canoes and hauling buffalo meat to make pemmican."

"Not in Halifax you didn't do none of those things."

"You're right. Out west and the grandmother that you remind me of is an Indian chief's wife, a great woman, with the name of Warrior Woman, who has taken scalps on her own right."

"A fighting woman, eh? Well, so long as you weren't trying to call me an old lady. You're part Indian, eh?"

"My mother is Assiniboine."

"That makes you one of them fellows out there they call Metis, half breeds."

Now Craig began to grow sensitive. Was she going to mock him? He started to move away from the bar.

"No, wait," she said. "No offense meant. You fellows have much in common with us Irish. I assume that's why you're here. O'Connor, shit, where is that kid? Kevin O'Connor," she yelled out.

"Here, you old battle axe," a young man screamed drunkenly from across the room.

"Lucky, you're where I can't reach you," Bella screamed back.

"It's indeed my good fortune."

"Well, do something to earn your keep. We have a young guest. I want you to take him under your wing and explain our cause to him." As she spoke she pointed to Craig.

The flushed face of the black-haired, brown-eyed youth broke into a grin. "Make your way over to this table, guest," the Irish youth called out.

Craig started to move in that direction when he felt Bella's clawlike grip on his shoulder.

"You'll be going nowhere without your paying first."

Craig reached into his pocket and handed her his schilling. She nodded at him and turned to serve another customer.

"An ale costs a schilling in this tavern?"

"No, it's two pence."

"Well, I'll be going nowhere without my change," he imitated her brogue.

Now it was Bella's turn to laugh. "Oh, I thought you enjoyed my company so much you were rewarding me with a generous gratuity."

"I love the cause, Bella, but the cause of my own pocket must come first."

Now she let out a roar of laughter. "Kevin O'Connor, you old misbegotten bastard, you take good care of this one. I like him."

She handed Craig his change. He took his mug of ale and joined O'Connor and his three companions at a table across the taproom from the bar.

"My name's O'Connor, Kevin O'Connor, though how you could miss that fact with that tub of lard screaming it all the way across the taproom I don't know. And these louts are my companions. Jim Hickey."

A large well-muscled redheaded freckle-faced man merely nodded at Craig.

"And Sean Lavery."

The second young man actually rose from his seat and made a sweeping eighteenth-century bow to Craig.

"The lad is a bit daft," Kevin explained. "He was on the stage in Dublin before he discovered a sudden necessity to be in Canada."

Craig nodded to the three young men. "Craig Miller," he said extending his hand.

O'Connor shook it as did big Jim Hickey but Lavery concluded that his bow was more than sufficient greeting. Besides he had concerns. "Miller, Craig Miller, that's not an Irish name. Have we a Judas in our midst? I'll be damned if it's not an English name."

"You're right. My family is from good Loyalist English stock."

"Shall I bash him and throw him out?" Hickey muttered.

Craig started to chuckle at this joke until he realized that the big man was serious. "That's on my father's side. My mother's an Assiniboine, a tribe that's been fighting the English since before Montcalm."

"This Boyne, does it have to do with the Orangemen?" Hickey looked even more menacing now. "My family lost everything it had at the Battle of the Boyne."

"Shut up, Jim," Lavery insisted. "Your family never had anything to lose in the first place."

Hickey looked as if he had been kicked in the shins but he became immediately subdued. He was like a giant puppy dog doing whatever Sean Lavery commanded him to do. He said nothing more.

"So you're just not another homeless man looking for something to belong to. No wonder Bella sent you over," said Kevin. "You Indians and us Irish are natural allies."

"How so?" asked Craig, still keeping his eye trained on Jim Hickey to make sure that he really was subdued. He had been drinking and he seemed to be a mean drunk and he was so huge.

"Because of the common enemy."

"Bella," Lavery called out.

"What is it, squirt?" she responded.

"Bring another round of drinks for us all."

"Not without seeing some coin of the realm first."

"You know it's against my principles to carry anything bearing the image of the English monarch. I have no money."

"Convenient principles you've got. Convenient for you that is. Well, I've got one of my own principles. That is, no money, no drink. Why don't you hit the Indian? He took some pence off me just a few minutes ago."

Craig nodded.

"Hooray," Kevin O'Connor shouted, "the drinks are on the Assiniboines."

From the whole of the taproom rose a mighty cheer. Craig panicked momentarily but then he realized that he had a half crown in his watch pocket. That should be enough. Even big Jim Hickey rose and clapped him on the back.

Bella's assistant started bringing trays of whiskey and ale

from behind the bar. Men grabbed at the glasses and at Bella's assistant, a pretty red-haired girl of about seventeen.

"Keep your hands off her," Bella screamed.

"I know," Sean Lavery called out, "she's reserved."

Bella gave him a wicked look. "I'll fix it so that, as they say in the Bible, your line shall no longer piss against the wall, Lavery."

Sean laughed and stuck his tongue out at Bella. The longer he left it out of his mouth the redder her face became. She was sure to step from behind the bar but Lavery seemed to know just what was going too far with her and suddenly he turned his attention back to Craig.

"Big Jim and I are going to the States next week. We're joining up."

"With the Yanks?"

"Who else?"

"But why?" Craig asked.

"We Irishmen must get our training," Kevin chimed in.

"We're going to learn tactics from the Yanks and then we're going back to Ireland and fight for a Republic. We'll all be officers in an Irish Republican Army," Lavery said. "Can't you see me now. General Sean Lavery."

"Me too," said Hickey.

"No, Jim, I'm sorry. There can only be one General Sean Lavery."

Jim was confused a second. Then he broke into a big grin. "I didn't mean I'd be you."

The front door of MacSorley's swung open just as Craig glanced in that direction.

"Oh shit," he said, staring at the newcomer. The three other men looked in the same direction.

"What is it?" Kevin asked. "It's surely not a man and boys are not welcome."

"That's no boy either," Craig said angrily. He rose and squeezed his way through the standing and laughing crowd of Irishmen. He grabbed the newcomer by reaching over someone's shoulder.

"Hold it, cousin," he said taking a handful of his own spare jacket which hung loosely from the newcomer's shoulders. Meg Brant turned her face toward Craig.

"What the hell do you think you're doing here?" he

shouted at her. The sound was drowned by a cheer as Bella's assistant finally reached the far side of the taproom with another tray of drinks.

"Get yourself out of here and get back home. What will Uncle Michael say if he finds out?"

"I'll tell him you took me with you," Meg said haughtily.

"He won't believe that of me," Craig responded.

Meg pouted. "You're right," she said finally. "But I won't go unless you come with me. I really thought I was a free-spirit, Craig, stealing your clothes and sneaking out of the house and following you here but I'm not as brave as I thought. I was really frightened out there in the dark street alone."

"I can't go now," Craig protested. "Oh damn, come sit down with us for a few minutes. Then we can go home."

He took her by the hand and led her through the crowd back to his table.

"Kevin, Jim, Sean, this is my little cousin Mark. Mark Brant."

"He doesn't even look Indian," Jim said studying Meg's face.

"Well, I am. My father was a Hebrew Mohawk."

"Ah hah," Sean laughed, "one of the descendants of the Lost Tribes."

Kevin studied Meg suspiciously. "There's more mystery here than we are being told. I suspect it is not age that would bar you from these premises," he paused and then said, "sir."

There was a commotion at the front door of the tavern again. The double doors flew open with a crash. Some of the stained glass clattered to the floor.

"Hey, what the hell . . ." Bella called. She did not finish her explanation. A young man's body came flying through the door and crashed into the first set of tables and chairs, overturning them along with mugs of ale and sending them and patrons scurrying in all different directions. The first body was followed by a second and then there was a rush of the largest black men that Craig had ever seen. They came swinging clubs made from barrel staves. One blow came crashing on an Irishman's skull sending blood flying through the air. Suddenly about ten Irishmen were down and bleeding.

Bella came, feet first, over the bar. Her enormous leg

swung up into the crotch of the nearest black man. He screamed in agony and fell to his knees holding his groin with both hands. A huge smile crossed Bella's face.

"Fuck up my place will you, you black bastards." A knee rose again and this time it smashed his face beyond recognition.

There was a woman's scream and Bella went berserk thinking it was her "assistant" who had been hurt. She tore into the attacking crowd in the direction of the scream. In fact it was Meg who had screamed as one of the black dock workers came charging toward their table. Craig grabbed her about the waist and pulled her from the seat and out of the way of the attacker. Instead the attacker was greeted by big Jim Hickey who rose to his full 6'4", dwarfing the large man who had come toward him. As Jim rose the expression on the black man's face changed from anger to awe and then finally to fear. He turned to retreat and soon smashed into Bella.

"Has this prick hurt my Phoebe?" she screamed. She reached for him but was cut down from behind by a flying table. The reprieved black man picked up a loose chair, turned swiftly and brought it down splintering on top of Jim's skull.

Hickey blinked in astonishment and then shook his head. His reactions were slowed but his intention was unaltered. He moved toward the attacker. The black man cursed and started to run away. His foot was grabbed from below by Bella reaching from out of the fallen tables and chairs. The bone in his ankle snapped with a sickening crack and the black man screamed in agony.

Kevin stood next to Craig. "I think we had best get out of here," he said, "A fellow could get hurt in here. Lavery," he called to his friend who was sampling drinks on other tables vacated by a great rush of his fellow Irishmen, "get Hickey to lead us out of here."

Lavery pulled his cloak from the back of his chair and theatrically turned it about on his shoulders. "Big Jim," he called, "let's be gone."

Hickey halted his pursuit of screaming victims and turned back to his friends. His eyes spread wide in surprise when he saw Meg. Her father's old hat, which had hidden her long hair, had been knocked from her head in the scuffle. If Sean Lavery was surprised he hid it well. "We must protect the lady. Irish chivalry, our honor demands it, Jim my boy," he called out.

With Hickey in the van the little group inched their way toward the rear door of MacSorley's. Kevin had fashioned a club out of a chair leg and brought up the rear immediately behind Meg who stayed as close as she could to Craig's back.

Hickey kept clearing people out of their path, white or black. He managed to pick Phoebe up off the floor on the way and threw her over his shoulder. One large black arm came crashing at him. He caught it in midair with his fist and twisted it. Craig could not tell if the owner of the arm screamed or not. The noise in the tavern was deafening and it was impossible to distinguish one scream or shout from another. Finally they reached the side door. It was locked. Hickey handed the unconscious form of Phoebe to Lavery and threw his shoulders into the door shattering it. It was a mistake. Outside of the door were at least fifteen black longshoremen kept out of the fray by the obstacle Jim had just removed. They came rushing forward with a force that even Hickey's enormous power could not resist. Jim, Sean Lavery, poor Phoebe were knocked backward into Craig. They all fell to the floor and were trampled by the onrushing black men.

The first through was flustered by meeting Meg as his first "Irishman." He was about to punch but at the last moment he pulled it. Kevin's club struck him on the side of the temple and he folded at the knees. Kevin reached around Meg's waist and pulled her off to the side. When all the black men had rushed through the shattered side door he calmly led her through it out into the pitch black of the alley.

"Quick, hold onto me," he ordered. "If we can get out to the street we might just get out of here without getting our heads bashed," he whispered.

"I can't," Meg objected. "Craig's still in there."

"Tough shit, it's each man for himself in there. My chivalry stops with saving women and children. Beyond that I don't go."

He stiffened when he heard the constable's whistle. "I've got to go. Are you coming with me?"

"No," she responded, "not without Craig."

"Listen, whoever you are. I've got very good reason for not

wanting to fall into the hands of any of Her Majesty's bloody loyal officials so I'll see you around." He moved further into the shadows and then disappeared from her sight. Now Meg was really frightened. She did not want to follow Kevin into the darkness. The light coming from the broken doorway drew her attention toward it but beyond the doorway the violence was terrifying. Timidly she peeked through the smashed door panel. She was nearly knocked over by a black man who rushed through the door and down the alley toward the street. She gasped when she saw Craig lying on the floor. His head was cut and his face was covered with blood.

She rushed to his side. He was groggy but conscious. She tried to help him to his feet but an unconscious Jim Hickey lay across his legs and she could not move him in order to free Craig.

Suddenly the room was filled with constables and some redcoated troops from the citadel. An officer was shouting orders. Someone shoved aside tables and chairs and a battered and bruised Bella MacSorley emerged from under the rubble.

"Bella," a British officer addressed her, "I warned you again and again about these brawls. Now this time I am taking you in."

She paid no attention to him but searched the room with her eyes. She saw Phoebe sitting on the floor laughing at a joke that Sean Lavery had just told her. Lavery looked as unruffled as he had before the attack occurred. He said nothing about the wooden splinters that pierced his buttocks when he was sent sprawling by Hickey's fall.

Bella rushed to Phoebe's side and helped her to her feet and covered her face with kisses.

"Bella," the British officer yelled again, "I'm talking to you. Didn't you hear me? I'm taking you all in."

"What else could I expect from an English pig like you?"

"Well, this is a den of Republican Irish thieves. You all, in your own way, belong in a jail cell and for some of you that will be the first step toward a noose. One need not be a prophet to predict that."

Craig froze. It dawned on him that the officer meant him as well; even worse he meant Meg too. He grabbed her by the elbow and tried to shove her again toward the rear door but it was too late. The officer had seen them.

"Constable, block that doorway and arrest those two trying to escape."

Craig gave up when he saw the man step into the doorway. Again the officer called out. "They must have special reasons for wanting to escape. There are fugitives from Her Majesty's justice in Halifax. We'll need to examine those two carefully."